Letters to Lovecraft

Eighteen Whispers to the Darkness

Edited by Jesse Bullington

Published by Stone Skin Press 2014.

Stone Skin Press is an imprint of Pelgrane Press Ltd. Spectrum House, 9
Bromell's Road, Clapham Common, London, SW4 0BN.

ISBN 978-1-908983-10-7

A CIP catalogue record for this book is available
from the British Library.

1 2 3 4 5 6 7 8 9 10

Printed in the USA.

This book can be ordered direct from the publisher at
www.stoneskinpress.com

Contents

Introduction

We talk a lot about Lovecraft these days, far more than people ever talked about him in his own time. We talk primarily about his fiction, the rich creative legacy he left behind for readers, writers, artists, filmmakers, game designers, and other dreamers. It is debatable whether any other single horror author has left such an impact on the genre.

We also talk about Lovecraft as a person. We do so in part because he was a patient mentor and warm friend to so many other authors of weird fiction. We also do so because behind his extraordinary creatures and impossible worlds lurked a disappointingly prosaic horror: a vitriolic bigot.

While Lovecraft the man and Lovecraft the artist are both worthy topics of examination, this anthology sets its sights on a less widely discussed portion of his legacy: his essay "Supernatural Horror in Literature."

The essay functions in part as a commendably thorough overview of Western horror prose and poetry up to the time of its authorship. Of more immediate interest, it also serves as Lovecraft's writing manifesto, his literary philosophy. Here one finds both careful, contemplative meditations and intractable thou-shalt-nots, often grinding up against one another in the same lengthy paragraph. His cataloging of weird fiction thus does double-duty, reinforcing his claims and serving as sterling examples of his golden rules... assuming you agree with his assessment of any given work. The essay is therefore a rewarding read for anyone with a taste for the horrific and the macabre, regardless of one's feelings on Lovecraft's work or person.

This is not to say that "Supernatural Horror in Literature" is perfect, merely that it offers a vast wealth of material for consideration, and that certain particulars of the text elicit common responses. Who cannot help but look up from the page and ponder Lovecraft's analysis of Edgar Allan Poe, a rare glimpse at one grandmaster's critique of another? What modern reader doesn't smile when Lovecraft roundly rejects notions that Percy Shelley coauthored *Frankenstein*? Who does not frown upon encountering his casual racial essentialism in discussing the supposed inherent nature of the fictions of various ethnic groups?

That's our Lovecraft. At his best, he was a charming, erudite gentleman enamored with both the art and the mechanics of writing; with the romance of tradition and the advances of science. At his worst, he was as odious as any of his monstrous creations, such as when he wistfully longed in one of his letters for a cloud of poison gas to blow over New York's Chinatown and "asphyxiate the whole gigantic abortion, end the misery, and clean out the place." There are those who question the relevancy of Lovecraft's personal sentiments when it comes to discussions of his work... yet given the predominance of such themes as the horror of the Other and degeneration through miscegenation in his stories, it seems naïve to dismiss his prejudices as but a minor element of his thought.

That said, Lovecraft's relentless racism, classism, sexism, and other -isms no more invalidate his literary legacy than the quality of his writing excuses his rabid subscription to eugenics. For all his warts, as an author he possessed great skill and even greater imagination. And to the contemporary writer of weird fiction, it is impossible to ignore the long, distended shadow he casts down from his spectral perch atop the gables and spires of witch-haunted Arkham. Or, you know, Providence.

Not that he seems in danger of being ignored these days. From plushy Great Old Ones to guest spots on popular cartoon shows, Lovecraft is becoming — horror of horrors! — *mainstream*. For all this Cthulhumania, though, how much of it actually stems from the substance of his fiction, and how much is superficial appropriation? Oh sure, godlike beings from beyond time and space *look* pretty cool, but what's going on behind the wavering tentacles? Is the extent of Lovecraft's legacy a few public-domain monsters?

Of course not. In "Supernatural Horror in Literature," Lovecraft offers us a continuing contribution to horror that is just as thought provoking and inspiring as any of his individual stories. If this were all that Lovecraft had left us, we would still feel his weighty impression bearing down on generations of writers.

To some extent, writing is always a dialogue with one's literary predecessors. Authors push and pull against everything and everyone that came before, engaging both their enemies and their heroes. This writerly exchange can be painfully overt or deftly subtle, depending on the author. The goal of this project is to make the literary conversation even more direct, but not by assembling a collection of essays responding to Lovecraft's. Nor will this be an anthology composed solely of new Mythos stories, or, shudder, Lovecraft pastiche — no, the purpose here is to compile a collection of artistic responses to Lovecraft's ethos, in the form of original fiction.

To that end, I asked eighteen of my favorite storytellers to read the essay and select a particular passage that resonated with them. Each then wrote an original story inspired by whatever quote they chose. Several of these literary responses were an affirmation of some claim made by Lovecraft that the author found particularly profound or representative of their own approach to fiction.

For others, their story serves as a rejection of a passage that they disagree with. Often it's a little bit of both. Each story opens with the quote that triggered it, followed by a brief introduction from the author.

Some of these authors are already established in the cottage industry that is modern Mythos fiction. Others have never ventured into that non-Euclidean sandbox. Hell, I knew that a few of the authors were not even fond of Lovecraft's fiction, but, again, I believe this essay to be indispensable reading for any working writer of weird fiction. What these artists delivered runs the gamut from white-knuckle weirdness in the woods to avant-garde apocalypses; from the bizarre to the beautiful; from a quiet paean in praise of darkness to a raging howl against the cold impartiality of the stars — sometimes all in the space of a dozen pages. This is what happens when you ask modern masters to engage with Lovecraft not by revamping or expanding on his fiction, but by cutting straight to the heart of his philosophy.

Something I was curious to see as the stories began trickling in was if and when overlap would occur. Not just thematically or content-wise, as is the case with all anthologies, but in terms of which Lovecraft quotes the authors selected. Would I end up with eighteen stories responding to the essay's most popular passage: *"The oldest and strongest emotion of mankind is fear, and the oldest and strongest kind of fear is fear of the unknown"?*

No. There is a little overlap, as several authors did focus on the same excerpt, but always to wildly different results. Not a single author settled on the aforementioned quote, perhaps because I scared them off it with my ranting, or perhaps because they recognized that there was much more to mine from the essay than its famous opening line. I suspect any parallels you find in the following stories will be every bit as intriguing as the divergences.

For his "Past Reno" and her "That Place," Brian Evenson and Gemma Files both engaged with a particular quote that could be taken in almost any imaginable direction, and yet both stories deal with adults returning to their childhood homes to settle their parents' estates. Evenson's tale is all about the journey back, an increasingly disquieting drive through the wastelands of the desert and the mind. Files's story, on the other hand, concerns itself with the arrival, as three siblings return home to their deceased parents' remote house in the forests of Canada. Both stories deal in fractured memories and fracturing realities, but are fundamentally at odds with one another: one ends where the other begins, so to speak. The strange synchronicity at play between the stories became more and more indicative of the project as a whole, the further I read…

Intriguingly, the passage from which Angela Slatter took her inspiration for "Only the Dead and the Moonstruck" overlaps with that of Files but not that of Evenson. While the aforementioned stories involve the homecoming of children, Slatter's focal point is the disintegration of any real sense of home when a child is taken from a family. Far more explicit in its Mythos lineage, Slatter's piece is nevertheless delicate as a fresh bruise as she weaves together overt Mythos monstrousness with the sort of honest, raw emotion that was as alien to most of Lovecraft's fiction as any Yuggothian fungus.

Three authors selected a quote asserting "the true weird tale" requires "a certain atmosphere of breathless and unexplainable dread of outer, unknown forces." Nadia Bulkin's "Only Unity Saves the Damned" certainly makes a compelling case for this argument. She deftly parallels the cosmic futility that exemplifies Lovecraftian horror with the grim inevitability of growing up in a small town where few can escape the social gravity well and move away. Robin D. Laws's historical maritime tragedy "The Trees" likewise proves the rule as we sail from a commonplace calamity in England to far weirder shores in a remote quadrant of the Pacific, but there is another unexpected, inexplicable connection to Bulkin's found footage… And then there is Paul Tremblay, whose "_____" cheekily bites her oddly familiar thumb at Lovecraft's claim as we join a bored father overseeing his kids' swim lesson at a suburban lakefront. Yet as our narrator is joined by a perhaps too-welcome visitor, curious clouds begin to edge in around the easy, sunny atmosphere, and despite the obvious differences we begin to sense points of intersection between Tremblay's tale and those of Bulkin and Laws.

Jeffrey Ford and Chesya Burke both selected a charming quote regarding the fertility rites of "a squat race of [pre-Aryan] Mongoloids." Ford focuses his deadeye on the notion of the "hidden but often suspected presence of a hideous cult of nocturnal worshippers," and delivers a wild ride through the history of a very particular sect: "The Order of the Haunted Wood." What begins as an amusing, absurdist romp takes on an air of inexplicable menace as the boner jokes begin to wilt and the atmosphere grows thick as intoxicating smoke spewing from a cultist's censer. Burke, on the other hand, settles on the casual racism of Lovecraft's quote, meeting the bitter WASP on his familiar stomping ground of eugenic thought with "The Horror at Castle of the Cumberland." The horror found in her period piece is not Lovecraft's favorite blend of polluted bloodlines and physical degeneration, nor does it lie on the intrusion of the supernatural into the mundane, though she is able to execute the latter with an expert hand. Rather, our dread wells up in response to the everyday sadism and hypocrisy of ordinary people in a small Southern town at the turn of the last century, demonstrating that depending on the interpretation, any faith can be as cruel as the worship of the Old Ones.

Given the sheer breadth of Lovecraft's essay, it is hardly surprising that most of the contributors chose quotes that did not overlap with anyone else's. Some went with a brief, concise supposition, such as Cameron Pierce's selection. His wry "Help Me" opens with the perfect lure for readers of Lovecraftiana — a man fishing on a desolate stretch of beach, what could possibly go wrong? — then sets the hook with his easy yet exact style, reeling you in with the inescapable awfulness that you almost saw coming, but didn't. It's a fish story to end all fish stories, and will either put you off seafood for good or send you straight down to the shore, tackle box in tow. Others went for airier excerpts, for instance, Livia Llewellyn's choice to open up her "Allochthon." Airy, though, is categorically *not* the word for her intense, richly rendered requiem for a woman suffocating in her seemingly humdrum life, a life that won't let her go; any air here is the toxic fume belching up from subterranean vaults. Pack a picnic basket and squeeze into the backseat, because we're all going on a trip to Beacon Rock you'll never forget.

There is a brooding philosophy at play in Lovecraft's work, and while the above stories dip in and out of it to various depths, few seem as downright eager as Nick Mamatas to plunge in and root around until he finds something overlooked… or perhaps heretofore avoided for a reason. Sharing baked goods and theories in "The Semi-Finished Basement" are a motley crew of four individuals far too realistically rendered to belong in any Lovecraft story, yet, in the end, he delivers a bitter draught that one could certainly accept as the "concentrated essence" of his inspiration. If Mamatas directs a microscope at the Mythos, Tim Lebbon calibrates a telescope toward entirely different systems. In "The Lonely Wood," we join an atheist in St. Paul's Cathedral, in mourning, in turmoil, and, quite possibly, in danger. Grief is a recurring theme in the collection, perhaps because losing someone we love is the sharpest fear many of us feel, and Lebbon brilliantly capitalizes on the all-consuming nature of it: a personal, private apocalypse can overshadow anything, shaking the faith of believers and rattling the conviction of doubters.

Orrin Grey and Asamatsu Ken both make the potentially catastrophic decision to tell stories where Lovecraft himself plays a role, but through their skill and originality manage to pull it off. Grey's "Lovecrafting" starts off on a familiar course before sharply veering us away from the over-traveled Lovecraft's-stories-were-real route, and the novel telling of the piece dovetails perfectly with the cinematic scope. It's a monster mash as only Grey can deliver, and never overstays its welcome or overplays its hand. Asamatsu's "Glimmer in the Darkness" rows us even further into those dangerous literary waters, with our young protagonist none other than Lovecraft himself. What's more, the story takes the title of this anthology literally, with Lovecraft's letters playing a role in the denouement. With an expert's finesse, Asamatsu imbues his story not with the expected over-the-top antics found in most stories where Lovecraft shows up, but instead cultivates an eerie weirdness that is all the more disquieting for its restraint.

Restraint is decidedly off the table in David Yale Ardanuy's "One Last Meal, Before the End." Using Lovecraft's analysis of Algernon Blackwood's "The Windigo" as a starting point, Ardanuy catapults us back to the final days of the 18th century, when an unexpected visitor arrives at a remote trading post. If you think you've had this particular meal before, you're in for a delicious surprise, as Ardanuy bastes the choicest historical details with icy dread, hot-blooded action, and a healthy pinch of the grotesque. Balancing out Ardanuy's eager willingness to peel back the frozen sod and show us everything wriggling underneath is Kirsten Alene, whose beguilingly sedate "There Has Been a Fire" operates on the logic of an opiate-addled fever dream rather than a nightmare. Alene opens her story of an aging professor of poetry with a quote from Lovecraft on the nature of verse, yet despite the slippery nature of the lyrical prose we never quite lose our footing... much as we think we might like to. Imagine the professors from *Gormenghast* holding a parent-teacher conference with Edward Gorey over the disruptive behavior of his daughter, and you're approaching the deliciously musty essence of the piece.

Then there is "Doc's Story," Stephen Graham Jones's shitkicker of a werewolf legend that sinks its canines into a Lovecraft passage meditating on the evolution of horrific storytelling from oral tradition to literary fiction. For all his obsessions with men becoming monsters and devolving into animals, Lovecraft himself never came within howling distance of a lycanthrope, but what really sets Jones's beast apart from the oeuvre of his inspiration is the human heart pounding underneath the fur. Jones demonstrates with understated brilliance and wit that while Lovecraft may have been a master at instilling readers with fear and wonder, he was far less skilled at actually making us feel for his characters. Perhaps this is something that really sets the modern weird tale apart from its predecessors, for, of all the differences between Lovecraft and the crew assembled here, one element that reasserts itself again and again is the emotional connection to the characters, be they doomed, saved, or everything in between.

At last we come to Molly Tanzer's "Food from the Clouds," which takes its inspiration from Lovecraft's opining that "much of the choicest weird work is unconscious; appearing in memorable fragments scattered through material whose massed effect may be of a very different cast." Taking this as an open invitation to spread a wider net, Tanzer goes on to provide a quote that sounds like it was lifted directly off of a tombstone in Arkham Cemetery but actually has a far humbler pedigree. After this preamble, we are rocketed not into a hazy past or a shimmering parallel dimension, but straight ahead into a dismal future London where society has cycled back around, rather than progressing forever forward. The easy tone and warm demeanor of her narrator coaxes us into peering down rabbit holes we should have left well enough alone, and, before the end, everyone will learn a hard lesson on the perils of poaching...

Which, really, is what we're all doing here — jumping the fence at that point in the hedge where the oak tree of Public Domain crashed down, clearing the way for amateurs and professionals alike to run riot in Lovecraft's private estate. Some are here to take aim at something very specific, others just want to stuff their game bags with everything they can catch, and for others still it's all about wandering around, taking one's time and admiring the old growth, seeing what pops out of the underbrush. Nowadays Lovecraft's Mythos has the character of carefully landscaped, manicured grounds that have been given totally back to nature and allowed to grow wild, with invasive species choking out certain strains that once dominated the terrain, old earth made fertile again by the clawing of hungry animals and curious hands, the borders of the original territory long overgrown with foreign flowers and toxic vines, until there is no telling how far one might travel and still find both feet planted in the nigh-boundless garden he left for us…

So to speak.

Love or loathe Lovecraft, one cannot ignore him — he simply looms too large over the landscape of modern horror. Regardless of your opinion of his fiction, I encourage you to pick up a copy of "Supernatural Horror in Literature" and engage with him at his most scholarly. That's what the authors assembled here have done, continuing the conversation with a man who loved his letters every bit as much as his fictions.

Lovecraft cautioned us not to expect "startling mutations" in the evolution of literary horror. I leave it up to you, dear reader, to determine from the following stories just how accurate this prophecy has proven. I will leave you with this parting rumination from his essay's conclusion, for like so many sentiments on the subject, none could voice it better than Lovecraft himself:

"Whatever universal masterpiece of tomorrow may be wrought from phantasm or terror will owe its acceptance rather to a supreme workmanship than to a sympathetic theme. Yet who shall declare the dark theme a positive handicap? Radiant with beauty, the Cup of the Ptolemies was carven of onyx."

Jesse Bullington
March 13, 2014

Past Reno

Brian Evenson

"Because we remember pain and the menace of death more vividly than pleasure...it has fallen to the lot of the darker and more maleficent side of cosmic mystery to figure chiefly in our popular supernatural folklore... [U]ncertainty and danger are always closely allied; thus making any kind of an unknown world a world of peril and evil possibilities."

What I like about this particular Lovecraft quotation is the emphasis it places on uncertainty and the unknown, which for me is what I like most about his work: the way nothing really happens in "At the Mountains of Madness," for instance, but he still manages to build up a genuine and haunting dread. The story below began with that, and with my memory of a trip my wife and I took through Nevada where small, strange things kept happening, things that didn't really add up to much and that, for the most part, didn't bother her, but slowly began to accumulate for me, making me feel like the world was off a little bit, a nagging in the back of my mind making me feel I'd entered into a Nevada that wasn't on any sort of map. Living in

Providence, Lovecraft's town, where people generally seem to drive as if they'd just taken a painkiller and a shot of whiskey and where, even after ten years, I still find it all too easy to get lost, I've come to feel that some places are, for a lack of a better term, weird. This story tries to capture the particular and peculiar weirdness of the West.

I.

Bernt began to suspect the trip would turn strange when, on the outskirts of Reno, he entered a convenience store that had one of its six aisles completely dedicated to jerky. At the top were smoked-meat products he recognized, name brands he'd seen commercials for. In the middle was stuff that seemed local, with single-color printing, but still vacuum packed and carefully labeled. Along the bottom row, though, were chunks of dried and smoked meat in dirty plastic bags, held shut with twist ties, no labels on them at all. He wasn't even certain what kind of meat they contained. He prodded one of the bags with the toe of his sneaker and then stared at it for a while. When he realized that the clerk was staring at him, he shook his head and went out.

I should have known then, he thought hours later. At that point he should have turned around and driven the half mile back into Reno and gone no further. But, he told himself, it was just one convenience store. And it wasn't, he tried to convince himself, really even that strange. It just meant people in Reno liked jerky. So, instead, he shook his head and kept driving.

It was the first time he'd left California in a decade. His father had died, and he'd been informed of it too late to attend the funeral, but he was driving to Utah anyway, planning to be there for the settling of the estate, whatever was left of it. He was on his own. His girlfriend had intended to come along and then, at the last moment, came down sick. What it was neither of them were quite sure, but she couldn't stand without getting dizzy. To get to the bathroom to vomit, she had to crawl. The illness had lasted three or four hours and then, just as suddenly as it had come, it was gone. But she had refused to get in the car after that. What if it came back? If it had been bad while she was motionless, she reasoned, how much worse would it be if she was driving? He had to admit she had a point.

"Do you even need to be there?" she had asked him. "Won't they send you your share wherever you are?"

Technically, yes, that was true, but he didn't trust his extended family. If he didn't go, they'd find a way to keep him from what he deserved.

She shook her head tiredly. "And what exactly do you deserve?" she asked. Which was, he had to admit, a good question. "And didn't your father tell you never to come back?"

He nodded. His father had. "But he doesn't have any say," he said. "He's dead now."

But in any case she had not come with him. And maybe, he thought now as he drove, his girlfriend's illness — miles before Reno — was the first indication the trip would turn strange. But how could he have known? And now, well past Reno, already having gone so far, how could he bring himself to turn around?

Back at the beginning, just past Reno, he drove, watching Highway 80 flirt with the Truckee River, draw close to it and then pull away again. Then he hit the scattering of houses called Fernley, and the river vanished too. For miles there was almost nothing there, just a ranch or two and bare dry ground. He watched a sagging barbed-wire fence skitter along the roadside, then, when that was gone, counted time by watching the metal markers that popped up every tenth of a mile. After a while those disappeared, too, leaving only the faded green mile markers, numbers etched in white on them. He watched them come, his mind drifting in between them, and watched them go.

He thought of his father as he had been when Bernt was young: a man who wouldn't leave the house without ironing a crease in his jeans. His boots he made certain were brought to a high polish before he left, even if he was just going to the back acres, even if he knew they'd be dirty or dusty the moment he stepped off the porch.

That was how he was. Bernt hated it. Hated him.

He remembered his father lashing a pig's hind legs together and running the rope over the pulley wheel screwed under the hayloft floor and winding the rope onto the hand crank. His father had made him take the crank and said, "You pull the bastard up and hold it and don't pay no mind to how it struggles. I'll get the throat slit, and then that'll be the worst of it done. Your job's nothing. You just keep hold to it until the fucker bleeds out." Bernt had just nodded. His father said pull, and he had started cranking. There went the pig up, squealing and spinning and flailing. His father stood there beside it, motionless, knife out with his thumb just edged over the guard and touching the side of the blade, just waiting. And then, with one quick flick of his arm, he opened its throat from ear to ear. The pig still struggled, the blood gouting from the wound and thickening the dust. Bernt couldn't understand how his father didn't get blood on his boots or his pants, but he just didn't.

It was always that way, every time he killed something. Never a drop of blood on him. Uncanny almost, it seemed to Bernt, and he had spent more than one sleepless night as a teenager wondering how that could be, why blood would shy from his father. The only possibilities he could come up with seemed so outlandish that he preferred to believe it was just luck.

He shuddered. He watched the mile markers again — or tried to, but they simply weren't there anymore. For a moment he thought he might have left the highway somehow, by accident. But no, he couldn't see how he could have, and whatever road he was on had every appearance of a highway. Then he flicked past a sheared-off metal stub on the roadside and wondered if that wasn't what had once been a marker, if someone had been systematically cutting them down. Bored kids, probably, with nothing to do.

He gauged the sun in the sky. It seemed just as high as it had been an hour before, not yet starting its descent. He checked the gas: between half and a quarter tank. He kept driving, wondering if he had enough gas to get to the next station. Sure he did. How far could it possibly be?

He opened the glove box to take out the map and have a look, but the map wasn't there. Maybe he had had it out and it had slipped under the seat, but, if it had, it was deep enough under that he couldn't find it, at least not while driving. No, he told himself, there would be a gas station soon. There had to be. He couldn't be that far off of Elko. It was less than three hundred miles from Reno to Elko, and he'd filled up in Reno. And Winnemucca was somewhere in between the two. Had he passed that already without realizing it?

He had enough gas, he knew he had enough. He shouldn't let his mind play tricks on him.

His father had told him that if he was going to leave he should never come back.

Fine, Bernt had said. *Wasn't planning to come back anyway.*

And then he had left.

Or wait, not that exactly. It had been so many years ago now that it was easier to think that that was how it had ended, but it hadn't been quite so simple. He hadn't said *Fine*. He hadn't said *Wasn't planning to come back anyway*. What he had said: "Why in hell would I want to come back?"

His father had smiled. "Thought you'd never ask," he said. "Come along," he said, and made for the door, waving to Bernt to follow him.

Perhaps an hour later — maybe more, maybe less, it was hard for him to judge time driving alone — he called his girlfriend to tell her that she had been right, that he shouldn't have come after all. He was hoping that maybe she would talk him into turning around, inheritance be damned.

But she didn't answer. Or no, not that exactly: the call didn't go through. It seemed like it was going through — he dialed the number, he heard it ring a few times, and then the call disconnected. His phone had no reception.

Well, what's strange about that? a part of him wondered. He was out in the middle of nowhere: of course service was bound to be bad. He'd have to wait until he was near a town, and then he'd try her again.

All that sounded right, rational, correct. And yet another part of him couldn't help but worry that something was wrong.

The radio, too, faded in and out, the same station one moment seeming quite strong and the next little more than static, and then quite strong again. *Not strange*, a part of him again insisted. Must be the mountains, he told himself, the signal bouncing around in them. He told himself this even though it seemed to happen just as regularly when he was in open country as when he was skirting a mountain or when one had just hove into view.

There were moments, too, when there was nothing but static. When he turned the knob slowly but found nothing. When he could press the search button, and his tuner would go through the whole band from beginning to end without finding anything to settle on, and would start over again, and then again, and again, and again. It might go on for five minutes or even ten, and then suddenly it would stop on a frequency that, to him, still seemed to be nothing but static, but it stayed there. After a while he became convinced that there must be something beneath the static, a strange whispering, that surely would slowly resolve itself into voices. Though it never did, only stayed static.

He checked his gas gauge. It read between a half and a quarter tank. Hadn't it read that before? He tapped on it with his finger, softly at first and then harder and harder, but the reading didn't change.

When he came to Winnemucca, he would stop for gas, just in case the gauge was broken. He probably didn't need gas to make it to Elko, but he would stop anyway. He tapped the gauge again. Had he already passed Winnemucca? He felt like he should have, but surely he would have noticed?

He watched his father check the crease of his trouser leg. He watched him stop on the porch and raise first one boot and then the other to the rail, quickly buffing them with the yellow-orange cloth draped there, and then he stepped off and went down the path leading out to the road.

Bernt followed.

"This here is all mine," his father was saying, gesturing around him. "This, all of this, belongs to me."

But of course Bernt knew this. His father had been saying shit like that ever since Bernt was a child. It was not news to him. When his father turned to see how Bernt was taking it and saw his son's face, his lips curled into a sneer.

"What in hell do you know about it?" he asked Bernt.

"What?" asked Bernt, surprised. "I know you own the land. I already knew that."

"Land," said his father, and spat. "Shit, that's the least of it," he said. "I own anything that comes here, plant or animal or man, including you. If you leave, it's because I let you. And if I let you, you sure as shit ain't coming back unless I say."

Almost before Bernt knew it, his father's hand flashed out and took his wrist in a tight, crushing grip. Bernt tried to pull away, but his father was all sinew. He nodded once, his mouth a straight, inexpressive line, and then he cut off the path, toward the storm cellar, dragging Bernt along with him.

No, he should have reached a town by now. Something was wrong. The sun was still high. It shouldn't still have been high. It didn't make sense. The gas gauge was either broken or for some reason he wasn't running out of gas. He tried again to call his girlfriend, and, this time, even though his phone didn't have any bars, the call went through. He heard it ring twice, and then she picked up and said *Hello*, her voice oddly low and almost unrecognizable — probably because she was sick, he told himself later. He said, "Sweetheart, it's me," and then the call disconnected. He couldn't get it to reconnect when he called again.

♦

His father took Bernt across the yard, pulling hard enough on his arm that it was difficult for Bernt to keep his balance. Once he stumbled and nearly fell, and his father just kept pulling him forward, and he had to struggle to stay upright. He got the impression from his father that it didn't matter to him if Bernt stayed upright or not.

They went past the barn and around to the back of it, to where the storm cellar was, a single wooden door set flat into the ground and kept closed with a padlock. Bernt had always known it was there, but he had never been inside. His father let go of his arm and thrust a key out at him. "Go on," he said to Bernt. "Go and look."

II.

Just when he started to panic, he came to a town. He didn't catch the town's name: perhaps the sign for it had been vandalized, like the mile markers. He came over a rise and around a bend, and suddenly saw the exit sign and the scattering of buildings below, windows shimmering in the sun. He had to brake and slide over a lane quickly, and even then he hit the rattle strip and came just shy of striking the warning cones before the concrete divider. But then he was on the ramp and going down, under the bridge and into town.

He drove in to the first gas station he saw. He stopped at the pumps and turned off the car and clambered out, only then realizing that the place was abandoned and empty, the pumps covered with grime, the rubber hoses old and cracked. He got back into the car and turned it on again, then drove through the streets of the town looking for another station. But there didn't seem to be one.

♦

What had he seen in the storm cellar? He still wasn't quite sure. He unlocked it and went down, his father standing with his arms crossed up top. It smelled of dust inside, and of something else — something that made him taste metal in his mouth when he breathed the air. It made his throat hurt.

He went down the rickety wooden steps until he came to a packed earth floor. There was just enough room to stand upright. Even with the door open, it took a while for his eyes to adjust, and once they had adjusted, he didn't see much. The floor was stained in places, darker in some places than others — unless that was some natural property of the earth itself. He didn't think it was. There was, in the back, deeper in the hole, a series of racks, and there was something hanging on them. He hesitated and from up above heard his father say, "Go on," his voice cold and hard. He groped his way forward, but, because of the way his own body blocked the light, it wasn't until he was a foot or two away that he realized that what he was seeing were strips of drying meat. Hundreds of them, sliced thin and sometimes twisted up on themselves, and with nothing really to tell him what sort of animal they had come from. Though it was a large animal, he was sure of that.

His mouth grew dry, and he found himself staring, his eyes flicking from one strip to the next and back again. He almost called out to his father to ask him where the dried meat had come from, but something stopped him. In his head, he imagined his father answering the question by simply reaching down and swinging the door shut and leaving him in darkness. The feeling was so palpable that for a moment he wondered if he wasn't in darkness after all, if he wasn't simply imagining what he thought he was seeing.

He forced himself to turn around very slowly, as if nothing was wrong, and climb up the stairs. His father watched him come, but made no move to reach out and help him as he scrambled out of the shelter.

"You seen it?" asked his father.

He hesitated a moment, wondering what exactly his father had meant for him to see — whether it was the strips of meat or perhaps something else, something behind the racks, even deeper in. But almost immediately decided that it was safer to simply agree.

"I saw it," he said.

His father nodded. "Good," he said. "Then you understand why you have to stay."

Bernt made a noncommittal gesture that his father took as a yes. His father clapped him on the shoulder and then began walking.

Why his father felt he understood, what his father thought he'd seen, what he'd thought the storm cellar had done to him, Bernt couldn't exactly say. Indeed, he would never be sure, and ultimately felt it might be better not to know. He went after his father back to the house and retreated to his room. From there, it was a simple matter to wait until dark and then pack a few things, climb out the window, and leave for good. He had never been back.

♦

After a while he gave up looking: the gas gauge read between a half and a quarter full still; probably he had enough to make it into Elko.

He parked in front of a diner on Main Street and went in. It was crowded inside, all the tables full. He sat at the counter. Even then, it took a while for the waitress to get around to him. When she finally did, he asked her about a gas station, felt it was par for the course when she told him there wasn't one. *Used to be one,* she said, *but gas here cost too much. Nobody used it, not with Elko nearby.* No, the nearest one was up the road at Elko.

"How far away is that?" he asked.

The question seemed to puzzle her somehow. "Not far," she said.

He asked what she suggested, and she recommended the soup of the day, which he ordered without thinking to ask what it was exactly. When it came it was surprisingly good, a rich orange broth scented with saffron and with strings of meat spread all through it. Pork, probably. It made his mouth water to eat it. It seemed a sign to him that his trip was finally becoming less strange, or at least strange in a way that was good rather than bad. When he finished he used the edge of his thumb to scour the sides of the bowl clean.

He sat there, far from eager to get back on the road. At the end, the waitress brought him a cup of coffee with cream without his asking for it, and before he could tell her he didn't drink coffee she was gone again, off to another customer. He let it sit there for a while and then, for lack of anything better to do, took a sip. It was rich and mellow, different from coffee as he remembered it, and, before he knew it, he had finished the whole cup.

It's okay, he told himself, and found he more or less believed it. *The strange part of the trip is over. Everything will be all right from here on out.*

He had written twice to his father from California. The first time was maybe a year after he'd arrived. He'd wanted for his father to know that he was all right, that he'd landed on his feet. He'd also wanted to gloat a little. Perhaps, too, he had still been curious. *What exactly was it that you thought showing me the storm cellar would do? What was it in there that you thought would keep me?*

For a month, maybe two, he had waited for a reply. But his father had never answered the letter. The only way he knew for certain his father had received it was because when his father died his aunt had written to let him know, saying that they'd finally gotten his address off a letter he'd written his father.

The second letter, years later, had been more measured, calmer. It was, as much as he could bring it to be, an attempt at reconciliation. It had come back to him unopened, *Return to Sender* written across it in his father's careful block writing.

Everything will be all right, he was still telling himself when he got up from the stool and made his way to the bathroom. He peed and flushed, then stretched. While he was washing his hands, he noticed the mirror.

Or *mirrors*, rather. There were two of them, one suspended over the other, a larger one with a small one screwed in over it so that the larger one looked almost like a frame around it.

He looked at himself in it, his haggard face, but his eyes kept slipping to where one mirror ended and the other began. Was it meant to be that way? Some sort of design scheme? Was the center of the larger mirror cracked or foxed, and the small mirror had been hung to cover that? Was there some kind of hole that the second mirror was hiding?

He reached out and grabbed the edges of the top mirror. It was affixed in each of its four corners by a screw that went through the corner of the mirror and then through a thin block of wood and then through the mirror behind it. He could just get the tips of his finger in the space left between the mirrors. He tugged, but it was bolted firmly in place.

When he let go, the tips of his fingers were black with dust. He washed his hands again, more slowly this time. His face, when he looked up this time, looked just as haggard. He turned off the taps, dried his hands, and left the bathroom.

♦

A moment later he was back in. He had the penlight on his keychain out and was shining it at the gap between the top mirror and the bottom one. He pressed his eye close, but no matter where he looked, no matter where he shone the light, the mirror behind it looked whole and complete.

III.

At first, he lied to his girlfriend, claiming he had gone to Utah and to his father's ranch for the reading of the will, but had received nothing. But then, when the box came, he finally came clean. It was an old box, starting to collapse, and smelled dank. It was very heavy. The words "Bernt's Pittance" were written on the side of it in his father's careful hand.

He left the box sitting on the table for a day and a half. The evening of the second day, they were both sitting in bed, both reading, when she asked him when he was going to open it. He had put the book down on his chest and had begun to talk. She had let him, had interrupted only once, and when he was done she had curled up beside him one hand touching his shoulder softly, and said nothing. That had surprised him — he thought she might be angry that he had lied to her. But if she was angry, she kept it to herself.

Of course, he told her, *nothing was really going on, it was just my imagination. It was just an ordinary trip. I was just noticing the things that under normal circumstances I wouldn't notice.* But as he told the story, moved bit by bit across the landscape between Reno and the small town whose name he had never quite figured out, it was all he could do not to panic again. He didn't believe it had been a normal trip. He believed it was anything but. And he believed that, somehow, his father was to blame.

The hardest part was explaining why seeing that, seeing the one mirror placed atop the other mirror, had been the thing that had turned him around and made him drive back to Reno, made him stop and rent a hotel room and drink himself nearly blind until he ran out of liquor and sobered up enough to realize enough time had elapsed to give his girlfriend the impression that he had gone to Utah. There hadn't, he had to admit, been anything really wrong with the mirrors — but that, somehow, had been *exactly* what was wrong with them.

That had been the one time she had interrupted him. "Was it like what you saw in the storm cellar?" she asked.

But what had he seen in the storm cellar? He still didn't know, and never would. Was that like the mirrors? No, that had been a hole in the ground containing curing strips of dried meat. How could twinned mirrors be like a hole in the ground and strips of meat? No, the only thing they had in common was that he felt like he couldn't quite understand what either one was telling him. That he felt he was missing something.

He left the café, climbed into the car, and drove. His intention at first, despite the way he was feeling, was to keep driving, to continue on to Utah, to see the trip through. But as he took a left out of the parking lot and headed down Main Street, he felt like he was being stretched between the mirror and wherever he was going now. That a part of him was caught in the mirror, and the link between that and the rest of him was growing thinner and thinner.

And so instead of getting back on the highway, he circled back to the café. He took the tire iron out of the kit nestled beside the spare tire and walked into the café and straight into the bathroom. He gave the top mirror a few careful taps with the tire iron and broke out each of the four corners, and then lifted it down and set it flat on the floor. The mirror beneath was complete and whole. This mirror he simply broke to bits, just to make sure there wasn't something behind it. There wasn't. Only blank wall. So he broke the first mirror as well. And then he left just as quickly as he had come, the waitress staring at him open mouthed and the burly cook hustling out of the building and after him, cursing, just as he turned the key to his car and drove away.

Even then, he might have kept going, might have kept on to Utah, he told his girlfriend. But the trip — all of it, not just that last moment of finding himself doing something he'd never thought he'd do — seemed to him a warning. It was a mistake, he felt, to go on. So, he turned around.

And indeed, almost before he knew it, he was back in Reno, the car all but out of gas. He found a gas station, then found a hotel and settled down for a few drunken days to wait. Both because he was ashamed that he hadn't gone all the way to Utah and because, to be frank, now that he was back in a place that seemed fully real to him, he was afraid to get in the car again.

But then at last, head aching from a hangover, he had climbed into the car and driven. A moment later he had crossed over the state line. He wound up into the mountains, went past Truckee, skirting Donner Lake, through Emigrant Gap, and then slowly down out of the mountains and into more and more populated areas, ever closer and closer to home. By the time he had pulled into their driveway, it almost seemed like he had made too much of it, that he just wanted an excuse not to go to Utah after all.

The more he talked, the more he tried both to explain to his girlfriend how he felt and to dismiss it, to relegate it to the past, the more another part of him felt the event gather and harden in his mind, like a bolus or a tumor, both part of him and separate from him at once. He did not know if speaking made it better or made it worse.

♦

When he was done, he lay there silent. Her girlfriend was beside him, and soon her breathing had changed, and he could tell she was asleep. He was, more or less, alone.

There was the box still to deal with, he knew. He knew, too, that he would not open it. He did not want whatever was inside it. In his head he planned how to get rid of it. Just throwing it away did not seem like enough.

Careful not to wake her, he got up. He slipped into his jeans and found his car keys. He put on his socks and a shirt, and at the door he slipped on his shoes.

No, he needed to get it as far from him as he could. He would take it back to Utah, back to where it came from.

♦

Or maybe not, he thought a few hours later, well into the drive and recognizing nothing as familiar, completely unsure where he was. Maybe not as far as Utah, but certainly somewhere past Reno. That would have to be far enough.

Only Unity Saves the Damned

Nadia Bulkin

"The true weird tale has something more than secret murder, bloody bones, or a sheeted form clanking chains according to rule. A certain atmosphere of breathless and unexplainable dread of outer, unknown forces must be present; and there must be a hint, expressed with a seriousness and portentousness becoming its subject, of that most terrible conception of the human brain."

Like Lovecraft, I'm not a big fan of clanking chains or, in this case, urban legends about dead witches. Politics teaches us that we fear what we don't understand, and simplistically scary stories, lodged in our preexisting understanding of the world, keep us tucked safely into our comfort zones. Genuine dread takes us beyond this zone and into the sublime. But there's a point at which I humbly diverge from Lovecraft: as horrific as outer, unknown forces are, I think that up-close-and-personal forces — the devil that knows your name — are actually the most dreadful. And I don't mean empathy. I mean that twinge of familiarity that lets you know that you were chosen, you were hunted — and you know very well what's coming.

◆

"Dude, are you getting this?"

Rosslyn Taro, 25, and Clark Dunkin, 25, are standing in the woods. It's evening — the bald cypresses behind them are shadowed, and the light between the needles is the somber blue that follows sunsets — and they are wearing sweatshirts and holding stones.

"It's on," says the voice behind the camera. "To the winner go the spoils!"

They whip their arms back and start throwing stones. The camera pans to the right as the stones skip into the heart of Goose Lake. After a dozen rounds, the camera pans back to Rosslyn Taro and Clark Dunkin arguing over whose stone made the most skips, and then slowly returns to the right. Its focus settles on a large bur oak looming around the bend of the lake, forty yards away.

"Hey, isn't that the Witching Tree?"

Off camera, Clark Dunkin says, "What?" and Rosslyn Taro says, "Come on, seriously?"

"You know, Raggedy Annie's Witching Tree."

The girl sounds too shaky to be truly skeptical. "How do you know?"

"Remember the song? 'We hung her over water, from the mighty oak tree.' Well, there aren't any other lakes around here. And First Plymouth is on the other side of the lake." The camera zooms, searches for a white steeple across the still water, but the light is bad. "'We hung her looking over at the cemetery.'"

The camera swings to Rosslyn Taro, because she is suddenly upset. She is walking to the camera, and, when she reaches it, shoves the cameraman. "Bay, shut up! I hate that stupid song. Let's just go, I'm getting cold. Come on, please." But Clark Dunkin is still staring at the tree. His hands are shaking. Rosslyn Taro calls his name: "Lark!"

The camera follows Clark Dunkin's gaze to the tree. There is a figure standing in front of it, dressed in a soiled white shift and a black execution hood. The figure reaches two pale, thin hands to the edge of the hood as if to reveal its face. And then the camera enters a topspin, all dirt and branches and violet sky, as the cameraman begins to run. Rosslyn Taro is heard screaming. Someone — the cameraman, or possibly Clark Dunkin — is whimpering, as if from very far away, "oh, shit, oh, shit."

And then the video abruptly cuts to black.

They called themselves the LunaTicks. Like everything else, it was Bay's idea: he named them after an old British secret society, supposedly "the smartest men in Birmingham." There were ground rules not only for their operations, but for life as a whole: if one got caught, the rest would confess or expect to be ratted out; where one goes, the others must follow. Only unity saves the damned, Bay said.

Roz's father thought the boys were a terrible influence on her. These slouching undead fools had metastasized at his front door one day when Roz was in sixth grade, with their uncombed hair and unwashed skin and vulgar black T-shirts. He'd made the mistake of letting the vampires in. Under their watch, his daughter's mood swings escalated from mild distemper to a full-blown madness. The charcoal rings around her eyes got deeper; her silver skull necklaces got bigger. She was vandalizing the elementary school; she was shoplifting lipstick. He'd tell her he was locking the doors at midnight and in the morning he would find her sleeping, nearly frozen, on the porch — or worse, he wouldn't find her at all. So he excavated her room, vowing to take the Baileys and the Dunkins to court if he found a single pipe, a single syringe. He gave up when she failed to apply to community college. The screen door swung shut behind her and he thanked God that he also had a son.

He was not alone. Bay's parents hated Roz and Lark as well; their hatred of the two losers who hung like stones around

Bay's neck was the only thing the former Mr. and Mrs. Bailey still shared. They tried, separately, to introduce Bay to different crowds: the jocks, the computer geeks, the 4-H club. Bay said he hated them all (*too dumb too weird too Christian*), but the truth was that they had all rejected him. Eventually Bay's parents gave him an ultimatum: *get rid of your friends, or we get rid of the car.* So the responsibility of driving down bedraggled county roads — and all roads lead to Goose Lake, the old folks said — fell to Roz and Lark.

Lark's parents couldn't have named Roz or Bay if they had tried. "There's that raccoon girl," they'd say, or "it's that damn scarecrow boy again," before drifting back into a dreamless sleep.

None of the LunaTicks would have graduated high school without the other two.

◆

The Goose Lake video went viral, and life started to change just like Bay predicted. They sent the video from Bay's phone to the local news and suddenly they weren't the LunaTicks or the "dumb-ass emo kids" anymore — they were crisp and poignant, *three local youths* who had *captured shocking footage* of their *hometown spook*. People on the street gave them second looks of fear and fascination. A couple reporters came out from Lincoln and Omaha, though their arrogance forbade them from understanding what this video meant to Whippoorwill. They were interviewed on a paranormal radio show, *Unheard Of*, based in Minneapolis. For the first time in their lives, they came with the warning label they'd always wanted. "The footage that you are about to see," dramatic pause, "may disturb you."

Bay had to keep from laughing whenever he watched the Goose Lake video, because of the absurdity of his perky little girlfriend pretending to be a dead witch — for Halloween last fall, Jessica had been a sexy strawberry. He was proud of her moxie, even though she'd whined afterwards that she smelled like a dead rat.

"When we make the real movie, I want a better costume," she said.

"We ought to hire a real actress for the real movie, babe," he replied.

The movie was his big plan for getting out of Whippoorwill. It was all that time spent working at the theater, selling tickets to the "sheeple." Said sheeple couldn't get enough of those found footage mockumentaries. But really, they had a lot of ways out of Whippoorwill. There was working on a Dream America cruise, or hitchhiking, or Greenpeace. There were communes and oil rigs. The LunaTicks would lie on the asphalt watching jets pass overhead and dream up these exit ramps out of car exhaust. *I can't wait to get out of here*, they'd say, smiling wistfully — they'd been saying it for years.

Lark couldn't stop watching the Goose Lake video. He got the file on his own phone and then showed it off like a newborn baby to his retired neighbors, the gas station clerk, the town drunk who sat outside the grocery store with a whiskey bottle in a paper bag. Lark always asked what they saw, as if even he didn't know the answer. No matter what they said, he'd shake his head and mutter, "That's not it." Bay said he was taking the method-acting thing too seriously.

Roz couldn't watch the video at all. This played well during interviews because she seemed traumatized, but after the microphones were off she was angry all the time. She wasn't getting enough sleep, she said. The silver maple outside scratched at her window, as if asking to be let in.

The town bent around them like a car wrapping around a tree during a tornado. Suddenly all these Raggedy Annies — *Raggedy Annie in my yard, Raggedy Annie in my attic, Raggedy Annie in the hospital when my husband passed away* — came crawling out into the sunlight. The entire town had grown up with the same story about a witch who aborted babies back when the town was still being sculpted raw out of the rolling prairie, and they all knew the matching nursery rhyme as sure as they knew "Happy Birthday"

— *we hung her over water, from the mighty oak tree / we hung her looking over at the cemetery.*

A girl from high school, an ex-cheerleader, chatted Lark up in the express lane at the grocery store where he worked. She was buying diapers, but she wasn't wearing a wedding ring. "Aren't you freaked out? God, I think I might have *died* if I had seen her." Lark said that wasn't part of the story. Raggedy Annie didn't kill on sight. The ex-cheerleader made a mock screaming sound and hissed, "Don't say her name!" She also said to meet her at The Pale Horse on Friday night, but she didn't show.

So Lark sat at the bar with Bay and Roz. The bartender said he'd always known that bitch Raggedy Annie was real. "Shit, man, every time I drive by Goose Lake, I get this weird feeling. I thought it was a magnetic field or something, like Mystery Quadrant up in South Dakota. But nah, man. Our fucking parents were right! She's our demon. She's our cross to bear, if you don't mind me saying. And the bitch can't let go of a grudge. There's just this one thing I don't get though… but why did she show herself to you? Of all the people who've been boating and camping out at Goose Lake, why *you* guys?"

What they knew he meant was why, out of all the great little people in this great little town, would Raggedy Annie choose these losers? Or was it like attracts like: yesterday's demon for today's devils?

On Monday Lark showed the video to a pack of shabby children in the candy aisle. Tears were shed; one kid pissed himself. As a furious mother hoisted her away, one girl pointed at Lark and shrieked, "Mommy, the tree!" Lark's coworkers would later say that they had never seen him look so freaked out, so cracked up. He started shouting — in *desperation*, everyone told the manager, not *anger* — "I know, it's the Witching Tree!"

The day after, Lark neither showed up for work nor answered his phone. He probably would have been fired anyway, given the children-in-the-candy-aisle incident, but Roz and Bay had to make certain he hadn't somehow died — a freak electrocution, carbon monoxide, anything seemed possible if Lark wasn't answering his phone — because where one goes, the others must follow. So Roz drove them to the Dunkins' house on the scraggly edge of town. No luck, no Lark. "I have no idea where he is," said Mrs. Dunkin, from the couch. It smelled more foul than usual. "But he isn't here, raccoon girl."

His parents had really let the yard go — the branches of a grotesque hackberry tree were grasping the roof of the little tin house, like the tentacles of a mummified octopus. They always kept the shades drawn, so maybe they hadn't noticed it. "Nice tree, Mrs. Dunkin," Bay said as they left, but she didn't respond.

Bay had the big ideas, but Lark was the smartest LunaTick. He slouched in the back of classrooms, mumbling answers only when forced. Most of his teachers dismissed his potential — as the twig's bent, so's the tree inclined, they said. But there was no arguing with test scores. When the time came to shuffle the seventeen-year-olds out of gymnasiums and into the real world, Lark got the Four-Year-Colleges handout instead of Two-Year-Colleges or The-US-Armed-Forces. He stared at it for a week before quietly applying to the University of Nebraska-Lincoln. If he stayed he knew he would end up like Roger Malkin. Bay would eventually get a job at the Toyota dealership, and Roz would marry some tool with bad hair, but he'd take up the mantle of *town drunk*. He had the genes for it. Roger would slur, "You's a good kid," and that meant they understood each other, damn it.

He told the other LunaTicks that he'd gotten into UNL while Bay was driving them to Dairy Queen. Bay was so upset that he nearly drove the car off Dead Man's Bridge, and that moment of gut-flattening fear was the most alive any of them had felt in months. "Come with me," Lark begged, but Roz just chewed her hair while Bay ground his teeth. They looked like scared rats, backing into their holes.

After the university paperwork started coming in — *Get Involved! See What's New!* — Lark realized that his life in Whippoorwill was a mere shadow of real human experience. He saw himself in an inspirational poster: teetering alone on a cliff, muslin wings outstretched, *DARE TO DREAM* emblazoned across the bottom. In what should have been his final summer in his hometown, Whippoorwill shrank and withered until just driving down Jefferson Street made him itchy, claustrophobic. He'd stand in the shower stall with the centipedes for hours, drowning out the coughs of his narcoleptic parents, willing the water to wash off his mildewed skin. *All this is ending,* he would think. *All this is dead to me.*

When he loaded up his car in August, his parents pried themselves off the couch to see him off. "You won't get far," his mother whispered in his ear as she hugged him, bones digging into his back, and from the doorway his father said, "He'll come crawling back. They always do."

And he was right. After Lark came home for winter break, he never made the drive back east. Classes were hard. Dorm rooms were small. People were brusque, shallow, vulgar. Everyone had more money than he did. The jocks who'd made high school miserable were now living in frat houses behind the quad. He hadn't made any real friends — not friends like Roz and Bay, anyway. They were waiting for him at Dead Man's Bridge after the big December snow, smiling with outstretched wool gloves. "We knew you couldn't stay away," Roz said. For a moment Lark considered grabbing both their hands and jumping into the river of ice below.

Raggedy Annie stood at the end of the bed. *It's Jessica,* Roz thought. *Jessica broke into my room and she's trying to scare me and she and Bay are going to laugh about this tomorrow.* She tried to open her mouth and couldn't. She tried to pry her jaw open with her hand and couldn't lift her arm.

The thing at the end of the bed — *Jessica, Jessica, Jessica* — stretched two bone-white arms to the black hood. Roz tried to close her eyes, but before she could, the hood was gone, and the face of the ghoul was revealed. She didn't know what to expect, since Raggedy Annie never had a face in the story — but it was her mother. She was glowing blue-green, like fox fire in the woods, and if not for that glow, her face was so flat and her movements so jerky that she could have been an old film reel. Her mother — who should have been a mile away and six feet deep in First Plymouth — opened and closed her mouth as if trying to speak, though only a hoarse, coffin-cramped gasp escaped.

Roz was a mess the next day. She forgot about makeup and coffee and straightening her hair. She forgot to call the landscaping company about getting the silver maple tree, the one that knocked on her window every night, under control. It was almost as tall as the chimney now; it was overwhelming the house. *The one thing I tell you to do*, as her father would later say. *You're just like your mother. Apple doesn't fall far from the tree, I guess.* She also forgot about the performance review that would have determined whether she'd be made accessories sales supervisor at Clipmann's, and ended up spending most of the review trying to save her job. "Are you on drugs?" her manager asked, disappointed. He'd made it clear how important it was for women to look put-together on the sales floor. "You look terrible."

Old Lady Marigold, who had nothing to do now that her husband was dead except rifle through clearance racks, found her listlessly hanging hats upon the hat tree. It looked like a headhunter's tower. "You shouldn't have messed with Raggedy Annie, Rosslyn Taro."

Roz squeezed the cloche in her hand and took a deep breath that was meant to be calming. "We didn't do anything to her, we just…" The calming breath hitched in her throat — memories of smearing the white shift in damp dirt, saying *hell no* she wouldn't wear it, watching Jessica slip it on instead — "We were just hanging out at Goose Lake and happened to…"

"You *must have* done *something!*" Old Lady Marigold squinted as if to see through a curtain. "You must have been trying something, you must have invited…"

"You care so much about her now, but the town elders *killed* Raggedy Annie, didn't they? Isn't that the whole point of the stupid story? This town will literally kill you if you step out of line?"

Old Lady Marigold pursed her wrinkled, wine-stained lips but held her tongue for fifteen seconds longer than normal, so Roz knew that she was right. Not that anyone needed Raggedy Annie to teach them that lesson — just live in Whippoorwill long enough for the walls to build up, either behind or beyond you. "It is *not* a stupid story. Good Lord, what did your mother teach you?"

She shoved the cloche into place. "My mother's dead."

"And you don't want to let her down, do you? Now Raggedy Annie was an evil woman, but her story is part of our story, Rosslyn Taro, and for that alone you ought to have some respect. You shouldn't have showed that tape to anyone. You shouldn't have paraded her around like a damn pageant queen."

Roz willed herself to say nothing. Bay had warned them about keeping quiet regarding Goose Lake, to make sure their stories matched. He was getting calls from famous television shows, *Paranormal Detectives*–type stuff. He kept saying *this is it*, but Roz couldn't help thinking that more publicity — more pageantry — would only make the haunting worse. Bay wasn't getting visits from anything pretending to be Raggedy Annie, so he probably didn't care. She'd asked him how they would explain Lark's absence, and he said, "Say he went insane, it'll sound creepier." She had never so much wanted to hit him.

"That friend of yours has been hanging out in Roger Malkin's trailer. What's his name, *Lark?*" Before he gave up the ghost several weeks ago, Mr. Malkin used to sit outside the grocery store next to the mechanical horses, drinking whiskey from a paper bag. Lark would be sent to shoo him away, but never had the heart to do it. "My hairdresser lives out in Gaslight Village, and she says you gotta get him out of there. The debt collectors are coming to get the trailer any day now."

She called Bay on her lunch break, to tell him that Lark had not in fact run off to Mexico, and ask him if Jessica still had the costume — her tongue no longer wanted to voice the hallowed, damned name of *Raggedy Annie*. "Because I think we should burn it."

Bay was in an awful mood, supposedly due to a severe toothache. "Don't flake out on me like Lark."

"I'm not flaking, I just think we fucked up! I think we shouldn't have done this!" She pulled back her hair, sunk into herself, felt the rapid beating of her heart. She thought she saw Raggedy Annie — *mom?* — at the other end of the parking lot, but then a car passed and it was just a stop sign. Talk about this, and she'd sound crazy. Forget sounding crazy, she'd *be* crazy. Another loony. Just like Lark. She had to use language Bay understood. "We should get rid of the evidence before anybody ever finds it."

"Well, I have no idea where it is. I haven't talked to Jessica since Tuesday. She's being a bitch."

If Lark was here, he'd say *no!* all sarcastic and wry, and she'd let out her horselaugh, and Bay would get pissed because he was the only one allowed to diss Jessica, and she'd say, "What do you expect with some nineteen-year-old Hot Topic wannabe?"

"She's never got the time anymore. She's always working on her damn terrariums." She heard him scoff through the phone. "Here I thought she hated science."

The next day Roz called KLNW news and said she wanted to come clean about the Goose Lake video. "Our first mistake was making the film at all," she said on the six o' clock news. "Our second mistake was showing it to other people. I just want to say to the entire community that I'm so sorry for lying, and I'm so sorry for any disrespect we may have caused." To the nameless, unseen power behind the visitations, she added a silent prayer: *Please forgive me. Please let me go.*

The Bailey family tree lived in Aunt Vivian's upstairs closet. Once upon a time, when Bay was young and bored and his parents were having it out at home, Aunt Vivian had unrolled it and presented it to him on her kitchen table. It was his inheritance, she said. Just like his father's Smith & Wesson and his mother's bad teeth. Aunt Vivian's lacquered fingernails ran from name to name, jumping back and forth in time. "That's your great-great-grandpa Johnny, he enlisted after getting married and then went and died in the War," she said. "And that's Laura Jean, she's your cousin twice removed. She wanted to be a movie star, but she only sang backup in commercials."

"Why is it called a tree?" little Bay asked.

"Because we all grew from the same roots. Lots of people draw their family trees starting from their great-grandpas at the top, as if all your ancestors lived and died just so you could be born, you special little cupcake. But that doesn't make a damn bit of sense. You start with the roots — that's Herman and Sarah Bailey, when they moved here from Ohio. The rest of us are their twigs. We grew out of them."

The chart indeed looked like everyone since Herman and Sarah had grown out of their subterranean bones, children sprouting from their parents like spores.

"Does that mean we're stuck here?"

Aunt Vivian cocked her head. "And just what is wrong with *here?*"

His parents had met in elementary school; they grew into a big-haired Stairway to Heaven couple with matching letterman jackets. *Whippoorwill born and bred*, they cooed, as if that was anything to be proud of. They'd disproved their own manifesto by the time Bay was old enough to dial child services. For a while he was the only one who heard the plastic plates ricocheting off the dining room wall, the *fuck yous* and the *just get outs*, the station wagon scurrying out of the driveway and jumping the curb. He wondered how to put that shit in the family tree. *Attention, the tree is currently on fire.* After the divorce severed his parents' bond, he imagined his own name gliding away as if it had never been rooted to this gnarled monstrosity that began with Herman and

Sarah. Yet nothing changed. He stayed tethered to the crown of the Bailey tree: a struggling, captive bird.

His father never liked it when he talked about New York, Vegas, Mexico. He would point a beer can at him and say, "You think you're better than this town? We're not good enough for you anymore?"

It seemed easier to say he was sick of "you fucking hillbillies" than to tell the truth. He knew that would get a response, probably a box in the ear for pissing on his surroundings. But what he really wanted to say was *You were never good enough for me. You were never good enough for anyone.*

Rumor had it that the weirdo living in Roger "Alkie" Malkin's trailer in Gaslight Village was an escaped convict. Tweaked-out gremlins in neon shirts sometimes snuck peeks through the windows, standing on their tiptoes in the muddy swamp grass that had swallowed most of the trailer's tires. The weirdo was usually sitting in the dark with a flashlight, watching something terrifying on his phone. The glow on his face was lunar. When he noticed them, he'd growl and scurry to the window and pull the curtains. The rumor adjusted — now he was a scientist from Area 51, on the run from the Feds.

But he was just a man — a boy, really — who had the misfortune of stumbling upon some hidden fold in the world that he couldn't explain, and knew of no other recourse than retreat. He was just Lark. When Roz knocked on the door of the trailer, distressed because she'd seen feet descend from the silver maple tree in her backyard, he opened the door. And when Bay banged upon the door an hour later, yelling that he knew they were in there, Lark again relented.

"The gang's back together," Lark whispered, trembling and huddling on the piss-stained carpet. He looked like death by then — he'd lost so much weight, so much color. But Roz and Bay were red eyed too. They hadn't spoken to each other since her confession to KLNW news. He had tried to contact her at first — called twenty-three times and sent seven text messages, including *Fuck you you fucking bitch* — but, within forty-eight hours, he was the one on KLNW, and Roz was the unstable nut job with the ax to grind. He swore to the town of Whippoorwill that the video was one-hundred-percent authentic. "Only unity saves the damned."

"I just got fired," Bay said in the trailer. "My manager says she lost *trust* in me since my friend *Rosslyn* went on TV and said we faked the entire Goose Lake video." Roz was clenching her stomach, refusing to look at him. "So thank you, Rosslyn. Thank you so much."

"I was desperate!" she shouted. "You don't know what it's like! You turn every corner and you wonder — is she gonna be there? Is she watching me? Will anybody else see her? And even after I said sorry, she still didn't stop!" She knelt down beside Lark and cautiously tugged on the hems of the blanket he wore like a shawl around his head. "Lark, I know you've been seeing her too."

Lark stared blankly at her, and Bay clapped his hands over his head. "You're unbelievable. It's not Raggedy Annie, fuckwit, Raggedy Annie isn't real! Remember? We made her! She's Jessica!"

"Yeah? And where is your little girlfriend anyway? She's a part of this mess, she ought to be here too."

Bay nervously chewed on his fingernail as he stalked around Alkie's trailer. It was empty save for plastic bags and cigarette butts and half-eaten meals: evidence of a life undone. "Jessica's gone."

The other LunaTicks were silent, but Bay slammed his fist into a plastic cabinet and snapped an answer to a question he'd heard only in his head, "I don't know where! She's just gone, she hasn't been to work, her parents haven't seen her… they think she got mad at me and ran off. When they looked in her room all they found were those… damn terrariums." Suddenly exhausted, Bay slid to the carpet and pulled off his black beanie. "They're all the same too. Just one tiny tree in every one. Looks like a little oak tree." The tiniest sliver of a bittersweet smile cracked Bay's face. "Like a tiny Witching Tree."

"Bay's right," Lark mumbled. "It's not Raggedy Annie. It's the trees. Here, look at the video again." He held up his phone and their no-budget home movie began to play. Roz and Bay were so hollowed out by then that they didn't have the strength to object to watching their little experimental film another, final time. They watched themselves skip stones across Goose Lake, watched the camera find the Witching Tree. They watched themselves act out the script they'd written at Jessica's house the night before — *"Let's just go, I'm getting cold"* — and watched Jessica stand ominous and hooded in front of the Witching Tree. And finally, they watched the branches of the Witching Tree curl, like the fingers of some enormous dryad, toward Jessica.

"Do you see the tree?" Lark whispered, like he was coaching a baby to speak. The leaves of the tree stood on end, fluttering as if swept by a celestial wind, trembling as if awakening. "See it move?"

"I don't understand," Roz whined. "It's the breeze…"

"No, no, no! Listen, I've looked this up, and these beings exist across the world, in dozens of civilizations across time… there's Yggdrasil, there's Ashvattha, there's Világfa, there's Kalpavrishka, and now there's… there's the Witching Tree." Bay was about to punch Lark in the face, and they all knew it, so he spoke faster. "These trees, they connect… all the planes of existence, the world of the living with the world of the dead. The Witching Tree is our Cosmic Tree."

Those words — *Cosmic Tree* — hung like smoke circles in Alkie's musty trailer. Jessica's terrariums. The trees that grew manic and hungry over their houses. The Witching Tree itself, eternal long-limbed sentinel of Goose Lake. And all roads led to Goose Lake…

Bay was the first to break the trance and grapple to his feet. He claimed not to understand what Lark was trying to say. He said he couldn't waste his time on this bullshit about trees, because what could a tree do to him? All he knew was that Lark and Roz had gone completely batshit, and now none of them were ever getting out of Whippoorwill, and was that what they wanted all along?

Did they want to be stuck in this inbred town forever, maybe open a tree nursery if they were so obsessed with greenery?

"… dude, what are you doing to your teeth?"

Bay was picking at one of his bottom canine teeth, digging into the gum, trying to rip it out. "It's the root!" he shouted through his bloody fingers. "It's fucking killing me!"

Bay waited until he'd returned home to extract the tooth. He was so distracted by the electric pain that he failed to see that the dead cottonwood outside his mother's house, the one that had broken his arm as a child, was growing green again. He used a pair of pliers and the bathroom mirror — the pain was nothing compared to the horror of enduring another moment with the tooth's ruined root in his skull. Yet even as he stared at the ugly disembodied thing lying at the bottom of the sink, he could feel the roots of his other teeth rotting. He didn't know what had happened to them — his bad teeth, his mother's teeth — but he could feel their decay spreading into his jaws, his sinuses. The thought of those sick roots growing into his bones — he saw them jutting out of his chin like saber teeth, drilling down in search of soil — made him want to die…

They all had to go. By the time his mother came in, he was lying delirious on the tiles, his teeth scattered around him like bloody seeds.

The day after Bay was committed to Teller Psychiatric, Roz drove alone to Jessica Grauner's house in the half-light. She went because only unity saves the damned, though she'd hated Jessica when she'd tagged along on the LunaTicks' vandalism operations and petty larceny sprees. Where one goes, the others must follow, and she neither wanted to follow Bay to Teller Psychiatric nor knew how to follow Lark into his rabbit hole. And she had the squirmy feeling that Jessica was still hanging around — *like Raggedy Annie hung from the Witching Tree?* — somewhere on the property.

Roz had been to this house twice — once for a grotesque house party while Jessica's parents were out of town, and once to prepare for the Goose Lake stunt. On neither occasion had there been a linden tree in the front yard, but now a full-grown specimen had broken through the earth to stand in proud, terrifying splendor before Jessica's window. Its roots bubbled across the lawn, disrupting her parents' carefully manicured ornamental ferns. A large, discolored knot peeked out from the linden's trunk — a malformed branch, right, a sleeping bud? But when Roz got close enough to touch it, she saw that it was a face: Jessica's face, her eyes clenched shut and her mouth stretched open in an anguished forever-scream. Roz ran her finger down one wooden eye, heard Jessica's nasal whine — *I smell like a dead rat!* — and quickly stuffed her hand back in her pocket, running back to her car.

♦

Roz's mother died during the Great Storm. She died at home, of cancer, while the world raged around them. Electric lines sparked, cars slid off roads, walls fell in, and smaller trees were torn out of the earth, but their older, larger counterparts miraculously survived. It seemed like a condolence card from God: *The world is filled with death, but Life endures.*

There were strange things said at the funeral. "She's waiting for you, in heaven." "We will all meet again, by-and-by." Roz hated to admit it — because who wouldn't want to see their mother again? — but when these words floated up on desolate roads at midnight, she was frightened. She wanted to hear that her mother was at peace, in a better place, had *moved on* — not that she was *waiting, lingering, hovering,* skeletal hands outstretched to receive her daughter as soon as death delivered her — no. That was ugly.

Her mother loved trees. They were her favorite thing about Whippoorwill. *Don't you love how tall they are, how old they are? These trees are older than all of us.* She was a native, so she had grown up with them — climbed them, slept in their nooks, taken their shelter, carved her initials into their skin with the neighbor boy. Roz's father had agreed to move to Whippoorwill before they got married because it was supposedly a good place to raise a family — what with the safe streets and heritage fairs and seasonal festivals — but when he wanted to move to Lincoln for the sake of a higher salary, her mother had refused on account of the trees. *But there are trees everywhere*, he said. *It's not the same*, she said. *These trees are my inheritance. They're the kids' inheritance.*

She had a special bedtime story about the Witching Tree. It had nothing at all to do with Raggedy Annie. It was about the men and women who first built Whippoorwill, back when America was young. They built the jail and they built the church, they built the courthouse and they built the school. And then they planted the Witching Tree, so after their human bodies died they would stay close to their children, and live forever.

Her father listened in once, and got so upset that her mother never told it again, and Roz never heard it again from anyone else. At middle-school sleepovers — before the other girls decided she was just too weird — they only ever whispered about Raggedy Annie, the abortionist-witch. When she asked about *that Witching Tree story* they would indignantly snap, "That *is* the Witching Tree story, dummy!"

But one time in high school when they were all smoking pot in Bay's basement, Roz tried to retell her mother's version of the Witching Tree story, what little she could remember of it. It turned out Bay and Lark had heard similar shit from their parents, once or twice. Bay and Lark were, first and last and always, the only people she could count on not to lie to her. Lark said, "It's a creation myth. And an apocalypse myth, too. The end and the beginning, the beginning and the end."

Dawn came, and they never spoke of it again. The Witching Tree story — the real one, the one submerged beneath the arsenic-and-old-lace of Raggedy Annie — was only whispered in the ears of Whippoorwill babies, so the truth would soften like sugar cubes right into their unfinished brains. These babies grew up and forgot except when they were sleeping, usually, but sometimes when they looked at the massive, infallible trees of Whippoorwill for too long, that primordial story writhed like a worm and they would shiver, listening to the leaves rustling like ocean waves, wondering who was waiting for them.

♦

Raggedy Annie stood, again, at the end of Roz's bed. Roz could almost hear her breathing.

"No," Roz mumbled to herself. "She's not real. Raggedy Annie is not real." And maybe she wasn't, but something stood there. Something had turned Bay into a pile of dirt in Teller Psychiatric. Oh, that wasn't in the official hospital report — the hospital said he somehow *escaped*, from the restraints and the room and the asylum, and the forest-fresh soil that had replaced him in the cot was — what — a practical joke? The LunaTicks knew all about those, but this was something else, something beyond. Roz closed her eyes, telling herself that once she opened them, it would be morning, and Raggedy Annie would be gone.

When she opened her eyes the figure was leaning over her, twitching. This time it wasn't her mother beneath the hood. This was the face that looked back at her in the mirror every morning, bleary-eyed and bloodless, sapped of life. It was her. Her doppelganger cocked its head to the side like a bird and stared at her with her own big black eyes — black, then blacker, in the face of the ghost. It was death looking down; she could feel that in her veins, because that wasn't blood roiling inside her anymore. It was sap. *Slow like honey*. Death leaned in, and Roz screamed herself awake.

It was midnight. Roz drove to Gaslight Village in a fugue, but Lark wasn't there. Alkie's trailer looked like it had been spat out by a tornado — it had been smashed nearly in half by a fallen tree. Branches had broken through the windows and now grew inside the trailer, as if they'd been searching for him. Her first thought was that the trailer had become his coffin, but after she scrambled to reach a broken window, cutting her hands on glass shards, she didn't see a body in the dark. No soil, either. There was only one place, unhappily, that he would have gone.

She could see the woods around Goose Lake stirring before she even got out of the car. For a second she sat behind the wheel, trying to delay the inevitable, hypnotized by the razor-sharp static that had overcome the radio, until she saw again the figure that she'd been running from since they made the video. Raggedy Annie was standing where the trees parted to make way for a little human path. The hooded ghost turned and disappeared down the trail, and Roz knew this would not end if she did not pursue. Where one goes the others must follow, and Raggedy Annie was one of them. The truth was she always had been. Raggedy Annie and her mother and father and brother and Lark's parents and Bay's parents and Jessica and Old Lady Marigold and Roger Malkin and everybody, everybody in this town: they were all in this together.

She willed her legs to move into the rippling chaos. As soon as she stepped foot on the dirt path the air pressure dropped, and her bones felt calcified in pain. She'd been hoping not to return to Goose Lake. She'd been hoping to leave Whippoorwill. She'd been hoping... *well*. Hope was just delusion that hadn't ripened yet. The forest didn't smell like pine or cedar or Christmas or anything else they could pack into an air freshener — it smelled like rot. A fleet of dead were howling overhead, and there was nowhere left to go but forward. Just like all roads led to Goose Lake, all of Goose Lake's dirt paths led to the Witching Tree, the oak to seed and end the world.

The Tree had grown since she last saw it. She felt the urge to kneel under its swaying, groaning shadow. Even as worms crawled out of cavities in its trunk, new twigs and leaves sprouted on its boughs. Lark was a dwarf beneath it, wildly swinging a rusty ax. Every strike was true, but he wasn't getting anywhere — not only was the oak enormous, but its bone-like bark yielded nothing except for a few brittle chips of wood. She could see this, even though she could not see stars through the foliage. What stars? The Witching Tree was everything in this world.

Lark looked up and tried to smile when he saw her through his sweat. He looked so weak and mortal, a mere weed next to the Witching Tree. "We can make it, Roz! You and me. Just you and me. You just gotta help me. Help me end this thing."

She shook her head. She could feel the Tree's roots moving like great pythons beneath the fertile earth. "I don't think we can, Lark… I don't think we're getting away."

Lark frowned and paused his work, catching the blade with his hand. "But if we cut it down, it ends," he said, and then cried out and dropped the ax. He was squeezing his left palm — he'd nicked it. Or it had nicked him, it was hard to tell. So the blade was sharp after all — just not sharp enough to slay the tower of space-time that was the Tree. He moaned and pressed his right hand into the wound. "Something's wrong," his voice warbled, holding out his hand. By the Tree's light, Roz could barely see it: dark amber where red should have been. It was sap. He was bleeding sap.

"Roz," Lark whimpered. He sounded like the eleven-year-old Clark Dunkin that she had happened to sit next to in sixth grade: sniveling and sullen but, still, full of a future. The years of dishevelment sloughed off in seconds, revealing the baby face below. Was this how the Tree could promise endless life, like her mother said? "Help me."

She blinked, and became faintly aware that she was crying. "Don't fight it."

Now roots were bursting out of his storm-worn sneakers, running wildly toward moist earth — they were trying to find some place to settle, to never let go. Lark was trying to shamble forward but he could only heave his chest, retching until he couldn't breathe. Tree bark tore through his jeans, and his arms finally straightened and seized and were destroyed — no, transformed. Only the human skin died. Lark arched his back and would have broken his vertebrae had they not turned to pliable wood; his mouth tore open and a dozen branches leapt from his wooden throat, sprouting blood blossoms. It was almost beautiful.

Roz was kneeling by then, in deference and fear. When Lark's screams finally stopped, she knew that it was her turn. Where others go, one must follow. She lifted her head and saw the great and gnarled Tree, glowing blue-green with something far stronger and far more alien than fox fire, achingly reach its branches toward her and then shrivel back. It was so jealous, so unsure of her loyalty. *"Roz-zz-lyn,"* her mother said, from somewhere in the rush of leaves, *"why d' you want to lee-eave us?"*

Roz picked up the ax. A wail swept through the branches, but Roz only threw the weapon into the murky green waters of Goose Lake. "I'll never leave," she said, and began trudging homeward. "I promise."

It was not a warm embrace. The Tree's branches bit deep into her back as it entwined her, and she soon lost the ability to see anything but heartwood. Still, she melted into the Tree as easily and completely as if she had never been parted from it. Little by little, the walls came down: the walls of Whippoorwill, the walls of her skin. *I'm scared*, she thought as the flesh of her tongue dissolved into sap, and though the only response she heard was a deep and ancient drumbeat pulsing from far within the Witching Tree, she finally understood.

Paul Tremblay

"The true weird tale has something more than secret murder, bloody bones, or a sheeted form clanking chains according to rule. A certain atmosphere of breathless and unexplainable dread of outer, unknown forces must be present; and there must be a hint, expressed with a seriousness and portentousness becoming its subject... Atmosphere is the all-important thing, for the final criterion of authenticity is not the dovetailing of a plot but the creation of a given sensation."

I agree in principle with Howard (can I call him Howard?) that atmosphere can be the all-important thing in a weird/horror tale. But the hopeless contrarian in me says, "Atmosphere, schmatmosphere," at least in terms of Howard's prescriptive usage of the term. I've had an editor (who might be the same age as Howard) tell me that the atmosphere of the weird is always and forever the most important aspect of every horror story, which is simply not true. In so many of my favorite weird/horror stories (from Shirley Jackson, Flannery

O'Connor, Richard Matheson, Stewart O'Nan, Peter Straub, and Kelly Link), *the source of horror is the subversion of the commonplace through accrued detail, the bathing in the mundane and everyday and then peeling back the veneer of perceived normalcy to show the truth: that there is no normalcy and that any notion of salvation and/or safety are the biggest lies. The atmosphere of horror in those stories is our own. Aye, that's the stuff.*

And when Howard writes: "The story — tedious, artificial, and melodramatic — is further impaired by a brisk and prosaic style whose urbane sprightliness nowhere permits the creation of a truly weird atmosphere," I like to imagine he's talking about my story!

♦

She says, "Hi, honey," loud enough to turn the heads of all the Moms at the small beach pond.

I do my own comically exaggerated double take. She sidles up next to me, gives me a quick kiss. If this had happened to the teenager-me (alas, that nerdy kid was lost to the world so long ago, and replaced by this older, crankier model), he would've instantly vowed to never wash his cheek, and then locked himself in the bathroom *not* washing his cheek.

"Um, wow, okay. Hi?" I stay rooted in my chair under the shade of a skinny tree, slouched like Sasquatch on injured reserve.

She laughs. "Nice to see you, too. Jeeze. Aren't you surprised to see me?"

"Well, yeah. Of course." The spot where she kissed me feels pleasantly swollen.

"It's too nice out, and I'm jealous that you get to be out here on a Wednesday while I'm stuck at work, so I left. I'm playing hooky. Shh, don't tell anyone." She winks and smiles.

"I won't tell. Dig the bathing suit, by the way."

"Har har, funny guy. I jogged down here: 4.6 miles. Aren't you proud of me?" Standing spotlighted in a sunbeam that burns its way through the thinning tree branches, she strikes a runner's pose. I smile. Or I leer. No, I smile and I leer like some smiling, leering, drunken, leering, douchey frat boy. Seriously, I have no idea what's going on or what it is she's doing and what it is I'm doing. She wears black yoga/running pants (I don't know the difference) and a baggy white tee shirt that modestly covers the *wonderful* (trying to be less of that frat boy, yeah?) swell of her butt. The tee has some logo above her breast that I don't recognize. Her brown hair flecked with grey is tied up in a ponytail, and I long to know what her hair looks like when let down. She's fit, pretty in an everyday way, and she doesn't look anything like my wife, Shelley.

I say, "Very. I'm impressed," and I do a quick impression of a cheering crowd and clap my hands together manically over my head, but then I get all self-conscious of my sun-starved skin, the arm-jiggle of my shoestring arms, and even my faded concert tee shirt, the band long forgotten. So, yeah, my half-assed push-ups and burpees three days a week aren't exactly remolding my clay. I sit up straight and pretend not to hear the beach chair's creaks and groans. Crossing my arms awkwardly over my chest, I say, "I get winded even driving that distance."

"Hot. Why are you sitting under the tree, in the shade? I mean, why bother coming to the beach?"

"What do you mean? I'm being sun responsible. Protecting my precious, delicate skin. And it's not like there's a line of willing volunteers to slather me in sun lotion. *It puts the lotion in the basket,*" I say, doing my best Buffalo Bill from *Silence of the Lambs*, and I die inside a little bit because I realize that even my witty pop-culture references are middle-aged.

"Ew. You're so creepy," she says but laughs.

"When we get here, the kids sprint ahead of me, kick off their flip-flops, and crop-dust the beach, dropping their shit everywhere on their way to the water. If I shout, 'Treeeee!' after them like a madman, then at least they somewhat group their stuff near this spot." I'm talking a mile a minute, and it's already the longest conversation I've had with another adult at this beach.

I pat the tree next to my chair. The pocked and scarred trunk crawls with big black ants. On cue, I twitch, flail, and then flick an ant the size of a dachshund off my leg, and I look so amazingly macho doing so.

"You don't have to justify your life choices to me, hon. How are the swimming lessons going?"

"Great. But I already know how to swim."

"Is Michael on the other side of the dock with the older kids? I can't tell who he is out there. All I see are heads bobbing in the water. Where's Olivia? Oh, there she is. Think she saw me walk in?" She waves.

Olivia happens to be looking at us both. She returns a distracted and hesitant wave back. Olivia has always been friendly, too friendly really; her enthusiastically returning a hand wave is generally as autonomic as breathing.

The woman says, "Oh my God, she's like a little teenager already. She's embarrassed I called out to her. That's not supposed to happen yet."

Olivia dives forward into the water at the command of the instructor.

The woman shouts, "You're doing great, honey!"

I cringe at how loud she is, and I do my best to ignore the reverberating shocks of her easy familiarity, of her kiss, and of her knowing who my kids are. The strangers on the beach are one thing (I don't really care what they think), but what am I going tell Olivia and Michael about this woman? Maybe the kids met her at the Matthews' party and I don't remember? It's possible, yeah? I hope. Doesn't explain why she's acting like she's my wife and acting like she's their fawning Mom and why I'm playing along.

Whatever strange act we're spontaneously creating together, it's wrong, very wrong, but my head is pleasantly drunk with it.

Olivia struggles to freestyle swim toward the young instructor. The woman says, under her breath so only I can hear her, "Olivia's arms are as stiff as boards. Shouldn't the instructor tell her to, I don't know, bend her arms?" She pantomimes the correct swimming motion.

"You'd think you'd get more from fifty-dollar swimming lessons at the Bracken Pond, right?"

"Yeah. Where else can you get your kids' two weeks of sun, doggy paddle, and E. coli exposure?"

"When you put it that way, it sounds like a bargain."

"Ug, I can't watch this. Can I go down there and help her?"

"She's fine."

"How old do you think the instructor is?"

"Dunno. Eighteen?"

"You wish."

Olivia's swim instructor, like the rest of the pond's lifeguards (who also serve as the swimming-lesson instructors), is thin and tanned, wears a tight red bathing suit, and moves with the coltish combination of gangliness and grace of late high-school and college-aged kids. And it's so goddamn depressing that my son Michael is only a handful of years and the great and terrible yawning divide of puberty away from being one of them. It's to the point where I try not to look at him when he's shirtless, afraid I'll see a dark patch of hair under his arms. Because then it'll be all over.

I say, "I'm going to ignore that creepy but accurate remark. And I can honestly say I do not wish to be eighteen ever again."

"Yeah, me neither." She steps confidently in front of my chair and sits to my right, on Michael and Olivia's beach blanket. The blanket is pink and, when folded up, looks like a piece of sliced watermelon. It's such a clever blanket. She looks around at all the beachgoers and says, "You really are the only guy, the only *dad*, on the whole beach. Lucky you. But come on, wearing those mirrored sunglasses outs you as a total perv. Or a narc."

My face fills with blood and heat, and I sputter into what's supposed to be self-deprecating laughter but probably sounds like emphysema. Christ, I'm melting into my chair like I'm a bowl of ice cream. I'm embarrassed not because it's clear she knows I've been… shall we say… *ogling* the teen lifeguards and beach Moms, but because my patheticness is so predictable and obvious.

Mortally wounded, I say, "No one says *narc* anymore. You're so not hip. And sunglasses are the windows to the soul."

She reaches across my lap and tickles my knee playfully. Her hand and forearm is soft and she smells like plums, or a sweet tea, or those purple flowers that used to grow along the fence at my grandparents' house. I don't remember the flowers' real name, but Grammy called them her garden mums. And I don't know why I'm thinking about Grammy's flowers when I should be simultaneously enraptured and terrified by the not-so-innocent touch of a strange woman.

"My hubby, the dirty old man." She holds her hands out and nearly shouts to the rest of the beach, "Stand back, ladies! He's all mine!" She laughs at her own joke.

The Moms sharing the beach in our vicinity: they pretend to watch their toddlers running amuck on other people's blankets and throwing sand (that fucking kid with the sharks on his bathing suit is such a pain in the ass, I seriously considered tripping him on the sly yesterday); or they bury their faces in magazines and beat-up paperbacks they bought at the grocery store; or they look at the pond pretending to be intently watching their kids ignore and give attitude to the swimming instructor; or they blankly look up at the blue sky for the clouds that will one day approach. I'm not being paranoid (okay, I am), but they don't look at me and certainly don't look at the woman. I swear they're actively avoiding looking at us. I feel them *not* looking at me, which of course means they are judging me, saying in their heads *we don't know you, and we may not have ever met her, but we know she's not your wife.* I know better, but, goddamn me, it's not an entirely unpleasant feeling.

I say, "The dirty old man says that's not nice at all, and take off your shirt." I think about returning her touch. A light tap on her shoulder, or maybe letting my hand linger there, to see if it feels different than when I touch Shelley.

She says, "I'm not nice, but that's why you love me."

"I guess so."

"Oh, don't be so glum, perv. Hey, remember that game we

used to play when we started dating? We'd be in a bar, and one of us would say, okay, the world outside just ended, everyone disappeared or died or whatever, and all that's left is us and the rest of the schmoes in the bar." She pauses so that I can remember, so that I can cognitively catch up to her in the memory. Of course I don't remember something that's never happened, but I nod like I do. I nod like I'm so pleased and satisfied that anything of what I said or did in the earliest days of our relationship was something worth remembering. I nod because she's offering proof that I still mean something to her.

"Yeah, wow. I remember."

"Then we'd ask each other to rank ourselves in terms of mate-worthiness."

"You were always top five," I say, and then I add a detail, an anecdote that belongs to Shelley and I. "Especially at that friend's wedding where that woman showed up wearing a tiny day-glow turquoise skirt and a pink North Face fleece."

"You're so awful. You can't make fun of her, she had — issues."

"Don't we all."

"Look around, though. Just think, if the world ended right now, and it was just all of us here on the beach left, then you'd be a lucky guy. You'd be — top three, easy."

"Gee, thanks. So you're saying I'm third in a three-man race behind the teen Adonis lifeguards."

"You're sort of Adonis-like, kind of. If you averaged those two kids together, maybe?"

"So I'm average-Adonis."

"Don't I know it."

"Yeah. I don't think they'd need my help to repopulate the species."

"Hey, you never know. I bet some of the Moms here would go for the more mature look. And top three is top three. What about me? Be honest. Where would I rank?"

Before today, this past weekend's party at the Matthews' house was the only other time I've seen her (and by *seen* I mean its literal, non-dating or non-affair usage; as in I *saw* her standing on the other side of the room, far away from me). The Matthews are the first family we've really gotten friendly with since moving to Wrentham three years ago. Michael and Olivia are approximately the same ages as their kids, and they all get along very well. Emily Matthews thinks Shelley is a hoot, and I get along great with Richard; we're planning to coach our sons' flag football team in the fall, even though I know nothing about football, or flags. Future flag-football fun aside, the move to Wrentham hasn't gone as expected. Our kids have had no problem uprooting and going to a new town and making new friends, but, for Shelley and me, becoming friends with other local parents and families hasn't been easy. Branching out and being more social in the community is one of our family goals of the summer. We're so cutely lame we even wrote out our goals on a piece of yellow paper; the list is magneted to the fridge.

So we went to the party, and I tried my best to smile and join in on the conversations about lawns and building stuff that I can't build. I don't know why it was such hard work. That's not true; I do know why it was hard work: whenever I was asked what I did for work (stay-at-home Dad with some SAT prep tutoring on the side), the blank stares and jokes were all the same. So I mostly kept to myself and kept a full beer constantly in one hand. I was totally blitzed by the end of the night. And not coincidentally, at that same end of the night, the woman walked in the front door along with a guy named Terrance. According to Richard, Terrance was a *good guy* and a recent divorcee. The break was not a clean one. The Matthews and just about everyone else at the party were good friends with both Terrance and his ex-wife Mary. Mary wasn't at the party, much to Emily Matthews' chagrin. I'd heard her complaining to Shelley about it as they worked their way through a bottle of red wine.

Anyway, I remember the woman walking in, wearing cut-off jean shorts and a white tee shirt, and her hair was up like it was now, and she held Terrance's hand. He smiled too, but it was a different kind of smile. After an awkward initial introduction ("Everybody, this is _____, and _____, this is everybody"), the party continued to go on around them as if they'd never arrived. I'm serious. Granted, I was all in the bag (see what I did there? as opposed to half in the bag?), but I'm not exaggerating when I say that, the party people, they shunned the new couple as though they were Dimmesdale and Prynne. Terrance and the woman banished themselves to the corner. The only person I remember talking to the woman was Shelley. Shells went right up to her, and they chatted while I stumbled around looking for shoes (it was that kind of night) and my kids, and not necessarily in that order. I was going to ask Shells what she and the woman were talking about when we got into the car, but I passed out.

I say to the woman, "On this and any beach at the end of the world, you are number one."

"Yay!" She holds up a celebratory I'm-number-one finger. "You're a horrible liar, but I'll take it."

"Do you mean I am horrible in addition to being a liar, or that I'm not proficient at lying?"

"Now I mean both."

"Fair enough."

Our playful conversation ends with the blow of the lifeguard's whistle. The swimming lessons are over. Half of the kids run out of the water like someone spotted a shark, others stay and thrash around like greedy parasites in blood. Olivia stands waist deep in the pond, arms wrapped around herself. She's shivering, and her lips are blue, but she won't come out of the water. You have to drag her out, or at least dangle a towel in front of her.

The lifeguard's trilling whistle explodes in my head and ends in a sharp stabbing point inside my ear. My head feels stuffy all of a sudden. Maybe I'm getting one of those summer colds. Wouldn't that be convenient? I try coughing; a precursor to an excuse. It sounds fake and as forced as the sheepish shrug and smile I offer to the woman who suddenly seems as equally unsure of herself.

A shiver passes through me, as though I'm empathically feeling Olivia's coldness. I say, "All right, I think we'll just dry off and head out. Go home. It's noon already. Leftovers, more juice boxes, sandwiches, two pizza slices left…" and I trail off in volume, my speech degenerating into a weird, bipolar lunch-word association game. I grab Olivia's Harry Potter towel and shake out the ants. "It was nice —," and I'm going to say *talking to you.*

The woman stands up quickly, brushes sand off her legs, and says, "It's okay. You stay. I'll bring her the towel." She takes Olivia's towel out of my hands, and grabs a second towel out of my beach bag.

She hustles away from my shady spot, and I hold my hand out like I can reach out and grab her, pull her back, and keep her chatting and sitting next to me on the blanket, because that was all just harmless fun. We were all safe that way. But not now: anything that happens next will be irrevocable. And as she walks away and grows smaller from distance and perspective, I briefly pretend my hand covers her up, a rare back-of-my-hand eclipse, and, because I can no longer see her, that means she's not really there and that I've imagined her. It's the only scenario that won't end badly.

My head buzzes, and swims, gets thicker. Maybe I'm becoming the hypochondriac Shells always accuses me of being; I open and close my jaw, pop my ears, and shake my head, and nothing feels like it works right. My neck muscles are tight and stiff, the ligaments turning to bamboo.

Olivia comes running out of the water and into the open towel that the woman holds out for her. Olivia doesn't hesitate. The woman kisses the top of Olivia's head, and then rubs the towel all over, drying her off. She says, "Go see your father. He'll help you get dressed." She wraps Olivia up tight in the towel, brushes the wet hair out of her face, and tucks loose strands behind Olivia's ears. The woman points at me sitting in my chair, and that's all I'm doing, sitting, watching. Olivia stumbles up the beach, wrapped in a towel cocoon. She's shivering when she reaches me. Her teeth click together.

I say, "You okay, Liv? Your teeth weren't made to smash into each other like that, you know."

"I'm cold." She worms an arm out of the towel and scratches behind one of her ears. Her hair falls in front of her face. She won't look at me. I don't blame her.

"Let's get you dressed. We'll get lunch at home. Okay?"

I hold up the towel around her as she peels out of her two piece and struggles into underwear, shorts, and a tee shirt. She's still wet.

The woman is down at the shore, and no one stands within ten feet of her. She's like a human crop circle, which would be a funny joke to tell her if it wasn't true. I suddenly want to take Olivia up into my arms and just run. Fuck the car and fuck this town and just run and never stop running until I'm somewhere else, nobody knows where, and only then will I maybe call Shells and tell her that I'm sorry for the rest of my life.

Michael comes out of the water, and the woman gives him a coy little wave. He smirks at her, that look that says he sees you, doesn't want to talk to you, not in front of anyone else, but he's still glad you're there. The woman sneaks up beside him and, in one motion, drapes the towel over his thickening shoulders and sneaks in a quick hug around his neck. He's already almost as tall as she is. He says, "Stop it," but smiles and gives an embarrassed little laugh. He rubs a spot on the side of his neck absently. He's always been a distracted, twitchy little kid, and now's a charmingly distracted, twitchy big kid, just like Shells. It's amazing how much he looks and acts like her. Michael lifts the towel off his shoulders and drapes it over his head. The woman walks next to him, and bumps her hips into his. From under his towel-hood, he laughs, and says, "Stop," again.

I turn my back to them; I can't watch anymore and can't think anymore. I hurriedly fold up the watermelon blanket, doing it all wrong, and it ends up as misshapen as an asteroid. I stuff it and the rest of the kids' stuff into the green beach bag. If I grab Olivia now and run, would Michael know enough to follow me? The left side of my face feels swollen, like I've been punched, and slack too, and Christ, am I having a stroke?

Michael's shadow falls over me. His is the only shadow there. He's alone, I think. If she's there she's not saying anything. I'm not going to look for her. When did this (this being whatever it was I thought I was doing, I don't know, I don't know) become such a horror show? Has it always been a horror show?

I tell the kids we're going home. I don't give them the option of *not* going home. Olivia and Michael walk around in front of me but don't say anything, and they don't look back at me. My eyes fill with tears, and my chest is tight with panic, everything in my head spinning so fast it can only fly off its track and smash into a million pieces.

Michael doesn't bother changing into his dry shorts and tee shirt. He'll sit in the car on his wet towel. Even though Olivia changed into her clothes, her wet towel hangs loosely over her shoulders: a limp, sagging cape.

"Come on," I tell them. I'm impatient. It's how I lie to them: Yes, Dad has done something recklessly stupid, but he can fix it when we leave here, when we get home. "Come on, now! Walk. Move. Let's get home, okay?" I don't ask them to help me carry anything, so my arms are full of all the stuff. We stagger up the small, sandy hill, and then through the fence to the parking lot.

The woman calls out to us from behind. We stop. She stands next to a boulder that demarcates one section of the parking lot. We're five cars away from our car. She holds up surrender hands. Her smile stretches out across the rest of the lazy summer afternoon, yes, but there's something sad in her smile too. It's an all-good-things-must-come-to-an-end look. I know that look, I do.

She says, "Hey, guys, forgetting something? You really going to make me jog back home?"

We wait and she catches up to us. She says, "You guys are so mean to Mommy." She pats my butt, reaches into my bathing suit pocket and grabs the car keys. "I'll drive."

We fall in step behind her. She opens the trunk, and I dump the chair and everything else inside. The kids dutifully climb into the back seat. They don't argue about who gets to go into the car first and who sits on what side like they normally do.

Earlier, when I parked, I forgot to leave the windows open a crack. The car is a sauna. I sit heavily in the passenger seat and sweat instantly pours off my face. I catch a glimpse of my left cheek in the side-view mirror: there's a puffy mass as red as a boiled lobster. My right eye is closing up.

There's an ant on my thigh. I try to pinch it between my fingers, but I keep missing it. I brush it off my leg to the floor of the car. We've already pulled out of the lot and onto the street. I hadn't noticed we were moving.

The windows are down. The woman is driving. I look at her. She's been crying, or maybe still is crying, because she wipes tears off of her face. She looks an awful lot like Shelley does when she cries but pretends not to.

She says, "So, um, how were the swimming lessons, kids?" Her voice is bright and cheery.

They don't say anything. I turn around and look at Michael. He's sitting ramrod straight in his seat, eyes open as wide as an ocean, and they are fixed on the woman in the driver's seat. His neck is patchy red, like he's breaking out in hives, and he shivers despite the heat. His bathing suit goes dark in the crotch as piss trickles down off the car seat and onto the floorboards.

I yell, "Jesus, Michael! Are you okay? I think he just had — had an accident?" My own voice sounds like it's coming from so far away. I look over at Olivia, and she's just like her brother. They twitch and convulse together like partners in a dance. Her shorts —

There's a sharp sting on my neck. Everything goes darker and fuzzier at the edges. I settle back in my seat. The woman's hand hesitantly returns to the steering wheel, and maybe I see something protruding from the pad of her thumb before she vines that hand around the steering wheel.

She says, "Don't worry, they're all right. They'll be fine." Her voice wavers and is at the edge of breaking. She covers her mouth and blinks back tears.

I shake and shiver, and it hurts in my bones, like I'm shaking hard enough that I might fall apart on my own.

She takes a deep breath, composing herself, and says brightly, "They probably just need something to drink, something to eat. Is anyone else hungry? I don't know about you guys, but I'm starving."

Allochthon

Livia Llewellyn

"[T]aking definite form toward the middle of the century, comes the revival of romantic feeling — the era of new joy in Nature, and in the radiance of past times, strange scenes, bold deeds, and incredible marvels. We feel it first in the poets, whose utterances take on new qualities of wonder, strangeness, and shuddering."

On this planet, in this universe, geology is geology — the land simply is, and it is nothing else. Mountain ranges and forests and "Nature" in its entirety are not sentient, they have no wisdom or knowledge to impart upon the world, and whatever emotional expectations each individual traveler draws from their journeys into the wild is of our making alone — the landscape "speaks" to us, but it's only we who are doing the talking. Or so we say we believe — I myself am not quite as certain, and I suspect many of us feel the same. Lovecraft certainly didn't believe this to be the truth of our world. "[T]here was a…cosmic beauty in the hypnotic landscape through which we climbed and plunged fantastically," Lovecraft wrote in "The Whisperer in the Darkness," "and I seemed to find in its necromancy a thing I had innately known or inherited and for which I had always been vainly searching." Time and time again, he wrote of the land around us as alive in ways we barely comprehend, watching us, calling out to us, drawing us in. How, then, can we really know for certain that the conversation is so one-sided, that those resplendent and horrifying feelings of mysterium tremendum et fascinans *that the supernal wilderness of the world draws from us aren't the cosmic answers to questions we instinctively ask? Living as we do today, in cities and suburbs subtly crafted as if to seem once removed from unstoppable Nature, we forget that we came from the land; we are wet mortal ghost-slivers of the geologic forces out of which every living thing evolved. The land is always with us, because it is us. And when, in ways wondrous and strange, we are called home, we have no choice but to go.*

◆

North Bonneville, 1934

Ruth sits in the kitchen of her company-built house, slowly turning the pages of her scrapbook. The clock on the bookcase chimes ten. In the next room, the only other room, she hears her husband getting dressed. He's deliberately slow on Sundays, but he's earned the right. Something about work, he's saying from behind the door. Something about the men. Ruth can't be bothered to listen. She stares at the torn magazine clipping taped to a page. It's a photo of an East Coast socialite vacationing somewhere in the southern tropics: a pretty young woman in immaculate white linens, lounging on a bench that encircles the impossibly thick trunk of a palm tree. All around the woman and the tree, a soft manicured lawn flows like a velvet sea, and the skies above are clear and dry. Ruth runs her free hand across the back of her neck, imagining the heat in the photo, the lovely bite and sear of an unfiltered sun. Her gaze wanders up to the ceiling. Not even a year old, and already rain and mold have seeped through the shingled roof, staining the cream surface with hideous blossoms. It's supposed to be summer, yet always the overcast skies in this part of the country, always the clouds and the rain. She turns the page. More photos and ephemera, all the things that over the years have caught her eye. But all she sees is the massive palm, lush and hard and tall, the woman's back curved into it like a drowsy lover, the empty space around them, above and below, as if they are the only objects that have ever existed in the history of time.

Henry walks into the room and grabs his coat, motioning for her to do the same. Ruth clenches her jaw and closes the scrapbook. Once again, she's made a promise she doesn't want to keep. But she doesn't care enough to speak her mind, and, anyway, it's time to go.

Their next-door neighbor steers his rusting car down the dirt road, past the edges of the town and onto the makeshift highway. His car is one of many, a caravan of beat-up trucks and buggies and jalopies. Ruth sits in the back seat with a basket of rolls on her lap, next to the other wife. It started earlier in the week as an informal suggestion over a session of grocery shopping and gossip by some of the women, and now almost forty people are going. A weekend escape from the routine of their dreary lives to a small park further down the Columbia River. The park is far from the massive lock and dam construction site, the largest in the world, which within the decade will throttle the river's power into useful submission. The wives will set up the picnic, a potluck of whatever they can afford to offer, while they gossip and look after the children. The men will eat and drink, complain about their women and their jobs and the general rotten state of affairs across the land, and then they'll climb a trail over eight-hundred-feet high, to the top of an ancient volcanic core known as Beacon Rock.

The company wife speaks in an endless paragraph, animate and excited. Billie or Betty or Becky, some childish, interchangeable name. She's four months pregnant and endlessly, vocally grateful that her husband found work on a WPA project when so many in the country are doing without. Something about the Depression.

Something about the town. Something about schools. Ruth can't be bothered. She bares her teeth, nods her head, makes those ridiculous clucking sounds like the other wives would, all those bitches with airs. Two hours of this passes, the unnatural rattle and groan of the engines, the monotonous roll of pine-covered hills. The image of the palm tree has fled her mind. It's only her on the lawn, alone, under the unhinged jaw of the sky. Something about dresses. Something about the picnic. Something about a cave —

Ruth snaps to attention. There is a map in her hands, a crude drawing of what looks like a jagged-topped egg covered in zigzagging lines. This is the trail the men are going to take, the wife is explaining. Over fifty switchbacks. A labyrinth, a maze. The caravan has stopped. Ruth rubs her eyes. She's used to this, these hitches of lost time. Monotonous life, gloriously washed away in the backwater tides of her waking dreams. She stumbles out of the car, swaying as she clutches the door. The world has been reduced to an iron grey bowl of silence and vertigo, contained yet infinite. Mountains and space and sky, all around, with the river diminished to a soft mosquito's whine. Nausea swells at the back of her throat, and a faint, pain-tinged ringing floods her ears. She feels drunk, unmoored. Somewhere, Henry is telling her to turn, to look. There it is, he's saying, as he tugs her sleeve like a child. Ruth spirals around, her tearing eyes searching, searching the horizon, until finally she —

Something about —

♦

— the rock.

Ruth lifts her head. She's sitting at her kitchen table, a cup of lukewarm coffee at her hand. The scrapbook is before her, open, expectant, and her other hand has a page raised, halfway through the turn. On the right side of the book, the woman in the southern tropics reclines at her palm in the endless grass sea, waiting.

Henry stands before her, hat on head, speaking. —Ruthie, quit yer dreamin' and get your coat on. Time to go.

—Go where.

—Like we planned. To Beacon Rock.

The clock on the bookcase chimes ten.

Outside, a plane flies overhead, the sonorous engine drone rising and falling as it passes. Ruth rubs her eyes, concentrating. Every day in this colorless town at the edge of this colorless land is like the one before, indistinguishable and unchanging. She doesn't remember waking up, getting dressed, making coffee. And there's something outside, a presence, an all-consuming black static wave of sound, building up just beyond the wall of morning's silence, behind the plane's mournful song. She furrows her brow, straining to hear.

Henry speaks, and the words sound like the low rumble of avalanching rock as they fall away from his face. It's language, but Ruth doesn't know what it means.

—Gimme a moment, I'm gonna be sick, Ruth says to no one in particular as she pushes away from the table. She doesn't bother to close the front door as she walks down the rickety steps into warm air and a hard grey sun. Ruth stumbles around the house to the back, where she stops, placing both hands against the wooden walls as she bends down, breathing hard, willing the vomit to stay down. Gradually, the thick, sticky feeling recedes, and the tiny spots of black that dance around the corners of her vision fade and disappear. She stands, and starts down the dusty alley between the rows of houses and shacks.

Mountains, slung low against the far horizon of the earth, shimmering green and grey in the clear, quiet light. Ruth stops at the edge of the alley, licking her lips as she stands and stares. Her back aches. Beyond the wave and curve of land, there is… Ruth bends over again, then squats, cupping her head in her hands, elbows on knees. This day, this day already happened. She's certain of it. They drove, they drove along the dirt highway, the woman beside her, mouth running like a hurricane. They hung to the edges of the wide river, and then they rounded the last curve and stopped, and Ruth pooled out of the car like saliva around the heavy shaft of a cock, and she looked up, and, and, and.

And now some company brat is asking her if she's ok, hey lady are you sick or just taking a crap, giggling as he speaks. Ruth stands up, and slaps him, crisp and hard. The boy gasps, then disappears between the houses. Ruth clenches her jaw, trying not to cry as she heads back around the house. Henry stands beside the open car door, ruin and rage dancing over his face. Her coat and purse and the basket of rolls have been tossed in the back seat, next to the wife. She's already talking up a storm, rubbing her belly while she stares at Ruth's, her eyes and mouth all smug and smarmy in that oily sisterly way, as if she knows. As if she could know anything at all.

The sky above is molten lead, bank after bank of roiling dark clouds vomiting out of celestial foundries. Ruth cranks the window lever, presses her nose against the crack. The air smells vast and earthen. The low mountains flow past in frozen antediluvian waves. Something about casseroles, the company bitch says. Something about gelatin and babies. Something about low tides. Ruth touches her forehead, frowns. There's a hole in her memory, borderless and black, and she feels fragile and small. Not that she hates the feeling. Not entirely. Her hand rises up to the window's edge, fingers splayed wide, as if clawing the land aside to reveal its piston-shaped core. The distant horizon undulates against the dull light, against her flesh, but fails to yield. It's not its place to. She knows she's already been to Beacon Rock. Lost deep inside, a trace remains. She got out of the car and she turned, and the mountains and the evergreens and, thrusting up from the middle, a geologic eruption, a disruption hard and wide and high and then: nothing. Something was there, some thing was there, she knows she saw it, but the sinkhole in her mind has swallowed all but the slippery edges.

Her mouth twists, silent, trying to form words that would describe what lies beyond that absence of sound and silence and darkness and light, outside and in her head. As if words like that could exist. And now they are there, the car is rounding the highway's final curves before the park. She rolls down the window all the way, and sticks her head and right arm out. A continent behind, her body is following her arm, like a larva wriggling and popping out of desiccated flesh, out of the car, away from the shouting, the ugly engine sounds, into the great shuddering static storm breaking all around. She saw Beacon Rock, then and now. The rest, they all saw the rock, but she saw beyond it, under the volcanic layers she saw *it*, and now she feels it, now she hears, and it hears her, too.

Falling, she looks up as she reaches out, and —

The clock on the bookcase chimes ten. Her fingers, cramping, slowly uncurl from a cold coffee cup. Henry is in the other room, getting dressed. Ruth hears him speaking to her, his voice tired water dribbling over worn gravel. Something about the company picnic. Something about malformed, moldering backwaters of trapped space and geologic time. Something about the rock.

Tiny spattering sounds against paper make her stare up to the ceiling, then down at the table. Droplets of blood splash against the open page in her scrapbook. Ruth raises her hand to her nose, pinching the nostrils as she raises her face again. Blood slides against the back of her throat, and she swallows. On the clipping, the young socialite's face disappears in a sudden crimson burst, like a miniature solar flare erupting around her head, enveloping her white-teethed smile. Red coronas everywhere, on her linen-draped limbs, on the thick bark of the palm, on the phosphorus-bright velvet lawn. Somewhere outside, a plane drones overhead, or so it sounds like a plane. No, a plain, a wide expanse of plain, a moorless prairie of static and sound, all the leftover birth and battle and death cries of the planet, jumbled into one relentless wave streaming forth from some lost and wayward protrusion at the earth's end. Ruth pushes the scrapbook away and wipes her drying nose with the edges of her cardigan and the backs of her hands. Her lips open and close in silence as she tries to visualize, to speak the words that would describe what it is that's out there, what waits for her, high as a mountain and cold and alone. What is it that breathes her name into the wind like a mindless burst of radio static, what pulses and booms against each rushing thrust of the wide river, drawing her body near and her mind away? She saw and she wants to see it again and she wants to remember, she wants to feel the ancient granite against her tongue, she wants to rub open-legged against it until it enters and hollows her out like a mindless pink shell. She wants to fall into it, and never return here again.

—Not again, she says to the ceiling, to the walls, as Henry opens the door. —Not again, not again, not again.

He stares at her briefly, noting the red flecks crusting her nostrils and upper lip. —Take care of that, he says; grabbing his coat, he motions at the kitchen sink. Always the same journey, and the destination never any closer. Ruth quickly washes her face, then slips out the door behind him into the hot, sunless morning. The company wife is in the back, patting the seat next to her. Something about the weather, she says, her mouth spitting out the words in little squirts of smirk while her eyes dart over Ruth's wet red face. She thinks she knows what that's all about. Lots of company wives walk into doors. Something about the end of Prohibition. Something about the ghosts of a long-ago war. Ruth sits with her head against the window, eyes closed, letting the one-sided conversation flow out of the woman like vomit. Her hand slips under the blue-checked dish towel covering the rolls, and she runs her fingers over the flour-dusted tops. Like cobblestones. River stones, soft water-licked pebbles, thick gravel crunching under her feet. She pushes a finger through the soft crust of a roll, digging down deep into its soft middle. That's what it's doing to her, out there, punching through her head and thrusting its basalt self all through her, pulverizing her organs and liquefying her heart. The car whines and rattles as it slams in and out of potholes, gears grinding as the company man navigates the curves. Eyes still shut, Ruth runs a fingertip over each lid, pressing in firm circles against the skin, feeling the hard jelly mounds roll back and forth at her touch until they ache. The landscape outside reforms itself as a negative against her lids, gnarled and blasted mountains rimmed in small explosions of sulfur-yellow light. She can see it, almost the tip of it, pulsating with a monstrous beauty in the distance, past the last high ridges of land. Someone else must have known, and that's why they named it so. A wild perversion of nature, calling out through the everlasting sepulcher of night, seeking out and casting its blind gaze only upon her —

The company wife is grabbing her arm. The car has stopped. Henry and the man are outside, fumbling with the smoking engine hood. Ruth wrests her arm away from the woman's touch, and opens the door. The rest of the caravan has passed them by, rounded the corner into the park. Ruth starts down the side of the road, slow, nonchalant, as if taking in a bit of air. As if she could. The air has bled out, and only the pounding static silence remains, filling her throat and lungs with its hadal-deep song. —I'm coming, she says to it. —I'm almost here. She hears the wife behind her, and picks up her pace.

—You gals don't wander too far, she hears the company man call out. —We should have this fixed in a jiffy.

Ruth kicks her shoes off and runs. Behind her, the woman is calling out to the men. Ruth drops her purse. She runs like she used to when she was a kid, a freckled tomboy racing through the wheat fields of her father's farm in North Dakota. She runs like an animal, and now the land and the trees and the banks of the river are moving fast, slipping past her piston legs along with the long bend of the road. Her lungs are on fire and her heart is all crazy and jumpy against her breasts and tears streak into her mouth and nose and it doesn't matter because she is so close and it's calling her with the hook of its song and pulling her reeling her in and Henry's hand is at the back of her neck and there's gravel and the road smashing against her mouth and blood and she's grinding away and kicking and clawing forward and all she has to do is lift up her head just a little bit and keep her eyes shut and she will finally see —

♦

Ruth's hands are clasped tight in her lap. Scum floats across the surface of an almost empty cup of coffee. A sob escapes her mouth, and she claps her hand over it, hitching as she pushes it back down. This small house. This small life. This cage. She can't do it anymore. The clock on the bookcase chimes ten. —I swear, this is the last time, Ruth says, wiping the tears from her cheeks. The room is empty, but she knows who she's speaking to. It knows, too. —I know how to git to you. I know how to see you. This is the last goddamn day.

On the kitchen table before her is the scrapbook, open to her favorite clipping. Ruth peels it carefully from the yellowing page and holds it up to the light. Somewhere in the southern tropics: a pretty young woman in stained white linens, lounging on a bench that encircles the impossibly thick trunk of a tree that has no beginning or end, whose roots plunge so far beyond the ends of earth and time that, somewhere in the vast cosmic oceans above, they loop and descend and transform into the thick fronds and leaves that crown the woman's head with dappled shadow. All around the woman and the tree, drops of dried blood are spattered across the paper like the tears of a dying sun. The woman's face lies behind one circle of deep brown, earth brown, wood brown, corpse brown. She is smiling, open-eyed, breathing it all in. Ruth balls the clipping up tight, then places it in her mouth, chewing just a bit before she swallows. There is no other place the woman and the palm have been, that they will ever be. Alone, apart, removed, untouched. All life here flows around them, utterly repelled. They cannot be bothered. It is of no concern to them. What cycle of life they are one with was not born in this universe.

In the other room, Henry is getting dressed. If he's talking, she can't hear. Everywhere, black static rushes through the air, strange equations and latitudes and lost languages and wondrous geometries crammed into a silence so old and deep that all other sounds are made void. Ruth closes the scrapbook and stands, wiping the sweat from her palms on her Sunday dress. There is a large knife in the kitchen drawers, and a small axe by the fireplace. She chooses the knife. She knows it better, she knows the heft of it in her hand when slicing into meat and bone. When he finally opens the door and steps into the small room, she's separating the rolls, the blade slipping back and forth through the powdery grooves. Ruth lifts one up to Henry, and he takes it. It barely touches his mouth before she stabs him in the stomach, just above the belt, where nothing hard can halt its descent. He collapses, and she falls with him, pulling the knife out and sitting on his chest as she plunges it into the center of his chest, twice because she isn't quite sure where his heart is, then once at the base of his throat. Blood, like water gurgling over river stones, trickling away to a distant, invisible sea. That, she can hear. Ruth wipes the blade on her dress as she rises, then places it on the table, picks up the basket and walks to the front door. She opens it a crack.

—Henry's real sick, she says to the company man. We're gonna stay home today. She gives him the rolls, staring hard at the company wife in the back seat as he walks back to his car. The wife looks her over, confused. Ruth smiles and shuts the door. That bitch doesn't know a single thing.

Ruth slips out the back, through the window of their small bedroom. The caravan of cars is already headed toward the highway, following the Columbia downstream toward Beacon Rock. They'll never make it to their picnic. They'll never see it. They never do. She moves through the alley, past the last sad row of company houses and into the tall evergreens that mark the end of North Bonneville. With each step into the forest, she feels the weight of the town fall away a little, and something vast and leviathan burrows deeper within, filling up the unoccupied space. When she's gone far and long enough that she no longer remembers her name, she stops, and presses her fingers deep into her sockets, scooping her eyes out and pinching off the long ropes of flesh that follow them out of her body like sticky yarn. What rushes from her mouth might be screaming or might be her soul, and it is smothered in the indifferent silence of the wild world.

And now it sees, and it moves in the way it sees, floating and darting back and forth through the hidden phosphorescent folds of the lands within the land, darkness punctured and coruscant with unnamable colors and light, its dying flesh creeping and hitching through forests petrified by the absence of time, past impenetrable ridges of mountains whose needle-sharp peaks cut whorls in the passing rivers of stars. A veil of flies hovers about the caves of its eyes and mouth, rising and falling with every rotting step, and bits of flesh scatter and sink to the earth like barren seeds next to its pomegranate blood. If there is pain, it is beyond such narrow knowledge of its body. There is only the bright beacon of light and thunderous song, the sonorous ring of towering monolithic basalt breathing in and out, pushing the darkness away. There is, finally, past the curvature of the overgrown wild, a lush grass plain of emerald green, ripe and plump under a fat hot sun, a wide bench of polished wood, and a palm tree pressing in a perfect arc against its small back, warm and worn and hard like ancient stone. When it looks up, it cannot see the tree's end. Its vision rises blank and wondrous with branches as limitless as its dreams, past all the edges of all time, and this is the way it should be.

Doc's Story

Stephen Graham Jones

"Witch, werewolf, vampire, and ghoul brooded ominously on the lips of bard and grandam, and needed but little encouragement to take the final step across the boundary that divides the chanted tale or song from the formal literary composition."

What that line cued up for me was that Sandman *issue, "The Hunt," with the Russian werewolves. Which is perfectly told — it's Gaiman — and leaves no room for any other story to even try to be told, right? A grandpa werewolf telling a grandkid about the glory days, with a surprise gift at the end. No room for anything else, I know. But I had to try. Not to one-up Gaiman, but to tap that same situation, see if there were other places it could go. Turns out there were, there are. And Lovecraft was right: with this kind of setup, very little encouragement is needed to take that step to the page. "Doc's Story" pretty much wrote itself, inside of two hours. But I'm always thinking about werewolves, too, so I never have to cut very deep to bleed their stories.*

♦

My grandfather was a werewolf.

Not by the time I knew him — transforming at his age would have been a death sentence — but my Aunt Libby and Uncle Darren had stories. Grandpa halfway up an old wooden windmill, howling at the moon, swiping at it with his claws. Grandpa on the porch one morning after two nights gone, his man-chin caked with blood, his whiskers not grown in like you'd think, him having run off into the woods without a razor.

When the hair pulls back in to wrap around your bones or wherever it goes, it's like a reset button, I guess. If you had a beard before, you'll wake without one.

One of those mornings, he had to go into town to the doctor, though.

Another thing you don't expect is the bugs. If it's summer or even a late fall without a hard enough freeze yet, the insects'll still be crawling, and if you pull a deer down, then, well, ticks, they just care that you've got warm, drinkable blood, and can't reach all your scratchy places.

What my Aunt Libby figured happened was that, while Grandpa was rooting around in the slit-open belly of a fat deer, one of that deer's ticks jumped ship, went to where the beating heart was.

It wasn't Lyme disease that sent Grandpa to the doctor, though. Wolfed out, his system probably could have kicked smallpox.

No, what sent him to town was that tick. When Grandpa fell to sleep on the porch, and his hair started slithering back into its pores, that tick was a cartoon character, climbing a tree that was sinking into the ground as fast it could climb, and then just riding that hair down.

It impacted itself in one of the wide pores on the back of Grandpa's arm, just under the shoulder. If it hadn't been headfirst, then it would have starved, shriveled up, turned to dirt.

Headfirst like it was, though, it could slurp and slurp and slurp, its sides and back swelling lighter and lighter grey, stretching that one pore wider than any pore was meant to, making Grandpa's whole shoulder throb.

The doctor took one look and said it was either pop her — he knew the tick was female, somehow — let her little tick-lings all pour out onto Grandpa's skin, and maybe into his blood, or he could lance her with something hot, killing the mama and boiling all the babies at once. Grandpa wasn't exactly sold on either option, so the doctor made the decision for him, heating up a piece of baling wire with his lighter and stabbing it in slow and thorough, then digging the head of the tick out with what looked like a dental hook.

Before he could antiseptic it, Grandpa rolled his shirtsleeve down over the fleshy crater so the doctor couldn't dab away the blood, maybe get some on himself. *In* himself. If you're born into the blood, you're fine, but if you catch it, then it's bad. Those werewolves, they never last long.

By the time I started coming around at eight years old, the scar on the back of Grandpa's arm from the tick was just a smooth little dab of skin that could have been from anything.

This is the way werewolf stories go.

You hear about it, hear about it, are breathing hard it's so great or so gross or so scary or so close, but then at the end, whoever's telling it pushes back a little like in satisfaction of a tale well told, nods at you like you've just got to believe it, now. Because it's the gospel truth.

Never mind any proof.

♦

Where this is going is my grandfather lying to me one afternoon.

I wasn't living with him, really. Where I was living was with my Aunt Libby, my mom's twin once-upon-a-time, but she had a job sewing bags of feed closed out west of town, and said she didn't trust that her ex-husband wouldn't come around while she was gone. And she didn't want me there for that.

Uncle Darren would have been my fallback there, but school was still in session, and he said the truant officer'd be all over him if word got around I was running produce back and forth to Tulsa with him three times a week.

"Produce," Libby had said about that.

"Produce," he had said back, but the way he looked away, I could see they were talking about something completely different. Something I was too young for.

Grandpa it was, then.

By that time he wasn't moving from his rocking chair by the fire much, and everything on his shelves I said I liked, he'd tell me I could have it.

The first time I took something — it was an old ceramic car that was a cologne bottle — I carried it around with me all afternoon, finally had to admit I didn't have anywhere to take it *to*.

My mom had been dead since I was born, and my dad was anybody. Aunt Libby said I was to call her *Aunt*, not Mom, but I still did sometimes, in my head. Anybody would. She was what my real mom would have looked like, if she'd lived through me getting born.

Her and Uncle Darren and Grandpa all shuttled me back and forth from school, and because I knew they'd have tried, I never asked them to help with my homework.

Werewolves aren't any good with math.

Not that Uncle Darren or Aunt Libby ever shifted anymore, mind. At least not on purpose. Sometimes, asleep, you can't help it. Or strung out like Uncle Darren gets on the road.

He's wrecked two trucks so far, is with his third company in five years.

Grandpa understands.

He's the one who tells them to save it, their shifts. He's the one always saying look what it's done to him.

You'd think he was eighty or a hundred, as frail and twisted up as he was then, but he was fifty-six.

It was because he hadn't had anybody to tell him, to warn him.

When you're wolfed out, running around the woods on all fours, snapping at rabbits and birds and terrorizing the villagers, you age like a dog. And Grandpa, as a young man, he'd always preferred to run his dinner down rather than work for wages to buy it at the grocery.

It had made sense. Until the arthritis. Until his skin turned to rice paper. Until his left eye glaucoma'd up like there was a storm building in there.

There was.

Two years after he got stuck with me those three weeks, he stroked out.

Aunt Libby and me found him half in, half out of the front door. Halfway between man and wolf.

"He was going for the woods," Aunt Libby said, looking there.

I did too.

Because we didn't need the questions — and the social security checks didn't hurt — we burned Grandpa on the trash pile a few times, then Uncle Darren showed up with a front-end loader, pushed the pile back and forth until there was nothing left anybody'd want to dig through.

This is the way it is with werewolves.

We don't have secret graveyards.

We move a lot.

And, I say "we," but my real mom, even though she was oldest, she was the runt of the litter. It's what Grandpa called her. And he'd always add how she was the lucky one.

Not all the children born to a werewolf are werewolves.

Even Aunt Libby and Uncle Darren, they've got half of my grandmother in them. You can tell when Uncle Darren lets his beard grow in, to prove to Grandpa he isn't shifting. It's tinged red, like Grandma was supposed to have been as a girl.

How she died, it was in another town, some rival pack. I'd never gotten the complete story of it back then, but I had enough.

Grandpa's gone hunting, and the other crew comes calling, and there's my grandmother standing in the door with three shots in her rifle, her three kids peeking around her skirts.

What Aunt Libby claims to remember is shifting for the first time right there in the front part of the living room, shifting a cool seven years before puberty, when it's supposed to happen. How she screamed and tore at herself, and this made Darren start changing early too.

And how my mom, she just stood there.

"Run," Grandma's supposed to have whispered down to them, and they did but they couldn't, they didn't know how to use their new legs, so my mom — is this why there's always a human in the litter? — she dragged these two little wolf cubs along, she pulled them by the shirts they were growing out of, she pushed them ahead of her, only stopped for a moment, when three shots fired off behind her.

That night Grandpa found the three of them, smelled them out from twenty miles of lost woods.

He was red to the shoulder, the other pack's blood steaming off him, and Aunt Libby said it was right then she knew nobody she ever married was ever going to be good enough.

Uncle Darren tells it different, but that's the way it always is with werewolves.

We learned thousands of years ago to always keep shifting, always keep the story changing.

That way nobody can pin it on you.

I was trying to do my geography, trying to believe that triangles mattered, were going to help me someday, when Grandpa's voice creaked that way it did, a minute or two before he got wound up enough to start saying whatever it was he'd thought of.

I waited it out, free-handed the angle of a corner out on my paper and erased it, drew it right beside itself, like tracing a ghost.

It was a blind stab at the correct answer, a bad guess, I knew, but if you erased enough, Ms. Chamberlain would give you points for effort.

Sometimes she'd have a baggie of shelled pecan halves for me too, for lunch.

"It was that time that one with the black tail came in smelling like skunk," Grandpa started off, laughing behind the words like it was all coming back.

I looked up to him and past him, to the fire. It was banked low, a "daytime fire," he called it. An old-man fire.

Such are the last days of mighty werewolves.

But there had been a time, I knew.

Each time I looked at him, I would try to see it.

"No, it was the *dock*-tail," he said, nodding to himself about it.

"Dogs," I said.

Dogs, he nodded.

You'd think a family of werewolves would have a soft spot for farm dogs, but it's kind of the opposite.

The dogs know, and never trust.

You smell like one thing, look like another.

"It was high summer," Grandpa said, licking his lips, his one rheumy eye shiny wet. "It was old Doc."

"For dock-tail," I filled in.

He nodded, shot me with his finger gun.

I sat back, hooked my arms around my knees.

"Done there?" he asked, about my homework.

Aunt Libby'd be all over both our cases if my geography wasn't done by the time she came in covered in feed dust, half the cattle in the county trailing her in the door.

"Done," I said to Grandpa, flipping the textbook closed to prove it.

He knew I was lying, but he knew that stories are more important, too.

"It was high summer," he repeated again, "and old Doc, he was what you might call an egg-sucking dog. Know what that means?"

I shook my head *no*, couldn't imagine.

"Chickens," Grandpa said, smiling in a way that told me clear as day that he was something of an egg sucker himself. "Some dogs, they can't keep themself out of the henhouse. They know it's wrong, they know they're going to get the business end of the shovel afterwards, but that don't change a thing, no siree. Once they look through the fence a certain way, then the deed, it's already half the way done."

"But you said it was a skunk," I said, squinting like trying to keep up.

"So I did," Grandpa said, rocking back. "What you got to understand about this, it's that Doc, he was of a *type*. It wasn't that he liked chicken meat or eggs so god-awful much, it's that he couldn't ever keep his nose out of trouble. And that's what finally did his dumb ass in."

He was still talking about himself here, I knew.

Aunt Libby'd told me once that all of Grandpa's stories, they were really complicated apologies. Most times to people who weren't even alive anymore. That that's how it is when you get old.

But she also said that if I listened, I might learn something.

I wish she'd been wrong.

Grandpa's story as it unfolded went around and around the house. This was what Uncle Darren always said anytime Grandpa got wound up, started remembering out loud.

"I don't want to go around and around the house with you, old man," he'd say, and slap his cap on his pants leg like killing a fly, or hammering a gavel.

But he did go around and around the house with Grandpa. He would.

Me too.

So there's Doc with his docked tail that hadn't really been docked with shears or a pocket knife to keep it from collecting burrs — it had been shot off with a twenty-gauge, from a neighbor who cared about his chicken stock — and he's traipsing through the woods. Partly because it's shady and cool back in the trees, and partly because there's nothing going on up by the house.

"When you're young, you like to roam," Grandpa said, looking me straight in the face to see if I was young or not.

My heart, it was out there with Doc.

Grandpa winked his blind eye.

Now Doc's on the scent of a bitch in heat, he thinks. Or wants to think. His nose to the ground, his ass haunched up in the air, that little tail working like a librarian's finger. Whining the way a dog will on the trail — exactly the way a wolf never would, Grandpa made sure I understood.

I might have been the kid of a human, but Grandpa still treated me like a werewolf.

It meant everything.

Soon enough, following his nose like that, Doc crosses the creek, winds into the part of the woods the neighbor's cleared of underbrush so his tree blind has lines of sight on everything.

Doc too.

Standing in the middle of the clearing is a king skunk, one of those ones with two stripes instead of just one. One of those kind that don't back down.

Doc's lip quavers, the growl building in his chest.

The skunk just glares across at him, not remotely concerned. Its feet, though, those tiny black claws — Grandpa held his own hand up to show, and for a breathless moment I thought his fingernails were going to curl around, that I was finally going to see it happen — they were gripping onto the top of the ground.

"Just like you have to anchor a cannon down on the deck of a ship," Grandpa said.

If he'd ever been on the open water or even to the Gulf, I didn't know about it.

I did know backhoes by then, though, and they had those robot arms that would reach out on each side, dig in.

It was the same way for that skunk, I knew.

He was about to deliver a payload.

Stephen Graham Jones

That night, Doc skulked back to the house whimpering.

His muzzle was still scarred from the last time Grandpa had had to take pliers to the porcupine quills barb-deep in that velvet black skin behind his whiskers.

Porcupines don't carry rabies, though. They can, I suppose, I'd just never heard of it.

No, rabies, it's what the bats bring to the coyotes, what the coyotes give to the prairie dogs, what the prairie dogs special-deliver to the polecats.

This skunk Doc had tangled with, it didn't *necessarily* have rabies.

But maybe.

And, when you've got dairy stock and other dogs and bats living in the attic, maybe's enough.

Grandpa didn't want to rouse Darren and Libby and my mom, though. They were still kids, and he didn't want to deal with the way they'd dive between Doc and the end of the gun, how they'd promise Doc was okay, never taking their own safety into account even for a slip of a moment.

The only way to tell for sure he didn't have rabies, it was either to wait for it to be too late or to cut Doc's head off, mail it into Tulsa for testing.

Either way, it was the end of the line for Doc. What had started with his tail was going to find completion after all these years.

Grandpa turned the porch light off, wrapped a bandanna around his face — even when not shifted, the smell of skunk still hurts — and hooked a finger through Doc's collar, led him past the barn.

What he had looped in the painter loop of his pants was a ball-peen hammer. Not one a working man would like, with a two-pound head that completes the swing for you, just one to bang something straight on the anvil.

It would be enough. More important, it would be quiet.

"Except," Grandpa said, laughing in his wheezy way — this was the punch line he'd been building towards — "after I hit Doc between the ears that first time, I like to have never got that next lick planted, let me tell you."

And he laughed and laughed, and the fire found a few pops of sap, and for a few moments I could see him out there, the silhouette of him anyway, holding the silhouette of a big rangy dog by the collar, that dog pulling him around and around, that long-handled hammer whistling through the air, trying to deliver its kindness down, and then trying again, all through dinner.

You have to smile, sometimes.

♦

Three years later Uncle Darren had found us a place outside Sprayberry, Texas.

All the trucks were oilfield trucks, their dashboards black with it.

He was running pipe now, back and forth to El Paso.

Aunt Libby was clerking at the gas station. They had a video shelf on the back wall, and she'd let me bring home the movies nobody'd rented that night, then sneak them back in her purse, "find" them behind the cereal or the soup cans if her boss was there.

This is what werewolves do.

Until one night Uncle Darren walked up out of the highway. It was just like the opening credits of a show I'd been watching on television, so that I felt the ground shift underneath me, like somebody had their hand on the channel dial.

Aunt Libby heard or smelled, came out, her hands dusted white with flour.

"No," she said.

Yes.

Hooked over Uncle Darren's shoulder was the creaky black belt of a state trooper. The pistol was still there in its molded holster, the handle flapping against his side every other step.

"Go inside," she said, pushing me away.

She should have pushed harder.

We didn't need anybody to tell us what had happened here.

For weeks now, Uncle Darren had been coming in from his runs cussing the smokey that'd been dogging him.

When Uncle Darren drove, he liked to drink wine coolers. Just to stay awake.

He'd been doing it so long that he'd become a real and true marksman, could hang a bottle out the window on his side, flip that bottle over the top of his rig, nail the mile marker reflectors each time.

And he never got drunk. It was just wine coolers, right? I wasn't near old enough, was just pushing twelve, but I knew they tasted like watered-down something else, I just wasn't sure what. But they sure weren't beer, or anything stronger.

This one state trooper who worked 20 just east of Stanton, he didn't agree.

Uncle Darren had taken to muttering how bears and wolves, they weren't *meant* to get along.

Whenever Aunt Libby heard him, well. It was *on*, like Grandpa would have said. Screaming and cussing, one of them storming out into the mesquite darkness.

Aunt Libby was right, though, I knew.

She'd always able to control transforming better than Darren. Like, she could get mad at somebody and *not* wolf out on them.

It kept the gas station from becoming a killing floor. It kept her boss alive, day after day. It kept his grabby hands connected to his pale wrists.

Uncle Darren, though, he'd taken to long-haul trucking specifically to avoid those kinds of confrontations.

Until this one state trooper.

Fifty miles behind him, I knew, his rig was cocked over in the ditch, the running lights on, the door swinging, the dome light glowing down on three or four bottles of what had been a six-pack. Of strawberry wine coolers.

That big chrome gas tank, it would be tacky with blood, I knew.

Maybe some splashed up onto the mirror, and the backside of the windshield.

Uncle Darren had torn through that trooper like the human sheet of tissue he was, and come out the other side with that thick black belt in his teeth, a prize.

Then he'd run up the yellow stripes until the pads of his feet were raw.

And then he'd stood, a man.

Aunt Libby didn't even stop from him being both naked *and* her own brother. She walked right out into the road, straight-armed him direct in the chest, nearly dislodging his trophy of a belt.

Uncle Darren was ready, but still he had to give a bit.

He tried to keep sliding past her, for the house, for clothes, for the suitcases because we were moving again, we had to, but Aunt Libby hauled him back, and I should have gone inside, I should have been inside watching a stolen movie about ninjas, I should have been inside already packing.

But I wasn't.

I heard.

Not the growling — it wasn't the first time I'd heard it from Aunt Libby — but the words. The human words.

At first Aunt Libby was talking low and steady, about how she had a good job this time, how this was a good place. How they were going to know who did it.

Like Darren, though, I wasn't really listening, here.

What I was doing was watching him.

I could see Grandpa rising up in his son. I was seeing Grandpa as a young man, itching to roam, to fight, to run down his dinner night after night, because his knees were going to last forever. Because his teeth would always be strong.

Darren's skin was jumping in folds, cringing back from the shift. Aunt Libby was pushing his every last button, and — he'd never been a talker — he didn't even have any good defense, aside from that Trooper Dan had been asking for it, that he'd been asking for it his whole life, and that they could go back now if she

wanted, they could steal a truck, fake a wreck. Pretend Trooper
Dan had been doing a ticket when a drunk veered, and, and —

Aunt Libby slapped him.

Her claws were out, too.

My eyes took snapshots of every single frame of that arc her
hand took. It was the first real wolf I'd seen. It was what I'd been
waiting for ever since Oklahoma, ever since Arkansas. Ever since
ever.

It proved that these weren't just stories, that they weren't just
excuses.

A piece of Uncle Darren's lower lip strung off his mouth,
clumped down onto his chest. The lower part of his nose sloughed
a little lower, cut off from the top half.

His eyes never moved.

By his legs, his fingers stretched out as well, reaching for the
wolf.

"*No!*" Aunt Libby yelled, stepping forward, taking him by both
wrists, driving her knee up into his balls.

It's another thing about werewolves.

Mid-shift, a knee to the balls can bring you back to the human
side of things. Pain is a weight. It anchors you.

Uncle Darren balled up, curled on his side there on the asphalt
where anybody could drive by.

Aunt Libby stood over him breathing hard, still growling, her
skin jumping in the most beautiful way.

All that bullshit about packs and dominance, alphas and
submission?

Right then I believed the hell out of it.

"You can't just say whatever story you want and make it true,"
she said, finally, about the wreck Uncle Darren wanted to stage.

"Learned from the best," Uncle Darren said, and Aunt Libby
whipped her eyes up. Right to me.

"'I found all three of you out there by the old — by the creek'…
is that what he used to say?" Darren managed to get out. "I mean,
I mean, is that what he used to *sell?*"

Aunt Libby was still staring at me. With her real self.

"Three shots," Uncle Darren laughed, still holding himself, speaking directly down into the hot black rock. But I could hear him. "There were three shots in that rifle, Lib, three shots, three shots and three *ki—*"

Aunt Libby kicked him before he could finish, but it was too late.

Three *kids.*

You don't tell your children to run, not when the wolves are at the door.

No kid can outrun a werewolf, much less a riled-up pack of them.

What you do is you deliver the only kindness you've got left. What you do is you hold each of their little heads and kiss them on the forehead, and then replace your lips with the open mouth of a gun.

But my grandmother hadn't gone all the way through with it. Grandpa had come home right at that moment, or they'd slipped away out a side window, or the other crew had come through the door, or Libby and Darren had changed, and fought her back with their sharp baby teeth, or — or a hundred other things.

None of which mattered.

Once you make a decision like that, you can't take it back.

And, because Grandpa had loved her and not hated her, I guess — because he understood — he'd made a lie up about that day. He'd made it sound good.

And it probably wasn't the first time. Or the last.

I could see it in the way Libby had slashed her eyes to me, tried to hold me with them. Tried to keep me from understanding. From seeing through.

"Doc," I said, in the new quiet Uncle Darren's pained breathing was spreading all around. "There never was a dog named Doc. We've never had dogs. They would never shut up if we did."

"Don't," Aunt Libby said, her mouth tight, like keeping a secret.

I turned, I ran.
She let me.

♦

The next few weeks were quiet.

We were living in the panhandle of Florida, slapping bugs off our necks every few soggy breaths. Uncle Darren was working the boats at night, like Grandpa never had. There weren't any cannons on them. Just contraband. It was why he had to work naked: so they'd know he wasn't smuggling anything himself.

Aunt Libby was taking coupons and making change at an oil change place. I worked down in the pit. I wasn't old enough, but they didn't have to pay me as much, so it all kind of worked out.

Down there turning my wrenches, that liquid clicking of the ratchets swelling up all around me, I ran through Doc's story from every angle I could, trying to peel it back to a different truth, a better truth.

All I kept hearing, though, was what Grandpa had really been telling me, his one eye pressuring up to burst back into his brain.

All I kept hearing was what he'd really been apologizing for.

My mom.

It had to be.

If Aunt Libby hadn't thinned her lips that night when I said Doc's name, I probably never would have completely flashed on what Grandpa was saying.

But she had.

Still, there was some assembly required.

Another story Grandpa told me, it did have proof, is maybe the only werewolf story in the whole history of werewolves to ever have proof.

It was where dew claws come from. Why they are.

On dogs, they're useless, just leftover. From when they were *wolves*, Grandpa insisted.

It was about birthing, about being born.

Just like baby birds needed a beak to poke through their shells, or like some baby snakes have a sharp nose to push through *their* eggshells, so did werewolf pups need dewclaws. It was because of their human half. Because, while a wolf's head is made for slip-sliding down a birth canal, a human head — all pups shift the whole time they're being born, can't help it — a human head is big and blocky by comparison. And the momma-wolf's lady parts, they aren't made for that. You can cut the pups out like they did for Grandma each time, just to be safe, but you need somebody who knows what they're doing. When there's not a knife, though, or somebody to hold it — that's the reason for the dewclaws. So the pup can reach through with his paw. So that one claw up on the back of their forearm can snag, tear the opening a bit wider.

That's the reason for the dewclaws. So the pup can reach through with his paw. So that one claw up on the back of their forearm can snag, tear the opening a bit wider.

It's bloody and terrible, but it works. At least for the pup.

And I'm reminded now each time I reach up to wrap the strap around a dull orange oil filter.

On my forearm, there are two pale slick scars that I'd grown up thinking were from the heating element of a stove in Arkansas, when I'd reached in for toast before I understood anything. Two slick little divots in my life that I always figured were my secret connection to Grandpa: he had a scar from a stupid tick, I had one from some stupid toast. It was the story I'd been told. I'd never had to call it to question.

Until now.

It wasn't a skunk-bit dog Grandpa dragged out behind the barn that night, to take care of in the most personal way.

I can see it now, in his words.

Some days it's the only thing I can see.

A woman starts to have a baby, a *human* woman starts to have a *human* baby, only, partway through it, that baby starts to shift, little needles of teeth poking through the gums months too early. It's not supposed to happen, but the wolf's in the blood.

The thing about that night in Sprayberry, when Uncle Darren came up the road naked, when Aunt Libby slapped him down, the thing I hadn't questioned at the time but couldn't get over now, was that I'd *heard* him talking low into the asphalt, from all the way back at the house.

I'd heard him without thinking, from farther away than a human should be able to.

My mom, I didn't just tear her open, I probably infected her.

Werewolves that are born, they're in control of it, or they can come to be, at least. They have a chance.

If you're bit, though, then it runs wild through you, it burns you up fast, and hurts the whole time. All you can do is feel sorry for those wolves. They never understand what's happening to them, just run around slobbering and biting, trying to escape their own skin.

That skunk, it *did* have rabies, Grandpa.

That skunk, it was me.

And so, the real story, it's that a father carries his oldest daughter out past the house, he carries her out and she's probably already changing for the first time, but he holds his own wolf back.

This is a job for a man.

He raises the hammer once but isn't decisive enough, can't commit to this act with his whole heart, but he has her by the scruff, and she's on all fours now, is snapping at him, her infant son screaming on the porch, her twin sister biting those baby-sharp dew claws off for him, and for the rest of that night, for the rest of his *life*, this husband and father and monster is swinging that little ball-peen hammer, trying to connect, his face wet with the effort, the two of them silhouettes against the pale grass, going around and around the house.

We're werewolves.

This is what we do, this is how we live.

If you want to call it that.

The Lonely Wood

Tim Lebbon

"But the sensitive are always with us, and sometimes a curious streak of fancy invades an obscure corner of the very hardest head; so that no amount of rationalisation, reform, or Freudian analysis can quite annul the thrill of the chimney-corner whisper or the lonely wood."

I think part of being human is the ability to wonder, and, whatever one's beliefs, I think there's always a part of our brains that revels in the unknown. Whatever our thoughts on the supernatural and religion, when we reach into the darkness, it's rare to find someone who isn't at least a tiny bit afraid that something out there will take their hand… and maybe pull. In this story I wanted to play with proof and doubt, and explore what happens when the two collide.

The timing was perfect. Some might have called it divine. But as far as Guy was concerned, he was just in time for a song.

On his own in London with a couple of hours to kill between meetings, he'd headed to St Paul's Cathedral. Marie had always wanted to go, but for some reason they never had.

He hadn't been there since a primary school trip when he was ten years old, and thirty-five years later he wondered how much it had changed. In truth, not much at all. Buildings as old and grand as this wore their age as a disguise from which time slipped away, years passing in a blink, centuries in the space between breaths. It bore scars from the war, its walls were stained with decades of smog and exhaust fumes, yet it stood almost aloof amongst those far more modern structures surrounding it. It had existed before them, and it would likely persist long after they had fallen or been demolished. The cathedral was timeless.

Guy found that funny. Not humorous, but in an ironic, isn't-it-typical kind of way. He saw the building as a vast folly erected to superstition and vanity. That it would outlast them all only gave its uselessness a deeper melancholy.

Yet it fascinated him, and he found the building truly beautiful. It was the same with any old building — castles, churches, old houses or hotels. They dripped with character and history, and he'd come to realise that it was the hidden things that fascinated him. St Paul's revelled in its beauty and majesty, but he knew that it had more secret places than most.

He'd toured the crypt, pausing beside Nelson's tomb, hurrying past Wellington's tomb when he'd found it surrounded by a gaggle of school children, resisting the lure of cake in the café, and, upon returning to the nave, he'd seen a girls' choir preparing for song. Tourists milled around, many of them listening to recorded information and looking at handheld gadgets that told them the history of this place as they walked. Guy thought that perhaps they might enjoy it more if they experienced it for real, but he wasn't the one to tell them. Others stood staring at the incredible architecture, graceful statuary, and vivid mosaics. But he decided to join those others who had taken the time to sit and rest.

That was another strange reaction that he was comfortable

with, and had never felt the need to analyse. Even as a non-believer, he found such places of worship incredibly peaceful and contemplative.

A moment after he sat down, the organ breathed, and the singing began. The whisper of a dozen headsets, the mumble of feet, the swish of coats, all were swept away. Guy sat quite a distance from the choir, but he could see the conductor clearly enough, and the first few girls in line, with their red gowns, flexible lamps, and song sheets. His vision became focussed and narrowed upon the choir as the first sounds soared, and a thrill went through him.

The organ notes and the caress of voices filled the cathedral. Guy shivered, a tingle that rose to his scalp and down his back. Calmness descended, a type of tranquility that he was not at all used to in his busy, full life. Not since his teens had he listened to music for music's sake — it was always background to something else, whether he was writing a report, cooking, or working out. Now he could not imagine doing anything other than listen. It was beautiful. It was art splashed across the air, perfection given voice and then allowed to fade away. He mourned every note that vanished, but then revelled in the new ones that sang in afterwards.

I want to hold onto this forever, he thought. He leaned back in the chair, tilted his head back, and closed his eyes. He could not make out any words. The hymn was probably in Latin, but meaning was unimportant.

Wonderful. Beautiful.

He opened his eyes. Above him was St Paul's huge dome, the Whispering Gallery encircling it at a lower level. There were several people up there now leaning on the handrail, looking down, swallowing up the transcendent song rising to them. On the walls lower down were immense paintings or mosaics of the four disciples that had supposedly written the Gospels.

"Come on, then," Guy muttered, surprising himself. He had no wish to disturb the music, but something was settling around him. At first it was a playful notion, an idea that if he was ever to receive the touch of Christ, or to find his heart opened to the God he had never believed in, now would be the time. He'd never thought himself an on-the-fence doubter, was comfortable in his convinced unbelief. Yet he'd often had that discussion with Marie — *If God exists, why doesn't he just tap me on the shoulder and show me the smallest sign?*

"Come on, here I am," he whispered. "Do your worst. Do your best. Just do anything."

Proof denies Faith, was always her reply.

Why?

"I'm waiting."

Nothing happened. Guy chuckled. Of course not. He stared up at the amazing ceilings above him, the incredible artwork, and marvelled at the dedication and commitment of those who had created it hundreds of years before. To build this place now would be almost impossible. The cost would be into the hundreds of millions, the skills all but vanished in a time of steel-and-glass altars to commerce and excess.

And suddenly, in that place of wonder and grandiosity, he felt a flush of disgust. How many lives had been lost building this place? He doubted they were even recorded. How much money spent while the rest of London had lived in conditions of poverty, filth, and plague? The true cost of places such as this was never known. The music and singing soared, and it felt like the only pure thing. He appreciated the beauty of the architecture, but he could no longer admire it.

Guy stood, chair legs sliding against the floor. One of the choir girls glanced at him — it must have been the sudden movement, she can't have heard his chair move from that far away — and he tried to smile. But she had already turned back to her music sheets.

The conductor waved, body jerking like a marionette.

The organ groaned and moaned, exhalations of distress given wonder.

Guy turned his back on the choir and walked away. He headed for the front of the cathedral and the impossibly high doors which were only used when *important* people came. Not people like him. But somehow he drifted to the left, and then he found himself at the entrance to the staircase that wound its way up into St Paul's massive dome, and the famous Whispering Gallery it contained.

He started up the wide spiral stairs. The risers were low, the stairs wide, so it almost felt like he was walking on the level. Each stair was identical to the ones just gone and those ahead — smooth concrete, narrow to the left and wide to the right, a dark line drawn along the stair's edge. His blood started pumping, heart beating. But Guy was a fit man, and his level of exertion was low.

The movement seemed smooth and almost distant from him, as if it was someone else walking. The steps passed beneath him as the tower turned and he remained in the same place, pushing the stairs behind and below him with his feet, turning, moving the tower while he himself remained immovable.

Nothing can move me from here, he thought, and a man ran past him down the stairs. He wore jeans and a leather jacket and was gone in an instant, but Guy caught a glimpse of his wide eyes and slack-jawed mouth, and smelled the rank odour of sweat.

"Everything all right?" he called after the man, but the figure was already out of sight. The muttered words in French that echoed from stone walls seemed disassociated from anything, mere phantom pleas.

Guy carried on climbing, soon entering that hypnotic rhythm once more. And he heard the music again. Each pulse of its rhythmic heart seemed to match a footfall, and he found himself humming along, an inaudible vibration that seated itself in his chest and travelled out through bones and sinews, veins and ligaments, kissing his extremities. *How can I hum to music I don't know?* he wondered, but then realised that he might know it after all.

All her life, his wife had wanted to hear him sing her own song. It had never been a big thing between them — no pressure, no major disagreements — but her devout faith and his lack of it had sometimes felt like a repulsion pushing them apart. He believed that she'd felt it much more than him. Sometimes waking up in bed, he'd wrapped his arm and leg around her, drawing her close, holding her there.

Thinking of Marie now almost caused him to trip. But the steps kept moving, and he felt himself rising.

Firmly though he did not believe, he couldn't help thinking of Marie still watching him from somewhere. Looking down. Being his guardian angel.

He chuckled, and even that seemed to match the music and singing he heard. *How foolish*, he thought. *She's dead, and the only person that matters to now is me. She's gone, and I'm the one hanging on.* But he couldn't shake that fanciful idea. Sometimes in the dark, alone and cold in bed, tears drying on his face, he spoke to her. He supposed it was very much like praying.

Footsteps approached from above, and they were breaking the rhythm. Sometimes they hurried, sometimes they dragged, and, just before he saw who made them, he heard a soft impact. He continued walking, rising, and a woman appeared on the steps before him. She was holding her hands against her stomach and repeating something over and over.

Guy paused and lifted the hair hanging down over her face. She looked up at him, still speaking, her words lost in a language he could not place. She looked terrified.

"What is it?" he asked. "What's happening?"

Because something was. Something had been happening since he'd sat down and started listening to the choir. He thought of the girl who'd looked at him then looked away again as he waved, and wondered whether she'd even been there at all.

"It's… all… real," the woman said, struggling to form the unfamiliar words before muttering again in her own language. She lowered her head and kept her hands clenched to her stomach. Maybe she was hurt, but Guy could not tell. He didn't want to touch her again. Something about her terrified him.

He moved on, and soon he came to a sideways branch in the stairwell that opened out into the Whispering Gallery. There were others there, at various points around the walkway. Some sat on the stone steps, heads back and eyes closed. Others hung over the cast-iron railing and looked down.

Guy reached for the railing and followed their gaze.

It was pandemonium. People, tiny people, ran back and forth across the mosaic floor of the cathedral. Some collided and fell, either getting up to continue their run, or remaining on the floor, curling up and hugging themselves into a ball. A small group of people knelt in front of the chairs and seemed to be praying. One man was splayed out with blood pooling around his head. Maybe he'd jumped.

The music and singing continued to soar.

"What's happening?" Guy whispered to himself, and a disembodied voice answered.

"This is it," the voice soothed. "This is the end. Now we all know the truth, and we can't be allowed to live." The speaker laughed. "What a load of shit!"

Guy looked directly across the wide dome at the man standing opposite, his head back as he guffawed.

"You believe a word of this?" the man asked. Guy could barely see his mouth moving from this distance, but the words were crystal clear. Even over the shouting. Even above the singing, and the laboured breaths of the organ.

"I don't know," Guy said, surprised at his doubt. "I don't even know what's happening."

"Go up," the man said. "See. See if you believe. I still... I..." Then he started walking around the gallery, and his words faded away.

Guy moved to the left, heading for the route up to the next level on the dome. He ran, passing people sitting silent and still, and others who were speaking softly. Maybe they were praying, but Guy didn't stop to listen. It had always been a private act for Marie, and he had respected it in others ever since.

The stairs to the next level were much narrower, stone treads worn down by a million footsteps over hundreds of years. Time weighed heavy. He hurried now, feeling a pressing need to discover what might be happening, even though he was quite certain he wouldn't want to know.

The choir's song and the organ's lament accompanied him on his climb. *Where is everyone else?* he thought. *Why isn't everyone climbing these stairs?* He paused to listen but heard only those haunting hymns, exultant one moment, screeches of terror and torment the next. That had always been Guy's problem with religion — the ecstasy and the horror.

He walked on, enjoying the feeling of exertion. He was sweating and panting. This felt good and right, and he only wished that he and Marie *had* come here together.

He reached the top of the staircase and emerged onto the external balcony surrounding the dome. To his left was the tall railing, heavy bars offering a partitioned view out across London like an old zoetrope. To his right, the dome, still exuding warmth from the day's sun.

And everything, and everyone, had changed.

"You're so bloody stubborn!" Marie said. There was a lightness to her voice, but he had known and loved her long enough to know that she was also frustrated.

Welcome to my world, he thought, and he said, "I'm not! Just because I don't suffer from blind, blinkered faith, you say that —"

"Blind *and* blinkered?" she asked.

"You know what I mean."

"Well, no, not really, 'cos like if you're blind, why bother being blinkered, 'cos if you —"

He leaped across the picnic blanket, rolled her over an open foil packet of uneaten sandwiches, and shut her up with a kiss. She fought him off, but he pressed his mouth to hers. She was tough and strong, but he could also feel her starting to giggle.

Birds sang around them. A gentle breeze whispered secrets through the tree canopy. This was their place, or, when Marie spoke about it, it sounded like Their Place. They'd come here on three occasions to spend time in the woods, and they did their best to ignore the scraps of litter and broken vegetation around the clearing, shoving aside the fact that other people probably also knew this spot as their own.

Their Place.

She pushed him off at last and peeled a flattened sandwich from her butt. She held it up, and it flopped down limp. She raised an eyebrow, and Guy burst out laughing.

"I believe in the god of limp sandwiches," he said. "I'll worship him forever, and sacrifice every third sandwich to his most glorious and —"

"Oh, fuck off!" she said, lobbing the bread and catching him perfectly across the nose.

They stopped talking and started kissing, and that suited them both just fine. In Their Place they found proof of love.

♦

London danced and sang. From all across that great city, voices rose, crying and chanting and singing, rippling over the built-up landscape like an ocean's tides. They sang of joy and wonder, delight and ecstasy. Down below he could see people in the streets around St Paul's, dancing and relishing this momentous, amazing moment. Most vehicles — cars, taxis, buses, and motorcycles — were motionless. London was still but for the people, and the birds that swooped and swerved along streets and around tall buildings. He knew London so well, and the feelings he usually experienced when looking out over the city from a high vantage point had changed. Usually he thought of the millions of people hidden away in the sea of grey buildings, working and striving to earn their keep, stressed and traumatised by whatever lives they had chosen or fallen into. A smog of desolation constantly smudged the city in his eyes, however clear the weather. He never *liked* that feeling, but struggled to work his way out from beneath it.

Now he thought of every beautiful, complex mind, every
cheerful thought, each wonderful story of every single person
he could spy down in the streets and the many more inside the
buildings. They were no longer grey lives. It was no longer an
anthill of workers edging towards extinction, but a sea of hope and
potential.

In Guy's mind it was a moment of pure revelation.

But also a time of pain.

Here and there across the great city, he saw the flickering
signs of small conflagrations. A couple of miles to the south, great
flames reached skyward, much taller than should be possible,
flexing and stretching in majestic slow motion like the fingers of
a fire-giant being born from the earth. Smoke rose around them,
deep black and almost oily against the sky, as if extensive piles of
fat sizzled and burned beneath them. What he had taken to be
musical accompaniment to the joyous ululations were the coughs
of thousands of windows bursting out beneath terrible heat.

The Thames flowed red.

Guy grasped the railings and pressed his face to a gap. The
feel of cool metal framing his face pinned him to reality, and he
tried to blink the sights away. They would not go. Neither would
the sounds of ecstatic song and breaking glass, nor the smells of
jasmine, rose petals, and burning flesh. He was a man who trusted
his own senses, and he did so now more than ever before.

Do your worst. Do your best. Just do anything, he'd said,
glibly challenging the beastly god he had never believed in. And
whatever Marie had believed, he had always attempted to keep an
open mind.

"Marie!" Guy shouted. He talked to her often in his mind, but
this was the first time since she died that he had cried her actual
name aloud. "Marie!" It felt good. It felt right, and he started to
run around the circular walkway looking for her.

Surely if this was some divine demonstration, a sliver of proof
for a world slipping into doubt, then Marie would be with him
once more?

That was what he required to believe and care. That would be his proof.

So he ran, calling her name, circling the balcony that skirted around the dome. There were others up here too. They were doing their own thing, and he ignored them as they ignored him. This was a personal time — whatever they saw, smelled, tasted was all their own. He saw one man praying and one woman hiding her eyes, and he wondered what he might be doing when this day was done.

"Marie! Where are you?" He ran on, and a transformed London lay all around. Eventually he came back to where he had begun, his route blocked by the entry lobby out onto the balcony. So he turned around and ran back again, calling his dead wife's name. Senses could be fooled. A mind could be tampered with, cajoled, distorted. But he would know Marie.

He circled around to the lobby, pressed his face to the railings once more, and London blurred in his tears.

"What is this?" he screamed. Voices sang in answer but he could not understand their words. *You never did*, Marie might have said, but that was only in his mind, a precious memory of her face and voice, her sweet smile and gentle touch.

The singing continued, a million voices rising in celebration, setting the cathedral behind him shimmering and crackling with an amazing energy. The flames rose in unison, dancing to their tune. It might have been proof undeniable, belief unstoppable. But in any world where Marie remained dead — in the face of any bastard god who could push her into the path of a foolish, drunken driver — Guy remained immovable.

He turned his back on everything, entered the dome, and started back down the winding staircase.

On that journey down the first staircase to the Whispering Gallery level, he met no one coming up. He was on his own. He moved quickly around the outer edge of the stairwell, using the wider part of the stairs so that he didn't trip and fall. He watched his feet, saw the steps passing below him and the core turning as he descended, and, for some reason, he came to believe that the drop below him was far, far deeper than it really was, and that if he fell he might tumble forever. It was dizzying and hypnotising, and he trailed his fingers along the outer wall where a million people had touched before. He brushed fingertips with every one of them.

He reached the Whispering Gallery level and moved out onto the inner balcony. All was silent. There was no one there, and looking down he could see no people on the cathedral floor below. The singing had ceased, the organ had breathed to a halt.

He felt completely alone.

"Hello?" he asked. He closed his eyes, and for a loaded moment that seemed to stretch forever, he firmly believed that he would be answered. But his voice whispered away to nothing.

He circled the balcony and started down the wide staircase that led to the cathedral floor. Every thirty steps or so he paused to listen. For voices, footsteps, singing, screaming, *anything*. Only his heavy, fast breathing broke the silence.

Moving faster, the steps speeding up beneath his feet rather than feet accelerating down the stairs, he finally tripped. A blade of fear sliced into his core, and in panic he held out his hands to break his fall.

He hit the steps and rolled.

Down… down… forever.

◆

When Guy was in his late twenties, a year after falling in love with Marie, he'd gone on a business trip to Scotland. He'd just started his own web consultancy business, and he was investigating the possibility of a partnership with another young, forward-thinking entrepreneur. He and the man had gone out on the town in Edinburgh, and Guy had learned his most important lesson of the day — never drink whiskey with a Scotsman.

Several pubs and a dozen single malts later, he was paralytic.

He'd made his excuses and stumbled back to his hotel room already fearing the next day's hangover. His head had felt like the only fixed point in the universe, with everything else in a state of turmoil. He fell twice on the stairs up to his room. Once in his room, he took a piss, drank a pint of water, then fell on the bed and went to sleep fully dressed.

He woke in the early hours. The headache throbbed in first, consuming his entire body, and then he heard someone groaning. He stirred quickly, fumbling for the bedside light, missing, rolling from the bed. Hurt his shoulder on the floor. Then he realised that the groan was his own, and he climbed slowly back onto the bed and turned on the light.

It melted his eyeballs to the back of his skull.

Squinting, slowly stripping off his shirt, he hobbled to the bathroom. Here he stripped naked and propped the door open so that he didn't have to turn on the harsh light. His head throbbed. His stomach churned. He burped and smelled whiskey, and groaned all over again.

As he took a piss, he stared at his darkened reflection in the mirror, and then he saw Geraldine. She was Marie's mother — funny, intelligent, a widow far too young, Guy got on with her amazingly well. He was already starting to think she might one day be his mother-in-law.

But now she was in pain. Her reflection was much hazier than his, as if in a much darker room, but he saw her features twisted in agony, her body shivering, and he pissed all over the floor.

Rushing back into the bedroom, his hangover seemed to have vanished instantaneously. Without stopping to think — how stupid this was, how unlikely, how bloody annoyed Marie would be when he phoned her in the middle of the night because of some weird just-surfacing-from-a-drunken-sleep dream — he dialled her mobile. He told her that there was something wrong with her mother, and, when Marie asked how he knew, he said he didn't know. Yes, he was still in Edinburgh. Yes, he'd been drinking, but no, he was sober now. No, he didn't know how, but could she just…?

Half an hour later, Marie rang from her mother's flat. She'd fallen down the stairs and broken both legs, and was suffering from concussion and shock.

Next morning Guy's hangover landed with a vengeance, and he spent the whole morning in his room puking, sleeping, and vowing that he'd never drink again.

Marie called it a miracle. Guy, who had time to think about it on the long train journey home, and who could not really remember if he'd actually seen Geraldine, or whether he'd been anything other than drunk when he called Marie, shrugged his shoulders.

"Just one of those things," he said.

He was lying on the cold stone floor, head lower than his feet, arms splayed out. He was still on the shallow staircase, but, ahead and several steps down, he could see the arch of the doorway leading back into the cathedral's cavernous interior. Light flickered in there, a thousand dancing candles. But it shifted slowly, almost sensuously, as if the air was almost still.

Groaning, Guy rolled onto his front and pushed down, lifting his upper body from the step beneath him. The stone was speckled with a few droplets of blood. He swung his legs around and sat on a step, then put a hand up to his face. His cheek was sore and bruised, nose a little bloodied. He looked at his watch — almost six p.m. He can't have been out for long.

Breathing softly, Guy stood, hand against the wall in case he was woozy. A dull headache thudded against the inside of his skull, each pulse matching the beat of his heart, but he did not feel unsteady.

Something had happened.

He started to shake, but it was nothing to do with the fall. This was uncertainty and fear. It was worry and confusion. The silence was wrong, the stillness was something that should not be. He walked down the final few steps and then stood in the arched doorway.

The cathedral was deserted. High windows let through a rainbow of light, subdued now that evening was falling. Dust motes drifted in the light, and tides of colour shadowed across the cathedral's interior. Around the central area, directly below the huge dome, giant candles burned in tall braziers, their flames almost motionless.

It looked like a place that had not been disturbed by human presence for years.

Guy took a tentative step out from the staircase enclosure and looked around. It was truly deserted. The choir stalls were empty. No songbooks were present, and the anglepoise lamps were all off and aimed down. The curve of seats where visitors could sit — where *he* had sat, head back, staring up at the mosaics of the four disciples and inviting something in — were empty, cushions hanging from small hooks on the seat backs. He turned and looked along the cathedral to the giant doors, only used now on occasions of high ceremony. Down there, close to the entry and exit, a rack of candles lit by visitors burned gently. Some of them had already sputtered out, and, as he watched, one more died a smoky death.

"Hello?" Guy whispered. His voice was quickly lost to the massive, motionless space. He thought of calling louder, but he was suddenly terrified of what might answer.

This was not a space meant to be so empty.

He started walking towards the exit, a hundred metres away. He looked around constantly as he went, not sure what he expected to see, not wishing to see anything. He passed the tombs of forgotten priests and looked away, catching stony movement from the corner of his eye. He walked across a solid brass grating that looked down into the crypt, but it was fully dark down there now, and anything might be staring back. He felt the air moving around him as he walked, but, when he looked behind him, he could see no sign of the disturbance he had made. It was as if he wasn't really there at all.

Guy paused and listened, head cocked on one side. Maybe everyone had abandoned this place when they saw what was happening outside. Maybe they'd vacated the cathedral to leave room for what might come next, or perhaps they had fled in terror.

He could hear nothing. In a space like this, there should have been echoes, whispers, the groan of memory or the reverberation of the building's great weight settling for another long night. But other than the frantic beating of his heart, there was utter silence.

He lit a candle. He should have felt ridiculous doing so, but it was all for Marie. He held the wick against another candle until it caught, then placed it gently in the small holder. Its flame shifted for a moment, as if excited at being given life, and then it settled into a steady burn, mimicking all the others. If he turned around and then turned back, he might even forget which flame was his.

The exit was close. He took slow, gentle steps, listening for any sign that the cathedral knew he was there.

"Oh, I thought I was the last one," the voice said, and Guy screamed.

The old man stood from behind the reception desk, hands held out, an apologetic smile on his lips. He looked so human.

"Sorry, mate, hey, didn't mean to startle you." He came out from behind the desk, hobbling with arthritic pain. "Where'd you come from, then? I thought everywhere had been checked."

Guy stared at the old man for a few seconds, certain that he'd see something horrible or terrifying. But the man's smile only faded into a troubled frown, and that made all of Guy's stress drain away. His shoulders slumped, and he chuckled, shaking his head.

"Sorry. I fell and banged my head, and…" He held a hand to his face and felt the bruise starting to form. The blood was already drying in his nose. "I'm sorry."

"No need to apologise to me," the old man said. "You're lucky! I'm just about to lock up, you could have been in here all night." He looked around and actually shivered. "Not something I'd like to go through."

"Something's happened!" Guy said. "Outside, something… have you been out? Have you seen?"

The man smiled and shook his head. "This is my place. I sit here from three till six, then lock up a little while after we close to the public. Nope. Not been outside. Though I hear it's getting cold."

"Have you seen Marie?" Guy asked. There was something about the security guard. Or perhaps it was merely Guy's own mystery reflected in the old man's eyes.

"No, no Marie," the man said. He turned and started walking, and Guy found himself compelled to follow. They reached a small side door set beside the circular entrance door, now motionless.

"But something happened."

The man turned and smiled.

"What are you smiling at?" Guy asked.

"You. Your face. Lots of people have stuff happen to them here, good and… not so good." He mused, looking over Guy's shoulder into the deep spaces beyond. "First time one of them's talked to me about it, though."

Guy frowned, trying to recall what he'd seen. Maybe the bang on the head was mixing things up.

"But there *was* something…" he said.

The man shrugged and opened the door, inviting Guy to step through. "Just one of those things," he said.

Outside, London roared.

The streets around St Paul's were buzzing with taxis, cars, motorcycles, buses, and cyclists braving the darkness with little more than flashing lights for protection. Horns blared. Tyres squealed, and someone shouted. Pedestrians weaved around each other on the pavements, some chatting and laughing, others focussed on getting home from work as quickly as possible. Shops around the cathedral were closed or closing, security grilles splitting the subdued lighting from inside. Restaurants and pubs spilled laughter and music across the streets. Streetlights glared, several flickering in their death throes. The smell of London was heavy and rich — cooking food, exhaust fumes, and an occasional waft of sewage beneath it all.

There was no singing, other than a drunk man leaning against a wall with his hat upturned on the floor. There was no dancing. There were no raised hands and joyful chants, no fires melting the city's distant shadows, and no impossibly tall flames licking at the underside of clouds. London was the place he had always known, loved, and hated.

But perhaps it was a very different world.

Guy had yet to decide.

Help Me

Cameron Pierce

"Therefore we must judge a weird tale not by the author's intent, or by the mere mechanics of the plot; but by the emotional level which it attains at its least mundane point."

The spectrum of emotion on display in Lovecraft is stunted at best, a consequence of his personal life and its effect on his concept of literature. But here, after drawing lines in the sand distinguishing his ideal weird tale from all other types of weird stories out there, he concludes that, above all, a weird tale must be judged by the emotional resonance in its peak of strangeness and otherworldliness. It's not about authorial intent, plot construction, or how painstakingly one mimics classic weird tales. It's about the emotions evoked by the weird.

The fishing town of Innsmouth is my favorite of all Lovecraftian locales, but having grown up on the West Coast, Innsmouth evokes in me memories of fishing with my father in San Simeon, California, a permanently cold and grey highway beach town known only for William Randolph Hearst's mansion and the zebras that still roam the former newspaper mogul's estate. When I think of San Simeon, my own private Innsmouth, I imagine my father, fishing alone in the cold surf, unaware of the unspeakable things lurking just beyond the breakers.

◆

The fish struck hard, and Jim Mulligan was nearly pulled off his feet, into the surf that crashed around his waist. A halibut, or perhaps a small shark. Whatever tugged at his line was certainly larger than the rainbow perch he'd caught all morning. He loosened his drag and let the fish peel off line. Ten, twenty, thirty yards… then seventy, eighty, ninety. Within seconds, the fish nearly stripped his spool bare. It showed no sign of slowing.

Jim tightened the drag and began to reel. At first the fish resisted, but, after several cranks, it turned tail and swam in toward the furthest breakers, toward shore.

Jim's heart thundered in his chest. His legs had gone numb from many hours taking a beating in the waves. Despite the perpetual grey of the sky, he had still managed to catch a sunburn. The dozen perch he'd landed would make a fine meal or two for himself, Jen, and their four-year-old boy, Jason, but to yield something bigger — that would make this whole vacation one to remember. A trophy lingcod. He licked his lips at the thought of the sweet, buttery meat.

The fish came in easily now. Maybe it wasn't as big as he first judged. Even though he loved nothing more than the feel of a fish on the other end of the line, disappointment rose within him as he considered the possibility that it was just another perch. Not that he'd complain. He came out to the beach, ditching his family's planned visit to Hearst Castle, in order to catch perch. Faced with the prospect of something better, though, he couldn't help feeling cheated. By who or what, he did not know. He'd felt a similar sensation of being cheated when they learned last year that Jason was autistic. The guilt of entitlement wore heavy on him, and for the moment he felt sorry for this fish, which had made a hell of a run and should be appreciated for what it was, not for what it might have been.

A black dorsal fin spotted red slashed through the waves breaking closest to Jim. The sight turned his blood cold. No fish he'd ever seen pictures of, let alone caught, possessed a fin like that.

He focused on the angle of his rod to the water, the buzzing of the spool sending his heart into his throat every time the fish held ground or fought to earn an extra few feet of line. Even though it feigned struggle, he knew it was gassed. The biggest risks now were it coming unhooked or a seal or shark swooping in for an easy meal.

He held his breath and prayed to the god all fishermen pray to.

Then a tail cut through a white-capped wave.

Holy fish gods in heaven — from the fork of the tail, Jim guessed the whole fish to be at least three feet long. Quite possibly four or five.

Some exotic type of giant rock bass? He did not have long to find out. The fight was almost finished.

He stepped backwards, then took another step, careful not to slip on any submerged rocks as he eased out of the sea and back to shore. To lose this fish now, especially after glimpsing that it was indeed something rare and wonderful, would be nothing less than tragic.

In spite of his cautiousness, his knees turned wobbly, and he collapsed to the sand when he saw the thing.

He was not sure what hideous detail he took in first:

The fish's humanoid arms and legs, clawing helplessly at the sand.

The razor-filled frown that ran like a knife gash across its cantaloupe-sized head.

The leathery, mottled skin, like that of a moray eel.

The dorsal fin that flitted open like a sail then shut again, timed to the hoarse breathing of the creature.

Its eyes, the bluest eyes he'd ever seen, that gazed at him with such despair.

Or perhaps before taking in any of the innumerable awful details of the creature before him, he registered that it spoke.

"Help me," the fish croaked. "Help me."

Pity for the creature swept over him, replacing the horror he initially felt. He fumbled about for his pliers and then set to removing the barbed hook from the creature's jaw. The poor thing whimpered as he ripped out the hook.

"I'm sorry," Jim said.

"Help me," said the fish.

"Do you want me to drag you back into the water?"

The fish shook its head sadly.

"Then what do you want?"

"Help me," it said.

"Help you how?"

"Take me home."

"But you live in the ocean, and I live in a town two hours from here. I'm on vacation with my family. I can't take you home."

"Take me with you."

"I'm out here catching dinner, not finding new pets. We already have a dog. And a cat. What am I supposed to do with you?"

"Eat me if you must."

"I'm not going to eat you." Jim shuddered at the thought. "Just tell me what you want."

"Help me."

"Look, I don't know what you want from me. I don't know that I can help you."

"Let's be friends."

"This is ridiculous."

The creature stared at Jim with its blue eyes, and he tried in vain to ward off that nagging sense of pity. Blood trickled from the hook wound in the creature's lip.

Jim packed up his fishing gear and hoisted the bucket, heavy with perch and seawater. He turned his back on the fish-thing and marched up the beach to his truck.

Then, sitting in his truck with his fishy hands clutching the steering wheel, he returned his gaze to the beach, where the sad creature still lay on the sand. Why did it not return to the sea? What the fuck was wrong with it?

Help me.

"Oh hell," Jim said. He climbed out of the truck and marched down the beach. He took the fish in his arms and carried it back to the truck. He plopped it into the half-full bucket with the perch, because, even though it seemed to breathe air just fine, he figured it might need water. It was a futile gesture. Hardly a quarter of the creature fit inside the bucket. It clutched the sides of the bucket, staring down at the dead perch with a blank expression.

As Jim pulled back onto the highway and drove toward the Motel 6 in town, it occurred to him that fear should have been his initial response to the creature. Why did he not fear it?

Because it's so pitiful, he thought. *It's just so damn pitiful. That's why I don't fear it.*

Back at the motel, upon lifting the hatch on the camper shell, Jim discovered that the creature had slunk out of the bucket and now cowered in the furthest corner of the truck bed, covering its blue eyes with its unsettlingly human hands.

It feels shame, Jim thought.

He turned his attention to the bucket and realized why. The perch were gone. The damned thing had eaten them.

"You son of a bitch," he said, and he dropped the tailgate and started to crawl into the back of the truck, prepared to beat the creature. But as he raised his left fist to pummel the thing, it whimpered and in a meek little voice said, "I'm sorry."

Jim lowered his fist and shook his head. "That was dinner."

"Eat me instead."

"No, I can't do that. What would my wife think if she saw you? What would you even taste like? What are you, anyway?"

"I'm a fish," it said. "Like you."

"No," Jim said. "I'm not a fish. I'm a man."

The creature uncovered its eyes as a crooked grin split across its face. A fleshy black tongue lolled out of its mouth and traced the peaks and valleys of its dagger teeth.

"Well then, I must be mistaken," it said.

All at once, the pity Jim had felt for the thing was replaced by a sickening dread that weighed on his chest like a sack of stones.

But it was too late for him. Too late for all of them. His wife, his son, the motel staff, the residents and vacationers in San Simeon, the state of California, the whole Pacific coast, the country, the continent, the world. They would all meet their doom trying to help this hideous thing from the sea. Jim realized this now, as if the thought were implanted in his mind by the thing itself.

"W-what do you want with me?" Jim stammered.

The creature lashed out, crossing the truck bed and locking its clawed hands around Jim's skull in a lightning flash. It must have weighed less than fifty pounds, and yet it was stronger than him, and it dragged him into the back of the truck with ease.

Darkness slid into the driver's seat of his mind, and Jim felt his chest collapse beneath the stones that seemed to weigh on him. His body turned out to be disposable, but he was too far gone to care.

He awoke some time later. The fading orange sunlight beamed through the windows of the truck. He felt cold anyhow. The creature knelt beside him. It smiled. He did not like that it smiled.

"Since you helped me, I have helped you," it said.

"Helped me how?"

"I have made you beautiful."

The creature held out the driver-side mirror for him to take. It must have crawled out of the truck and broken off the mirror. Jim wondered if anyone saw it. He guessed not. They would've shit themselves. *No*, he realized, *they wouldn't have. They would've helped it. Like I did.*

"I don't want to look," Jim said. Even as he said it, he was snatching up the mirror. He was still human. He was sure of it. He still felt human. Why should he not look human too?

In the mirror, staring back at him, he saw the unnamable fish he'd pulled from the sea. The wretched creature he'd try to help, that now sat there grinning at him like a fucking dummy.

"Help me," he said. He said it again and again, louder and louder, until he was screaming and thrashing about in the back of the truck, throwing himself against the windows and floor and ceiling, hoping to crush his own skeleton or whatever it was inside that made him so hideous to look upon.

If someone would just fucking help him.

Hotel staff and guests began to gather in the parking lot, pointing at the truck. Surely they heard his screams and noticed his thrashing. Why did they not help?

"Help me."

All the while, the firstborn, as he thought of it now, remained completely still beside him, its eyes closed and an atonal thrum emanating from its lips, as if it were meditating.

"Help me!"

Then he saw her.

Julie.

She said something to the crowd, and they shook their heads at her, refusing to help. Alone, carrying their son in her arms, she moved toward the truck. Julie, his sweet and tender wife, had come to help.

As she lifted the hatch of the camper shell, Jim licked his razor-sharp teeth and opened his blue eyes wide, for best effect. "Help me," he said to his wife.

He was ready to return home.

Glimmer in the Darkness

Asamatsu Ken

Translated by Raechel Dumas

"For those who relish speculation regarding the future, the tale of supernatural horror provides an interesting field. Combated by a mounting wave of plodding realism, cynical flippancy, and sophisticated disillusionment, it is yet encouraged by a parallel tide of growing mysticism, as developed both through the fatigued reaction of "occultists" and religious fundamentalists against materialistic discovery and through the stimulation of wonder and fancy by such enlarged vistas and broken barriers as modern science has given us with its intra-atomic chemistry, advancing astrophysics, doctrines of relativity, and probings into biology and human thought."

Translator's note: A careful balance of historical material and bizarre imagination, "Glimmer in the Darkness" offers a glimpse into the minds of early twentieth-century Americans, capturing the complex range of emotions experienced by those who lived through this period of rapid technological innovation. This piece also offers a unique perspective on H. P. Lovecraft, a writer whose oeuvre, it would seem, was informed as much by his personal demons as it was by his keen interest in the possibilities embodied by scientific inquiry. In addition to Lovecraft's essay, Mr. Asamatsu would also like to acknowledge his debt to John A. Keel, whose Operation Trojan Horse: The Classic Breakthrough Study of UFOs *served as a source text for this story. "For a time I questioned my own sanity," Keel writes, describing his conversion from skeptic to conspiracy theorist. "I kept profusive notes — a daily journal which now reads like something from the pen of Edgar Allen [sic] Poe or H. P. Lovecraft."*

♦

The man who entered the café was dressed in a brand new black suit and wore a shiny derby. Over his left hand hung a pristine coat — also black — constructed of thick cloth. Among the shop's patrons, only two noticed him: the waiter and a young man of nineteen years of age, who sat in the corner, relishing a bowl of ice cream. It was December 25, 1909, Christmas afternoon.

A swarthy Oriental — probably a Japanese, though possibly a Chinese — the man in black was of a sort clearly not permitted to enter a place like this. He wore a bewildered expression and glanced about restlessly, as though seeking someone's assistance. The youth quietly raised his right hand and beckoned him over. Appearing as though he had been rescued, the man at last removed his derby and approached the youth's table.

"Er… I'm quite unaccustomed to shops like this." The man seemed to be suffering from a respiratory illness, for he loosened his collar with a gasping wheeze. He asked the waiter, who had arrived to take his order, to bring him the same thing the youth was eating. Somehow or another, it appeared as though he didn't know the term "ice cream."

"Are you an Oriental?" the youth asked. If he were Japanese, he would by all means listen to him. Ah, the beauty of a haiku's meter and moment, the strange folklore of Lafcadio Hearn. Were the man Chinese, he hoped to learn something of Daoist magic. The youth was a poet.

"Yes… no. I'm from Boston. Tiny Smith's the name."

"Mister… Tiny Smith?" The youth raised his brows. Being so tall in stature, the man was anything but slight. And Smith? Perhaps he was of mixed blood, part-Oriental and part-English.

"Well… uh, it's…I have a government job." As he said this the man pointed to a three-pointed insignia attached to the lapel of his business suit. In the center of the isosceles triangle was the image of an eyeball. The youth recognized the symbol. It was a Freemason's mark. His Grandfather Whipple, who had died five years prior, had frequently shown it to him, when he was a young boy.

"A Boston Mason then?" the youth pondered as he gazed at the man's swarthy visage.

Before long the waiter returned and placed the ice cream in front of Tiny, who picked up the silver bowl with both hands. He opened his mouth wide, as though to swallow it whole.

"Excuse me, but… you don't use a spoon?"

"Huh?" Dabbing ice cream from around the perimeter of his mouth, the man raised his face.

"A spoon, a spoon," said the youth, showing the man his small piece of silverware. "Use this!"

"Huh? Ooooh, yes. Of course." Tiny clumsily grasped the spoon and, restlessly turning his head to survey his surroundings, began downing his ice cream. As he watched Tiny, the youth developed a steadily swelling sense of anxiety, a feeling as though he were being slowly but steadily crushed. The man was somehow abnormal. Somehow… mad.

Mad.

You're too ugly to go out in public! From somewhere his mother's voice resonated. *Howard! What a face! With your twisted nose and flattened chin…*

Mad!

A sick feeling arose in the youth's breast, and he grew nauseated, though the sensation was not merely a response to the memory of his mother.

Tiny had moved toward him now, and a terrible, sulfurous stench poured from his mouth as he spoke. "Incidentally, that invention — the flying machine constructed by that Worcester inventor — haven't you seen it?"

"Right... the flying machine. No, I haven't. But if I'm not mistaken, there's an article about it in today's issue of the *Journal*." Saying this, young Howard pulled a copy of the paper from beneath the seat next to him and handed it to Tiny. The large man opened his eyes wide and began reading voraciously. His queer expression prompted Howard to avert his eyes, and he looked out through the café window at the expansive winter sky on the other side. It was covered in greyish-white snow-laden clouds, and it seemed as though at any time snowflakes would begin to dust the ground.

"A flying machine..." Howard muttered to himself. An enormous flying machine piloted by a Worcester, Massachusetts, inventor had recently become the talk of the town and, indeed, the entirety of the East Coast.

It had begun on September 8th, in the open sea surrounding Long Island. That night members of a sea-rescue crew reported having heard a thunderous engine reverberating high in the black sky overhead. The account of a rescue worker named William Leech appeared in the Long Island and New York papers. On the same day, an amateur scientist in Worcester proclaimed to reporters that this was the invention of the century.

The inventor in question was the executive vice-president of Worcester's Sure Seal Manufacturing Company, Wallace E. Tillinghast. He claimed to have invented a flying machine with the power to transport three individuals, weighing up to two hundred pounds each, a distance of three hundred miles, at an average speed of one hundred twenty miles per hour, without replenishing the fuel. Moreover, Tillinghast reported that, on the 8th of September, he had taken his machine on a test flight, circling around the Statue of Liberty, venturing as far as Boston, and returning to New York, all without landing.

"They say Mr. Tillinghast's flying machine is a monoplane," said Tiny, "with a seventy-two-foot wingspan and a 120-horsepower engine. In all, it weighs 1,550 pounds. And it can even take off from an area just under seventy-five feet and travel at two miles per minute… if this is true, what an amazing invention!"

Young Howard's pupils glittered behind his rimless spectacles. Like most youths of the early twentieth century, he embraced the hope that the practical uses of scientific technology had no bounds. "It seems this sort of technology interests you greatly."

Tiny folded up the copy of *The Providence Daily Journal* and placed it at the corner of the table. "I like science. Astronomy above all else. Do newspapers and magazines also run astronomy columns?"

"Ah… astronomy. Well, it's a young science but a promising one. So, what kind of column?" For a brief moment Tiny's eyes emitted a bewitching light, but Howard didn't notice. Howard brought together his hands and, with a dreamy expression, continued, citing the most mainstream journal he could think of. "For example, a column in *Scientific American* asserts that because of the high likelihood that a ninth planet exists beyond Neptune, astronomers ought to combine their intellect and endeavor immediately to discover unknown planets."

Just as Howard said the words "ninth planet," Tiny produced a sputtering, violent cough. He removed a pristine handkerchief from the pocket of his business suit and covered his mouth. "I see, I see. Sounds like an interesting column… A ninth planet, eh? Hmm. Indeed, quite so. So that's what the astronomers have been up to. They ought to discover Pluto sometime soon, then."

"What was that?"

"That is, the ninth planet! Pluto is…"

"Pluto?" Howard gazed questioningly at Tiny's upturned eyes. As though he had made some error, Tiny screwed up his lips and hurried to correct himself. "Oh! Err… well… it just struck me. Being the next planet after Neptune, it seems Pluto would…" Then, as if to change the subject, Tiny returned to the topic of the flying machine. "Nevertheless, well, to be sure, the biplane took flight in Paris in 1906, and only three years later a monoplane… that's progress in the true sense of the word, and this is a marvelous affair for us Americans in particular."

Howard nodded.

"They say Mr. Tillinghast is creating new models one after the other! On the 20th, at a wharf in Boston, a bright light was seen flying by at an incredible speed, but this must have been one of Mr. Tillinghast's new models, right? I saw the same thing in Boston — wow, it was terribly bright! I hear that in Little Rock, Arkansas, some sort of shining cylinder was also seen on the 20th, around one o' clock in the morning. This must have been Tillinghast's invention, too, eh?"

Howard knit his brows. The flying machine in Boston had been witnessed on the 20th at one in the morning. Considering the distance between Little Rock and Boston, even a model that boasted a speed of one hundred twenty miles per hour couldn't have made it there and back in such a short span of time.

"Umm… it seems that it was spotted in Rhode Island, as well. If I'm not mistaken, in a place called Pawtentas or something like that."

"Pawtucket," Howard corrected him.

"Ah. New York's *Tribune* reported that in Pawtucket, on the 21st, just after one in the morning, a red light was seen advancing southward. All of the witnesses identified the outline of a flying machine against the background of the starry sky."

On the evening of December 22nd, the flying machine had made an appearance in Marlboro, Massachusetts. Shining a searchlight toward the sky, it proceeded from Marlboro to Worcester, where it danced for a few moments in the sky — and then disappeared. Two hours later the flying machine reappeared, its high-powered searchlight licking across the streets of Worcester as it circled four times, high up in the sky.

As a matter of course, reporters had intruded upon the mansion of Tillinghast, who had been performing test runs of this marvelous flying machine. But in the great inventor's absence, his wife had greeted the journalists in the foyer to speak on his behalf: "My husband understands the mission he must carry out. When the time comes, he will discuss the matter."

It seems Tillinghast was more interested in showing off his great invention before the general public than he was in holding a press conference. On December 23rd this strange, luminous body was witnessed throughout New England. Starting in Boston, the flying machine soared through the sky to Marlboro, and from there traveled through South Framingham, Natick, Ashland, Grafton, North Grafton, Upton, Hopedale, and Northborough. On the following day, December 24, 1909, Providence's *Daily Journal* recounted the incident: *Observers reported that the light was generally fixed, but sometimes it emitted glimmers, and once or twice flickered out completely.*

"But can it be true?" Howard said. On the table sat four bowls of ice cream.

"True… meaning…?"

"'The test flight on the 23rd had nothing to do with me.' Mr. Tillinghast said this in his comment in yesterday's *Journal*." Though Howard had interrupted him, Tiny resumed listening without any indication of annoyance. "He wasn't in Worcester that night — we can't say where he went. Maybe he was flying through the sky above the town, but that's also impossible to say. And that being the case, perhaps someone other than the Worcester inventor is operating these machines. Nevertheless, that amazing invention — here and there and all over New England — must be easy to build and fly, eh? Personally, I wonder if Tillinghast might be using a hot-air balloon or something to perpetrate a hoax."

Tiny flatly denied Howard's suggestion. "The luminous body seen on the 21st flew against the wind — it couldn't have been a balloon. Besides, did you know that Tillinghast has a hangar in the outskirts of Worcester?"

"No."

"A *United Press* correspondent ascertained that a hangar has been constructed in the mansion garden of the president of a telephone company in West Boylston. This company president is named Paul B. Morgan, and he is a close friend of Tillinghast's. The reporter seemed concerned that this flying machine is somehow unordinary — Morgan's company employees had been engaged in secret operations in the hangar. It seems likely that Morgan is Tillinghast's patron. Apparently the *UP* reporter who discovered all of this was arrested for trespassing and is being held on charges related to the violation of Morgan's property... and the secrecy of this project. Perhaps the country is also banking on Tillinghast's invention."

Howard stopped the hand that was conveying the ice cream toward his mouth. Might this Tiny Smith character not be a governmental agent deployed to observe Tillinghast's invention? Just last night, on Christmas Eve, the flying machine was witnessed shining its searchlight throughout the Rhode Island, Connecticut, and Massachusetts regions. Unfortunately Howard had been feeling poorly, and from early evening onward had remained curled up in bed, leaving him unable to observe this marvelous invention.

According to Howard's mother, his aunt Lillian had witnessed it and, "in a state of excitement unbecoming of a doctor's wife," as she put it, had rushed out into the garden and bathed in the luminescence of the searchlight. Howard stretched his hand toward the copy of the *Journal* that sat before Tiny. He felt as though there was something portentous about Tiny's way of speaking, about his terribly detailed understanding of the particulars surrounding Tillinghast.

Portentous? Had Tiny misspoken when he had said "Pawtentas" instead of "Pawtucket"? Clearly he'd said "portentous." How ominously sinisterly astonishingly strangely terrifyingly imposingly mad!

Eventually you'll go mad, as well. So mad that everything will cease to make sense. Bedridden. Just like me. Again his mother's hysterical, piercing voice vibrated in Howard's eardrums. At the same time, he was attacked by a chilling sensation, as though his abdomen were being caressed by a terrible hand.

Like that of his father.

As if to rid himself of the hallucination of his mother's voice, Howard casually shook his head. Sarah grew quiet. He loosed a deep sigh and looked back at the open spread of the *Journal*.

> *Tillinghast is still reticent. Since the enigmatic luminescent body was first witnessed, the infamy that has begun to dog him has placed both his work and home lives in jeopardy. He is not even permitted an hour of tranquility. Two or three people seeking information are constantly in his office. The doors of his workplace and his residence alike are closely guarded by mysterious men.*

"This says he's closely guarded by mysterious men…" Howard turned his eyes up toward the black-suited man sitting before him. Tiny awkwardly scooped at the melting ice cream and continued to shovel it into his mouth. Shortly cropped, coarse black hair. Swarthy skin, like that of someone afflicted with a liver condition. Upturned eyes. A pointed chin. A seemingly brand-new business suit. An immaculately white collar. A perfectly knotted necktie. *The devil was a black man.* Howard recalled a passage from Cotton Mather's *The Wonders of the Invisible World*, which had been in his grandfather's library. During the Salem witch trials, an accused witch had made just such a declaration.

This is absurd… I'm a materialist — I don't believe in demons and the like! Were I some Pawtucket fisherman's wife I might just take one look at Tiny and, wondering if he doesn't possess cloven-hoofed feet, demand that he remove his shoes and show them to me!

Cloven hooves — a sign of the devil, like being cursed with sulfurous breath… Sulfurous breath? That's precisely how Tiny's breath smelled.

Mad.

— Or a nightmare, perhaps? Howard was exasperated, but what did it matter? Night after night he was plagued by scream-inducing nightmares… ever since the old woman's death this had been the way of things! Sarah's voice echoed in his head, his brain vibrating with each reverberation. Nausea and vertigo simultaneously surged forth, and Howard let the newspaper fall from his hands. A parched voice assaulted him, frighteningly loud.

"You dropped it," Tiny said as he lifted his face from the bowl of ice cream. Those eyes stared intently at Howard.

Just like the eyes of a hypnotist. Eyes that seemed as though they could render anyone who stared into them entirely open to suggestion.

Howard peeled his eyes from Tiny's face and leaned over to retrieve the paper. He picked up the copy of the *Journal*, and, as he lifted his head, Tiny's legs struck his gaze. Thick green wires were coiled against the inner part of both legs, which peeked out from beneath his trouser cuffs. The wires originated in Tiny's socks and had been concealed beneath his trousers. Now, it looked as though they were crawling into his body by way of the flesh around his calves.

Howard held his breath and adjusted his spectacles. Pitch-black shoes, polished to a high shine. Short black socks. Green wires, hidden beneath trouser cuffs — this was mad! Tiny Smith was queer in the head. What else could have inspired such outrageous behavior as running wires into his body?

Howard straightened back up in his seat. Tiny took out a small memo pad and made some notes. The page was filled to the brim with tiny letters that Howard had never before seen.

"Well… before long I'll have to start heading back."

Howard began to rise, but Tiny's words reined him in. "Be that as it may, a little longer won't hurt." Tiny turned toward the waiter. "Hey! Bring us another round!"

Howard timidly lowered himself back into the chair. Tiny crossed his unusually long, narrow fingers, placed them on the table, and spoke in a low whisper. "There are a great many things out there resembling Tillinghast's flying machine, things from the cosmos — so it seems. What do you think of, say, the chances that something will arrive here from the ninth planet?"

"Like a monoplane? Seems unlikely. Scientists claim that any human being who rides a vehicle whose velocity exceeds sixty miles per hour will disperse into particles! A little while ago, I asked if the Worcester inventor might not be a fake, and you asserted that he could fly at one hundred twenty miles per hour. Though I'm not entirely convinced, I admit it might be possible. But in the void of space, there isn't any oxygen. It's filled with ether. How could one operate an engine in that sort of environment?"

"Well, say one were to implement a device that resists gravity or something of the sort…"

"Isn't that the plot of a Wells novel? Look! An anti-gravity metal, like Cavorite in *The First Men in the Moon*. Nothing like this actually exists. I'll permit that Wells is a great author, but he's not a scientific type."

"I also enjoy Wells. Especially *War of the Worlds*… It's interesting. And I think so-called Martians really exist."

"I'll concede the possibility that Mars is home to a very few plants — things like mosses — along with lower-class insects. But intelligent life… absolutely not."

With an air of admiration for Howard's coolheaded tone, Tiny began taking notes in his memo pad. "Your literature, too, is undoubtedly deeply scholarly. When writing novels and the like…"

"No," Howard said, shaking his head sadly. "I don't write novels. I don't have the talent. As a child I wrote a lot of things, but I burned and trashed all but two of those scribblings. Now, aside from penning the occasional poem, I'm detached from literature…"

"You surely have the eye of a poet. You might just become a great bard, à la Longfellow!"

"How's that?" A dejected expression appeared on Howard's face. Owing to his nervous disorder, he had left high school in the middle of the term, and, with his hopes of entering Brown University quashed, the possibility of becoming a renowned poet or the like seemed unlikely. "Well, if you'll excuse me." Howard stood up to leave.

Tiny turned to face the tall, lanky man's back. "Thank you for such a wonderful time!" he said. "Might I have your name and address? I'd like to write to you after I return to Boston."

Howard turned and, with a weak smile that betrayed his feelings on the matter, consented. "Angell Street, number 598, Providence. The name's Howard Phillips Lovecraft."

Tiny jotted in his memo pad, whereupon an awkward smile — entirely like a clown's mask — arose on his face. "I swear it — you'll become a great poet or scientist. Goodbye. Stay well. Mister Lovecraft!"

Howard bowed and pushed open the café door. He fell into a daze, as though he were viewing the street corner in the lingering evening through a veil of melted copper. He advanced slowly along the mud-slushed pavement.

Mad!

Having walked about a hundred meters, the inside of his head began to flicker. How did Tiny polish his shoes to such a glittering shine? How had he traversed this terrible, muddy road without a single speck of muck clinging to his shoes?

Mad! Impossible!

Terrified, Howard turned his head and glanced back.

Pluto? A devil dressed in black? The smell of sulfur? *War of the Worlds?* Monoplanes in great numbers, headed toward the earth?

Tiny's figure appeared on the porch of the sidewalk café. A black automobile pulled up silently, and a door opened in his direction. Tiny raised his right hand to Howard, gave a salute, and casually disappeared into the car.

Eight years later, Howard Phillips Lovecraft resumed writing fiction at the behest of his friend W. Paul Cook. He subsequently became a regular contributor to *Weird Tales*, which was launched in 1923, and gained a favorable reputation among a limited number of enthusiasts. Many young writers adored him and asked him to look over their own works.

Lovecraft had many close friends with whom he exchanged a great number of letters. The correspondences that accumulated over the course of his forty-six years of life were astronomical in number, and it is presumed that if we were to compile them all, the collection would exceed fifty volumes. But among these letters, there is not one addressed to a man named Tiny Smith. And in the end, Tiny's promised correspondences from Boston never did reach Lovecraft. Moreover, Lovecraft remained silent concerning his encounter with this queer man.

But in the year 1930, in an exceedingly unusual science fiction piece, the specter of Tiny returns in the form of a fictitious pseudo-human character. The story, titled "The Whisperer in Darkness," is an invasion-themed story concerning a Vermont occultist who battles a monster attacker from Pluto until he is finally defeated, with his brain sealed in a cylinder. In this narrative, Lovecraft describes an enigmatic figure who collaborates with cosmic life forms, a mysterious conspiracy involving the interception of letters and parcels, and humanoids that perfectly resemble people — all with the characteristic force of Lovecraft's mature literary style.

The great inventor Tillinghast, always at the core of Lovecraft and Tiny's conversation, officially announced his flying machine at the Boston aviation show, which ran for a week beginning on February 16, 1910. After informing the newspaper reporters of his invention, he disappeared for all eternity from aviation history. He was forgotten by the general public, and, even among those old-timers who had experienced these events firsthand, talk of his great invention eventually subsided.

In 1909, the aircrafts exhibited in broad daylight before the attentive eyes of laymen were all biplanes. That is to say, they conformed to the model designed by Orville Wright. Society had to wait until the Great War to witness biplanes that could achieve speeds exceeding one hundred twenty miles per hour.

The development of monoplanes with a wingspan of seventy-two feet was achieved in the 1950s. The Douglas had a wingspan of seventy-five feet. Incidentally, a monoplane with a seventy-two-foot wingspan, a weight of 1,550 pounds, and the abilities to take off from an area under seventy-five feet and travel from Little Rock to Boston in just a few minutes was at the time, and continues to be, scientifically unfeasible.

Sixty-one years later, the mysterious flying body witnessed throughout New England in December of 1909 came to be referred to among American UFO researchers as the "Massachusetts flap." Aberrant records concerning the incident have been compiled, and, if one consults the *M* heading among these files, Tiny Smith's true character may be revealed: an MIB, that is, a "Man in Black." These were the mystery men who materialized before UFO witnesses. Seizing UFO photographs and pieces of evidence, sampling correspondences, wiretapping phones, and making malignant threats, these men instilled fear in UFO investigators. There is viable evidence that any number of researchers were assassinated by the MIB, as well.

New York–based MIB researcher John Keel chronicled the features of the MIB in detail. The characteristics he describes include dark skin and Asian features. They also wore brand-new suits and rode in old-style Cadillacs, always working in groups of two or three. Their bodies emitted the strong odor of sulfur or ammonia. At times it appeared as though they could predict the future, and in these moments they experienced slips of the tongue. Some wore clothes that would become fashionable years down the road. The majority posed as government agents…

It appears as though the Massachusetts flap was burned into Lovecraft's memory. In one bizarre story from 1920, he presents his own response to the affair. The tale is one of an inventor who renders visible a dimension of existence that cannot be apprehended by the human eye. Together with his friend, the man conducts experiments with his device. But because the physical laws of our dimension are duplicated on the other side, the inventor's body is destroyed — more specifically, it wastes away. The story concludes as follows:

> *It would help my shaky nerves if I could dismiss what I now have to think of the air and the sky about and above me.... [T]he police never found the bodies of those servants whom they say Crawford Tillinghast murdered.*

The Order of the Haunted Wood

Jeffrey Ford

"Much of the power of Western horror-lore was undoubtedly due to the hidden but often suspected presence of a hideous cult of nocturnal worshippers whose strange customs — descended from pre-Aryan and pre-agricultural times when a squat race of Mongoloids roved over Europe with their flocks and herds — were rooted in the most revolting fertility-rites of immemorial antiquity."

What drew me to this quote was the idea of a hideous nocturnal fertility cult that has survived secretly through centuries. The word fertility made me wonder what it could refer to in a story, and I was thinking that while watching the news and eating my dinner. In the space of a half hour there were three commercials for drugs treating erectile dysfunction. It took a while, but, eventually, I said, "Oh, yeah, fertility." The creepiness of the ads made me ponder them in light of the story idea. What I noticed was that whatever they were about, they certainly weren't about fucking.

♦

The past evolves into the future, and, with training, one can spot it in its new guise, the way a dinosaur can be found in a raven by a paleontologist. As with creatures, so with traditions. The ancient moves among us in our rituals. One of the most fruitful of enterprises a scholar can undertake is to trace the trail of evidence from the dawn of humanity to this very moment.

Take for instance the Order of the Haunted Wood, a secret society that is still not widely known but whose influence has been persistent. Its traditions and rituals go back, most likely, to some pre-language era when humanity was barely out of the trees. The purpose of the Order was, through the use of supernatural forces, to bestow fertility on those of its members who needed it. In clandestine night meetings, they summoned the spirit to enter the bodies of the afflicted, and, as Baron Menifer recorded (1453) in his *Practices and Preachments of the Order of the Haunted Wood*, "that which lay down, rose up."

There are scant accounts of the group's doings through the centuries, because it was frowned upon for members to speak openly about its affairs, but there were enough initiates who broke with that code to allow a basic understanding to be able to now be pieced together. Literal mention of the Wood died out somewhere around the beginning of the 20th century, although some scholars point to a notice in a local newspaper from Manhattan in 1972, a tiny piece in its want ads that read, "TOOTHW, midnight, Wash Sq. Prk," as evidence of the society's continued existence.

One need not grasp for such flimsy proof of the society's pervasive influence, though. All one need do is turn on the television, sit back, and, before long, on any channel, you will come across a commercial for a product that addresses the problem of erectile dysfunction. These commercials, whether the viewer knows it or not, are bursting with the symbology and ritual of the Order. There are those who *will*, but I won't go so far as to suggest that the Haunted Wood is directly behind these products and their ads. I subscribe to the notion that what is played out in the seemingly insipid dramas of these minute-and-a-half promos comes from a kind of collective unconscious, an ancient spell that has twined its way through the history of male minds to blossom anew, metamorphosed, in the *fleurs du mal* of advertising.

You know the commercials first by their music. Notice the snare drum played softly with brushes at a calm but steady pace while the flute and saxophone carry a lilting metronomic harmony. The setting is always well-to-do, upscale, in living rooms and kitchens furnished as if from the pages of *Better Homes and Gardens*. The implicit message is the poor can't afford an erection, and, since it is always a male and female couple, none but heterosexuals deserve one.

There is a fellow, too well dressed for home, in a V-neck sweater and khakis, hair slightly greying but perfectly in place. He has all his teeth, and they are pure white. There's a smirk on his well-tanned face. He is watching his wife at some menial task, for instance, as in the recent spate of commercials for a product called Doalis or its fast-acting co-product, Dofran, loading the dishwasher. Her age, the crow's-feet, the frown lines, seem to have been applied by a makeup artist with a gracefully subtle hand. Her hair is done in a youthful style, mid-length, without adornment. He leers as she bends over in her camel hair slacks to place a glass on the upper rack, but it slips out of her hand and falls to the floor, shattering.

She winces, and he gets a silent chuckle out of it. He shakes his head in a condescending manner and then slowly approaches her from behind. He is smitten by her ineptitude. As he draws close and wraps his arms around her, a friendly but warning male voice says, "You never know when the call to action will be upon you. Sometimes it arrives, like a thief in the night." She turns around, surprised by his embrace with a look that is disturbing in its glee. They laugh. Cut to a shot of them cleaning up the glass, he with the broom, she with the waste pan. "Be ready," says the disembodied paternal voice, "for those moments when the

Jeffrey Ford

unexpected becomes a reality. Just take one Doalis with a glass of water twelve minutes before the event for desired results."

In the next scene, they sit down on the couch in the living room, and she pours him a glass of water from a pitcher. They laugh. The voice returns with a litany of side effects — stuffy nose, failure of vision or hearing, high blood pressure, low blood pressure, testicular alopecia, stroke, cardiac arrest, bleeding from the anus and/or ears, liver failure, dizziness, homicidal thoughts, terminal halitosis, or an erection lasting more than six hours. Then the music comes up. The woman makes a foolish face, and they continue laughing. "Doalis," says the voice, "or, for readiness in three minutes, try Dofran." In the last scene, we see both the woman and the man, from behind, each naked in their own separate barrel, facing a blazing sun.

The first thing one must know in order to follow any analysis of this drug commercial in light of its Haunted Wood influences and shared symbology is that in the rituals of the Order there were absolutely no women present. It is the one element of the ritual that has remained completely intact through time. In its most ancient practice, the part of the female partner was played by a male member of the Order wrapped in an animal skin. Later, in agrarian culture, the woman was a straw-filled scarecrow with a painted face and an apron. Late 19th century iterations of the female entity called Vigra were dress-making dummies and early store-window mannequins. If one studies closely the woman of the contemporary television ad, it is evident that neither is she an actual woman but an avatar of Vigra as well. What woman laughs so much where humor is so blatantly absent? A madwoman? No, a goddess of laughter, confabulated by the male psyche from the misty dawn of consciousness. She traditionally laughs at the subject before he achieves an erection and laughs when he has one.

Baron Menifer described this sacred trait of hers as "the eternal jocularity; a song of cosmic futility." Vigra is an agent of chaos (the shattering of the glass akin to the shattering of the world), but also a bringer of water. Bear in mind, though, she does not participate in the sexual act, but instead is the physical manifestation of a creative force that through her supernatural presence awakens a dreaming sex from hibernation. Ejaculation is withheld by the subject in order to bestow that gift upon the real partner.

The moniker that eventually coalesced around the cult, for it had many names throughout the centuries from ancient Egypt to the culture of the Picts, the Order of the Haunted Wood, comes from Gotland, an island that lies off the coast of Sweden. In the 1400s there was a wealthy Dutch nobleman, Fabianus Adelheid II, who kept a large forested estate on the island's southern shore. He only stayed at the castle once every three years, and, for the autumn months he was in residence, there were visitors from every part of the world. These were the first international meetings of the Order, then known to its members by a passel of different titles, although they shared the same ritual. It so happened that the forest surrounding the estate was haunted.

Apparently, Adelheid's father, who was a member of the Estates General of the Burgundian Netherlands, established the place as a hunting retreat. The patriarch's first wife, Leentja, in six years of marriage, never became pregnant. The councilor was impatient for a male heir, and so, one day when taking his wife out riding on the estate, he brought her to a secluded part of the forest and supposedly strangled her so that he might marry anew without the bother of beseeching annulment. Her body was never recovered, but, in the years following, her spectral form was often seen, flitting among the fir trees, weeping. To be fair to poor Leentja, whereas her husband was not, when Fabianus was born to the new wife it was whispered by all that he bore a closer resemblance to a local swineherd than his father.

I mention this morsel of history in relation to a number of aspects of the commercial. First and foremost is that the Order held its rituals in a clearing in this forest. The music described above, with its reliance on the lightly brushed snare drum, is reminiscent of the practice of "tapping the tree," wherein members of the group lightly struck a fallen log with branches of dead leaves in an incantatory rhythm meant to enhance the concentration of all present and to coax natural energy from the setting. The lilting sound of the flute is, of course, the wind in the trees, and the saxophone is the distant weeping of Leentja.

In a clearing of the Haunted Wood, the subject was stripped naked and made to wear a pair of strange crystal spectacles known as the Dimsight, which fractured his vision of the waking world and prepared him for the nightmarish reality of the summoned realm of the supernatural. As the Syrian merchant Abdul-Basir Fakhoury, once a subject of the ritual as a guest of Adelheid, attested in his deathbed memoir about the Order, *The Summoning of Desire*, "To see through Dimsight was to see reality splintered and replaced with the liquid flowing energies of night's domain." Let us not forget that before these spectacles were donned, the subject was administered a honeyed dough ball brimming with hallucinogens like foxglove, belladonna, and minced pieces of the mushroom *Stropharia cubensis*. The subject was given clear water from a nearby stream to wash this down. I know you must be ahead of me here and have already noted that the images of water and drug have their equivalencies in the commercial, but did you guess that the shattering of the glass by the woman in camel hair slacks stands in for the fracturing of reality by the Dimsight?

To fill in some finer points not so readily evident, I return to the reliable Baron Menifer and his invaluable book. In the words of the good Baron:

Never having been at a loss to raise the rooster, myself, although always willing to lend assistance to a fellow in a woebegone condition, I can only give second-hand accounts of what the subject of the ritual experienced when wearing the Dimsight and three sheets to the wind from the effects of the ingested honeyed ball we knew in each of our given languages as The Load of the Toad. A stately gentleman, who had been a librarian in the far-off university/trade city of Timbuktoo, part of the Songhai Empire, and went by the name of Modibo, told me, through an interpreter, "The mind boils, the heart toils, breathing is foiled and the breeches are soiled. My multifaceted vision suddenly shattered and I beheld Amna (his culture's name for the entity Vigra). She was both old and young, beautiful and frightening, with mid-length hair and dressed in a cloak of camel hide. She moved around me, laughing, laughing, laughing, till her laughter bored into my mind. I felt it traveling down my backbone like a caravan of ants, through my blood like a fleet of burning ships, to gather in my nether regions and sprout a grove of agonizing thorn trees. I cried out, feeling I was drowning in magic. Before I succumbed to my pain and fear, Amna ripped off her face to reveal she was a man in disguise, the Lord of Death. As I slumped to the forest floor, the bone-faced specter recited the fatal possibilities of the ritual, the Two Dozen Errant Paths to Destruction. It was made clear to me in my thoughts that my only salvation was in an erection."

You can readily match the camel hair slacks with the camel hide cloak. The laughter, I've discussed already in relation to Vigra. This brings us to Lord Death's recitation of the Two Dozen Errant Paths to Destruction, which, of course, is now represented by the litany of side effects. Contemporary pharmaceuticals have whittled this list down, as in the case of Doalis, to about a dozen and a half dangers. The progress of modern science. Certainly, though, Death is still at play in the ritual. In 2000, one well-known brand of drug meant to combat erectile dysfunction resulted in the deaths of over five hundred of its users. Imagine what the yearly tolls are now. And what of that disembodied voice in the commercial, the one now warning and paternal? Is this the evolution of the voice of Death? Jimmy Stewart from the 6th dimension? No longer does the cosmic spirit of Mr. Mortality command with inevitability and wrath, but now minces out warnings with a postmodern bourgeois inflection. I'm guessing that you have already apprehended where my train of thought is heading. If not, stare out the window and wait for it.

I'm moving on to one of the most significant correlations between the ritual of the order and our contemporary advertisement. As mentioned previously, the last scene of the commercial shows the man and the woman, naked, each standing in their own separate barrel, staring into a blazing sun. A curious way to end a piece that hopes to ultimately engender togetherness of a most basic sort. The iconography of the scene is rich with the spirit of the Haunted Wood, because what was noticed through time by the members of the secret society was that, although the ritual worked and an erection resulted, there was also a kind of vague apprehension that the supernatural power that produced it brought with it a kind of consciousness and gave the impression that there were now three rather than two in bed. The Order termed this threesome The Trinity. They came to understand that it was really an ancient cosmic entity out of Nature that was performing intercourse with the partner. The couple are in a blaze of passion, as the couple are in the blaze of the sun, yet they are also separated, not only as in the commercial by barrels, but also by the presence of Lord Death, who, if I may for once be straight forward to emphasize a point, is doing *all* the fucking. The Order, discovering this dread reality, accepted it as the price of the ritual.

Recently, a group of a hundred men were given samples of Doalis. They were later interviewed as to its effectiveness and asked to speak candidly about the experience. One statement by a retired diplomat, William Cottly, is enough evidence of the similarity of the drug's effect with that of the ritual. "Things are definitely popping," he said. "Doalis, like Mussolini, keeps the trains running, each boner like a moray eel in rigor mortis. But now, when I do my wife, she is constantly looking through me and whispering gibberish as if someone else is present. My dick burns from within with a dry heat. These are mere inconveniences, though, in light of the results." And so, a bona fide endorsement from a high powered professional man, but reaching the same exact conclusion as the ancient Order of the Haunted Wood. The past, my friends, is with us.

Only the Dead and the Moonstruck

Angela Slatter

"Children will always be afraid of the dark, and men with minds sensitive to hereditary impulse will always tremble at the thought of the hidden and fathomless worlds of strange life which may pulsate in the gulfs beyond the stars, or press hideously upon our own globe in unholy dimensions which only the dead and the moonstruck can glimpse."

Yes, children will always be afraid of the dark, and that's because they're smarter than adults. Men — and women — with "minds sensitive to hereditary impulse" are rare. As we grow, our minds fill with logic, with reason. We learn to explain away all the things that go bump in the night, all the items that disappear for hours or days and then are found returned to where we first left them, and the people we meet who don't seem quite... grounded, who have one foot on this firm earth, and with the other straddle those gulfs beyond the stars. They mean us harm, the strange things, although modern storytelling would have us believe otherwise — that ghosts protect us, that vampires want only to date us, and that creatures from outer space desire nothing more than to phone home. The dead and the moonstruck envy our very breath, our very solidity.

In our willful blindness, we leave ourselves open to threats we refuse to even countenance. We assume everything is harmless — unless it carries a chainsaw — until it is too late.

But children see between worlds. They hear the ringing of the dead bell across the empty gulfs and know that something wicked this way comes. They hear the gentle tap-tap-scrape of nails upon glass reaching across dimensions, looking for a way through, a way in. Children are generally smart enough not to open those windows, those doors, but adults… adults will let the thing in because they are too proud to do what should be done: hunker down by the fire, ignore the summons, and pray until daylight comes and breaks the hold of the night. Yes, children will always be afraid of the dark, but sometimes this prepares them for survival.

Becky heard the clink of the beer as he tried to slide it silently out of the fridge.

"Put it back," she said, "or I'll tell Mama."

Micah swore almost under his breath, but loud enough for her to hear what he thought of his little sister. The bottle made an angry sound as he replaced it; then there was the soft thud of the juice bottle and the little fermented sigh as he uncapped it that told her it was almost out of date. She knew without looking that he was drinking straight from the carton; it was the kind of thing he did nowadays. She heard him slip back onto his chair and start hacking at the fried chicken on his plate. On her lap, Riddle, the fat ginger cat, stirred and sniffed, settled again, knowing that no food escaped the boy.

She tuned out the noises of her brother's meal and watched her mother, as she always did, through the sunflower gauze curtain. Becky wasn't sure if Suellan knew she was there, but she thought not; the woman was too focused on the sky. The stars were bright the night Aidan, Becky's eldest brother, had disappeared, and Suellan, by her own admission, couldn't help herself, not even two years down the track. Not even a new town, new house, new life, could stop her from going onto the narrow porch, a glass of red in hand, after she'd served up their dinner (always late, always around nine) and taken a few bites of her own, to stare upwards, judging the quality of starlight, hoping that one night they'd shine bright enough for her boy to find his way home.

And Becky understood. She understood a lot of things: that her mother hadn't believed the police when they'd said Aidan had run away, nor when they changed their story to *abducted*. That Suellan sure as hell hadn't believed them when they'd tried to tell her that the decomposed body lying on the steel tray at the Arkham morgue was all that was left of her son after he'd finally been found in the river. After all, she'd said to Becky's father Buck, there was really only the right forearm with enough pale, puffy skin left to show the places where it seemed something had suckled and bit with all those tiny ring-a-ring-a-roses of sharp teeth, and that could have belonged to anyone.

It didn't matter that the ragged clothes wrapped around the rotted form were identical to Aidan's. Didn't matter what they told her about DNA. Didn't matter when they said Aidan wasn't the first Essex County boy to whom this had happened. Didn't matter that she'd eventually given in to Buck's pleas that they move, start again. Becky remembered her father asking *Didn't the other kids deserve a future that wasn't overshadowed by their brother's passing?* but she couldn't recall her mother answering.

Didn't matter, Suellan told Becky and Micah more than once, coz one day their big brother was coming back, and he'd know where to find them because of the starlight, because it would lead him home. To her.

"You got homework?" Becky asked Micah and received a grunt, which she interpreted as *yes*, and said, "Leave it on my desk."

In Suellan's memory, Aidan was fifteen forever, unchanging and perfect, filled with potential and always *just* on the cusp of returning; she had hung onto that idea, but Becky could see what it did to Buck. He'd given up, in the end; she and Micah had come home from school one day, and he told them. Wanted them to understand he couldn't bear it any longer, couldn't bear Suellan, how she'd brought everything with her, the sadness, the baggage, the hurt, everything they'd needed to jettison if they were to become light enough to keep living. He said things like that sometimes, poetic things, pretty things, useless things. Buck had taken just two suitcases, and the new house was as cluttered as the old with golf clubs, wetsuits, tennis rackets, the speargun Suellan had given him one birthday so he could take the kids snorkeling. So many discarded things spilling from the garage and into the laundry, taking up corners and shelves, because Buck's wife couldn't be bothered to get rid of it all even after he left.

Suellan had continued to function, though, and Becky was grateful for that, grateful that her mother could hold down the freelance copywriting jobs and work from home, get paid a good wage, with a healthcare plan and all. She looked after her remaining offspring, and Becky knew she tried hard not to punish them for being Buck's kids, or for not being Aidan.

"Any more chicken?" asked Micah, surprisingly articulate when he wanted something. Becky, having eaten two packets of Red Vines after school, wasn't hungry. The cat began to purr, a low thrum that sent gentle vibrations through her knees.

She shrugged, didn't take her eyes off Suellan's thin shoulders and narrow back. "Have mine."

Adolescence had changed Micah in a way it hadn't for Aidan, making him a surly, slouching, testosterone-scented troglodyte. But Becky, with love and guilt — so much guilt! — reminded herself everyday to cut him some slack. They'd both suffered from the loss of Aidan, but Micah had taken Buck's desertion especially hard. He wore T-shirts and jeans that had belonged to his brother. Sometimes their mother's eyes caught on a shirt, recognition sparked and so did a tear, but she didn't say anything, just watched Micah as if she imagined he was her lost child.

Becky wondered if the terrifying transformation that had taken Micah would affect her, too. She had a year before she became a teen, and she watched the time pass with a kind of resigned fascination. Maybe there wasn't anything she could do about it.

"Can you hear that?" Micah asked, words pushed out around masticated chicken and crumbed crust. Becky didn't turn, just tilted her head and listened carefully.

"Nope. You're hearing things. Did you leave the TV on?"

He didn't dignify that with a response; the television was always switched off as soon as dinner was on the table. Becky didn't get resentful like others might; she was a good student, a good daughter, a good sister. She was patient with her mother and brother, and accepted her self-imposed burdens and duties, and she did it a lot out of love, but even more out of guilt.

Because Becky had seen the girl and told no one.

From her bedroom window, she'd watched Aidan leave the house and wander down the path that starry night. Seen the dim shape of someone waiting outside their fence, where the porch light was weakest, where the gloom hid the sloping bank and the river that was sometimes sweet, sometimes salty coz it ran out to the sea not so far away. Seen it resolve itself into a strange-looking girl who drifted back and forth, as though she swam through the air. Becky almost called out, but then saw her brother lift a hand to the visitor. She couldn't see his face, but she thought he was wearing that shy smile he had, and went straight to the girl's arms and snuggled right into her as if it was the place he most wanted to be. It was then Becky realised what had drawn her to the window in the first place was the girl's song, guttural, like one frog calling to another.

And that girl with skin as pale as a fish's belly, thick lips, and wide-set protruding eyes that even in the moonlight appeared to have no whites, had looked up at Becky's window. That girl seemed to see her, even in the darkness, even through the lacy curtain. And that girl smiled slowly to let all those tiny teeth catch the rays of the moon and stars.

And Becky had peed her pants.

And Aidan hadn't come home.

And Becky had never told.

She'd never told because inside her head she'd heard the girl's voice, her words all wet and throaty and slow. Words that numbed Becky's mind until everything the girl said was reasonable, a seed planted that kept the younger girl's mouth shut forever afterwards, because Becky knew she'd made a bargain, and, if she broke it, she would lose even more than she already had. So, she let Aidan go and was grateful to have kept Micah.

Behind her there was a burp, deep and long, the kind produced only by the stomach of a teenage boy. The kind that penetrated the double glazing and made Suellan startle and shiver. Becky shook her head and threw Micah a withering glance. He shrugged and stood, leaving his plate where it was. That was okay: it was her week to stack the dishwasher. He took the distance to the living room in two long strides.

"Don't forget your homework," she called after him, but the only answer was the thud of his overly large sneakers on the carpeted stairs. She listened, tracking him along the corridor, into his room, out again, to hers, door thrown back to hit the wall as always, then three steps to her desk. She imagined the harsh whisper of the school books hitting the cheap laminate, then Micah's footsteps as he retreated to the bedroom set up just as it had been when he'd shared with Aidan at the Arkham house. Bunk beds and the two desks cramping the much smaller space, walls covered by the same posters, shelves heavy with the same baseball mitts, interesting rocks, pieces of driftwood, and assorted sporting trophies. As if Micah was wrapped in an Aidan-cocoon. He'd be asleep soon; he slept so much, early and late.

"Frogs are going crazy out there," said Suellan and slammed the kitchen door. Riddle, startled, dug his claws through Becky's skirt and into her thighs, but didn't bother to leap off. Becky bit back a curse and looked reproachfully at her mother. Suellan smiled, leaned down, and scratched her shocking-pink nails along the amber fur.

"Stupid cat," she murmured, then switched her attention to

Becky and ran her fingers through the girl's mouse-brown hair. Becky, like Riddle, closed her eyes for a few seconds, just that tight temporal sliver when everything was okay: the darkness behind her lids was warm and the hand upon her was gentle. For that tiny moment, there was comfort and things were all right. Then Suellan moved away, and Becky heard the sound of her wine glass being set carefully on the bench, then the running of water into the tumbler her mother always took up to bed, to wash down the tranquilizers the doctor kept giving her. "Night, Becky."

"Night, Mama. Lots of stars tonight," she said but got no response. When she opened her eyes, Suellan was gone, moving silently as always on her long legs. Becky blinked, and couldn't remember the last time she'd felt a goodnight kiss on her forehead. She sighed and rose, dislodging the cat, who squeaked indignantly. "Oh shush, hair bag."

Riddle sat in front of the cat door, as if threatening to desert, but he'd never used that exit in his life, preferring to yowl until someone opened the people door for him, and he wasn't about to change habits now. He began to wash his ears, watching as she packed the dishwasher, which took more time than it should because they only ran it once a day. Becky didn't mind. It was quiet time for her to plan, to get her ducks in a row. She always did her homework as soon as she got home from school, so there would just be Micah's — it was Tuesday, so probably algebra and English.

She slotted the last coffee mug into place then put the soap tablet in the tiny box that was supposed to release as soon as she closed the dishwasher. Becky remained convinced it sometimes hung on for a while, freeing the thing only when it felt like it. Just like she was certain the fridge light stayed on that little bit longer, to assert some kind of independence. Straightening, she peered out the window into the shadowy garden.

Becky took in the colour of the night, how it changed the objects it touched: the swing set she hardly used anymore; the folding sun chairs; the defiantly unhappy *Rosa rugosa* bushes; the palings leeched silvery by salty air. Sand blew up from the shore and piled against the fence, crept through to make the lawn grainy. She looked beyond the yard, out to where the land fell away and a path led down through a thin barrier of shrubs and stunted trees until it met the beach proper. She stared and stared, lost focus and fell into a kind of trance until something pale ran right past the pane, leaving a smear of after-image on her surprised gaze.

Becky gasped and stumbled back, then leaned close again and scanned the empty 'scape. Something else moved further away, between the trees, paler still, glowing, and then it was gone. At the door there was the sound of the handle being tried, and Becky turned; she didn't know if Suellan had locked it when she came in. Becky always checked just before she headed upstairs, and sometimes it was locked, others not. The doorknob rotated, slowly at first, then faster as it became obvious that the latch held and whatever was attempting to get in became increasingly frustrated.

She had only just begun to savour her relief when the square-cut flap at the bottom of the door was pushed open, and a greenish-grey hand with long nails and webbing between its fingers darted in, found Riddle's fat rump, and dragged the surprised animal out before he managed even a squeak of protest.

Reaching out, her first instinct was to open the door, try to save the cat, but the cold part of her brain said *no*. It stayed her hand, and she backed away, spun on her heel and ran up the stairs, past Suellan's door — experience had shown that her mother would not be roused until the sun came through her window in the morning — into her own room. Becky crouched by the window, peering over the sill, trying to see where the thing was.

And there it stood, in the middle of the yard, head raised, flattish nostrils dilating as it drew in great lungfuls of sea breeze. Becky thought it — *she* — wore a dress, something long with sleeves, something bleached. In its — *her* — arms was the cat, who lay frozen as the talons brushed up and down his pelt. Only the gleam of moonlight in Riddle's eye told Becky how afraid he was.

The house was locked, thought Becky, *they were safe*.

It couldn't get in; everyone else was asleep.

There was just Riddle, poor old Riddle, and he was a goner.

Becky bid him a silent guilt-ridden goodbye, and slumped against the wall. In her heart she was affronted that the thing, the girl, had broken their bargain; that she'd come seeking again, but she knew she shouldn't have been shocked: hadn't she spent all that time reading after Aidan had gone, researching in the library? Hadn't she seen a pattern?

Disappearances stretching back so far that those old microfiched newspapers called it the "the Harvest" or "The Arkham Harvest." Didn't she find over one hundred years of reports saying annually how baffled the police were? It didn't matter that they'd moved, because Kingsport wasn't so far from Arkham, as the crow flies… or the fish swims… and hadn't she'd found evidence of teenage boys vanishing not just here but across the length and breadth of Essex County? All the strange girl had to do was follow the path of starlight and the scent of Suellan's longing, to come up from the cold waters and trek along the beach until she reached their front door. All she'd had to do was wait, bide her time until Micah had ripened, until he was giving off those odours and hormones that said he was fresh meat.

But the house was secure, and Micah was asleep, wrapped in that heavy, unbreakable teenage-boy sleep that rivalled Suellan's drugged slumber. Becky just had to wait. Sacrifice the poor old cat and wait for the dawn, figure a solution tomorrow when the sunlight burned away terrors. The rush of adrenaline began to wear off, and, in its place, came the sluggish flow of exhaustion. It crept through her limbs, and she closed her eyes. She sat there in front of the window so long that she began to drowse, head drooping; from somewhere a song seemed to start, at first lulling her, numbing her mind, calming her until she had almost slipped to the bottom of night's well… but then she realised that the beat was wrong. It wasn't a lullaby, or a comfort, it was familiar and the memory of it made her shudder and fight, swim up from the darkness and wake.

The girl had begun, at some point, to sing: a siren song of amphibian longing, a soothing, a calling, a summoning, so low at first that Becky barely heard it. But it had gotten louder, triumphant, and then Becky had recognised it. She wondered if Aidan had fought or simply given in because it was easier than anything else, because the tune had convinced him to go quietly as easily as it had convinced her to let him go.

Then she heard, quite distinctly, the slap of large bare feet on the linoleum downstairs, the kitchen door being unlocked and thrown open to bang against the wall. She struggled up as if swimming in glue and stared down through the glass, watched as the girl's smile widened and she opened her arms to the boy covered only by his ratty boxers. Riddle, released, sped back into the house, a streak of frantic flame, passing Micah as he padded into the yard.

It was only when they'd trudged off into the gloom that Becky found she could move freely again. She took the stairs so fast she almost fell, yelling without hope that Suellan would wake. Sprawling into the kitchen, she hauled open the cutlery drawer, looking through the knives, rejecting each one because none seemed big enough for the task at hand. Then, as she sobbed, she remembered all Buck's abandoned things, the remnants of him that haunted the house: the golf clubs, the tennis rackets. The speargun, that waited atop the laundry cupboard, where Suellan had stashed it when Becky was smaller and unable to reach, but now… She'd grown just enough that she could jump and tap the handle visible at the edge, just enough to dislodge it; one more jump and it dropped, followed by one — only one! — of the spears. But she didn't have time to climb up and see if there was another; she had to get out, out, following her brother and the girl. Becky slid that precious bolt into place, just as her father had shown her.

Outside, the clouds had covered the moon and the stars had dimmed, so she ran in the direction they'd disappeared, guided only by the textures under her bare feet: grass soft then gritty; then small stones, some sharp, some smooth; then coarse sand as she found the path; and finally the shingle itself with all the fine loose particles that made movement so difficult. And it was dark, so very dark, and she couldn't make out anything in that blackness as she hefted the weight of the gun and felt… not the trigger, but the button, the button of the light Buck had fitted to the weapon. She remembered how proud he'd been when he got it to work. Becky pressed the switch and a weak yellow light leaked. She swept the pitiful circle ahead of her, across the beach until she found them in a huddle halfway to the water, as if the girl couldn't wait.

Micah was draped across her knee and left arm; her right steadied his shoulder, while her head bowed over his chest. Sensing the pale wash of light, the girl lifted her face, and Becky saw how full of teeth her mouth was. And her tongue, her long tongue, the tip of it suckered lamprey-like to the boy's bare torso. Becky screamed, and the girl hissed, dropping Micah to the sand and standing, arms at her sides, the bat-wing sleeves of the dress spread.

Becky fired. She had the girl dead to rights, and the barb flew straight, but at the last moment she shifted like an eel, and the spear went through the wing of her sleeve… no, not a sleeve, Becky realised.

Webbing.

The webbed skin tore and the girl shrieked, flapping the left arm against her side in pain, making the wet hole bigger, bigger. Becky took her gaze from the girl, just for a second, to see if Micah was moving, but she couldn't tell. Then the girl, the thing, moved faster than Becky would have thought possible and rushed towards her, the uninjured arm striking out and connecting with Becky's jaw. She saw starbursts against her eyelids, and she wished as hard as she could that she'd had more than one spear.

Becky dropped the gun, and the light flickered off, and it didn't matter that she opened her eyes, because clouds had rolled in and the night was pure pitch, and all she knew was that the girl was looming above her, and then the breath *whumped* out of her as the creature settled on her chest. Then there came the oily sting of something attaching itself, snake-like, to her shoulder, between the neck and the collarbone, and Becky couldn't believe how much it hurt. She couldn't believe Micah hadn't been yelling and screaming when she'd found them, not with this happening to him. She wondered if the girl would just injure her badly, incapacitate her, then make her watch as Micah was taken; wait until her heart, already battered by the loss of Aidan, was broken completely, and only then kill her.

And Becky could feel something other than blood flowing from her: life and energy were drawn out, replaced by pure anguish, because she knew she couldn't do anything to stop it.

Then, as despair settled on her, heavy as the girl herself, the clouds were caught by a new wind, and pulled apart. The moon and the stars were revealed in all their shocking brightness, lighting up the stage of sand and sea as if it was an open-air theatre, and the girl, her tongue releasing Becky and falling limply away, froze.

Becky twisted, finding the girl easy to throw off. She half-scrambled, half-crawled towards Micah but, realising the beach was brighter than it should have been, she glanced around. A shape, in the form of a young man, drifted over the waves and the sand, untroubled by salty water or grit, for he floated above both. As he drew closer, Becky recognised him, and whispered a silent apology for ever doubting her mother.

It was Aidan, drawn home, but Aidan remade, with starlight and moonlight running through him.

Aidan, but Aidan as if he wore light as a shroud.

Aidan, but Aidan as if his life, his death, his afterlife were transparent layers. Becky could see the skeleton innermost, then the pale muscle and flesh, then the punctured, suckled-upon skin holding all the marks to show how he'd died, and, finally, the astral radiance that wrapped him all round, and shone from his eyes and his mouth and his nose. His light began to pulse and pulse and pulse.

And the sight of him, oh! The sight of him made the girl, who'd taken his life so boldly, cower and shrink.

Becky smiled at her eldest brother, but he didn't smile back, didn't seem to see her, just concentrated on the girl, as the shining intensified and then blazed out surely as a solar flare, engulfing everything.

Becky was blinded for long moments. When she at last blinked away the searing whiteness, was able to focus and remember what had happened, she became aware of a scent: ozone and fried fish. Not far away she saw Micah, sitting up as if waking, rubbing his head. She struggled over, hugged him until he laughed and told her to stop. And they found they were both crying.

"What happened?" he asked, and she didn't know how to explain.

Then she realised that the beach was still lit, though moon and stars were once again hidden by clouds. She turned and found Aidan, hanging in the air a few feet from them. She wondered if he would fade, disappear, his work done, his siblings saved. But though they stared for a long minute, then another, then another and another, their brother, transparent and luminescent, remained in place.

Becky didn't know what was worse: having sacrificed him, or having him back. The remorse that made its home inside her welled up and stuck in her throat. Did he know? Did Aidan know what she'd done? What was he, now? Swallowing, she made a decision, and, with halting steps, Becky approached. She reached out and took Aidan's hand, which was as fragile and airy, as cold and sharp, as she imagined starlight to be. She tugged at him, and he floated along beside her. Micah stood, watching, waiting, afraid to touch.

"What do we do?" he asked, and Becky shrugged.

"Tell Mama she was right."

That Place

Gemma Files

"Because we remember pain and the menace of death more vividly than pleasure, and because our feelings toward the beneficent aspects of the unknown have from the first been captured and formalised by conventional religious rituals, it has fallen to the lot of the darker and more maleficent side of cosmic mystery to figure chiefly in our popular supernatural folklore. This tendency, too, is naturally enhanced by the fact that uncertainty and danger are always closely allied; thus making any kind of an unknown world a world of peril and evil possibilities. When to this sense of fear and evil the inevitable fascination of wonder and curiosity is superadded, there is born a composite body of keen emotion and imaginative provocation whose vitality must of necessity endure as long as the human race itself. Children will always be afraid of the dark, and men with minds sensitive to hereditary impulse will always tremble at the thought of the hidden and fathomless worlds of strange life which may pulsate in the gulfs beyond the stars, or press

hideously upon our own globe in unholy dimensions which
only the dead and the moonstruck can glimpse."

Like any kid who grew up on C. S. Lewis (my favourite was
The Magician's Nephew), *I've always wanted to write something
involving a portal universe, one of those stories where people stumble
sidelong and end up somewhere completely different, awful in the
oldest sense of the word. For me, Caitlin R. Kiernan's "Onion" sets
the standard, though I also mention* Elidor, *by Alan Garner, in
the text, because its mixture of numinous terror and gritty realism
has stayed with me since only slightly after my initial tour through
Narnia, leaving me with a lingering fear of looking through front
door mail slots. As for how the Lovecraft quote ties in, meanwhile
— why it suggested to me that this might well be the time to act on
these impulses — I think it'd have to be the line in which Lovecraft
says, "[I]t has fallen to the lot of the darker and more maleficent
side of cosmic mystery to figure chiefly in our popular supernatural
folklore. This tendency, too, is naturally enhanced by the fact that
uncertainty and danger are always closely allied; thus making any
kind of an unknown world a world of peril and evil possibilities."
Stay out of that wardrobe, kids.*

♦

So say two sisters finally come back home, after their parents
die — twins. Their names are Holly and Heather. They have a
younger brother, Edwin, whom they haven't seen for some time.
Estrangement's grown up between them all, for no apparently
good reason. It's sad, but these things happen.

Holly and Heather attend university in Toronto. They also
room together, because why not? They've always been like that.
They can't ever remember being apart.

Edwin never went to university. He finished high school, then
trained as an auto mechanic, so he works all year round. He does
most of his calls along the rural routes of northern Ontario, circling
the area where they used to live, in Lake of the North District; his

specialty is extending the life of trucks and four-wheelers, fighting planned obsolescence on behalf of people who can't afford to trade up. Distance is an issue, up there. If you can't drive, you can't do much of anything.

One night Holly gets a call — it's Edwin. *Mom and Dad are gone,* he says. *Accident, out near Overdeere. Black ice pile-up. You need to come into town to hear the will read, then muck out the house with me.*

The girls know this isn't going to be easy, either way; it's not like their parents were hoarders, as such, but they did tend not to ever get rid of anything. There's a lot of stuff to appraise, most of it probably worthless, except on an emotional level. But it's got to be done.

We'll live there while we do it, Heather decides. *Go up just after midterms, spend a few weeks. It won't take longer than that. Not if we don't let it.*

"Town" is Chaste, up past Your Lips, almost to God's Ear. Five traffic lights, a church, a school, a gas station strip mall, and a clinic that does double duty for Quarry Argent. Around it, there's a network of small farms, plus acres of uncut woodlots. Cabin-style houses here and there, like the one they grew up in. It took thirty minutes to drive to the town limits, then twenty more to walk in, so days started early, up before dawn. Insects singing in summer, dark and cold and silent all winter.

Hope the fireplace still works, Heather says.

Funeral's already happened: cremation. The lawyer's office is in the strip mall, right next to a hardware store. Edwin's waiting outside, their parents' shared urn under one arm. The reading's brief — three-way split. The lawyer suggests they sell the house as soon as possible, and they agree, once it's cleared out. They sign, initial, and drive up, Edwin leading the way.

The house looks the same

The house smells the same.

The air is full of dust, already. It hasn't been that long. Does this happen, when people die? Does dust just fill the air, like you're breathing in their ashes?

Edwin puts the urn on the mantel above the dusty fireplace. *I was thinking we could scatter them in the garden*, he says, *but we'll have to wait for spring. Too cold, right now. Earth's frozen.*

Yes, Holly agrees, while Heather says nothing.

She's looking at the urn, its dull silver curve. Thinking she can almost see something reflected there, besides them, but unsure of what.

So say they work all the rest of that day, as the light slowly dims. Outside, overhead, grey clouds scud a mackerel sky. Inside, Edwin, Heather, and Holly are going through closets, pulling out drawers, looking under sinks and poking around cabinets, finding spaces they barely remember existing. Every inch of secret room packed tight with boxes, bags, piles of paper. It's amazing what stacks up.

Why would they keep all this? Heather asks, amazed.

Edwin shrugs. *Why wouldn't they?*

It's a valid question.

Upstairs, under the bed in their parents' room, they find the box. It's plain cardboard, with both their names written on it: *Holly & Heather, 1995*. When Holly opens it, it makes an odd little sound, like a sigh.

It contains a collection of seemingly random objects, some broken and melted, all discoloured, as though exposed to bright sunlight for long periods of time before being stored. Some sort of tin, slightly flattened; a necklace with two clear, cracked plastic beads; a handful of shells and stones, still crusted with dirt. A doll's hairbrush. A stiff gilt ribbon. And also two folded sheets of paper, worn along their creases, like they've been kept inside a wallet. Opened, these turn out to be covered in rambly, vaguely familiar writing, too large for an adult's... Holly think it's hers. Heather thinks so, too.

Go there, the top of the first one says. *Throw each piece down, as you do. A trail. Breadcrumbs.*

Wind the string (and there is string, Heather sees now. It used to be purple) *around three corners. Wait.*

Words will come. Say them.

Let it form.

Never knock first. Wait until THEY do.

Wait again. Until THEY go away.

Open.

And on the second page, nothing but this — a warning, one can only assume:

If it's That Place, then <u>don't</u>.

The *don't* is underlined, three times.

They all three examine the box and its contents for some time, Edwin watching his sisters, as though waiting for them to speak. Eventually, Holly asks: *What is this?*

I don't know, Heather replies. *Some kind of game? We made this, though. And I don't remember…*

… ever playing anything like this? Me either.

Those rules are crazy. It's like we were high when we wrote them.

Heather shakes her head. *That's how you wrote till you were ten. Unless you were doing stuff you never told me about, "high" didn't come into it.*

But you must've been there too.

Been where when? When this got made? I don't —

Holly turns the box lid over again, pointing out: *Not the rules, no, but this here — that's not just labelling. That's our* names, *the way we used to sign them. Mine, and yours, too. See?*

Yeah, sure. Like you say, though… I don't remember.

There's a snort, then; a swallowed laugh, curt and ugly. It comes from Edwin, who they turn to look at, as one. He raises his eyebrows.

Seriously? is all he says.

◆

An hour later, they're sitting at the kitchen table with a gas lantern turned up high and a whole sheaf of crumbly newsprint spread out in front of them. Edwin took the file from a drawer in their Dad's desk in the icy little add-on office he built out back when the girls were eleven, looking out onto the not-so-distant fringe of almost all-conifer woods. Now that most of the leaves have fallen except for the evergreens, you can just make out a pale little smudge halfway up the sloping rock face that marks where they once set up a wooden card table and used it for shelter, sitting beside each other under its shade, staring down at the house from up high. It was blue once, but age and weather have chewed its planks almost bare.

You don't remember any *of this,* Edwin repeats, finally, after they've told him that several times. *That seems… no, seriously?*

We don't, Holly says. Heather snorts.

It's a joke, she tells her sister. *He's making it up.* She gestures at the articles Edwin's been showing them, the documents, the photos. *Not the getting lost in the woods part, obviously — we could've blocked it out, trauma, all that. Just… everything else.*

Why would I lie? Edwin demands.

Another snort. *Why* wouldn't *you?*

What the file says is that when Holly and Heather were nine years old — Edwin was seven then, odd man out since birth — they disappeared for roughly three days, seventy-one-and-a-half hours, after having "gone for a walk" one afternoon. That they were found in a clearing, one the adults searching for them had already covered, marking it off their maps a good thirty-five hours earlier: dirty, unconscious, mildly wounded (scrapes, bruising, a long scratch down Holly's cheek, which may have created that faint scar she's never known how she got) and starving. Having lost so much weight, in fact, that it almost seemed they'd been gone for far longer.

What Edwin says, however…

You used to play the game, all the time. You'd never let me play. It was something you made up one day, passing the paper back and forth, like you were writing a story together. Words just appearing in your heads, like you were being told them.

Oh, you are so full of —

You said it opened a door to somewhere, Edwin goes on, undaunted; probably gives him immense pleasure just to say it out loud, after all this time. *Someplace that scared you, but you kept on going back again and again, probably because it did scare you. And I wanted to go too, 'cause I wanted to do everything you did, but you told me it wasn't a good place to go. Said if I did, they'd know I wasn't supposed to be there, and they'd get me.*

"They" who?

How'm I supposed to know? He looks down at the table, taps the closest headline: *GIRLS RECOVERED UNHARMED. This is where you did it, right here, where they found you. Not at first — used to be you'd go upstairs, into the attic, till you caught me sneaking up after. That was when you took it outside, into the woods, up past the old table. Up over the rock, with that clump of three trees.*

Holly shakes her head. *Okay, Ed, Christ. That's more than enough.*

I'll show you. You think I can't? Take you right fucking there. Been there enough times, since.

Sure you will, Heather mocks. *The scary place in the woods! The door! Fucking Narnia.*

Holly laughs. *Fucking* Elidor, *sounds like.*

They grin at each other. Edwin sit there sullen, arms crossed — twice as big, not that that counts for much. Bent in on himself like he's already eaten so much of his own rage, over the years, it's gestating inside him; has to hug himself hard, or it might break free and flop out, spraying everywhere.

You two, he says, to no one in particular.

None of them will be able to remember how they got there, later on. Just that they're suddenly standing there, bundled to the eyes, breath puffing out like steam, rising ghostly into the black, black sky. The clouds hang heavy except where they gap here and there, wind torn. Through these few rips, patches white with numberless stars can be glimpsed, finally freed to reveal themselves now that the city's light pollution's been peeled away by cold and distance — sharp, small, glinting bright. Pins, velvet set. Weasels' teeth.

Three trees and a dip, a crevice full of dirt and leaves where two rocks meet underground, grinding against each other. Frost on the bark, odd speckles of snow. A ferocious lack of light, so deep it almost becomes a fourth presence, pooling between them in that triangle, that inverted chalice.

Here we are, Edwin tells them, unnecessarily, as Holly feels the hair on her neck — hood hidden though it might be — start to lift.

This is bad, Heather says, equally unnecessarily. *This is…*

(fucking *terrifying*)

And they don't even have to look at each other, don't have to say it at all: don't know why, could care less, but they just *can't* stay. Wild horses couldn't keep them here one single moment longer, let alone their stupid-ass "little" brother, whatever goddamn game he's playing — there's nothing to be done but turn, grab hands, and run, run and keep on running. Back down the path, 'round the rock, past the table. Back to the house, the warmth, the light.

… the worst place on Earth, Holly thinks, as Edwin falls behind, startled by the sudden swiftness of their mutual retreat; he's yelling something after them now, but the wind has it, snatches it from his lips like a great, black, invisible hand. And they're long gone, anyhow.

Back at the house, they fall into bed, clutching each other, hearts hammering. Every breath seems to shake the world, drawn and let go in a shudder. There's no way they'll fall asleep, not tonight — maybe not ever again, if they can't get back to Toronto fast enough, once the sun's finally up.

That's what they think, at any rate. Until, inevitably, they do.

◆

And when Holly wakes up, much later, she's alone.

◆

Four in the morning, probably. The whole house is cold, dry, empty. Dim, but not exactly dark — there's light coming from somewhere, all right. Awful light.

Holly has trouble making herself get up, let alone open the bedroom door, but she does. She has to. And the first thing she hears, stepping out into the hall, is the sound of something crunching underfoot.

She looks down, squints. Can just make out a trail of objects, leading to the attic stairs.

Throw each piece down, as you [go there], her mind whispers, unprompted. A *trail. Breadcrumbs.*

It's the stuff from the box, definitely. She doesn't have to look closer to know it.

Names in her throat, caught and choking: *Heather? … Edwin?* But she can't let them go, physically *can't*. Not when who even knows what might be nearby but hidden, all unseen. Might be —

(watching)

(listening)

(*waiting*)

Holly swallows, so soft she can barely feel it. Directs her feet along the prescribed path, one reluctant step at a time. And as she follows, tracing the route Heather must surely have set out for her, she finds herself wondering, resentful —

How could you start without me?

— and almost freezes in realization's wake, shockwave rocking her top to toe. Thinking, helpless: *Oh God. So I do remember…*

… a bit, something. Not enough.

Up the stairs, one half at a time, braced tight against any creak, each puzzle piece increasingly leaf- or dirt-encrusted, increasingly deformed, as though they've been buried and trodden on since she, Heather, and Edwin first pawed through that stupid box. A curl of formerly purple string lies outside the attic door, question mark–curled, frayed at one end; not cut. Sawed, or bitten through.

Wind the string around three corners. Wait.

Her hand is on the door, pushing. It falls open without a sound.

Inside — still cold, still dim. The light increases. This is where it's coming from.

(Of course.)

The rest of the string, already wound, maps a rough triangle on the floor in front of one wall, the one without a window. Stone piles form corners, three to five stones each, uneven granite eggs, earth-smeared. Somebody (Heather) has obviously already skipped over *Words will come. Say them,* for which Holly can only be grateful, though she thinks she can almost feel those same words — or similar ones — plucking at the corners of her brain's folds.

Let it form was the next instruction, as she recalls. And… it has.

There's a door sketched on the wall, six feet by two, complete with lintel and threshold, even a knob. From a distance it looks spray-painted, scratched, its slightly uneven dimensions filled in with greying black, but, as Holly draws closer, she sees it's actually more incised or even *burnt* into the plaster. Worn, like it's been there for years.

She and Heather were up here yesterday, though, when the wall was clean. Empty.

The rest of the list plays itself out as she stands there, not wanting to come any closer. Four final groups of instructions, paragraphed, like so —

Never knock first. Wait until THEY do.

Wait again. Until THEY go away.

Open.

If it's That Place, then <u>*don't*</u>.

Them, Holly thinks, over and over, frankly unable not to. *That Place.* And she stands there not knowing what to do — there's not exactly a smell, maybe the memory of a smell… like the woods. That place in the woods, the hollow, the three trees. Shadow of leafless branches above, ruin of fallen leaves below.

(*The worst place in the world*)

So she stands, and she doesn't knock, and she waits. And then, finally — from behind the door, deep under the plaster, or somewhere even further than that — she hears her brother Edwin's faintly wavering voice reverberate, struggling through, as though the wall's a skin he's trapped behind. As though it's a metaphorical stand-in for the flesh cradle they all once shared, both separately and together; the slightly bulging membrane of their dead mother's womb, fresh-wrapped in architecture.

Open the door, man. Holly, I know it's you, gotta be… just let me back in, please. They*'re coming.*

And: THEY, she thinks. *Them. That Place.*

(*don't*)

She swallows again, throat scratchy. Manages to ask, at last —

Is Heather with you?

A pause. *Dunno*, Edwin says, finally, before she can convince herself he was never there at all: quieter, faster, growing panic threading through each new word, tightening till they start to ruck. I *went in looking for her, found* them *instead, and now — they've seen me, they're coming. I think they have her…* please, Holly, let me the fuck back in! *Please!*

Barely a whisper now, but if it was written down, it'd be underlined — four times, maybe five. And Holly knows she should do something, anything, though she isn't sure what. But…

Shouldn't've gone, she finds herself thinking, with a dreadful lack of sympathy. *Not when you saw where it was. We told you not to.*

And what did we think we were doing, anyway? Playing this game… all of it? Where did we want to go?

Anyplace, perhaps, so long as it was different. Not that we could have known where we might end up, when we began.

(A wardrobe, a door in the wall, a blister; a mirror turned window, different on the other side. Three trees, a wood between the worlds. Narnia. Elidor. Charn.)

We didn't know, though.

(No. Of course not. But —)

— THEY did, I'll bet.

And she can't move, and the light, the *smell*. *So* horrible. The very worst. And then —

— her brother starts to scream, high and thin and anguished, more like an animal than a man. And after he stops, stops short, as though the sound itself snaps in half, there simply *are* no other noises, just nothing. This deafening silence, where surely there should be noise.

So: Holly stands there frozen, hand half reaching. And then there's a grinding noise, plaster dust sifting, spotting the floor like snow. And then...

... the drawn-on handle begins, very slowly, as if manipulated *from the other side*...

... to turn.

The Horror at Castle of the Cumberland

Chesya Burke

"Much of the power of Western horror-lore was undoubtedly due to the hidden but often suspected presence of a hideous cult of nocturnal worshippers whose strange customs — descended from pre-Aryan and pre-agricultural times when a squat race of Mongoloids roved over Europe with their flocks and herds — were rooted in the most revolting fertility-rites of immemorial antiquity."

I entered the horror genre a fresh nub, having read many of the classics of horror literature but feeling as if most of it didn't relate to me in my life. One of the good things about being a newbie is that more experienced writers are quick to tell you the "must read" titles, whether you ask or not. Atop each and every list thrown my way was H. P. Lovecraft. I had not read him, so I quickly picked up everything I could find. I read, with growing trepidation, the descriptions of those things that Lovecraft feared. For me, those fears sounded all too much like... me. Brown people and black people and yellow people, and Jews, Lovecraft believed, would corrupt the good, decent Aryan race.

Lovecraft, it seemed, feared me and those like me. More importantly, horror (and speculative fiction generally) had built an entire genre around this fear of The Other. The hoard, the zombie, the monster, the fear of anything that isn't white, pure, and virginal.

So my question, when confronted with the above quote was: What happens when you're a member of a corrupt system and you gain the knowledge to resist it, as Lovecraft did? What happens when that system is unopposed, left to continue unchecked, unchallenged? What happens to later generations who refuse to confront it?

So for this piece I did something that I rarely do; I wrote about white people. A white man. A man who has the choice, as Lovecraft did, to accept or reject the ideologies fed to him by society.

Understanding society as I do, it is, even for me in writing this, a difficult choice.

◆

Edgar Kay Morrison died for the first time on August 13, 1900. He would die many nights after that, it would seem, always for the same reason. He was an enigma to some; to others, an evil devil sent to bewitch; and still yet, a prophet to most. However, on that night, he was none of those things. He was a seven-year-old boy who thought God had sent his chariots down for him, on the count of him having been such a good boy all his years.

At least that was what his momma whispered in his ears as he lay there wrenching in pain. The cramps started in his legs two days before, and had quickly taken over his body. That was when Momma sent Papa to get Doc Warner. He would know what to do, she said.

"Calm yo self, boy. God ain't gonna set no pain on you, as you cain't take." Even as his momma spoke, another cramp seized his body. "Them chariots gonna be worth all this if they get you tonight," she sounded so sure, but he saw tears rolling down her too-pale cheeks.

Edgar closed his eyes. He didn't want to see her this way. He felt guilty. His sister had died just the year before, and his momma had stayed in bed for two weeks. She had cried so much that she said she had run out of tears. He didn't want her to go through that again.

The pain — like a lead pipe snapping down on the small of his back — seized him again, and his body contorted; his arms flailing behind him, his head thrown back. He looked for all the world as if he were trying to roll himself up in a big ol' ball, backward. His fingers were knotted in peculiar shapes, and he couldn't get them to move.

"The devil," his younger brother, David, whispered from somewhere behind his head.

"Shush up, boy. Now go on over there and get me something to put under his head. Go on now."

David watched for another moment, and as Edgar screamed again, he jumped and ran into the other room. He didn't come back for a full ten minutes, when he did, the only thing he brought with him was the old thick Bible, which was the only thing Momma had gotten from her father when he'd died twenty years before.

Momma took one look at him and shook her head. "Get... Give me that thing." She took the Bible from David, and placed it under Edgar's head. "This here will give you comfort in your time of trouble." She told him, kissing his hand and touching the Good Book.

Outside, thick drops of rain hit the crude windowpane that Papa had cut himself just the year before, before Edgar's sister had died. David went to the window, rubbed the condensation off, and stared out into the night. He was scared. Edgar couldn't blame him, but what he couldn't make out was if the boy really thought that he was the devil.

The wind hit the old wooden shack hard, rattling the whole thing, breaking through the door, and engulfing the whole room with its power. Momma ran to the door, trying to close it as the rain rushed inside. It covered Edgar's feet, but he didn't mind. He relished the coolness of it.

Late August in Eddyville, Kentucky, often brought thunderstorms and wild winds. Eddyville was a prison town. The Kentucky State Penitentiary dominated everything, and the town completely revolved around the massive stone structure that oversaw the township. Although the prison could be seen from every corner of the city, the stench of town never managed to leave the muddy grounds of the prison. But now Edgar smelled it, the rot of street funk that fed from the normal hardworking people. It was overpowering. It had taken over the room within a few dog seconds. And that was fast because everyone knew that dogs didn't live as long as people did. The smell was kinda like dead things — lots of dead things — as if they had gotten in under the floorboard and taken up there. Like that coon had back two summers ago. It just lay under there and died. Papa had the hardest time getting that thing out of there.

But this was worse. Much worse.

Another seizure overtook him, and he got this feeling all over him. Like something wasn't right. Like something wasn't never going to be right, not ever again. He closed his eyes and felt cold; not like the rain had been, but like the coldest night of the coldest winter. Kinda like that, but not really. This was something else, something bad.

Inside his head something broke. He lay there just knowing Momma had been right, God was coming for him. Somehow, he was all right with that. Sometimes, as Momma said, people weren't long for this world, which is what she had said to herself about Cilia, his little sister. Maybe this was true for him, too.

Just then Papa appeared, Doc Warner right behind him. He helped Momma with the door — it took both of them to close it. The wind fought them, but Papa was strong.

Inside the room, the smell itself seemed to resonate from Edgar, and the doc checked him for wounds that may have gone 'grene. His mother assured the man that he had not been injured.

"That smell," the old man said, "it's not right. Something died." The doc looked around.

"Musta got under the house again," Papa said, "Them damn coons."

Lightning struck somewhere outside, which was followed by a loud boom. It was close, too close. It was coming for him. *They'll come for you*, the voice in his head said. *Some people just are not long for this world.*

His daddy was still pointing toward the floor, as if he were illustrating his point, and, as Edgar looked down, he saw a shadow move across the floor. It was small and almost unnoticeable at first, but, as he watched, it grew bigger, climbing the wall to within a foot from the ceiling. It stood there, still, unmoving, watching. It was only a shadow, but he knew there was something unnatural about it, something wrong. The dark shape grew even larger, getting its strength from the people within the room. From him, Edgar knew. No one else in the room seemed to notice the shadow. This scared him more than anything. There was something there, watching them, but only he knew it. Only he saw it.

Maybe it had always been there. Maybe he was the one changing. As he thought it, he knew this to be true. He knew somehow that the thing there, above their heads, was somehow eternal, not unnatural at all, but that it was hiding away, in the shadows, watching them, always. It was inevitable. He saw something wild and longing, something deep, a knowledge not afforded to man. He *felt* like this thing had been there longer than any man, and would be there well after every man had gone. He knew he was getting a glimpse of something forbidden, and, for his part, it would cost him his life.

He lay back accepting this, the one gift given to the dying, the one truth. He lay there taking that knowledge to what he thought was his death.

The book beneath his head grew harder with each moment, as if the thick pages were *on* his head instead of beneath it. He sensed knowledge of not only the being above him, but of other things as well. Big things. Smart things.

It was the book, it was too heavy. Too big. Too many words; too much knowledge.

He wiggled his body until his head was no longer on the book, but beside it. He touched it, closing his eyes to finally allow the inevitable to come, but wanting to know the Good Book was near him. In the distance somewhere, he heard his mother gasp, as the doctor told them he didn't think Edgar would make it too much longer.

"Not another child of mine," the woman said to no one but God — or the devil. She said she had given Him all she had to offer, but her son was not for sale. That was how she had put it, "My boy is not for sale."

Just at that moment, another great gust pounded on the house, blowing open the doors as they rocked back and forth on their hinges, the house shaking and rattling as if it were coming apart around them. His brother screamed and rolled himself up into a ball right on the floor, holding his knees to his chest. Almost simultaneously, the dark thing dodged at Edgar, and before he could even move, it had seized him. Grabbing a hold of him, mind and soul. Edgar couldn't see or hear anything going on around him.

The boy felt a longing so old and deep he couldn't control his emotions. Inside, he cried and screamed and pleaded, as things he didn't know or understand fought to control him. It was knowledge too great for any man to bear, he realized. And still yet, he was no man. He tried to move, but his body was no longer his own.

Suddenly a bright light blinded him, and he could feel it engulfing his heart and soul. It seeped from his pores and into his humble room, in the small shack that he shared with his family. If Edgar had been aware, he would have seen the doc, his father, brother, and even his mother, repel from his dead body as if it were diseased.

Finally Edgar *knew*.

After what seemed like a lifetime, he opened his eyes and fully expected to be sitting at the gates of heaven, surrounded by thousands of Good Books as far as the eyes could see. Instead, he awoke with his mother and father and brother staring at him. His mother's eyes were red and stained with tears.

"Woman," he said, "why are you crying?"

His papa had always called his momma quick, and this was no different. She looked at him and at the Bible he clutched in his hands — the one she said she couldn't get him to read within a month of Sundays. "Rabboni?" she asked, quoting what Mary said to Jesus after he had risen. It meant *teacher*.

"I have seen the Lord," Edgar answered. It was the same answer her Savior had given in her precious book.

Edgar hated going into town with his mother anymore. He thought he must hate it almost as much as the woman did herself. She said that it stank from the unclean denizens that roamed the streets where they didn't belong. There were too many people, too many that did not worship Christ as they should, or not at all. Instead they littered the streets, speaking in dozens of strange tongues, begging for food, needing things that they wanted others to give them after a hard day's work. Too many people had relocated to Eddyville to be closer to their pathetic family members, criminals serving out long sentences for offences that ranged from petty theft to murder, and everything in between. It was said that a life sentence there was no different from a death sentence. And that sat just fine for most people in those parts, considering they were talking about convicts.

Edgar, however, had begun to see other things, too. It had been two whole weeks since he had died and come back to life in his humble home while his mother cried on her knees beside him, and now Edgar had changed. The shadows that had appeared that night had not gone away … they had multiplied. The vestiges of the unclean masses of Mongoloid people who walked the streets during the day only fueled the impure nocturnal worshipers feeding from their obscenity and misery, unseen, unknown. They watched him, darting from dark corner to dark corner, mocking him. He'd tried to look away, pretend he hadn't been awakened to their presence. But he couldn't; he saw them. And what's more, he was sure that they *knew* he saw them, too.

Edgar was glad that they didn't have to go into town very often. Most anything they needed they got from the farm, a mule, chickens for eggs and meat, and Betsy the cow for milk. Momma even made lye soap at home, by pouring water over wood ashes. Edgar and his father hunted, rabbits and some deer, but not too often, gunpowder not being something they could grow in the stubbly fields. Tobacco brought in the money, what little there was of it. They'd barter some things. Anything else, they just did without, mostly. Once or twice a year, Momma would shop at the store for a big bag of flour and cornmeal, which would last them half a year or so. She brought him along so that he could carry it for her.

The dry goods store, Charlie's, sat just off the main street, opposite the courthouse. Compared to that grand building, the goods store looked like a shack house with one door and one large window, which sat oddly in the frame. It had been broken more times than most people could count, and so Charlie, the owner, had stopped spending extra money on fitted panes, and he'd just tell them to give him whatever they had cheap. Behind the store, the dirt road led to a loading dock of sorts for wagons and dark folk who saw fit to shop there.

Inside, the store was dark and smelled liked smoked meat. The shadows moved oddly in the corners. They shimmered, getting lighter and darker as Edgar moved through the door of the store, following dutifully behind his mother who fondled her apron too much and carried three dozen brown eggs. His mother walked up to Charlie, who stood behind the counter counting coins. She smiled, but her lips were cracked, dry. She looked too old, too worn.

"How you do, Mr. Charlie?"

The man didn't look up, but nodded toward her direction.

"I have some eggs for fair trade, sir."

"How many?" The man stood up, looked at the woman.

"Three dozen."

He sighed. "The price of flour and cornmeal has gone up to two dollars, that's not a fair trade."

"I…" His mother looked around the store for a moment. "I… I will need a little time to come up with the money, you see."

The man looked at her coldly, "Your credit is not as good here as it once was. I cain't extend you more credit."

"I'll pay it back, Mr. Charlie. I always pay it back."

The man looked to the ceiling and then to the floor, sighed again. "Okay. But just the flour and cornmeal. Nothing else."

His mother thanked the man and walked toward the back of the store. Edgar watched her go, her back more bent than it had been when she entered.

A short, muddy colored man and little girl slid open the back barn-like door and stepped inside. The man was dirty, his nails and shoes caked with filth. His daughter was just as grimy, her dull eyes darting back and forth, not focusing on anything or anyone. She had a useless lazy eye.

They looked wrong. Didn't belong.

"What you wont, boy?" Charlie noticed them as soon as they came inside.

"New shirt." The man's English was broken. Wrong.

"Ain't got none."

The man looked around the store, then pointed to a few white men's shirts on the shelf toward the back of the store. "One of those. Just fine."

"Ain't got no shirts. Do you have money?" Edgar moved so that he could better see the pair. His mother was somewhere in the back of the store.

The man stared at Charlie for a while, moved his lips to speak, thought better of it, and grabbed his child's arm. "Good day."

"Oh, no you don't. I asked you a question. You got money? What you doin' with money? Where you get it, boy? From me? You stole my money, boy?" The white man was screaming while he grabbed his would-be customer's grimy overcoat. Several of the people in the store ducked around shelves of canned foods and bagged goods, staring at the wretched man and his plaintive offspring.

The shop owner began rubbing his hands along the man's body, searching him. "What you do with it?"

"Nothing," the man said calmly, reached, again, for his child.

People were watching. A white man with a big wide-brim hat walked over and grabbed the dark man, helping Charlie search him. He pulled a few dollar bills from the accused's pocket and held it up for everyone to see. Then the white man in the hat reached out and slapped the dark one, hard. He almost fell to the floor before he caught himself; his daughter never let go of his hand, and helped him to his feet when his legs wobbled too much for him to stand on his own.

The girl clutched her father. "Stop it!" Her voice seemed so tiny in that room of shouting men. Suddenly a woman walked up and pushed the little girl to the floor. Her dress flew over her head as she fell, her bloomers showing for everyone to see, and her butt hit the floor hard. She was, it seemed, as pathetic as her father. "Where the rest of my money, boy? Where's my money?"

It all happened so quickly. Several people rushed in and stopped Charlie and the other man from hitting the poor slob any more, but his face was already swollen and bloody. The sheriff broke through the crowd, stared at the scene, and sighed, "What happened? What's going on?"

Burly white arms were holding on to the beaten man, keeping him on his feet.

The whole time, the poor fool didn't say a word. Edgar wondered why he didn't just offer Charlie the little bit of money he had, and maybe the shopkeeper would let them go.

The sheriff asked again. "What's going on here?

Finally the man spoke, his lip broken in two places: "Just misunderstanding," he said simply. The shadows scurried around the man's feet, feeding from his misery.

His daughter wiped the dirt from her butt and made her way over to him, trailing dots of blood behind her. She was the only movement in the whole store, and it seemed as if everyone was frozen in their spots. Her eyes darted back and forth between the men and her father.

"I saw him take it," a voice from the back spoke up. A familiar voice. Edgar's mother. The woman walked up slowly. He had never noticed how slight she had become, how her limp had worsened since last he noticed, her back a bit more hunched. "I was watchin' him close when they come in. He took money right off the counter there. I saw it."

"There was money right there on the counter, is true." A small woman from the back ducked around the canned corn. "I'm…I'm sure of it."

Edgar thought back to the moment he entered the store. He remembered… There had been coins, no bills… He was sure, they had been on the counter, just as the woman said. And his mother wouldn't lie. She had been in the back of the store, but maybe she had come back up without him noticing. Why hadn't he noticed? He had been so busy watching those damn shadows, which had now gathered around the grubby, beaten man and his little girl's feet. Perhaps, Edgar had been wrong. Perhaps the creatures were not feeding from this man at all. Perhaps, they were a part of him. Perhaps they were a part of them all.

Edgar nodded. He'd seen them take the money all along. He just hadn't realized it.

The sheriff was a big beefy man who didn't carry a gun — said he didn't need one — but he carried a wooden ax handle. The hickory was polished to a shine, and smooth and yellow like churned butter. "Y'all sure? You saw these two take that money?"

Nobody said anything at first.

"Yes." Edgar's mother was sure.

"Yes." The small woman was sure.

"… Yes." Edgar was sure.

The thief rubbed the sweat and dirt from his face, reached for his daughter's hand. The girl grabbed it, clung to her father while the darkness clung just as tightly to their souls.

The sheriff carted them away, two fewer leeches sucking the lifeblood of natural society.

◆

He began to hear them after that. The treacherous songs of a fallen, squat race of Mongoloids who had once roved the Earth. He knew them now. He heard every formerly muted whisper, every foul threat against humanity within their painful cries.

Whispers. Whispers.

He heard them all the time now. They called to him. Filling his head with foul thoughts. Putting doubts in his mind. Making him question all of the things that he knew to be true.

Rabboni. He was the teacher. The one who could lead others. His mother assured him of this. She knew. He knew.

But, dear *God, the voices*. They mocked him.

He lay in the bed in which he had first died only weeks before, again writhing in pain, again lost to all around him. His mother placed a wet cloth on his forehead, assuring him that "this too shall pass, son."

She was so sincere. But the voices in his head made him doubt her, challenge every word. Did it matter if it'd pass, when his pain was so great now? Was this the excuse that you give when you have no answers?

She touched him again, her hands feeling like rusty nails over his skin. He moved away from her touch. She looked at him, hurt. "Everything happens for a reason. Everything."

Yes, mother, but whose reason? Edgar's thoughts had long been out of his control. His body ached, a painful reminder that he was to suffer as Christ had suffered. Or, he reasoned, a reminder that every word from his mother's treasured book, every word that lingered in his head like a heavy burden, was written, forged, just like his schoolbooks. And just like his schoolbooks, they taught a specific knowledge.

The aches in his body would not let up. They had taken over, and it no longer mattered that he could not feel his mother's touch, that he did not *want* to feel her hands further corrupt his flesh, and his mind. She had lied to him, deposited secret messages into his head that could not easily be removed. He was not taught to love, as her precious book demanded. He hated. With all of the power that he had within him. He feared. Feared things that he could not see or understand. Knowledge was the enemy of his mother's teachings, and so she had kept him stupid. Accepted nothing less than his acquiescence.

"No!" He screamed out in pain. Not the pain of his body, but that of his thoughts that were betraying everything that he had ever known, ever understood. What was there in life if not his understanding of the Good Book?

And, yet, he knew the Bible now. The words swam around in his brain, mixing with the memories of what he had been always been taught.

Edgar, like the Lord he knew, had been put here to suffer — and suffer, he did. His body twisted and contorted in a way that would never have been possible if he'd had full control over his limbs. Seeing this, his mother said a silent prayer, asking Jesus to protect Edgar, beseeching the Son of God instead of the Lord himself. But somehow they had become one and the same in his head. Or, had they always been so? He could not remember any longer. Could not distinguish his old memories with his new ones, his old understanding of things with these new corrupted thoughts.

The shadows, they taught him. *Who are the least of these?* The Mongoloids, the hordes of dark flesh that seek to undermine good society. *Where can they be found?* He knew the answer. Right outside, in the sewers and gutters where all trash can be found, with the least of these.

For God shows no partiality. Unless of course man is White — pure.

Pain gripped him, and he rolled off the hard lumpy mattress onto the harder cold floor. Edgar's brother David, who had watched on silently, made no move to help him. The boy now scorned Edgar as he did others. His mother rose laboriously to her feet, stared down on her fallen son. He feared for a moment that she could read his mind, see his corrupted thoughts. But she could not. No one knew his vile memories.

Edgar pulled himself up to his knees, staring into the woman's eyes, reached out to her. She touched him, and his skin burned under her fingers. He did not pull away, did not reject her. He could not; she was all he had known. How do you reject that which is engrained?

Edgar turned and looked to the ceiling, imagined white clouds, fluffy, pure. "Why have you forsaken me?"

The Lord did not answer.

They decided to hang the pair of thieves in the public square outside of the penitentiary the following Saturday, reasoning the daughter was accomplice to her father's crime. Edgar's mother got herself dolled up in her best Sunday clothes to attend. She had Edgar and his brother wear their Sundays too. Everyone who had been in the store was to testify before the town; presumably the crooks would confess, but, even if not, they were to be hanged by the neck until dead.

They were an example. A warning to other Mongoloids and Negroids and heathen who would think to move to Eddyville to corrupt the people there. Corruption was just another word for sin. The shadows were vivid, loud and demanding, that morning. They screamed unimaginable things in his ears, condemning him, mocking him.

Edgar and his family took the buggy into town instead of walking the seven miles. This was a special occasion, and his mother didn't want to get her good clothes dirty in the muddy streets. His father pulled the buggy into an empty spot directly opposite the prison. Edgar jumped down from the carriage and then helped his mother down. He stared at the giant building as if he hadn't seen it before.

Called Castle of the Cumberland, the prison sat high on the hill overlooking the Cumberland River. The giant had taken more than six years to finish and had killed many workers helping to build the structure in record time. Everyone knew the old state penitentiary in Frankford had been a disgrace. The conditions had been called "inhumane" by the newspapers, and had forced lawmakers to quickly find another solution.

That solution was Eddyville and its new castle.

The building stood over the top of the trees, staring up like a vengeful child. When he had been small, the children all told stories of the old, narrow cell house, which led underground from the prison proper, into the hills. They called it "the dungeon," and said that was where the guards chained unruly inmates. They said that you could sometimes hear the cries of the hopeless men at night, their wails calling out over the waters of the Cumberland.

In town, people were gathering around the prison, waiting for the show. The shadows lay at their feet, as if they were ordinary, normal vestiges from the sun's radiant glare. They were not. They were evil. They sought the souls of every living being in attendance. Perhaps they would get them.

Thunder broke the quiet, and Edgar looked up, hoping that the rains wouldn't come the way they had the night before, and the day before that. A thin cloud passed in front of the sun, and he realized that no rain would be forthcoming that day. He said a quick prayer, thanking God for that.

The thunder had come from the massive building, as if the walls themselves were moaning. The giant steel doors swung open, releasing the doomed from their temporary cages into the arms of their final embrace — the ropes around their necks.

Edgar and his family crossed the street, and narrowly avoided getting run down by a grand four-horse buggy that raced toward the prison. On the other side of the road, a woman carrying a small child pushed past them, trying to get closer to the gibbet. She smelled of old, dirty things. Tears streamed down her face as she looked away from the show that had begun to unfold.

Three guards and a tall man in a top hat led the condemned man and girl out from the prison gate. The woman beside Edgar let out a loud gasp, reaching absently for the pair whom she would never embrace again. Her family, Edgar reasoned. Somehow he had not thought that there would be people to mourn them. As he watched them, he was surprised to see how tiny the girl looked. She couldn't be older than twelve, although she was small even for this generous estimate. The girl followed her father, silently to her death. She knew what would happen to her, he could see the look of resolution on her young face.

The terrible, terrible whispers of the revolting shadows filled his ears, his head, his thoughts. He could hear them mocking him.

The doubts rushed back to him: *Will you testify? Will you?*

The crowd of people was thick toward the center of town, and people were talking and laughing as if they were there to see a Broadway show in New York City. Several more thunder-like sounds rose over the crowd from the state penitentiary. Every time, all conversations would pause, and people would stare at the building hoping things were getting started.

Finally the man with a top hat and suit of clothes that were years out of fashion appeared over the high stone wall. He waited a moment for everyone to quiet down before he spoke.

"Good evening, everyone. As you all know, I'm the commissioner of Lyon County, Saul Williams." People began clapping and shouting the man's name. Smiling, he said, "Now quiet down, folks. We'll be getting this show underway here soon." Everyone laughed and clapped for a long time. Edgar just stared. "Also, when we're finished, we'll have a viewing. You'll all be able to see the bodies for yourselves. No pictures now."

Suddenly the father dashed forward, nudging his child to the side, behind him. The crowd jumped, afraid that he'd come for them. Edgar stared, he wasn't afraid. "I confess." The man's daughter broke down, crying. He turned to look at her, then back to the crowd. "I did it. I did it. I took that money. It wasn't mine. And I took it…" He looked down, glanced for a moment at his child. "My daughter. Did nothing. She didn't know. She's fourteen. A child. Spare her." No shadows stood beneath his feet, only beneath the crowd's.

The woman beside Edgar held her breath for a moment. No doubt that she was torn between wanting her daughter to be spared, but not wanting the man who had spawned her to die. Edgar turned to look at her for a moment. He saw her, as if for the first time. Her face was red from the tears and the emotion. Her gown was worn and caked with dirt at the bottom, though this was probably her best dress. She had a scar down her left cheek, from a lashing, perhaps. It had healed wrong, thickened. Her eyes were swollen from the tears, but clear. She would watch every moment, remember. Most of the people there would have forgotten within a week's time. Edgar wasn't sure if he could forget.

For a very long time, there was silence. Complete silence. Even the shadows surrendered to the moment.

"No," the girl spoke loud enough for everyone to hear her. "No. He didn't."

With nothing left to say, the man in the top hat spoke: "Now, if we can have those who will testify step up? Speak your piece before the good people of this town so that they know the crimes that have been committed by both this man and his offspring."

One by one each of the people who had been at Charlie's that day told what they saw, as they saw it. The father and daughter were a gang of roving thieves by all accounts. They were vestiges of an undeveloped people who needed to be extinguished from the earth, or at least from Eddyville. This was the day to begin the purge.

After the others had spoken, Edgar stepped forward. He looked to the girl and then her father and then back to the girl again. Too small. Sick. Unhealthy… Unclean. After a moment, he opened his mouth to speak his truth. The shadows and the people of Eddyville were there to receive it.

Jesus wept for man in the Bible.
Edgar never fully understood why.

Lovecrafting

Orrin Grey

"The appeal of the spectrally macabre is generally narrow because it demands from the reader a certain degree of imagination and a capacity for detachment from every-day life."

When I was rereading Supernatural Horror in Literature *prior to writing this story, I was expecting to find more of Lovecraft's weird racial essentialism than I remembered, and I did. But I also found this odd streak of proto-geek pride running through it, with his continued insistence that there was something unique and special about people who could appreciate a good supernatural tale. That's what stuck with me, and the seed of this story, which had already been germinating in thematically appropriate ways in my head, came to full flower from there.*

It's a scene straight from the pages of one of Gordon's earlier, more lurid stories. The graveyard scene. Dana and Conner as the latter-day resurrection men, tramping across the swampy ground in the pissing rain with a battery-powered lantern and shovels that they picked up at Home Depot.

Dana's hoodie is pulled up against the weather, her glasses spattered with drops that she can't wipe away completely because her sleeve is too damp. She wears black leggings under her jeans for warmth, but you can only tell in the places where her jeans are worn through. The shock of purple in her otherwise brown hair is hidden by the darkness and the wet.

Conner is a good foot taller than Dana, wide at the shoulders. If he were a character in a movie, he'd play basketball or football, be wearing a letter jacket. Instead, he plays chess and video games, can't stand most sports, though he's been known to do Frisbee golf on occasion. He wears a leather jacket that repels the rain, and one of the shovels is over his shoulder, while Dana carries the lantern and the other shovel. His jacket hangs unevenly due to the weight of his father's Colt .45 in his right pocket.

The lantern's light is golden and seems very small in the graveyard, picking out just the edges of tombstones that seem to lurch out of the darkness in its uneven light, leaving everything else to shadow and rain.

DANA: Fuck Gordon for this, y'know?

From the tone of her voice, and from Conner's non-reaction, you can tell it's not the first time tonight that she's said these words.

DANA: Fuck him for leaving this to us, and fuck him for convincing us to do it in the first place. And you know what? Fuck him twice for knowing that we *would* do it.

Conner doesn't say anything, just trudges on ahead while Dana stops to wipe off her glasses again, this time taking them off and fishing under her hoodie for the edge of her relatively dry T-shirt.

DANA: He really is the Danny Ocean of this little trio, and no mistake.

CONNER: Frank Sinatra or George Clooney? Not that it matters much, I just call dibs on not being Sammy Davis Jr.

DANA: Not really any good parts for me, though I'd take Julia Roberts over Dana Phillips right about now.

CONNER: Maybe that's what the next one of those movies oughta be about. Grave robbing.

DANA: It'd be a change.

Both of them stop, the banter dead on their lips. They've come to wherever they're going, now. The lantern swings in Dana's grip, the radius of light moving up and down, revealing the inscription on the stone before them, then hiding it again. In the light the stone is fresh, smooth and unblemished, and the name on it is clear: Gordon Phillips.

CONNER: I guess this is where we start digging.

DANA: Roshambo to see who goes first?

from *"The Transition of Jacob Cutter"*
by Gordon Phillips

His own hands began to disturb him. When he looked at them now, he no longer saw them as hands. To him, they appeared to be something else, pincers or tendrils or things with sucking pads. The hairy claws of an ape, the digging appendages of a mole. He knew that he was wrong, that they were still just hands, and, when he concentrated, he could still see them as he knew they must look to others, but the other image was always there, superimposed, like a double exposure in an old film.

They still worked like hands, he could still grab and manipulate things with them. Before Catherine left, he could still hold her hands in his, still touch her skin, but he always knew that the other hands were lurking there, beneath the surface, itching to break free as soon as he let his guard down.

And worse, they no longer felt like his hands. Not just that he could feel their wrong texture, shaggy or squamous or chitinous or gelid, but that they never seemed like he was really in control of them. Oh, they made no overt move against him, but he still felt that it wasn't he who governed them. It was like watching the hands of your reflection in the mirror, or, closer still, watching some stranger mimic your every movement. The stranger may do everything that you do, just as you do it, but there is always the knowledge that at any moment they may stop. That thought carried with it a subtle menace, somehow more frightening than if his hands had suddenly leapt up of their own accord to strangle him.

He grew to hate his hands, and everything that he relied on them to do. He could no longer bring himself to type, and so deadlines came and went. He stopped using his phone, stopped checking his email. His computer sat dark and silent. He imagined cobwebs gathering on it. He lay in bed, curled into a ball with his hands clasped between his knees to still them, though he knew they weren't moving. He thought about movies that he'd seen with possessed hands in them, and about the carving knife in the kitchen drawer, but he never went to get it, because he knew, even then, that cutting off his hands wouldn't help.

It was in him everywhere…

A cheap-looking hotel room, two weeks earlier. Less a setting from Gordon's fiction, but maybe a crime scene in a low-budget television police drama. There's only one bed, with a confetti-colored comforter, and Conner sits on it, almost lounging, his foot hanging off, his sneaker brushing the carpet as he kicks his foot back and forth, back and forth. The light inside the room is buttery and dull, the light that creeps in from outside is cold fluorescent blue, the kind of light that makes you think of morgues in movies. That's the association that'll stick.

Dana paces in front of the big double window. The thick hotel drapes are pulled closed, but they hang slightly askew, letting the blue light in around the edges. Her circuit takes her from one taupe wall (the one with the TV and a generic painting of nightingales perched on branches) to the other taupe wall (with a matching painting, whip-poor-wills this time, and lamps screwed into the wall above the bed, casting that yellow light). Back and forth, back and forth, like a mannequin on rails, like Conner's foot.

DANA: Why would he break into a cemetery?

It's the first time in a while either of them have spoken, they've been inhabiting their own frustrated silences, each doing their own mental pacing, but the question doesn't seem to startle the quiet. Instead it's so expected, it feels almost rhetorical.

CONNER: You know why.

DANA: Because of some stories? That doesn't make sense.

CONNER: Gordon never made a lot of sense.

DANA: More than this. Did they tell you how he got hurt?

Conner shakes his head, not long, just a brief motion, one side to the other, not interrupting the rhythm of Dana's pacing, or of his own swinging foot.

CONNER: Just that he fell, somehow, getting over the fence. A night watchman caught him, I guess, scared him off. Gordon ran, and the guy went after him. Gordon was trying to get over the fence, and then at the top, he must've just fallen. They think maybe he hit his head.

DANA: It doesn't make sense.

CONNER: It made sense to Gordon. Sense enough for him, anyway. You read his email. He was going to prove something to himself, one way or the other. If the body was there, if everything was as it was supposed to be, then great, he was wrong, he was crazy, high-strung, over-imaginative, like everybody always said. If not, if he found what I guess he was expecting to find, then he was right, at least, and he had proof. Maybe not that anybody else would buy, but maybe enough for him.

DANA: Did he actually think he could do it? Dig up a body without getting caught? Especially *that* body?

Conner is quiet, just the swishing of his shoe on the carpet. Back and forth, back and forth. It calls to mind a pendulum, a metronome, the ticking of a clock, the inevitable passage of time, the grinding approach of death. As if it's triggered by the association, the ticking of the clock on the wall becomes audible in the silence between the two friends, measuring out every beat of time that passes before Conner replies.

CONNER: I don't know what he thought. I talked to him last, what, a week ago? I drove by his place. It was a mess. Old containers of takeout food, the whole bit. Cluttered, like it got when he was working, but different too. Not just junk. He had these books. Library books, some of them, and others books from his collection, pulled down off his shelves and stacked everywhere. Lovecraft, Bierce, Poe, Machen, that lot. Biographies of them, too, collected letters.

DANA: Not unusual reading for him…

CONNER: No, but it was different, like I said. He had it all marked up, Post-it notes stuck to everything, highlighters out. All these notes on legal pads. He must've used up half a dozen of them, all stacked next to his desk. He was working something out, working something up.

DANA: Doesn't sound all that much different than anytime he was working on a story.

CONNER: I know it doesn't, but it *was* somehow. I can't really explain it. It just *felt* different. You know in movies when they go into the room of someone who's been working out a conspiracy theory, and there's a big board with newspaper clippings and whatever else all connected up with pins and yarn? This felt like that, though not on some big board. Just, kind of all over the room.

DANA: And whatever it was he was working on, he thought he could work it out by digging up Lovecraft's body?

CONNER: He kept talking about how they all died. He had them memorized. Lovecraft dead of cancer. Poe of "congestion of the brain." Blackwood of cerebral thrombosis. Leiber of some unspecified brain disease of his own. Hodgson killed by an artillery shell in Belgium, Howard by a self-inflicted bullet to the brain, and Bierce unaccounted for somewhere in Mexico. But who knows what would have become of them had nature been left to take its course?

Dana stops pacing. She's standing by the air conditioner unit, the blue morgue light from outside catches half her face, throwing the rest into shadow.

DANA: But Gordon didn't think that's what they really died of?

Conner doesn't answer right away. He looks down at his foot, going back and forth, and he seems to become aware of the ticking of the clock, and from outside in the night the sound of cicadas, rising up suddenly. He stops moving his foot, leaves it frozen in the air, and looks up at Dana as he answers.

CONNER: No. He said that something was growing inside them.

from "The Mimic Rout"
by Gordon Phillips

When I venture out of my apartment now, which I do only rarely and by the gravest of necessity, I no longer see the people around me as I once did. They appear to me not as they look to each other, nor as I had always imagined them before, but as they truly are. Maimed mannequins, their crumpled faces merely pallid masks from which vacant sockets gaze.

They move with the slumping, quivering gait of broken animatronics in some sideshow spookhouse. Mindless brute creatures, their puppet strings extending unbroken into the black abyss of the heavens, toward which they cast their scripted prayers and their rote imaginings.

I always felt apart from the world, never like I belonged. I always thought that this was a defect in me, that I was a round peg in society's square hole, but now I know the truth. The other entities that inhabit this world, the others I thought of as peers and friends, coworkers and family, are in fact simple automatons, eking out a pointless existence at the behest of invisible masters they will never know or understand. The only exceptions are myself and those like me. Finally, I see us as we truly are, as well. Not the plastic flesh that we wear to blend in with the puppets, but our true forms, bulbous and many eyed, squirming and creeping and flying, sending out our own ghostly light. Each of us different, each of us truly unique, as the staggering mannequins only imagine themselves to be, but we are bound together, siblings in our difference from that mimic rout.

And when the day comes that the marionette throng sees us for what we truly are, we will seem as monstrous to them as they now seem to me. And though they are mindless things, they unconsciously abhor that which reminds them of their sameness, and so when they know us they will turn on us like the maenads who tore apart Orpheus, and, like that ancient poet, we will be rent asunder and destroyed, though even the rocks and trees refuse to strike us.

I know that this is the fate which awaits me. I see it each time I venture out of my apartment. I see the hatred there, in their blank faces on the bus and at the grocers. They hate me for my difference, even though they don't yet know it, and one day soon they will unmake me.

Curtains. Applause.

Dana's apartment, a month before that. A nice enough place, but small. The apartment of a student, maybe someone working her way through medical school, or law school. Light blue walls, white trim. It's dark. The only sources of illumination are the cold morgue light that comes in through the blinds, and the cone of yellow made by a small bedside lamp. A digital clock on the same bedside table says that it's three in the morning.

Dana is in bed, the phone pressed to her ear. Her glasses are off, lying on the table next to some change and her keys. It looks like maybe she got in late. There's a jacket draped over a chair at her desk, a pair of jeans in a pile on the floor next to it, though the room is otherwise neat. The dimly lit spines of the books that line her headboard aren't the kinds of things that Gordon writes. Not even a Stephen King novel to be found. Dashiell Hammett, Truman Capote, James Bond.

We can hear Gordon's voice from the other side of the line.

GORDON: Dana, listen, I'm sorry I woke you.

DANA: You said that already.

GORDON: Yeah. Look, it's just, I need someone to talk to. Need to talk to someone.

DANA: Isn't Conner around?

GORDON: He's out of town. He didn't answer. Look, I know you don't care about this stuff, but, please, Dana, just let me talk, okay?

Dana flops back onto the bed, switching the phone so that it's pressed to her other ear. She pulls the blanket up to her shoulders, closes her eyes.

DANA: Sure, bro. Go ahead and talk. I'll mumble now and then, so that you know I'm only half-asleep.

GORDON: Okay, so you're familiar with the concept of the muse, right?

DANA: "In spite of Virtue and the Muse…"

GORDON: Right, sure. But what if we've had it backward all this time? What if there's no external muse, what if instead it works the other way around?

DANA: Conner really is the better person for you to bounce story ideas off of, kid.

GORDON: This isn't a story idea. I mean, it's also that, kind of, it's been in all my stories lately, but it's just… just an *idea* idea. Just hear me out, okay?

DANA: Mmkay.

GORDON: Okay, so, what if instead of something else making us write, we're making something *by* writing. Not just making up fictional characters and worlds and whatever, but actually making something real. I mean, imagination, that's a kind of energy, right? And energy can be neither created nor destroyed.

DANA: That's matter…

GORDON: Whatever. Anyway, energy doesn't just dissipate. It goes somewhere, does something. It changes things, makes things happen, right? Imagination is a kind of radioactivity. It throws off sparks, hurls out bits of itself that get into everything around it, causes mutations. Or hell, maybe it isn't anything like science at all. Maybe it's an evocation, a magic spell. Maybe you put the right words down in the right order, and you call something up from somewhere, conjure something. Or maybe there's no difference, really, magic spell or radiation. Black mewling god at the center of the universe or the spark of creativity in the human brain. Maybe it's all one and the same.

DANA: Look, Gordy, I can't understand this kinda stuff when it *isn't* three in the morning, okay?

GORDON: I know, Dana. I just… I'm scared there's something wrong with me.

Dana smiles, though her eyes stay closed, and, when she speaks, she sounds a little more awake, a little more herself.

DANA: There's always been something wrong with you, bro. Have you talked to Dr. Sherman about this stuff?

GORDON: Yeah, a little. But it usually works better when I write it down, channel it into the work, y'know?

DANA: Or call me in the middle of the night?

GORDON: Or that, yeah.

There's a moment of silence and the sound of the connection becomes audible, a distant crackling, like tinfoil being crumpled at the bottom of a mine. Dana starts to sit up in bed again, opens her eyes. Outside, the cicadas are singing.

GORDON: Dana, I'm sorry.

DANA: Don't worry about it, kid.

But the connection has already been broken, and the phone that Dana holds in her hand is now dead.

from "The Congregation"
by Gordon Phillips

Comes now the Congregation, into this great space. They are of every shape and description, and they shine with their own inner light, like creatures of the deepest sea, like the algae that makes glowing waves upon the ocean at night, like fungus and fox fire and will-o'-the-wisps, like corpse candles and the flames of St. Elmo. They move in every way that a creature of the earth can move. They creep and scuttle, float and fly and drift and slither. Here the carapace of a crab, there the legs of a spider. Fins decorate backs, tails drag along the cold stone floors. Eye stalks waver in the darkness, and vestigial limbs grope at the air like antennae. Some are heavy and segmented, as many-legged and compound-eyed as insects. Others ooze like the cephalopod. Still others touch the ground not at all, but drift through the benighted atmosphere like jellyfish in a tidal pool. Each is different, no two the same, though they carry with them a similarity that is not of genus or of species but something else. A kinship of spirit, in the way that couples long married may come to resemble one another, or a pet grow to echo its master. They are alike only in their strangeness.

As each one crosses in front of the altar, a momentary flicker can be discerned, a glimpse of some other body, some other place. Boxes buried in the ground, caged up in the dark. Not broken open, because the creatures can pass as wraiths when needed, for they are made of sterner stuff than the merely material world. One, a squat thing, crab-like and knurled with knobby eyes, brings with it an image of a cave somewhere in Mexico, and in that cave a body that is no longer truly a body, but an empty cocoon, like the husk that a cicada leaves behind on the bark of a tree.

They gather in a great circle, this eldritch congregation. Though their speech is not the speech of men, their words not those of any earthly language, they make themselves understood to one another. Their ranks part open to admit another member to their gathering. Its form is as strange as any, and its inner light glows as bright. As it passes the altar, an image is shown of a box being lowered into the earth, and then it creeps forward among them and is made welcome.

The graveyard again. The lantern is sitting on Gordon's headstone near where Conner's jacket hangs, throwing its light into the hole that Dana and Conner are digging. It is getting deep now. Conner stands in the hole up to this shoulders, the shovel in his hands rising and falling like the head of a pump jack as he throws dirt onto the growing mound at the side of the grave.

Dana sits on the edge of the pit, leaning against the headstone. The rain has stopped, and she's smoking one of Conner's cigarettes, even though she quit smoking six months ago. When she draws on the cigarette, the molten orange glow illuminates the lenses of her glasses, makes them opaque.

DANA: How long do you think he knew?

CONNER: That he had cancer?

Dana nods, draws on the cigarette, holds the smoke in her mouth so long that she coughs a bit when she finally blows it out, taking the cigarette from her lips and offering it to Conner, who wipes his wet mouth on his shirtsleeves. He takes it from her, pulls on it, and hands it back.

CONNER: He didn't think he had cancer, you know that.

DANA: So you think he really believed all that shit? That stuff in his stories, that stuff that he told us?

CONNER: You think so, too. If we didn't wonder, at least a little, we wouldn't be out here in the asshole of midnight, digging up your brother's grave.

DANA: Touché.

She stands up, brushing off the backs of her pants and taking another pull on the cigarette as she does so.

DANA: Okay, Herbert West, I think it's my turn to dig.

But before she can begin to climb down into the hole, Conner's shovel drops again, and, instead of sinking into the dirt with its usual quiet shunk, it raps like the fist of a midnight caller on the front door of Gordon's coffin. The two share a glance, Conner standing in the sucking mud at the bottom of the grave, Dana looming above him, cast in chiaroscuro by the lantern's light. In that look is the knowledge that this is the last opportunity for turning back. Dana puts her hand on the other shovel, and drops down into the damp earth at the side of the coffin. The smell is stronger now than it seemed before. Not a rotting smell, just the loamy scent of turned earth.

They work in silence, and once the lid of the casket is clear, they both stand on either side, looking down at what they've uncovered.

CONNER: This is it. Do you want to do the honors?

Dana nods mutely. She grips a shovel in both hands, opens her fingers one at a time, then closes them again the same way, like a batter stepping up to the plate.

DANA: So it's just going to be his body in here, right? He won't even be rotted much yet. He'll probably smell like an old folks' home, or something. That's all we're going to find, right?

She looks at Conner, but it's obvious that he doesn't have anything to reassure her with. He reaches up, and, from the pocket of his leather jacket, he pulls out his father's pistol.

DANA: Okay, I'm going to do it. Are you ready?

Conner nods, and Dana takes a deep breath. The casket comes open with a wrenching sound, like the lid of a crate being pried up. Conner and Dana are both breathing heavily now, almost panting. The rain has stopped. Their feet make squelching sounds as they shift in the dirt. In the trees around the graveyard, the cicadas have begun to call.

DANA: Oh shit.

The lantern tumbles from its perch above them, and the bulb shatters with a flash on the base of the headstone. Darkness rushes in behind it, and it's hard to say if there's a dim glow from the grave, or if it's just the lingering image of the light on the rods and cones of your eyes. In the dark there's a crack of thunder, maybe, or maybe it's the sound of the pistol going off. The cicadas are screaming now.

Curtains. Applause.

One Last Meal, Before The End

David Yale Ardanuy

"Another amazingly potent though less artistically finished tale is 'The Wendigo', where we are confronted by horrible evidences of a vast forest daemon about which North Woods lumbermen whisper at evening. The manner in which certain footprints tell certain unbelievable things is really a marked triumph in craftsmanship."

Blackwood's "The Wendigo" is one of the first western uses of the northern Native American legend, and a truly frightening tale of possession and subtle transformations. While I agree with Lovecraft on the quality of the work, it is worth pointing out that Algernon Blackwood uses the least grotesque aspects of the legend's attributes, leaving out the most notorious elements of the myth: the cannibalism, bloodlust, and sorcery of the windigo. Lovecraft rightfully praises Blackwood's tale, but fails to realize the actual scope of the mythology or the extreme terror the Native Americans' held for both the spirit and the transformation of the windigo. Lovecraft describes the tale as "amazingly potent," but disarms that statement by describing the myth as some ghost story that lumbermen swap around the dinner table. This description by Lovecraft is woefully slight when compared to the former mass belief among Algonquin, Ojibwa, and Cree Native populations, as well as its historical realization many times over. So, amazingly potent, yes, but poison and desserts can both be potent. The windigo myth is concentrated terror, and firmly rooted in the North American historic record.

♦

February 22, 1799: Iron Knife trading post, twelve miles north of Lake Superior.

♦

The day started as every other had for the past few weeks, dark and freezing. The old pine boards of the wall, dryer than any Jesuit tract, concealed the cabin's outer logs and the merciless cold beyond. Placing another log in the iron stove to warm the room, I recall I cut my hand on an especially jagged piece of wood. Yes, I remember it, not the pain, but the taste. Oh, and what a taste it was... or rather, what it became later in my memory, at least. I remember the events perfectly, lest you doubt my mind, it is the memory of... *other* things that has changed. The taste of beef, venison, fowl, is as ash, now, and they bring on a great sickness if consumed. Human blood is unspeakably delicious to me now, and it is difficult to resist the urge to drink from my own arm. I digress, forgive me, I will return to these matters later.

As I was explaining, that wound marks the beginning of the destruction of my life, and my soul. A moment later my boss, the trading post manager Sabian Ruelle, came in from his chambers.

"Morning Andre," Sabian said. "Colder than a witch's tit, it is. How about you making us some coffee?"

I asked him how he slept, I recall. A few moments later we were drinking coffee and discussing the burn of our tobacco pipes, enjoying one of the few pleasures available in the region.

The main door resounded with a series of loud bangs, which startled me into spilling my coffee all over my hand. I remember again tasting the splinter wound as I put my burnt finger in my mouth. How delectable the memory is… pray, pray, forgive me… But yes, Sabian opened the door and a snow covered Indian burst in.

That Indian was an Algonquin called George Red Foot, a good trapper and well liked in the region for his fairness in dealings amongst the other tribes. He carried a solemn and fearful expression along with his load of furs and bags.

"Sabian, I am here to trade my furs, I am leaving," he blurted out, clearly in a great hurry to start the exchange.

"Why are you here so soon?" Sabian asked. "The season's not over, and those furs will hardly fetch more than your current debt to this post."

To this his expression hardened, and George said, "I will do just fine. When I leave here I will be alive to work again somewhere else."

"What is threatening you, George?" Sabian raised an eye at me, as though I might shed some light on this Indian's panic. "Other Indians? Early bears?"

"My partner Francois has frozen inside." This George said with such severity that even though I did not understand his meaning, not then, a chill ran down my spine.

His queer phrasing stirred up a deep worry in my breast, and I asked, "How did he catch his death? Falling through the river?"

At this George's expression changed into a mask of stark terror. "He is not dead, his… his *heart* has frozen." His voice dropping to a whisper, he said, "He has joined with the Ice and become windigo."

"Windigo?" I said, and George hissed at me:

"Do not speak it out loud, ever, or it will know you. It will come for its due."

"Andre, start weighing out this fur," Sabian said as he directed George over to the stove. Offering some tobacco, he said softly but still loud enough for me to hear. "What's really going on, George? You can't seriously mean to take off in the dead of winter!"

"Francois is gone now," George said softly. "I am moving on as soon as you pay me for my furs. My wife Moon Bird is waiting for me outside right now."

"All weighed out, sir," I called over.

Sabian gave George his shrewdest stare, one he often gave me when bluffing at cards, and said, "Francois owes this post a great debt of furs, George. If you would collect them for me before leaving the area, I would pay you one-third of their value."

George's already unhappy expression soured considerably. "You would pay me to kill myself? How generous the white man becomes when he requires the death of the Indian."

"What are you on about?" Sabian asked, taken aback. "I have only been fair with you, and every other Indian in the region. If you really believe your partner is a mortal danger to you, why don't Andre and I take you back to his cabin, so we can all settle this matter together? Surely the three of us would be the equal of one demented old man!"

"I wouldn't go back if you had three hundred men." He stated this flatly, with resigned conviction, and moved to the front desk where I worked. He received his trade value in tobacco, corn meal, black powder and shot, then walked to the door. He paused there, and, looking back at me over his bundle of supplies, said, "Do not go there for the furs, Andre. They are lost now, as lost as Francois and his debt to this post. It is better that you leave, too, before death finds you. Or worse. You may have forgotten your people and ways, but the spirits have not."

With that he left, closing the door quietly behind him.

"What do you think?" I asked Sabian.

He sighed. "We must at least attempt to get Francois' furs. If he has gone soft in the skull, well… then we may have to do him violence, if he tries to visit it upon us first. But he's no spring chicken, between the two of us I'm sure we can catch him alive. After that, well, we can turn him in to the Jesuits near the lake mission, see if they can't help him. They've reformed worse than a dotty white man, eh?"

Sabian did not sound as though he relished this course, but we both knew that as post captain he must acquire all debts by contract or lose his own profit, and possibly position as well. There was no way around it: we would be going, at least for the furs. Had I known then the horror that awaited us, all the money in the world would not have lured me there.

As we readied our gear, I recall asking Sabian, "What was that windigo business he was talking about? He seemed terrified by the mere mention of the name?"

"Oh, it's just some old Indian myth," said Sabian dismissively. "Folks who spend so much time alone in the wilds, they start acting like beasts themselves. The Indians think they are possessed… you know, like a werewolf or something."

"Windigo." The strange word felt cool on my pipe-bitten tongue. "Huh."

"Shouldn't you be the one telling me about it, anyway?" He said in that imperious way he got, when he felt like putting the spurs to me. "Being part savage yourself, I'd have thought your head was filled with tall tales of witches and windigos and wolf spirits, all that rot. Or did your heathen daddy only teach you how to cheat at cards and guzzle firewater?"

"Father Orleans told me plenty of stories about spirits and witches, but only those from the Gospels," I said, refusing to rise to his bait. I'd told him twice before it was my mother who had been Indian, which was once more than I felt I needed to. Orphaned at an early age, I had been dealing with folk like Sabian almost all my life. "And growing up with the Jesuits, most of the card sharps and drunks I met were white men who came begging at the mission. I won't remind you again, Sabian: I'm a Christian, not an Indian."

"You're red as old George's feet, my boy," he said in his superior way. "Doesn't your Bible say something about accepting that what we cannot change?"

I glared at him and sipped my coffee, now quite cold.

"Half-breed, whole Christian, what's the difference?" Sabian said, happy to play the peacemaker now that he had gotten my goat. "Hell, Andre, it don't matter to me. Only thing I care about right now is going out there to get those furs. Probably old Francois' just gone crazy — that codger's been out here a sight longer than me, and I've been out here a sight longer than you. Alone in the wilderness with nobody but the beasts and the Indians for company will do that to a man."

"Two of the same thing, isn't it?" I said sarcastically, but, as usual, my comment went right over Sabian's head.

"If he is mad, we need to get him to the mission before he chews up those furs, or something equally deranged. It also occurs to me that that damned Indian George Red Foot might've killed his partner, and told us a whopper to put us off the scent. If *that's* the case, then we need to know so we can send word for his arrest before he gets too far. We had best hurry up and get out there."

"Windigos and werewolves," I grumbled, stowing a bottle of whiskey in my bag so we would have something with which to tempt Francois into letting us into his cabin. I recall how safe we were then. We should have left with George Red Foot and his wife. Instead, I shouldered my pack for the trip and contemplated whether all Indians were insane to some degree, or only George Red Foot.

We started out at mid-morning and traveled north about six miles, where we stopped at the Eight Stones River crossing to rest and eat. Francois' home was located about three miles away from that point, due east along the river. I recall the weather was pleasant along the way; a warm sun had miraculously appeared for most of our trip and the duration of our rest. I remember the air had a deliciously crisp taste, heavily scented with spruce and pine. I was considering how fortunate we were to have had such splendid weather after months of brutal winter, when Sabian reminded me of the grim task at hand. We continued on in hopes of reaching Francois' cabin before nightfall.

As we walked along the river, I remember noting an abundance of trees snapped in half at mid-trunk, some fifty feet from the ground in some cases. Following my gaze, Sabian said, "It's the ice and the wind that does it. The tops freeze up with ice and snow, then the wind comes through and snaps off the tops. Just like you or I would tear the drumstick off an overcooked chicken."

He said this easily enough, but the remark disquieted me. As we walked I imagined some monstrous hand reaching down from the sky and tearing treetops off to stick in its mouth, chewing the bark and ice as a man might relish the crispy skin of a roasted hen. With these and other dark thoughts did I wile away our march.

Looking back on it now, it seems that as we drew closer to the damned place a pallor of cruel wickedness settled on to both my thoughts and the landscape. All around, the broken trees increased in number, and large formations of ice hung from the pine boughs and clung to the trunks, or reared up from the ground. It was almost as if they had frozen in specific places in a vaguely organized way. It struck me as… unnatural.

Francois' cabin appeared as we rounded a large patch of granite boulders. It was a small shack, perched quaintly atop a rise, at the edge of a steep, tree-covered embankment, overlooking the frozen Eight Stones River below. No smoke rose from the cabin, a truly ominous sign as few veterans of the northern winters would be foolish enough to allow their fire to go out before the first thaw of spring.

"What a wretched little place," Sabian remarked. "Hopefully it's dry inside."

I briefly imagined old Francois inside, raving mad in the dark. A thought that startled me with its clarity, a thought I quickly shut out.

As we approached the cabin, a distinct quiet fell over the area. Only our breathing and crunching footsteps in the snow made any sound. The snow around the cabin was deep and undisturbed, which struck me as odd — no one had come or gone from the cabin in some time, so when had George Red Foot last checked in on his partner?

Then I noticed something else — the lack of birds. Most animals were silent for the winter, the exception being the ravens and magpies that hang about settlements to rob scraps of food. At the trading post, they were ever present and sometimes quite loud... yet it seemed that there were no living creatures within a mile of Francois' cabin, save Sabian and me. As we stopped halfway across the clearing to peer at the dark structure, the silence enveloping us was absolute — we could not even hear the wind, which had harried us all along our hike.

"The door is open." Sabian's whisper sounded like a yell in the unnatural stillness, and I hushed him, startling myself with my own volume. We un-shouldered our muskets as we approached the cabin's face, making our way in total silence. I was reminded momentarily of a tomb or mausoleum as I looked at the cabin's open door and the black interior beyond.

Sabian lit a lantern as I stood watch over the doorway, expecting at any moment to see Francois charge forth. Nothing stirred, and, under the soft glow of the lantern, we entered the cabin. Inside was a sight that defied logic, that inspired true horror. The cabin itself was unremarkable in its design, a single room with a hearth at one corner, having the usual trinkets and gewgaws that Indians and mountain men hold dear hanging about the room. The horror lay on the floor, and the image has been seared into my mind ever since.

A corpse of an Indian woman, Francois' wife perhaps, lay sprawled in the middle of the cabin. She was... *encased in ice*, from the waist up, but, to our extreme revulsion, her legs, where exposed from the frost, were stripped of all flesh. The bones themselves were gnawed and ragged as if some predator had chewed the flesh directly off. An expression of mortal terror was quite literally frozen onto the dead woman's face.

I looked away in shock as Sabian staggered past me, heading back outside. I moved for the door, fearing to be in the half-eaten corpse's presence a moment longer. As I stumbled away, I began to hear the sound of rushing wind and cracking trees, accompanied by a shrill howling that chilled me to the bone. I followed Sabian outside into the clearing immediately in front of the cabin, shivering even before the wind and unspeakable cold hit us. Sabian stood in the snow as the howling wind hit us, looking like a man on the verge of total panic. I was nearly stricken as well.

The shrill howl evolved into a ghastly scream, a sound utterly alien from any wind I had ever heard. The trees surrounding the cabin first bent to an impossible degree in the gale and then began to snap apart, blasting like gunshots as their trunks split. Then, above us, from the wind-thrashed and shattered treetops, Francois appeared, descending like a monstrous bird. He shrieked as he was borne through the air on the ferocious wind.

Francois landed in the snow next to Sabian. I told myself it had been a trick of the wind and the fading light, that the deranged trapper had merely been hiding up one of the pines and now jumped down upon us… but I could not convince myself, not even for an instant. I could not even believe this was still Francois.

I remembered Francois as aged but hardy; a somewhat stocky, short, black-haired Frenchman; what I saw now looked nothing like this memory. The thing that I saw was a horrible parody of the once rugged trapper, having more in likeness to a frostbitten corpse than any man still living. He… no, *it*, was at least eight feet tall, but dreadfully thin, as if it had existed in a state of starvation for months upon hungry months. Broken and jagged teeth were plainly visible; the thing appeared to have chewed its own lips off. The color of its skin, having the texture of the frozen dead, ranged from a light greenish blue along the length of the limbs and torso to a dark bruised purple that was reminiscent of deep internal trauma at the neck and abdomen. Stark naked and still howling that wracked, chilling wail, Francois, or what remained of the man, glared with a demonic mania at Sabian. It brandished a length of jagged bone.

Sabian, realizing his doom was at hand, raised his musket in a belated attempt to shoot the horror. Before he could, the fiend stabbed him in the neck with what I now saw was a broken section of clk antler. The prongs of the antler pierced Sabian's neck in two places, causing him to choke and gurgle. The blood spray from the wounds hit me directly in the face, burning my eyes and creating a ruddy haze that stole the clarity of my sight.

Sabian's awful death rattle and the howling of the monster seemed to come from all around me. In a panic I raised my musket and fired in the direction I perceived the sound of its madness. As soon as I took the shot, all sound faded, and, as I wiped the blood from my eyes, I prayed that I had struck Francois... Then the monster leapt upon me, screaming anew and clawing at my face with its foul, ragged hands. Blinded and hysterical, I grappled with it, staggering backwards in the snow.

In a new revelation of despair, the ground disappeared, and I rolled down the embankment beside the cabin, the monster riding me all the way. Bouncing against trees and off of rocks as we tumbled down the slope only seemed to excite the wretched thing, my own body singing from the cruel bludgeoning of the fall. Its unholy mouth came at my throat, its lipless maw giggling as its teeth brushed my neck...

By sheer providence, I landed a blow squarely to the bottom of its chin as we rolled, and it fell off of me as we skidded to a stop on the frozen river. The ice bruising my already battered back caused me to cry out in pain, and the monster laughed as though in true revelry. Frantically wiping the blood and snow from my eyes, I could perceive its unnatural shape rise up from the ice. Thoughtless as some hunted beast, I scrambled up and fled from that terrible shape, that grotesque laughter. Over the sound of my boots reverberating against the frozen river, I heard it chant in a hissing croak, some unspeakable phrase that cooled my strained, burning heart. The utter wickedness of the phrase was... imparted to me, even though I understood it not. Then the ice beneath my feet broke, as if in response to the blasphemous voice... or in revulsion from it.

The cracking ice sounded like the scream of a swine under a butcher's knife, and I fell through, into the lightless, deadly cold of the river. I felt the cut of a thousand razors as the black water enveloped me, stabbing into my very brain. I began to thrash in my heavy garments, once so warm yet now prohibiting any movement that might save me as I was pulled down by the iron-heavy wool and leather.

A rock battered my scalp, stunning the fight clear out of me. As if in a dream, I drifted back up on the sluggish current, facing the ice above me as the river carried me ever closer to death. What I saw shocked me back into the full horror of the situation. Staring back through the transparent, snow-dusted ice was the grotesque face of Francois, following my progress downstream as I endured my ignoble death. I recalled that, from above, the ice was clouded and difficult to see through, but the thing that was Francois appeared to mark exactly where I was, having no trouble seeing through it. Its horrible shape and scratching claws, silhouetted against the last light of the setting sun, made me thank God in those final moments that I would be drowned and lost to its incomprehensible, evil plans. A numbness came over me, so comforting as to feel almost like warmth, but then I was thrust out of the water, to be again battered against stones and ice.

By some miracle, or curse, I was cast down a series of small waterfalls where the river coursed down a sheer slope. Even as I realized what was happening, I became lodged in a crevice of stone and ice. I began to panic again, my heart beating frantically, from both the returning cold and from the terror of imagining the beast attacking me while I was pinned. Wrestling my way free of the cracked ice and jagged stones, I pulled myself out of the river and onto the sheer bank. Then the cold came in earnest, stealing all use from my limbs and causing me to shake so violently that I began to chip my teeth against one another.

I gave up, God forgive me, I resigned myself to death, and waited for the monster to come and kill me, to have its reward after so long a chase. It never came, however, though even from such an impossible distance I could hear it feasting on Sabian, howling and screaming with cannibalistic, manic joy at the night-shrouded forest.

I regained my senses to some small measure, and tried to drag my freezing body to some place where I could hide, and find some relief from the merciless cold, but all ability had departed me. My frozen hands could not even close around the roots that hung down beside me, let alone drag my weight. So I lay waiting for death in whatever form it would take.

Death never came, despite my wounds, despite being sheathed in ice-stiffened, waterlogged wool, and I passed the night in a state of madness. I could hear animals bleating and scratching all around me throughout the night, and other, stranger noises that had no explanation in either reality or dream. This deep in the Northern winter, the animals must be sleeping or else stalk silent as ghosts through the forests, but the tumult they made around me had the wanton air of a revel.

Then I heard a voice whisper my name. In all my many years of devout prayer, never had I heard an answer from my Savior or his saints, but, now, in my most desperate hour, I swear I heard an outer voice with perfect clarity... but this was not the voice of my Lord, or any of his servants. This was not even the voice of Lucifer, questing after my soul. No, I knew as soon as I heard that loathsome, wicked voice murmur my name that it came from someplace far, far closer than Heaven or Hell, and yet infinitely more remote...

It spoke to me not of sin or salvation, but of boundless, frozen gulfs. Gulfs of ice at the top of the world, from which every herculean glacier and humble icicle originates. The voice told of ancient hungers and unspeakable rites. Rituals where I might live forever, with limitless power over both man and nature. I had no choice, it whispered, only a choice to die as prey or haunt the frozen forests as it required.

The light of day eventually came, revealing a great abundance of animal tracks all around the area I had passed the night. They seemed to range through the entire natural animal kingdom, and yet further still. Humanoid footprints having only three toes and vague slithering as if great serpents had passed just beside where I lay. I marveled over the tracks as dawn came in earnest, creeping over the cursed and frozen forest.

Rather than putting my miseries to an end, daybreak brought with it fresh agonies. The sun shone down through the screen of icy branches, breaking upon me and creating an uncomfortable warmth that brought with it debilitating nausea. In time I clambered up and attempted to retreat into what shadows remained, away from the scalding light. My strength had returned sufficiently to stand and walk, but the oppressive heat of the dawn caused a new weakness in my muscles. I fled in to the darker areas of the forest and shed my frost-rimed coat. I ignored the fact that deep snow was all around me as I panted from the ever-rising temperature.

By midday the blazing of that sun caused me to collapse, in a state near death despite the blankets of snow I pulled over myself. As the day waned on and the sun crossed the sky, the heat gradually decreased. By late afternoon I was able to emerge from the sheltering snow and stand again without swooning. As the stars came out, I began the long walk back to the river, and from there retraced my way back to the post.

During the interminable hike, a hunger began to grow in the core of my body. It was a sharp and gnawing sensation, and, as I pushed myself onward, I dimly recognized that I had never before known true hunger. The ache of the need had reached a maddening and torturous state by the time I reach the pickets of the fort; a deep clawing agony nearly crippled me as cramping pains began to throb from my abdomen.

As I broke in the door of the cabin in my haste to enter, I marveled at my strength. The door had resisted me no more than a dried twig might. Forgetting this I all but ran to the larder. Within, a rank smell assailed me as I flung the contents around, too desperate to wonder how cured meats might have spoiled so quickly, intent only on the quest for anything palatable. Everything in the cabin sickened me with their noxious smells, but I was so hungry I forced some pemmican in my mouth. I chewed it voraciously, but, before I even swallowed my first mouthful, I vomited forth vile bluish-black phlegm and lay shaking violently on the floor.

After a time the sickness passed, and I noticed a smell so delicious I nearly wept. I realized the smell was coming from my own arm, which I had sliced open in my thrashings around the cabin. It was a shallow cut, barely more than a scrape, but I silently rejoiced as I gnawed at the wound, tasting the very essence of my soul…

I came back to myself, then. I realized what I was about for the first time since coming to the cabin of Francois, and a terrible horror came over me. What was happening, I wondered, then I thought of the warning of George Red Foot…

I had noticed how much smaller the cabin seemed, but only now saw that it was I who had grown. No fire burned in the hearth, but the heat in the room was sweltering. I knew then that I had become doomed by whatever curse had afflicted Francois. I despaired momentarily on my lost future, on my lost *humanity*… and then became resolved. An abiding hatred began to rise up within me, for myself, for Francois, and for that unhallowed voice that spoke to me of the frozen abysses in the north.

I knew then that I must end my own life before I killed an innocent or, worse yet, caused another to follow me into this icy hell. I resolved to put a lead ball in my head, but first I must complete this record… It is a warning for those who might find my body, yes, and also a testament as to why a true Christian would commit such a sin. I have no choice. This is not my fault.

So here I am at the end of my tale, and my hunger has only increased with each word. I can smell a scent in the air as I write these final words. I hear the jingling bell of one of the Jesuits' ponies coming through the yard — Brother Dunn, perhaps, capitalizing on the unseasonably good weather to acquire some new furs for the mission.

The pistol is beside the inkwell on the desk, waiting to end my life… but I am so hungry.

Now his feet are tramping through the snow, approaching the cabin. His voice quavers as he calls through the ruined door, "Is anyone there? Sabian? Andre?"

The pistol looks so heavy, and my arm is so tired from writing all this down. I will eat just once from this visitor, so I will have the strength to kill myself. One last meal and then oblivion, I am sure whoever has arrived will understand. I could never end my life with a hunger so great, and this visitor smells so appetizing. A scent that causes my teeth to ache and my mouth to water with anticipation.

Yes, one last meal for the condemned, and then the end.

There Has Been a Fire

Kirsten Alene

"Just as all fiction first found extensive embodiment in poetry, so is it in poetry that we first encounter the permanent entry of the weird into standard literature."

Lovecraft is one of the first authors to obliquely and obtusely communicate monsters, villains, and the ultimate source of psychological and supernatural horror as female. Big, fat vagina monsters are all over the place, and, if a woman appears, she's either evil or she's bringing evil with her.

He's a product of his time and place, and so are his ideas, or whatever. But that specifically, it's not an indication of sexism, it's an indication that he is a participant in a trend that starts, as he states himself, in poetry. The things that lurk unseen in the darkness, the things that watch you with cold indifference from the woods/ice/ mountains/space/ocean are by far the weirdest, the most terrifying of all.

The trend of verse historically is toward the alienation of people, things, and ideas that threaten society. Verse functions as a very basic way of teaching people what is good for them and what is bad, what is safe and what is dangerous.

And when, in poetry, women suddenly become separate enough from the functioning world of men that their actions and motivations are mysterious and unknown (when they enter, really, the realm of the weird), they quite quickly become terrifying.

I have been growing bats in the attic of the faculty hall for a long time. The warm, humid atmosphere suits them, and they appear to flourish under my care. Sometimes I take their soft, fat mammalian bodies in my hand and press their chests against my cheek. They are paralyzed by the smooth softness, and the only part of them that moves is their heart, which beats as fast as the vibrato of a piccolo. The morning that the sun rises orange through the rosary window on the fourth floor of the faculty building, I am tending the bats in the attic, and I miss what transpires on the first floor, in the faculty lounge.

Someone rushes up the stairs to tell me, "Anna Beth, there's been a fire. Anna Beth, there's been some sort of fire."

Downstairs the hallway is blackened and crumbling, but the walls are all intact. Teachers and students, a few aids, and a school nurse are walking around the place, expressing their dismay and despair by guttural emissions, which together add up to a general monastic hum.

Under the remains of a light fixture, which sparks benignly overhead, is a small blonde thing with ashes fluffing out from her head in a halo. She's very dirty, and the other faculty members do not approve. Who does she think she is, running around setting fires and then becoming blackened by them? She's just ruining the whole atmosphere of tragedy, standing there getting everything dirty where there wasn't any dirt before.

The host of helpful faculty members who supposedly appeared when the explosion sounded are closing in on me, relaying information they think must be relevant in catlike whispers near my ears so that no one else will hear and take credit for their powers of observation.

"A sign like a snake and a cross," says one.

"And the smoke was a bright reddish green, Anna Beth, tinged, a chemical reaction of some sort."

"I was, of course, preparing for my lecture and then the sound… like an elephant trumpet."

"Like a bassoon."

"Like a man screaming."

Then, the only really relevant piece of information comes from Peabody, a professor of Japanese ceremonial dress: "I think a man was inside."

The little blonde child turns slowly to face Peabody. My first instinct is to remove her from the nurse's claws, which are grasping at her, searching for wounds. But when she opens her mouth to speak, she no longer looks vulnerable at all.

"There was a man inside," she says, "I saw him run out. He ran out."

Quiet descends over the assembled disaster response. Then another rumbling hum as whispers race like snapping synapses from head to head.

The girl is installed in my office. When actual firemen arrive, followed closely by insurance lawyers and a foreman, I return to the attic where my bats are swaddled in their wings. They rustle softly, sway together and whisper as I close the door. My feet are sore from climbing up the stairs and back down and up again. Smoke from the fire is beginning to seep through the rafters and up into the attic. If they smell a whiff of smoke too strong, they'll all fly out the window in a second.

I sit for a moment, waiting for them to smell what I smell. There's a mouse sound, the creak of the stairs to the attic and then they smell it and, in a frenzy of leathery wings and soft, hot bodies, they rush over and past me, bursting through the window and down clumsily like a landslide.

When I inherited the office fifty years ago from a retiring astronomer named Getz, it was hung with papier-mâché planets, all in rows and spirals. They weren't mine, and they didn't have much to do with medieval rhetoric, but I liked them, so I kept them. The girl in my office is turning the planets around with one hand, inspecting them or making them turn. As I expect, she knows nothing. Is confused. Her hands shake, but her voice is not small or weak. To others, this behavior is not alarming.

I give a lecture on a poem by John Donne. I read it to the class in a deep voice, but it still sounds a little ridiculous coming from my mouth, which is lined and creased like crumpled silk now. "'I'll undoe the world by dying; because love dies too.'" These words mean a little less than they ever did, which was never very much, now that no world could ever be undone by me, nothing annihilated by my inaction, nothing invented by my action. The chance for any teaching or making is past.

The culprit is not caught. No one is in hand. At the faculty meeting, held in the fourth-floor restroom, above the sounds of construction below in what was once the faculty lounge, Peabody is enraged. "Something must be done," he says.

"Hear hear!" they shout.

"Must be done!" they shout.

"Something!" they shout.

On a morning when I am in the bat room, watching other bats fly back in through the open window, each giving me a look as it passes that says: "Yes. Hello. Here again? Yes hello, we recognize you," someone calls from down below:

"There's been a fire," they call, then add, almost as an afterthought, "there's been some other sort of fire."

I release my current bat and say goodbye.

The fire is a tree. It has exploded from the inside out. It has been struck by lightning. I try to explain to Hammer, the professor of meteorology. "This looks like lightning," I say. "Doesn't it look a lot like lightning, like it was struck by some sort of… like it was lightning."

But he doesn't see it. "Foul play," he mutters, and the others take up the phrase.

"Foul Play."

"Fow-el Puh-lay."

"Fowl."

"Fowel."

"Fow-el Play."

"This is the second fire," says Professor Peabody later as he is sitting beneath Saturn, sipping a cup of tea and thumbing through a treatise on the invention of balloons as a fashion accessory.

But this is not the second fire. It is the fifth. And the third fire is the sixth. Someone is setting fire to the campus, circling closer to the center. The ghostly girl from the faculty lounge has not been seen. She is setting the fires, says Peabody, "It's definitely that girl. What was her name?"

"I don't remember," I say. I do. It was Lys.

"What did she look like, again? I can hardly remember."

"I don't remember." But I do.

"We should put up a notice. What did she wear?"

"I don't remember."

I do. She was blonde and small, with huge penetrating eyes, a vacant stare, and a snake-like, up-curved mouth which, when open, said only frank and honest things.

There were no lines on her face, not even a crease across her closed eyelids.

She was either a ghost or a skeleton. Maybe a mummy. Maybe a witch.

She was dressed in a modest white skirt. She wore a furry sweater with a shape knitted clumsily on the front. The silhouette of a spider or a moth.

From my office I can hear my bats fluttering above. Peabody sighs. "That's just too bad," he says. "I'm up for review, and I'd like to be the one that catches her."

When he says "catches," it sounds very exciting. I feel a little thrill. I feel like a fox who is about to start running. Waiting for the sound of the horn and the first patter of hounds' feet in the brushes.

At night, stretched out under Venus with my toes tapping Betelgeuse, I can hear the building moan. And beneath the building sounds there is another sound, like a monastic whispering again: the sound of many voices saying different things together.

Against the gooey inside of my eyelid, Lys is pressed, her face growing lined and crumpling, her eyes sinking back into grey circles like my circles. Her voice falling in pitch until it is low enough for a poem to make sense, but not low enough to make it sound powerful.

Then she grows young again, from a pile of dust, she rises up new and shimmering, with an infant alabaster softness, then slick like a sea creature, and moving quickly.

Waking from my half dream, with a sheen of nervous sweat seeping from my creases, I peer down the hall. Lights flicker in the work zone that was once the faculty lounge. Outside, through the glass front doors, I can see the burned tree, still smoking slightly, and beyond that another plume of fresher smoke curling up angrily into the night. It is a new moon, and my bats are sleeping, fat from feasting last night, snoring gently and rocking themselves in their sleep.

The night without any bats in it feels empty. I am alone in the building, alone on the campus, alone watching a few things burn outside.

I turn around to close the door to my office and catch a flicker of movement. Lys is standing there, at the other end of the hall. Her hands are clasped in front of her. My heart jumps, while my lips part and I am about to say hello. She bends a little, takes a step forward.

There is no Lys at the end of the hall. Just a lingering film over my vision from the dream. Still, I say, just in case: "Hello?" She turns and runs down the stairs at the end of the hall.

I am reading another poem, but the class is a council of shadows spread around me in the basement of the faculty building. "She is all states, and all princes, I," I say, but again the words sound strained and small pushed from between my leathery lips, bolstered by only an asthmatic breath after climbing down all of the stairs. Once again my feet are sore, and Lys has reappeared as a simple addition to the shadow council wreathing around me.

"'Thy duties bee to warme the world, that's done in warming us.'" We set it all on fire.

In the morning, my back is as sore as my feet. I've slept all night on the couch in my office, my left foot on Betelgeuse, my right foot under Mercury (a tiny granite-colored ball with a chip out of one side).

Peabody is at the door, knocking gently. "I remember when this was Getz, he'd be in here every morning, just getting up for a shave when I arrived." He sighs. "I guess it's the planets?"

For weeks I am nightly hunted by dreams of that shadow council, as pieces of the world burn around me. Here and there a desert fire, here and there a house burned down. The only other men likely to have noticed anything at all are the firemen, muted by the demands of their business and their heavy fire helmets. Fires in the sewer under the chemistry building. Fires under the cafeteria. Spontaneous combustion, oven fires, gas leaks, burning paper, burning cloth, the library, the groundskeeper's cabin. Dream fires and real fires are interchangeable.

"'I have always found that Angels have the vanity to speak of themselves as the only wise; this they do with a confident insolence sprouting from systematic reasoning.'

"Fear of the unknown," I explain, my hands folding in on themselves like a dying insect's wings, "Fear of the unknown arises with segregation. The expression of fear and horror is blankness. Through poetry comes the first real rhetoric of alienation."

No one is listening. Again, I am not sure which students surround me. *Ah*, I think, glimpsing the narrow shoulders of the lineless Lys. *It is the shadow students.*

Back in the attic with the bats, their little grasping fingers end in talons like a bird's. Their faces are expressionless where before they were welcoming. When I hold a body to my cheek, warm and soft in my shaking, gnarled hand, it seizes, tremors pouring through it, and it dies.

The body slips through my fingers to the floor, a little crumpled form in a plume of dust. I feel disgusted, ashamed, small, and I climb back down the ladder. Lys is standing there, her eyes wide and hot. She has been waiting for a century, and fires are already snapping behind me. Smoke fills my lungs, and I cough, wretch, and vomit on the ladder.

Bats are silent when stirred by fire, as if they do not want to be followed. As if to disappear obscurely is not horrible to them, to blink out of the world of the living without sounds or protests, without waking a person, is an admirable aim.

Bats fall through the open attic door, accompanied by soot and ashes, which cling to the white skirt of Lys and the laces of my orthopedic shoes.

All the bats are dying. I can hear their soft bodies thumping against the latched attic window.

Lys is muttering witch-like behind me.

Peabody will find me in the office in the morning, one foot on Betelgeuse and one under Mercury, my head in the crook of my arm, too old and beauty-less to launch a ship.

We are sitting in the office. Lys's hand is on the earth, turning it sideways. She is imagining the earth's axis shifted, gravity reversed, sloughing off the occupants into the void and cluttered space of the office. She is smiling, her skin creaseless.

"They sometimes speak, you know," she says, "but in foreign tongues and not to ears that hear the things that escape their lips. They waste away when they fail to divert the objects of their attention. When they do not produce obsession, they do not affect the world of man. Like the white lily pitching herself from the balcony into a shallow river when Lancelot decides he's not interested in all that."

She shakes the earth, little specs of dust blow out. "It is a good way to do what you want. It is how I have transcended the basic function of my gender and become an open gateway to an amoral paradise. Was I expected to waste away from lack of reciprocal attention? Was I expected to perform that ancient function of servitor? Was I expected to transform into the match for another terrible face, when I had already been molded by desire, into the object of the first one? To invent, and practise this one way, to annihilate all three.

"When he said that I — in that pinkening garden as the sun was setting to the triplicate harmonies of church bells, birdsong, and the highway — when he said that I was beautiful, was all the momentum of my body created or abolished?"

Eventually the smoke clears. Shook loose from the papier-mâché earth, I am drifting fast away. But the office is full of particles, not like empty space, and friction slows my momentum enough that I drift off to sleep.

In dreams the soft, warm mammalian bodies of the bats are pressed up against all the skin of my face, bleeding their softness and youth into me with the whir of their heartbeats like the engines of music boxes. Lys is not slighted but loved, and I am not old but young. I feel their little bat eyes on me, greeting me and recognizing me, and they are all soon fat and slumbering in the rafters.

I wake later to sirens, screams of outrage, and the monastic whisper-hum that happens when many people say different things together.

The Trees

Robin D. Laws

As maddening as it is influential, Lovecraft's essay shows the hazard of the writer turned critic. He takes his own vision and preoccupations and prescribes them as essential to his genre:

"A certain atmosphere of breathless and unexplainable dread of outer, unknown forces must be present; and there must be a hint, expressed with a seriousness and portentousness becoming its subject, of that most terrible conception of the human brain — a malign and particular suspension or defeat of those fixed laws of Nature which are our only safeguard against the assaults of chaos and the daemons of unplumbed space."

Lovecraft's horror is invasive: it comes from the Outside, from the reaches of space, or from the long list of ethnicities he counts as the Other. When it comes from within us, we discover that we were the Other all along — an ape- or fish-man, not the mystic yet noble Northerner we thought we were all along.

An alternate conception of horror would find that the unknown force is within us. Not an entity from the outside, but what we decline to acknowledge about ourselves.

The essay's influence arises from his establishment of a weird horror canon, and his practical writerly assessment of its members' works. Among the writers who owe their current reputations to it is William Hope Hodgson. I thought of him, and of the opening of The Boats of the "Glen Carrig," as this story took shape.

I do not assume that either Lovecraft or Hodgson would have wanted to read this story.

♦

Contrary to what his uncle told the crimp, Will Dowland had never been to sea. For this reason it did not strike him as remarkable that nearly all of the *Dido*'s crew had sailed on her before. As a shipwright, Dowland knew the vessels but not the men upon them. Because Uncle Edward lied to get him added to the manifest, Will imagined it a difficult matter to gain admission to a ship's crew. Only during the voyage, as he heard the men's stories of press-gangings and fraudulent recruitments, did he discover otherwise. Most captains hungered for men, and left port shorthanded. It was not until months later, on the island, that Dowland came to fully realize why the *Dido* would be different, why so many who had crewed her previous mission, which left England three years prior, would so avidly arrange their affairs to do so again.

He did, however, detect a tension among the men even before they left the Portsmouth docks, reminding him of his drinking days. Specifically, of the pregnant interval when all could tell a fight brewed, before the first blow was struck.

Will asked his uncle about it.

"We expected our old captain," Edward said. "The captain makes all the difference. This new one, this Codrington, who's to say? Sailors resist uncertainty."

Will watched the men, as they went about preparing the ship

to haul anchor, watching Captain Codrington. Tall, thin, Roman-nosed, the captain stalked across the deck like a raven.

Though they stood well out of the captain's earshot, inspecting the masts for signs of disrepair, Will spoke quietly. "The old captain, what was it they liked about him?"

"Clement," Edward said, "showed flexibility."

He ended the sentence with a finality that told Will to stop asking questions. They had to maintain the deception at least until the ship left port. Once underway, the *Dido* would not turn back to put off a carpenter's mate who lacked experience.

The Dowlands had already checked the state of the vessel the day before, and the day before that. But when shipping out, it was well to look busy, if only as a show of respect for those who did have work to do. Overall the Dowlands had found the *Dido* in good order, though they'd referred several spots in the hull to the attention of the caulker. Their jobs would not begin in earnest until the ship hit its first squall. Until then, Edward, who as ship's carpenter held the rank of warrant officer, superior even to the bosun, would project serene confidence in the condition of the ship. If Will stuck by his uncle's side and did not embarrass him, he could by stages assimilate the details of shipboard life. He regarded himself a quick study, a judgment his uncle shared. By the time the *Dido* faced the treacheries of the Horn, he would be ready, not only in appearance, but in fact.

A muttonchopped man, his reddened, bulbous nose preceding him like a figurehead, spotted Edward and hastened beside him. Edward introduced him to Will as the ship's surgeon, Dr. Lynas. Lynas assessed the younger Dowland with hazy disinterest.

"Any word on what went awry with Clement?" he asked Edward.

"Fell off a horse," Edward said.

Lynas shook his head. "Damn fool." He peered at Captain Codrington, a stray, rheumy tear gathering in his left eye. "What have you heard of him?"

"Very little. Jackson's brother served with him briefly, on the *Centaur*, where he was a lieutenant. He made scant impression."

"We'll have to take his measure," Lynas said.

"Naturally," said Edward, declaring the subject closed.

Lynas turned to Will. "Your uncle has done you a great favor, shouldering aside that ox Hannan to install you as mate."

"I thought he might benefit from distraction," Edward said.

Will gazed back at the red roofs of Portsmouth. "I am a recent widower."

Emotion came easily to Lynas' voice. "So young. A terrible pity. Childbirth?"

Will nodded. "We were expecting our first."

The doctor gripped Will's shoulder. Up close, he reeked of rum. "Trust in Edward, dear boy. He does right by you."

◆

Ever since his uncle announced his plan, Will had worried for his sea legs. If he fell too deeply into sickness he would reveal himself as a tyro. As the *Dido* hugged the African coast, others fell wretchedly ill, supposedly hardened tars included. Aside from the odd bout of dizziness, Will held steady.

For whole hours each day, he did not think of Elizabeth or of the baby. Then it would occur to him that he had forgotten his grief, and it would double back on him. In his solitude it did not occur to him that the crew did not seek his company, that he, like the captain, was held at an arm's length of suspended trust.

One, other than his uncle and the doctor, took pains to befriend him. This was Wearn, youngest of the three hydrographic surveyors aboard the ship. He fixed on Will as being of similar age and station, master of a skill that put him above the common sailor. Soon Will learned more than he cared to of sounding lines and channel depths. Gradually he came to value the whey-faced surveyor's gift for prattle. In its soothing dullness, it bore Will away from morbid thinking. In return, Will showed Wearn how to smack a biscuit on the side of the ship, dislodging its resident weevils. This trick he passed off as his own, although he had learned it from his uncle only days before.

At Cape Verde, the *Dido* left African shores for the open ocean. With nothing but water in all directions, and sky above, Will let himself fall into an automatic state. At night he might briefly be visited by the urge to sob, and, in dreams, Elizabeth once or twice came to him to remind him that she once had lived. But all in all, the spell the voyage was meant to have on him took hold. It blurred time for him as they reached South America, paralleling its coast from Brazil down south to the Horn. As they approached this place of fabled navigational peril, Edward, who as protocol demanded had been keeping company with his fellow warrant officers, resumed his presence in Will's daily routines. Lazy days would end when they hit the storms. Booms would bend and shatter. Masts could fall. Lynas was the ship's doctor, but the Dowlands, uncle and nephew, were doctors of the ship. On its health, the lives of all depended.

Yet the Horn, in its caprice, withheld all but the mildest of its assaults. The *Dido* sailed up South America's western coast after only three days of repair work.

After the ship turned at Peru into the open Pacific, a shift in mood intruded on Will's isolation. The tang of coming violence Will perceived at Portsmouth resurfaced. Throughout the voyage Codrington had conducted himself as any sailor could wish, neither cruelly punitive nor dangerously lax, yet the men regarded him with increasingly sullen apprehension. Crewmen whispered together, stopping when Will neared. He thought to go to his uncle, but needed greater grounds for it. As a warrant officer, Edward would be obliged to report the obscurest hint of mutiny.

Halfway between Peru and the islands, fever swept the ship. A third of the crew, the Dowlands luckily excluded, fell ill with it. Rumor spread that it was the plague; Dr. Lynas called all hands on deck to assure them otherwise. A landsman died and was buried at sea. The other victims were laid up for a week or so — except for Codrington, who could not shake it and remained abed, ceding command to the main master, a taciturn man named Tozey.

Lynas caught Will staring at the captain's closed cabin door and startled him by sneaking up behind him and breathing a rum fog into his ear: "Worried, young Dowland?"

Will made an awkward spectacle of himself, turning toward the surgeon even as he backed away. "Hoping the captain recovers, doctor."

"As am I, surely. It blots a surgeon's résumé, to lose his captain, no matter how arbitrarily."

"Could it be something in addition to the fever?"

"You're a medical man now, Dowland?"

Will couldn't understand why he was still talking, but he was. "Nothing was… for example, introduced into his food?"

"Are you asking me, young Dowland, if the captain has been poisoned?"

"Just a funny hunch. Maybe I have a touch of fever myself."

"I'll come round later to examine you," said Lynas, as Will slipped away.

About an hour later, his uncle came to him, features stony. "The doctor tells me you think Codrington has been poisoned."

"I have no cause to think that," Will stammered.

"That is good. Because he hasn't. Coincidentally. Simply lingering fever, nothing more. Which is as fine a sign that Providence smiles upon us as any I could foresee. For his sake, Will, hope he stays that way. For yours, wait and see. Soon you'll receive the gift I brought you all this way for. And then you'll understand. Until then, be smart and wait and watch."

◆

Two weeks later, Codrington died in his sleep. During the funeral, Will could tell that his uncle and the doctor were both studying his attitude. Recalling pale Elizabeth in her coffin, he wept. If they took that in some unkind way, he did not care.

Tozey, now ranked as captain, ordered a quick sail to a place he only called "the island." The others clearly knew what this meant. They sprang to action with a ferocious joy.

Three days after Codrington's sea burial, an atoll hove into view. Palm trees densely covered all but a crescent-shaped sliver of beach. Tozey issued orders to drop anchor, but these were superfluous, the men complying before he gave them. The crew clambered into the boats. Edward shouted for Will, who stepped quickly to his side, as affected as any by the excitement running through the crew. Edward directed him to join him, Lynas, and half of the other warrant officers. Then he handpicked a group of strong rowers to take the oars. After some confusion and bustle their boat was lowered into the water and they were off for the island.

"It's beautiful," Will said, stepping onto the shore. Warm, fragrant air blew through his hair.

Some men threw themselves into the shallow water around the island, splashing and hooting. Others set themselves firmly on land, jumping up and down on it, delighted by its solidity. Still more rushed into the stand of palms, pressing themselves up against the trees' smooth, green-barked trunks.

Scarlet fish, two hands long, teemed unsuspecting around the splashing men, who reached down to grab them up barehanded. Sailors produced baskets from the boats to hold the wildly flapping fish.

Midshipmen Enticott and Moore supervised the construction of a bonfire. Keech played on his flute; Rudge, on his drum.

Expectant gazes fell upon Dr. Lynas. He pointed to the sky. "We're here ahead of schedule. The moon has to be right."

"How far ahead of schedule?" demanded a black-bearded foretopman, who Will had never before heard speak.

Captain Tozey stepped up beside the doctor. "Two weeks or so. We made the cape faster than hoped."

A discontented mutter rumbled through the crew.

"The moon will reach the necessary phase sooner than that," Lynas said. "As long as it is waxing, we shall be set. So we can try in eight days."

"Should we cut them now?" The foretopman again.

Lynas shook his head, waving his hands for further emphasis. "No, no, no. Leave them for now. They have to be fresh. We cut them the day of."

Edward saw the question forming on Will's face. *The day of what?* Edward clapped his poor, sad nephew on the back. "You'll see soon enough."

The rest of the crew shared in the amusement. Over the next eight days they made a special point of smirking at him, reveling in his ignorance, and the change that would come when it was lifted from him. Every time he sought to wring from one of them the secret of this inexplicable stop in this isolated place, their amusement grew. As they poked at him with their elbows and made references that meant to mystify him even further, they treated Will with a previously absent camaraderie. He had never sought it, but now welcomed, in this hidden paradise, the pleasure of their fellowship. For the first time, they invited him to smoke with them, in the custom of friendship that united all English sailors.

"I wish it was my first time," he heard Keech say to Rudge, clearly about him. "Can't wait to see his expression."

The days passed in a sort of suspension, both elongated and without time. Again Will detached from his sorrows, now with bliss in place of numbed dullness. He swam. He ate fire-roasted fish till his stomach bloated. He drank deep from a heretofore unrevealed rum reserve. As never before, he broke free of his reserve, joining the men in the bawdy songs of his youth.

Will awoke one morning to a series of not-so-hesitant prods from a naked big toe. Wearn towered over him, grinning. "The doctor says it's time to start." Will tottered to the shore, discreetly relieved himself, then loped on bare feet to the doctor and his uncle, who stood at the treeline's edge. Edward patted the trunk of a palm, which they surveyed with admiration. "We picked a fine one for you."

Lynas crouched down to draw an invisible line with his finger, near the base of the trunk. "You must be careful to cut above the root line, but not too far. Make the cut as even as you can, all the way around."

"An even cut renders the pleasure all the more sublime." Edward handed him an axe.

"But why?" Will asked.

"You'll see," said Wearn.

"Do you know what this is?" Will asked him.

He nodded.

"The senior surveyors let it slip," Lynas tut-tutted. "You're the only one left to surprise."

"So I cut down the tree, and then what?" Will saw that the other men were ready to cut their own trees, one apiece. Each had an axe of his own.

"Every man must take his own tree," said Lynas. "Or that's how it was taught to me."

"What are you on about? Taught by who?"

"A native fellow, from the islands hereabouts, who we saved from his people. A sorcerer, they called him."

Trees began to fall. At Edward's urging, Will got to work. The wood's green softness made an even cut difficult, but as a capable carpenter he did better than most.

"Now," said Lynas, "you must with ever more perfect care cut the tree's hair." He led Will to the leafy top of his felled palm. "Pare away each frond as tightly as you can. For this, it is better to use a knife."

Will did as instructed, whittling down the stubs where the fronds radiated out from the treetop. Lynas produced a stone bowl, decorated by a circular pattern from which swirled a stem of snake-like forms. In the vessel a hot paste steamed, giving off a heady odor of sweat and rotting flowers.

"You paint this on the cuts, both at the base and at the top. Thickly, as you would applying a healing salve."

"Never have I been party to such an elaborate jape," said Will.

"Do it," said Edward, and he did.

"Now take one of the fronds to the fire and set it alight. Then bring it back here," the doctor said.

When he had done so, Lynas directed Will to set the paste alight. A choking black smoke arose from the gluey spots where the cuts had been made. The flame consumed the paste but not the wood. "Like cauterizing a wound," said Lynas. "Now, the step on which all else turns. Do this well, and you'll thank yourself for it. Using the knife, bore one hole about this wide…" With thumb and forefinger, he made a circle just under the diameter of a crown coin. "About six to seven inches deep, let's say. But be careful not to drill all the way through, because after you're done, you'll turn the trunk over and do the same on the other side."

Will flushed and threw down the knife. It landed point first in the sand. "This *is* a joke. And a filthy one, at that."

The doctor uncorked a rum bottle, took a swig, and wiped his mouth. "It's anything but, dear boy. So you'll do it, and do it right."

"That's what they're all so excited about? Knocking down trees and carving them into dirty statues?"

Edward pulled him aside. "Will, you have trusted me this far. Humor me for just a few hours, and do as the doctor asks."

Will crossed his arms. "All of you have entered into a conspiracy against my dignity."

Edward pointed to the rest of the crew, knives already boring into their tree trunks. "You think I could impel all of those layabouts, and the officers and captain too, to such extraordinary lengths, merely to play a prank on you? What effort does it cost you to play along? A little carving? And who do you think these old tars are, that any immodesty on your part could possibly strike them as worthy of a second glance?"

"Explain your purpose, uncle, and I'll gladly obey."

Edward moved closer to him. "They've only now come to like you, boy. Show some fellowship. Or you'll learn what it's like to be confined to a ship for month upon month with forty nail-hard men who think you a prig and have little to occupy their idle time."

The hot sensation in Will's neck and cheeks had only intensified. "Pretend to be amused by this then?"

"Put on whatever show you like but do as the doctor says. Or you'll force me to turn my back on you."

Will knelt and began to carve. The wood gave way easily to his blade.

"At more of an angle," said the doctor.

When Will had finished with the two holes, Edward leaned down to inspect his work. "We are all men here," he said. What this statement explained, Will did not deign to ask. Edward's shrug suggested that Will's work, if not his best, would prove sufficient. "Now lie down next to it," Edward said.

Will began to compose an objection, but saw that others of the men were already doing so — embracing their trees from a prone position.

"It is for purposes of measurement," Edward said. He turned to Wearn. "You'd best start on yours, boy." Bobbling his head in compliance, Wearn bounded off. "I also do not have all day to supervise you, Will."

Suppressing a sigh, Will laid alongside the tree trunk. With the tip of his own axe, Edward cut a mark into the bark, at about the level of Will's mouth.

"Now cut another hole here," Edward instructed.

This too Will did, at which point Edward and Dr. Lynas went off toward other trees.

"What now?" Will called after them.

"Patience, boy," Edward replied.

As the sun fell, turning the western sky a golden orange, the doctor called for the men to drag their trunks together onto the beach. They arranged them in a circular pattern, with the top ends pointing inward around the fire. Lynas had doffed all clothing save for his breeches, which he had retied into a loincloth arrangement, and also his hat. In other circumstances, Will might have considered the result comical.

The men heaped the bonfire with the slats of empty barrels. Burrows, the surgeon's mate, stripped as Lynas was, held a squirming burlap bag. He reached in, hand trembling, and snatched out a rat — undoubtedly taken from the ship. It reared and flailed, trying to bite him. Burrows stabbed it with his pocket blade. When it had completed its death throes, he slit the creature's throat and handed it to Lynas, who let the blood dribble onto his back, his shoulders, and down his torso. The doctor flung the dead rat aside; Enticott kicked its body into the sea.

Lynas threw back his head and cried up to the new moon. He spoke in a lilting tongue Will did not recognize, its rhythm, however hoarse and shouted, recalling the lapping of the waves. The others stared up at the moon along with him. Across its bright surface a dark shape briefly pulsed. The men hollered and clapped. Lynas silenced them with a snap of his fingers and continued his invocation. Only when he reached a note of crescendo did he step back, bow his head, and signal to the crew that they could now disperse.

The men pulled their felled trees from the circle, dragging them to various points throughout the isle. They reassembled for more drinking and singing, accompanied by Keech's flute, and sometimes Rudge's drum.

Gradually each stumbled away to lie beside his tree.

Will, who had left his tree by the fire, remained busy of mind and fell asleep on the shore only as dawn glimmered in the east.

By the time he woke noon had nearly arrived. A quiet had settled on the men. Even those who were catching fish did so with a settled determination, the only sound they made the plashing of water as they waded through it.

Will wished to unburden himself. Thinking better of approaching either Lynas or his uncle, he found Wearn, still sprawled beside his tree.

"The surgeon has called the devil down on us," Will said.

Wearn smacked the glue of sleep from his lips. "What are you blurting at me, Dowland?"

Will crouched over him, "What would you call that, last night, but the worship of Satan?"

Wearn sat up, forcing Will to inch back. "It's nothing of the kind. The doctor explained it all to me."

"Blood sacrifice?"

Wearn waved dismissively. "Of a rat? We're up to our neck in them."

"Chanting in an indecipherable tongue?"

Wearn eased himself to his feet. "It's the native tongue, from around here." He ambled for the shore, Will dogging his heels. "Nothing to do with the devil. Ask the doctor, he can explain it better than I. Out here, the laws of God and Satan don't apply, as they would on Christian shores. Here we are ruled by moon and sky and water. All Lynas did was ask a gift of the moon." Wearn reached the water's edge, dropped his drawers, and loosed a healthy stream of piss. "I look forward to collecting that gift. Let yourself enjoy this, this… period of exemption. Who deserves that more than you? Your sorrows will still be waiting for you on the pier at Portsmouth."

As he stalked away from Wearn, Will thought he saw twin whorls forming over the slitted mouth carved into Burrows' tree trunk.

Will found a place of privacy at the island's northern tip, a jut of unstable sand surrounded by placid water. He went back to the fire only to cook his fish. The men hewed to their new silence. If they took note of his worried demeanor, they did not see fit to approach him about it.

That night, Will considered sleeping on the sand jut, but abandoned the idea for fear of rolling off it into the sea. For want of a more favorable spot, he wandered back to sleep beside his crude joke of a native idol.

He jolted awake while it was still dark. Low grunts and exclamations sounded all around him. His vision adjusted to the faint light cast by the coals of the dying fire. All around him the sailors of the *Dido* had mounted their fallen trees. They thrusted into the holes they had carved, bared arses convulsing in the tropical air. Will blinked, thinking himself dreaming, but this did not dismiss what he saw and heard. He flattened himself into the sandy soil and tried to ignore the obscene exclamations.

When morning finally arrived, he headed for the sand spit, where he intended to pray. Strewn in his path lay snoring men, trousers at their ankles, wrapped around the tree trunk idols.

These had changed in the night.

The idols had ill-formed faces now: round swirls for eyes, slight protrusions of the bark where noses ought to be. Raised, bumpy lips surrounded the mouth slits. Further down a pair of nipples manifested itself at approximate breast height. The shapes of the trunks themselves had altered, narrowing to form a waist then swelling again into a pair of hips around their carven cunnies.

Will turned back to look at his own trunk. It too had undergone the changes, though to lesser extent. The eyes had only begun to take definite shape. The nipples were but dots, the widening of the hips barely detectable.

Will lurched for the nearest axe. Raising it above his head, he rushed for his idol. A powerful force intersected with his jaw. He went flying onto the sand, landing on his tailbone. The axe lay a yard from his landing point. It was the black-bearded foretopman who had laid him low, and stood over him, ready to pummel him further.

"Fool!"

Edward and Wearn ran to intervene. The foretopman held off. Not wanting to provoke him, Will stayed down. His jaw throbbed; never in his life had he been hit that hard. This man could beat him to death with a few well-placed blows.

"We'll see he doesn't distress them," Edward told the foretopman.

"I'll not give him no second chance," the tar growled, moving away.

Wearn pulled Will to his feet. Edward jabbed him in the chest. "Take this blessing or leave it alone, but do no harm to your woman."

"Woman?" Will managed.

"The magic links them. When harm is visited on one, the others become distressed, and lose receptivity."

"Receptivity?"

"Don't ask any more questions," Edward said. "Fit in."

Will looked past his uncle to see that the entire crew had gathered to observe them. He could not mistake their presence for anything other than a threat. "I am sorry," he said. "I didn't expect this. If I understood more…"

Edward raised his voice for all to hear. "You're not to harm your woman, and especially not the property of any other man in this crew. Your lapse was borne of sudden shock, and will not be repeated. Correct?"

"Yes sir," answered Will, also projecting his words.

The group of men broke up, but, underlining the point, the foretopman and three others remained in threatening conference. Glances shot his way communicated what would happen if Edward failed to control him.

"I misjudged you," said Edward. "I did not think you the sort to recoil when presented with man's earthly heaven."

This island was rather the opposite of heaven, Will thought, but did not say.

"I never loved a woman as you did Elizabeth," said Edward, "I admit to finding greater peace among whores than in the sitting rooms of respectable ladies. Always have done. So seeing you so dreadfully pained, I put myself in your position and asked what I would want. I reckoned you would see the magic of this place as I did. No whore is as pliant and yielding as these girls here. Now it is plain: I could not have been more mistaken. I am not asking you to forgive me, because I meant well. Many a shit deed is performed with good intention. I beg you, though, don't let my mistake lead to the shedding of your blood. That I couldn't bear. Take your gift or leave it alone, but don't interfere."

"I promise," Will said.

With the so-called women to consort with, the sailors no longer drank quite so much rum. Nor did they keep so careful a note of each man's share. Will could thus sneak more than was his due, and keep himself soused throughout the day. This retreat into drunkenness, as far as he could tell, dulled the concerns of his watchers.

By the afternoon some of the ordinary sailors allowed themselves to copulate with their idols in the day's full light. Some concentrated purposefully on a single hole, while others athletically made the rounds. Will saw that the others had a way of looking through them when they did this — a privacy based entirely on pretense. Aping their discretion, he sank down next to his tree and hoped that sleep would take him early.

On the next day, his idol had transformed by degrees. Its face had gained detail; its outline had shifted further toward the feminine. Those belonging to the other men, who had been so assiduously fucking their tree trunks, displayed pronounced alterations. Wood and bark had fallen away from their faces, giving them dimensioned features. With blank, staring eyes they beheld the heavens. Their mouths opened and gaped. The beginnings of hands appeared at the sides of the trunks. Lines of separation, suggesting legs, ran down from their clefts of Venus.

Will went straight to the rum barrel.

The foretopman lay nearby, his member hanging limp from his unbuttoned trousers, his arm wrapped around his tree's plump wooden breasts.

"Get too drunk and you can't perform," he said. "Don't want to disappoint her."

Will lifted the barrel lid to skim its contents into his tin mug. "I have forgot your name."

"Veasey."

"Well, Mr. Veasey, do you care what I do or don't do with that thing, if I don't get in your or anyone's way?"

Veasey patted his idol. "Lucy don't like to be called a thing."

Will, afraid he would make a face at this, drank from the mug. "Lucy, is she?"

"It's more like loving if you give 'er a name." It might have been a trick of the light, but it seemed Lucy's face shifted from one unreadable look to another.

"I will consider that, Mr. Veasey," Will said, tottering.

Despite himself, he overheard enough to learn the names of other men's trees. Wearn called his Marie; his uncle, Charlotte. The doctor's was Rachel, which Will gathered was the same name he had given his idol the last time the crew of the *Dido* anchored on the island. That gave rise to other questions, which he both did and did not want the answers to. He drank more.

Three more nights passed, and three more days, in which the trees steadily took on more of the outward aspects of women. They might have been easier to take if their expressions showed any softness or accommodation. Instead they retained their original blind, gaping stares.

"How can you do it?" he asked Wearn.

Wearn laughed, as if they discussed nothing more than a preference for sherry over ale. "How can you not?"

"This is madness."

"You haven't tried yours yet, have you?"

"Of course not!"

"Try her, you'll understand. Never with a woman back home will you feel such perfect ecstasy."

"How can that possibly be?"

Wearn caressed the trunk of his idol, which they sat by. "Your wood girl, she exists because of you. And for you. Only for you. You feel that when you're, you know, inside of her. Her each and every movement, it is exactly right for you, at the moment she does it, so fine and so exquisite."

"They move?"

"Yes, they move, you dolt. That's why until you have her, you cannot understand."

Will studied Wearn's statue, wondering if it could tell what they were saying. "How can you, Wearn? Such grotesque visages!"

Wearn regarded his tree nervously. "Sssh. Don't say that."

"See? You're afraid of them. They're not girls. Not women. They're monsters. They're waiting until our… activities have completely transformed them, given them enough shape to get up and walk about the island. And then slaughter us."

Wearn clamped a hand over Will's mouth. "If you say that again around Marie, I'll have to do you as Veasey did."

Late that night, as the men on either side of him pumped into their wooden girls, Will heard a soft voice in his head.

Why haven't you named me?

He hit himself on the back of his head, to stir himself from the nightmare.

The voice kept on: *My sisters all have names.*

Shut up, he thought.

What have I done to offend you?

I'm going mad.

What about Elizabeth? You could call me Elizabeth.

There was a rock in his hand, ready to smash its face, before he remembered the danger of such an act and let it drop into the sand.

Please love me so I can be like my sisters.

He ran to the shoreline and dunked his head in the water. When he came back, his tree's face had gained delineation. Or it was his mind tricking him. With hardly any light, it was free to invent.

I won't call you Elizabeth, he thought at it. To stop you from calling yourself that, I'll dub you Nancy.

He heard nothing more from the voice, so he immediately marked it as a drunken hallucination.

In the morning he awoke naked from the waist down. Milky issue spilled across the idol's hips. Shame came over him like a nausea. He wobbled to the shoreline to throw up, but couldn't, even after sticking his finger down his throat.

He had, after all his resistance, done the terrible deed. He'd been drunk and perhaps acting in his sleep but it didn't matter. The same crime the others had committed was now his, too. He imagined himself with a pistol at his temple, pulling the trigger. "I'm so sorry, Elizabeth," he said. Then he recalled his nakedness and rushed to put his trousers on.

The next night he lay next to Nancy, heart thumping. He had already done it. He could not now be further damned. He should at least then understand what he had done to himself. He waited until the sailors around him fell quiet and silently climbed onto his idol. He would not redouble his sin by using the mouth or arse.

As soon as he entered her, a jolt coursed through him. He came without stopping. He tried not to cry out, but it was useless to suppress it.

He pulsed until he ached. An unthinking peace washed through him. He would not let it take him, as it was a falsehood, and he, a weakling and a coward, whose promises to himself held neither substance nor value. He rolled off of Nancy and soundlessly wept.

♦

The bosun's mate clanged a bell. He shouted for the men to rouse themselves and ready for departure. They had already overstayed. Any longer and the bad weather would start. It was time to say goodbyes.

Veasey, among others, shouted in protest. The doctor settled them down. If they made trouble now, they wouldn't be allowed back the next time.

The men took their idols and again dragged them to the beach. Numbly, unnoticed tears wetting his cheeks, Will followed suit. Not until the torches came out did he apprehend what saying goodbye entailed.

"Now form a tight circle," Dr. Lynas, himself a touch weepy, declared. "This is where it went bad, the last time."

"What are we doing?" Will heard himself asking.

Veasey stood beside him. "You can't want your Nan to die slow and painful."

"Nan? How do you know that?"

"They talk to each other," he said. "Now show some respect." He tossed Lucy into the central pile of tree trunks. Cracks had appeared in her drying bark.

Edward put his hand on Will's shoulder. "Steady now."

"How can we do this?"

"What do you mean?" his uncle asked.

"We've been calling them women. And now we're... we're to do this?"

Unlike many of the others Edward maintained a stolid composure. "They're not women. They're trees."

Veasey gestured to Will's trunk. "Want me to?"

Will couldn't answer, which Veasey took as a request for help. He easily lifted the idol and threw it onto the growing pile.

The last of the trees to join the pyre was Wearn's. Sobs wracked him; snot trickled from his nostrils into his mouth.

This time there was no ritual. "Thank you, girls," Lynas said. He threw the first torch onto the pyre of carven trunks.

The idols screamed. Before, Will had heard only whispers in his mind. This though was a real sound, keening and angry. With a whoosh flames enveloped the stacked trunks. Their shrieks reached a crescendo. Most of the idols burnt where they were. But in a handful of instances, wooden arms and legs cracked forth to separate themselves from the wooden trunks. These trees, perhaps the most loved, crawled toward the circle of men, waving flaming appendages. Veasey and others stepped up with axes, chopping them apart. Will did not see a man who wasn't yelling or wailing. Even his uncle had dropped to his knees and cried out some unintelligible apology.

Yellow flames wreathed Will's idol, Nancy. Her mouth worked up and down as she howled to him for rescue. He stood paralyzed, watching as she burned. Her trunk toppled from the rest and rolled toward the water. Now Will regained his volition and ran to her. He picked up the log, searing the skin of his hands. Vaguely aware of a chorus of shouts, he cried out her name. His fingers blackened. "Nancy," he said, and hurled her back into the fire. "I couldn't help it. I couldn't help it."

Lynas pulled him from the circle to treat his hands. His rashness would cost him a month in bandages.

When all of the logs had been reduced to ashes and charcoal, the group turned for the boats. Dazed, Will followed his uncle.

"They weren't persons," Edward said, not to Will but to himself. "Not persons."

The rest of the voyage gave Will ample time to imagine punishments for what they had done, all of them imminent. In every creak of the ship, he heard the coming vengeance of the wood spirits. Or whatever those beings were. At any moment the *Dido* might come to life and choose to shake itself apart. Or merely steer itself for a shoal, so that all would drown at sea.

North of Australia, his stomach began to bother him, and he understood that the girls had all placed seeds inside each of them. When they finished germinating, they would burst forth in a shower of viscera and torn flesh, the bodies of the transgressing men their food and soil. From their too-deserving carcasses, a breed of bark-clad demon would emerge.

Then his gut ailment cleared up.

Whenever the surveyors left the ship for shore, Will feared that they would not return. The women, migrated into fresh wooden bodies, would be there as ambushing sirens, ready to kill as they had been killed.

Twenty-three months after its original departure, the *Dido* docked safely in Portsmouth. Unusually for such a lengthy voyage, only two who left did not come back — both taken by fever long before the island and the sins performed there.

Will now realized that the wood nymphs had waited till they reached England. The crew would go their separate ways, and then, one night, a letter would arrive telling him that Dr. Lynas had died coughing up leaves, or been found as a patch of viscera in a forest, surrounded by fresh roots. He would contact Wearn, but he would be dead too, and race to find Edward, only to arrive too late. It would start happening at the next new moon. Equally likely, the terror would come for them years later, a decade hence or even more. All that was certain was that the men of the *Dido* had cursed themselves on that nameless isle, and that a price would sooner or later be exacted from them.

But none of that ever happened.

Food from the Clouds

Molly Tanzer

"[M]uch of the choicest weird work is unconscious; appearing in memorable fragments scattered through material whose massed effect may be of a very different cast," *wrote H.P. Lovecraft in his essay "Supernatural Horror in Literature." How true; after all, when I think of times I've been creeped out while reading, Christopher Priest's The Prestige comes to mind. What so frightened me was a scene absent from the film version, where one of the narrators recollects an encounter with a curious and horrible machine one dark night. Priest's transmission of the sense of remembered fear experienced by a child was superb, and extremely affecting, especially being so unexpectedly located in a science fantasy novel about rival stage magicians feuding.*

Similarly, I was also unsettled by something I ran across while reading the introduction to Richard Jefferies's two most famous sentimental pastoral works, The Gamekeeper at Home / The Amateur Poacher, *though the quote in question was from another piece of his nature writing, "My Old Village":*

"No one seems to understand how I got food from the clouds, nor what there was in the night, nor why it is not so good to look at it from out of the window. They turn their faces away from me... perhaps after all I was mistaken, and there never was any such place... and I was never there."

For Jefferies, the above terror was over the prospect of being the only man alive who truly appreciated the natural world. Even so, I think his remarks resonate as easily in that context as in that of any number of "Lovecraftian" narrators — and is perhaps all the uncannier for being a dark moment of dread evoked while perusing a nature lover's remarks on beechnuts and duck hunting...

I never used ferrets until I teamed up with Burderop. Always preferred the snare. When you use a snare, it's all on you. If you misjudge the width of your loop, or set the wire at the wrong height, it's your fault — yours alone. If you don't come home with something for the pot, if those what rely on you are left wanting... carrying that burden by yourself, it makes you strong.

With a ferret, finicky things, the blame for an empty sack can just as easily lie with them. They're not obedient like a dog; in fact, they're more particular than a cat, and without that feline charm that makes you willing to forgive their quirks. Not being pets, really, it's hard to justify keeping ferrets without tipping your neighbors or landlord to what you do in your hours off — and then there's the process of getting them to a likely spot for a night's taking. Stuffing what are essentially half-domesticated weasels into a sack has never been my idea of fun. And while Burderop never minded muzzling them, I found the process of looping twine around their fangs and knotting it behind their ears completely terrifying. I always ended up bitten and scratched, and somehow worrying *I'd* hurt *them*.

But once I'd decided to throw in my lot with Burderop, well, I was already putting my faith in another, wasn't I? Ferrets seemed like the last thing I should be worried about when I considered everything that could possibly go wrong during the shift from self-reliant entrepreneur to being half of a pair. And wouldn't you know, that ended up being the case — though to be fair, what happened… it wasn't her fault.

◆

Before our alliance, Burderop stuck mainly to the ruins of Southwark and the Borough, where the silt washed up by the Thames during the flooding from the comet's impact all those decades back had helped the trees grow tall and the thick grasses thrive. Those areas by right belonged to the governor of the Old City, but were so diverse, and so overtaken with the kind of wilderness beloved of leveret, culver, and hedgehog, that a legion of game wardens could hardly have kept it secure. Not being a sportsman, the governor employed two.

Burderop made a fine living selling easily caught game, creatures that lived their lives in peace before they saw the shining red eyes; felt fangs at their neck. Totally respectable. But as for me… I don't know. There's nothing wrong with a bit of rabbit. It wasn't that. And it wasn't that I was braver. Stupider, maybe. I liked to poach the game what belonged to the families who were wealthy enough to still own private land, but couldn't afford the move to New London. Something about helping myself to whatever was being stocked in the sprawling estates built around the once-public green spaces gave me a thrill. But it wasn't all about brashness. If you knew where to go — and were good at not getting caught — you used to be able to trap practically anything nice to eat inside the Old City. Pheasant, hare, partridge, and peacock thrived alongside all the pigeons and rats. And why shouldn't they, being cared for more thoughtfully than most people?

Anyways. It was late November or early December. Cold, nasty, wet, windy, utterly miserable, of course. By then, Burderop and I had been poaching together for… on to ten months, I think, and even with having to handle ferrets, I was enjoying myself. Enjoying how lucrative our partnership had proven, is what I mean. We'd had different beats, as I said, so combining our understanding of what was to be had, and where, and when, vastly increased our take. That spring we'd gathered more eggs than we could sell or easily eat ourselves, which meant pickled eggs, a rare treat. In the summer, we delighted our clientele with young rabbit and all kinds of fish — proper fish, not the scary ones like what come out of the Thames; in the fall, acorn-fed partridge and fat squirrel. I swear, the faces of our district's public-house regulars looked plumper from the good meals they were getting. They looked… *happier*. Not having rat 'n' neeps for your Sunday roast does that for a body. Warmed the heart, like doing charity work. Well, charity work that lines your pockets in the process. So, better, even.

I looked happier too, I saw, when I came across the odd mirror. I'd lost a bit of the pinched, nervous look one acquires, being alone in the world. Having Burderop around to give me a boost over a wall; a second set of eyes and ears for spotting trouble — it was lovely. More than that, Burderop was fine company, and not hard to look at. I don't know where she found that country squire's tailcoat, but she looked well in it, with her hair cropped short as a boy's, the mismatched Doc Martens, and those tight pants with the subtle clingy stretchiness to them that you can't find anymore. Those pants… it's not just that I liked to look. They were clever. A decoy. Even with my wealth of experience with moochers, when I heard from a friend that Burderop and I shared "a mutual interest in the natural world," I said I couldn't believe it. You couldn't hide a thing in those trousers of hers.

Turns out she'd sewed pockets into the lining of her coat. An old-fashioned trick, but it worked great.

You really never can tell, can you? After all, when I knew her well enough to relate the story, she laughed and said she'd felt the same about me—save that for her, it had been the assumption I wore far too much tailored tweed to get up to anything illicit.

"Shows what you know," I'd replied. We were roasting pigeon wings in the nave of some ruined cathedral to pass the time during a sudden downpour. "It's the tweedy ones you have to watch out for. The only point to cultivating a proper appearance is deflecting suspicion of villainy."

Idyllic, I know. Two young scamps with vim and wit in equal measure, dedicated to the same purpose! We were great. We were better than great. We were *unstoppable*. The Robin Hood and Little John of poaching. The Burke and Hare of, well, hares. The Plunkett and MacLaine of mooching.

It couldn't last.

I'd picked my favorite beats due to their tricksiness, you see, so, after multiple nearly perfect raids on the urban estates of the Old City's elite, things, well, they got to feeling too easy. Together, me and Burderop robbed the best game from within St. Pancras, where the Earl of Somers Town employed an unknown number of reputedly ruthless groundskeepers to protect what was his; stolen what we wanted from sprawling, unkempt Ranelagh Gardens, where Lady Walters hosted dinner parties in the ruins of the old Royal Hospital, the highlight of which were allegedly her cook's famous Fricassee of Poacher. We'd taken from Russell Square Wilds while lights blazed in the Museum Palace, and from the Wreckage of Lincoln's Inn, close to where the Royal Courts of Justice would try rascals like us, had we been caught.

And as if we hadn't already enough feathers in our caps (and in our pockets), we staged a coup, hitting Holland Park and Ladbroke Square in one night, despite it being known that Sir Mark of Newton had trespassers brought before him so he could shoot them himself. Our bravery was rewarded: I came away with pockets full of mushrooms, three ducks, and a goose; Jeffries with a hare in each tail of her tailcoat, as well as what we surmised was an escaped chicken shoved down the front of her shirt. And her sack full of ferrets, sated on blood and sleeping nicely. Yet, as we ambled our way down Hornton to the High Street station (the District line was still working back then), I felt the familiar itch. I was restless. Dissatisfied. *Bored*.

I needed something more. Some hint of the former danger.

And it wasn't like I didn't know what I wanted… I just couldn't see a way to mention it. Not without starting a row.

"What?" asked Burderop. I flinched. I'd been thinking too hard. She could always tell when I was thinking. "Surely you're not disappointed?"

"Hardly," I replied, trying to sound jolly.

"Then what?"

I shrugged. Carefully. Lots to balance.

"Out with it, Bottleton." A quick sidelong glance at her face, all shadowed and sickly under the green light cast by comet-shards stuck into what had been gas lamps showed that she was not going to let me off with a shrug.

I chose my words carefully, so as not to give offense.

"Working with you has made this almost too easy," I said, lightly I hoped. "Where's the fun in life without a challenge?"

She sucked her teeth. "Pure privilege, that's what that is."

"Eh?"

"Eating's not "fun" when you eat well all the time, maybe. Try subsisting for a few weeks on what you can scare up at the markets. *Then* tell me if easy takings are boring."

I'd bungled it from the start, as usual. Now she looked sour as those little apples we'd gleaned from some nobleman's orchard a month or so back.

"I didn't mean —"

"Then say what you mean."

"Fine." I inhaled deeply. "Look. We've properly sacked this city, haven't we? Sacked it like… Crusaders. Turks. Whatever you like."

"Yeah?"

"Every spot worth beating, we've beaten."

"I know one we've missed."

My spirits rose until she slapped me on the back of the head. Hard.

"Hey!"

"What? It's a spot worth beating."

Molly Tanzer

"You're very clever." I couldn't rub where it throbbed due to being so laden down. "All right. Fine. There were *two* unbeaten sites worth a beating in this city. Now there's one."

I took a few steps before I realized she wasn't beside me. Turning, I saw her, hands on hips, sack of ferrets gently banging against one thigh.

"Where," she said.

I swallowed. Decided to go for it.

"There's one place we haven't been, and you know it."

Realization dawned. I could tell, because she looked like she was about to hit me a second time.

"You're a fool," she said. "There's no way. No one's been in there since they walled it in. We'd know!"

"Come on," I urged. "Let's hit Hyde Park."

She opened her mouth to speak. I couldn't tell what she was about to say, and, before she could say it, we heard the distant rumble of an automobile. We'd already tarried too long in an unsafe place, with far too much contraband on our persons should we be rumbled, so we left the matter unsettled. Burderop tugged on the brim of the tweed flat cap she always wore and scurried off into the night. I made haste to our former goal, the Kensington tube stop, alone, as was our usual method when some trouble seemed likely.

My heart was beating with the exhilaration I so missed as I fled down the steps, tipped the gatekeeper before jumping the jammed turnstile, and slid down the balustrade to the right platform. I knew I had to hit Hyde Park or die of longing. I can't explain it except… well, it felt like when you've a serious letch for someone. You can fuck around as much as you like and still feel unsatisfied. And I knew that, unlike the times I'd felt like that — all right, I admit it, like with Burderop — I couldn't just wait this one out.

♦

Turned out I needn't have worried. Once she realized the depth of my determination, she agreed to come along. Grudgingly.

Made me wonder how things might have gone had I been brave enough to bring up the other… though that's not the kind of thing one wants to experience grudgingly. Anyways, I got an earful of how this adventure was the stupidest idea in the universe, but I was used to getting an earful from her by then, and was too excited about getting my way to really listen.

I can't remember when they walled in Hyde Park, just that it'd been done long ago at the behest of its owner. Except that unlike nearly every other estate, which had signs warning about trespassing and family crests plastered all over the place, no one knew who owned Hyde Park.

And it wasn't just what had been Hyde Park proper, I should say — the wall encircled a huge area in the center of the city, stretching from the former edge of Kensington Gardens nearly to the Thames, narrowing like a wasp's waist at Duke of Wellington Place to expand around St. James's and the Green Park. We just called it Hyde Park for the ease of it.

It was the single largest private space in the Old City, as well as being the best fortified. And yet, despite this obvious challenge to rogues and mischief makers, I'd never met a soul who'd been inside… or even tried to get in there. Maybe it was the height of the razor wire–topped walls. Or maybe it was the sheer volume of creepy stories about the place. Haunted, *infested*, that sort of thing. Personally, I suspected it was nothing more than the richest hunting (or poaching) in the city, but I'd heard everything from it being a den of cannibal cultists, mutated from eating comet-dust, to a portal to another world.

Burderop told me yet another rumor as we crept through the moonlit streets around to what had been Hyde Park Corner, the just-visible ruin of the Apsley House looking like some nobleman's folly beyond the wall, jutting out perpendicularly from the western corner of the great gate. She said she'd heard a huge chunk of the comet had splintered off during the impact and landed in the center of the Serpentine. The king was keeping it hidden just in case some international tribunal ever successfully challenged

England's exclusive mining contract over what had become the world's only decent source of renewable energy.

As she spoke, I eyed the fortifications. I'd picked this as "the spot" for a few reasons. First and foremost, there were very few streetlamps. Additionally, Piccadilly had been blocked off by the new wall, and Knightsbridge largely destroyed by overgrown tree roots pushing up through the asphalt and between paving stones. It would be impossible for anyone to come speeding along in a coach and see us up to no good. Also, I'd spied an overhanging tree branch poking through the barbed wire atop Apsley Gate that looked a likely aide in getting across — oh, and the barbed wire wasn't concertina-style, as it was along some portions. Like everything else built in the Old City since the impact, the wall had been thrown together with whatever was around at the time, and with a minimalist approach to resources.

"Well," I said, "if we find some big chunk of the green stuff, let's see if we can chip off some. Bet it'd sell even better than pheasant on the black market."

"Cross that bridge when we get to it," said Burderop, giving me an exasperated look as a gust of wind kicked up, nearly blowing my trilby off and away forever. "You know what your problem is, Sam Bottleton? You want everything."

I considered this. She was right, but I didn't feel like admitting it.

"Mm," I said. "Ready?"

"No," she said, heaving herself up onto the stylobate. "But let's go ahead anyway."

I had with me the scrap of Turkish carpet I always used to get over barbed wire, rolled into a tight cylinder and tied in such a fashion that I could sling the rope across my chest, bandolier-style. After checking to make sure it wouldn't come undone, I stepped into Burderop's cupped hands. Being the larger and stronger of us, she gave me a powerful boost that sent me close to flying. I scraped my cheek before I found my grip more than halfway up the stones that had been mortared between the columns of the gate, but I didn't complain. Such inconveniences are all a part of the business. Digging my gloved fingers in between the cracks, I pulled myself higher, grateful for the layers of tweed between myself and the freezing wall.

"Hurry up!" I heard her hiss. I gritted my teeth, biting back a retort, instead channeling my effort into getting my foot secured on the lip of the architrave. That gave me enough leverage to scramble atop the cornice, and extending my reach high enough to grab that branch. Only a few feet of it hung over the razor wire — I had to be careful; completely sure of my next move. I'd seen a friend die of lockjaw, and had no wish to go that way.

One-handed, I unslung my rug and threw it over the wire to protect myself from the barbs. Once the carpet was in place, I could lean against it, using the tension to half sit and swing my legs over the top. Nimble-footing it sideways, I got close enough to edge along the bough so I could shimmy down the trunk of the tree whose branch had been such a help, then jumped the rest of the way.

Beyond checking that I wasn't about to come down in a lake or through the roof of a gamekeeper's cottage — or a cannibal cultist's shack, I suppose — I hadn't really scoped my surroundings. Haste had been paramount. A quick look around showed me I'd landed in a pretty typical park. Nothing spooky or abject — just a dark, quiet wood. So I looped a long length of rope around the base of the linden and threw it back over the wall for Burderop. Moments later, I saw her pulling herself overhand up and over the carpet, bag of ferrets on her back like I'd worn my rolled-up rug. Freeing the rug, she tossed it down before dropping beside where I stood at the base of the tree.

"All right," she whispered, eyes darting around every which way. "What's the plan?"

"To our right are the former Apsley House gardens," I whispered back. "According to my map, if we head left, there should be the remains of paths that will take us to the Serpentine. A long lake," I clarified, when Burderop looked mystified by this. "I say we just…

255

Molly Tanzer

take a tour. See what's to be seen, right? If we come upon a run, we'll set snares — or let your ferrets do their thing — but this place is supposed to be *huge*. We might want to just explore first."

Burderop grumbled something about a waste of a night, but I ignored her. The danger, the uncertainty, it was making me feel alive again. Like Eve exploring the Garden of Eden once she knew there was a tree of knowledge hidden somewhere. I glanced up, and every leaf looked like a yawning black hole in space, the moonlight bending around them impossibly. It made me feel wild, free. I had to see more — felt an irresistible compulsion to see it all. Pushing heedlessly through the brush, I came upon the broken remains of a road, and on the other side of it lay yet denser woodland.

"Let's go," I whispered, mostly to myself, and made a break for it. The heels of my brogues fell like hammers on the shattered asphalt; I could hear Burderop panting behind me. I realized the strange sense of exhilaration I was experiencing was doing things to my senses, judgment not excepted. Still, I pressed on, winding between oaks and slipping in amongst low bushes, until I came to a circular clearing bordered by four overgrown stands of bare, thorny rosebushes, with a fountain, dry now, of a fish and a sea nymph posing together in the center. There remained some rotted-out benches for admiring the scenery. Inspired, I jumped up on the lip of the fountain and imitated the nymph's pose, one hand behind my head, the opposite hip cocked out.

"Are you insane?" Burderop hissed at me, pulling at the hem of my trousers. "Get down, *now*. Someone might see us! Might have seen us already!"

She had a point. But the more I saw of it, Hyde Park looked so unkempt as to cast doubt on the rumor that it was an immaculately curated hunting ground. I almost said as much, but caught myself in time. I knew mentioning my observation would almost certainly have Burderop clamoring to leave immediately — she so hated to come home empty-handed. She was close to putting her foot down already, I could tell.

"The map said if we carry on this way…"

"Damn your map!"

"Steady on," I said. "Let's —"

"This is stupid! Haven't you noticed?"

I hopped down off the pedestal. "Noticed what?"

"Are you daft?" She shuddered. "It feels dead in here!"

"Eh?"

"I dunno!" She looked up and around where we stood, up at the leaves and then back to me. She was afraid of something, I realized. I'd never known Burderop to be afraid of anything. But something had spooked her good and proper. "It's a… *dead…* place," she said. "Not like, where the dead are buried. Animals live in graveyards, and the trees feel… alive."

I put my hands on my hips and shook my head at her. "Trees feel alive, do they?"

"Shut up! Just listen!"

I stood very still and listened. Beyond the pounding of my heart and the squirming ferrets rubbing against the burlap of Burderop's sack, I couldn't hear anything strange. Then I realized it wasn't that I couldn't hear anything — there was nothing to be heard. That was admittedly queer. It had been quite a windy night when we approached Hyde Park, but now we were inside the walls it was deeply, perfectly still. Not even the leaves at the very tops of the trees were rustling.

"Let's go in deeper," I advised, more madly curious than ever.

"I don't know. This place…"

"Come on," I urged. "Just a bit further. If we don't see anything soon, we'll call it a night. All right?"

She inhaled; bit her lip. Then she nodded. "But for pity's sake, try to be a bit quieter?"

"I promise to be the very soul of discretion."

And I kept my word, as we stepped off the path and back into the woods. I watched where I stepped, moved as quietly as possible, and looked around carefully when crossing any roads. But being more judicious also made me more aware that Burderop was right

— we made the only noises, and there was no sign anywhere of other living creatures existing anywhere inside of the park.

Then all at once the dense foliage opened up, revealing a black expanse of still water. In the distance I could see a flat bridge, the space under its supporting arches lighter than the lake. This must be the Serpentine, I was sure of it — and said so.

"Hey!"

This time it was Burderop who cried out heedlessly. She was pointing at something; I peered along the line of her finger, but could see nothing but a burned-out structure with an octagonal roof.

"What?"

"I saw a rabbit." She broke from the treeline. I followed after. "Oh, there's a warren, look!"

Along the foundation of the octagonal building there were indeed a series of likely looking holes. Burderop was nearly ecstatic, was already unslinging her bag of ferrets, but now I found I was the cautious one. It was odd to see rabbits burrowing so close to water, and I said so.

"Well, didn't you say it was a man-made lake?" She looked up from messing with her nets.

"Oh. Mm. That must be it."

"All right," she said, and I could tell she would tolerate no further discussion; she was totally focused on the task at hand. That was Burderop's talent. "I think I'm ready to let Ghost and The Duke go." She looked up. "Hey, if you want to keep, you know, *exploring*, I can do this on my own. It's not a huge run."

"Really?"

"Sure," she said, generous now that she was happy. "Just don't stay away too long."

I didn't need further encouragement. I stepped carefully away from the netted warren just as Burderop withdrew The Duke, an enormous pale hob, and untied his muzzle with her teeth. She set him in front of the hole and he vanished down it, fur rippling, moving in that way that ferrets move, like he was actually a liquid.

I headed left, around the southern edge of the long lake. The trees had grown thick nearly up to the very bank, and dead moldering reeds clogged the shoreline. Here and there I could see a rusted-out fence, a reminder that once people had come here all the time, perhaps to eat their lunches, or just enjoy the odd spot of good weather, and had to be prevented from swimming.

It was startling to me, how beautiful the sky was above me. It was a clear night, and the smile of a moon cast a silver sheen over the whole world. Away from the ground light of the Old City streets I could see more stars than usual; there were whole constellations I'd never seen before. Save for the crunching of my shoes in the gravel that had been a walking path long ago, the night was perfectly silent. Nothing moved. Beautiful, peaceful. I'd never felt so free, so utterly surrounded by *nature*. To think I felt myself familiar with the wild places! I'd never even seen a patch of sky that wasn't hemmed in on one or more sides by buildings.

I realized I felt *alone* for the first time in my life. Shocking. And while I knew somewhere nearby Burderop and her ferrets were hunting, it was so very silent I could almost believe I was the only living thing left in the world. It was the queerest feeling I'd ever had in my life.

Reaching the bridge forced me from my reverie, as I had to make a choice. Looking back the way I'd come, it seemed about the same, turning around or crossing and circling back to where I'd left Burderop. I hadn't been gone *too* long at that point; I figured she wouldn't be missing me yet.

Beside and slightly below where I stood lay the Serpentine, totally black, perfectly smooth. Tranquil. I think that's what made me do it — what appealed to the strange, reckless mood that I was in. Picking up a stone that lay by the side of the path, I stepped onto the bridge proper and walked across the flat expanse until I was in the very center over the water.

I set my stone on the railing and looked down — only to look away quickly and rub my eyes. Something felt… wrong about the surface of the lake, and, glancing back, I realized it wasn't moving.

At all. Steeling myself, elbows on the balustrade, I craned my neck out and over. The water was so motionless it wasn't even lapping at the bases of the arches that supported the bridge. I told myself that was absolutely impossible, and reached for my stone. Almost to prove it to myself, I dropped it in.

The stone hit the surface without a sound and lay there. Atop the water.

"No," I whispered, my heart pounding. And yet, I couldn't deny my own eyes when it slowly began to sink beneath the surface, as if it were being engulfed by tar, or maybe golden syrup. Then it was gone, leaving no trace it had ever been there.

Being alone in the world seemed vastly less appealing after that, and I took off toward the opposite side of the bridge at a healthy trot — not really running, but definitely moving faster than I had been. Burderop, I reckoned, had been right about this place. I didn't like it anymore. Not at all.

The sudden clattering behind me brought me up sharp, not two meters before I reached the far side of the bridge. Part of me — most of me, really — did not want to see what had made the sound — wanted to just keep walking and not look back. But my curiosity won out. Slowly, I turned.

My stone. It was the stone I'd dropped into the water. Lying there, pale and smooth, in the exact center of the bridge.

Some sound escaped my throat, and I nearly tripped over my own feet in my haste to get the hell away from there. My only thought was *get off the bridge*, but as I turned back around, there, blocking my way, was something, something thick and bubbling, like living treacle, pulling itself up and onto the bridge with long, sticky arms. I nearly fell over in my haste to not run straight into it.

That's when I heard Burderop start to scream.

Back the way I came, then — I jumped over the stone, lying still and clean, and got off the bridge at last, pelting pell-mell along the disused walkway. Burderop was screaming and screaming, it was the only sound I could hear other than my labored breathing and soles slapping on dirt and shattered concrete.

"I'm coming!" I called into the silence, but it felt like the air swallowed my words as I spoke. My lungs were burning like a fire by the time I rounded the last corner, where I saw Burderop on her arse, scrambling hand and foot away from something black that bubbled out of the holes she'd sent her ferret down. There was no sign of The Duke except for a few patches of white fur scattered about.

I felt sick from running, from the sights I'd seen, and from what was before me now. "Hold on!" I shouted, as the whatever-it-was slithered over the grass toward my only friend. One leg buckled as I stumbled on the uneven ground, but I kept moving despite the pain. I had to get to her, help pull her out of its reach — but before I got close enough to grab her hand, it wrapped itself around her ankle.

I've often thought back to how coolheaded she remained right then. Instead of totally losing it she tried to sit up and untie her Doc Marten… but reason had no place in Hyde Park that night. Whatever it was that had her foot quickly engulfed her hands and spread up the rest of her leg, clear up to the knee. Trapped, Burderop let out a shriek as it pulled her down what we'd foolishly thought was a rabbit hole. The tunnel was too small for her to fit, and I felt momentary hope that I could get her before she was dragged under, could pull her free. Then there was a great sucking sound, and she was gone. I could hear her bones snapping in the overwhelming silence as it pulled her underground.

The only thing that indicated she'd ever been there was her cap, upside down on the lawn.

I ran toward the hole, not away from it, as would have been sensible. As I drew nearer, I saw Burderop's ferret sack poking out from under a bush. The fabric seemed to squirm, and I nearly stomped it right then and there. Ghost wriggled her way free, still muzzled, before I could.

"Ghost," I breathed, taking the jill into my arms. "I'm so sorry."

She coughed. I almost laughed, it was such a normal sound. I untied her muzzle, thinking that would help her, but she coughed again. I scruffed her, holding her up in the weak moonlight to make sure she wasn't choking on something… which is when I saw it coming out of her mouth, black and sinuous.

I dropped her and ran for it, ran harder than I'd ever run, before or since. Back the way I'd come, crashing heedlessly through the undergrowth, and up the tree, not even bothering to grab my carpet. I just hauled myself up the trunk fast as I could, and clung there until I could work up the nerve to hurl myself over the edge of Apsley Gate, where I came down hard on my right leg. I heard the bones breaking before I blacked out.

They found me the next morning, but by then it was too late to save it. The doctors were so apologetic. I told them never mind, they'd done their best, and I was grateful to be alive. They said that was the spirit; promised that enough practice with the crutch and I could do just about anything I wanted. And that turned out to be true. I'd lost my taste for poaching.

The Semi-Finished Basement

Nick Mamatas

"[D]iluted product can never achieve the intensity of a concentrated essence."

It's always strange to be asked about inspiration and ideas. It doesn't happen often, the joke about writers constantly being assailed by questions like "Where do you get your ideas?" and "Is this story semi-autobiographical?" aside. When Jesse Bullington asked me to participate, I looked through "Supernatural Horror in Literature," and the above phrase popped out at me. At first I thought I might do something about fuzzy Cthulhu slippers and all the little Lovecraftian jokes and goofiness, which supposedly bother hardcore Lovecraftians (I don't care one way or another.) Then I thought about all those dumb neckbeards who run around actually claiming to worship or venerate Cthulhu as part of some metaphysical Satanism, but I couldn't bring myself to care about that either. It's not like the actual Lovecraft stories are really all that concentrated an essence of evil or universal disinterest. Stories are always entertainments; some people are just entertained by their own existential irrelevance.

The phrase "Everything happens for a reason" has always annoyed me though, and I've often wondered what it would take to get the phrase banned from the English language. And who can think about the actual concentrated essence of evil without thinking about the Holocaust? And then I started writing…

♦

There were other groups all over the world, or so the members of the group would have liked to think. It wouldn't be fair if they were all alone, all alone with the unbelievable truth.

And statistically, it was impossible that the four people in this room — two women, two men — were the only ones who had noticed the great change. And if there were others, it stood to reason that they would have found one another, formed groups. Met once a month, to talk about it, three months running, like this group had.

Maybe one of the groups was comprised of important people. Philosophers and scientists, poets and soldiers. People dedicated to getting to the bottom of what had happened, to setting the world aright.

This group, with its two women and two men, was not that group. It was, when all was said and done, more of a support group.

"So, anything?" Lurlene asked. The group met at her house, because she kept it neat and always offered snacks and soft drinks — diet soda pops and lemonade from a powder mix. Her husband kept guns, and that made the two men feel safer. They met in the basement for the same reason. It was hard to feel safe in a room with windows these days.

"I like these blondies," Nashawna said. She licked her fingers. She only felt safe, irrationally so, when Lurlene's black cat jumped into her lap and made himself comfortable, and purred. Which he did at the start of every meeting. He was there now, so Nashawna held her blondie in a napkin with her left hand.

Aaron looked at Nashawna, and the black cat, and the blondie, and said, "Ha, that should be a brownie."

"Don't," Nashawna said.

Lurlene glanced back and forth between the two of them, and then stared meaningfully at Stewart. "Forget that, Aaron. Just tell them what you recall."

"The crawling chaos," Aaron said. "I've been thinking a lot about Egypt lately."

"It's in the news, darling," Lurlene said. She always tried to calm Aaron down, since, if she didn't, then Stewart would start fuming and arguing. The worst thing to do with a paranoid schizophrenic is to simply disagree.

"All sorts of things are going on in Egypt," Nashawna said. "That's nothing."

"Don't the Egyptians hate the Jews?" Aaron asked. His eyes glanced from Nashawna to some empty space off to the left, above his head. He was asking the entities for a refresher on the geopolitics of anti-Semitism.

"The Egyptians," Stewart said, his jaw clenched, "were the first to make a peace treaty with Israel. But of course that was years ago. Many things have changed." He looked at Lurlene, then Nashawna, then he exhaled sharply through his nose. "But I wouldn't say that Egyptians — as a people — hate the Jews — as a people, again — especially."

Stewart and Aaron had similar noses. They were brothers. Aaron was about eighty pounds overweight, and an unruly beard sprouted from his neck. Stewart was muscular under his tight shirt, like a swimmer, and his knee twitched nervously.

Lurlene was a slow thinker. A slow speaker. Not unintelligent in the slightest; just extremely careful. "The crawlin' chaos. You said it came from Egypt before, right? Before the news started over in Egypt."

"But what does that have to do with —" Nashawna started. It was hard to believe even now. "The change."

That's what they called it. In the great scheme of things — and there was a great scheme of things, everyone in the group was sure of that now — it was a little change.

During the Second World War, which was still called the Second World War, Hitler, who was still widely considered the most evil man who had ever lived, began a campaign of extermination against European Jewry. As part of this program, he had built many concentration camps, and above the gates of several of them was emblazoned a slogan.

And that slogan was *Nichts geschieht ohne Grund*. Nothing happens without reason. Or, in the American idiom, the idiom of this quartet of seekers, "Everything happens for a reason."

These four remembered, they knew, that until recently, all the history books, all the pop culture references, all the eyewitness accounts had been different. *Arbeit macht frei*. Work will make you free. But now, that phrase had been erased. Erased and replaced.

Aaron snorted. Maybe snorting was a genetic predisposition. "It has everything to do with the change. Everything." Nashawna sat back, biting her lip. It was going to be a long meeting. Aaron launched into his monologue, gesticulating and pointing at an imaginary whiteboard in the air, connecting all the dots. The crawling chaos out of Egypt; oil as the black blood of the earth, not from dinosaurs but from other… creatures whom had been erased and replaced by the dinosaurs as part of the great trick.

"Wait one minute now," Lurlene said. "Are you saying that when the change happened, dinosaurs were introduced as well? Do you know about something other than dinosaurs, from out of the distant past?"

"Well, don't you?" Stewart said. His hand was up, in front of Aaron's face. When Stewart took charge of a conversation, he committed entirely. Lurlene wanted to tell him to mind his manners in her house, to remind him that she called the meetings, that she ran the group.

"I do," Nashawna said. "The devil. The devil put the fossils in the ground to fool us, to convince us to turn our backs on God and follow Darwin and secular humanism." She petted the cat, picked it up and nuzzled it. "And now look at where we all are."

Stewart had found Nashawna via her church newsletter — it

had made a local stir when she dared headline a column about the good and bad news of the congregants "Everything Happens for a Reason." He had sent her an email of support after she became a social media laughingstock. Lurlene had found Aaron at the local Wendy's when she bumped into him and caused him to spill his pop all over his shirt and sweatpants. He said that it must have happened for a reason, and Lurlene had forgotten to act offended. Aaron wore sweatpants everywhere. Always navy blue. Lurlene hoped that he had lots of pairs.

That was where they all are. A group of four. Lurlene was the leader because she made the calls to bring everyone together; she wanted answers.

"The dinosaurs," Aaron said, "aren't a lie per se. I mean, even 'Everything happens for a reason' isn't a lie per se. Yeah, I know. No, I don't wanna…" He muttered a few other things. More arguments with the entities he was sure bedeviled him.

"He means," Stewart said, "that even before the change, some concentration camps had similar slogans over the gates. *Jedem das Seine*, over Buchenwald's gates for instance."

"That means 'To Each His Own,'" Nashawna said. She let the cat down finally, and he ran off into the shadows of the basement, behind the washer-dryer. "I got Rosetta Stone," she explained.

"Yes, but it means something like 'Just deserts,' okay," Stewart said. "And —"

"Nyarlathotep!" Aaron squawked. His hands started trembling. "The God of a Thousand Forms! Dinosaurs, pharoahs! And you're talking of, of, of…"

"Have a blondie," Lurlene said. She leaned over with the plate, and made a point of showing off her cleavage a bit. She was no psychiatrist, but she knew Aaron well.

He took the blondie and muttered, "Desserts, just desserts. I'm trying to tell them something and I get a blondie." He chewed. "Okay, okay, I'll eat it."

"Anyway," Stewart said, annoyed. Arch disgust was set into his frown now. Maybe he would have strangled his brother, killed him, if not for Aaron's occasional burst of signal amidst all the noise of madness. Since the change, it was easy to get away with doing all sorts of crazy things for no reason. Murder, riots, rape of babies, cleansing the countryside of the neighboring peoples — nobody even asked why.

But only because they knew the answer: there was no why. A shrug. Eh, no reason.

Maybe that's why Stewart didn't kill his brother. He actually had reason to.

Aaron's beard was flaked with blondie crumbs. He cleared his throat and said, "I bet there's a group in Egypt. There's a fuckin' group in Egypt." Then he peered at Nashawna. "Hey, Rosetta Stone, you know Egyptian now too? Eh? Eh? Wanna go with me, get lost under a pyramid?"

"I am getting real tired of this," Nashawna said. Her face was locked, expressionless. "Real damn tired."

"We need him," Stewart said, quietly.

"Why?"

"Look, whoever, or whatever, did the replacement for lack of a better word, they changed perceptions all over the world. They rewrote history. Or it rewrote history. Aliens, the Devil, who knows."

"The crawling chaos," Aaron said.

"Anyway, the issue is a matter of perception. We know it already. Nashawna, you think God protected you. Fine. Lurlene, you had that car accident, you were in a coma when it happened. And I, well, I was just convinced by my brother. But he knows something. He knows it, and he can find the others out there, or convince other people too."

Aaron tittered, scratched himself. It wasn't accidental. He was putting on a show.

"There's an article I just read about human consciousness," Aaron said. "Scientists don't know where it comes from, but it has to come from neuron activity. We've all been short-circuited in a way."

"God short-circuited me?" Nashawna asked.

"You know — you say it yourself. You've been slain in the spirit. It's like having a fit."

Nashawna stood up quickly, her legs strong and thick. "It is not like having a fit. Don't blaspheme. I can take it from him —" she pushed her palm in Aaron's direction, "and the Lord can take it from anyone, but I can't take it from you."

"It's neurological. Like a seizure. Fine, believe that God made that neurological 'god part' of the brain, like a phone jack installed in your head. I…" he trailed off.

Nashawna stepped up to him, her hand raised high. "You keep talking about things happening for reasons. I don't need a reason to slap you silly, but I've got one —"

"Nashawna, please," Lurlene said. She stretched her arm and took Nashawna's hand, gave it a squeeze. She stood from her chair and put her other hand on Nashawna's shoulder. "I need you here. I can't do this group otherwise." She shifted her position so her shoulder and broad back were to the men in the room and mouthed, *Don't leave me alone with them.*

Things were quiet for a long moment, then the cat padded upstairs.

"I don't like this anymore than anyone else," Stewart said. "Aaron's probably immune because he's schizophrenic and, well, schizophrenia is genetic. Partially genetic. Maybe I'm persuadable because I was partially immune. Partially…schizophrenic. Schizotypal. But I think that's the key."

"To what?" Lurlene asked, turning to face Stewart. The basement seemed so small, and dark, with the two women standing. Like an interrogation room, but everyone was simultaneously the cop and the suspect.

"Finding other groups."

"Oh yeah, is everyone in Egypt schizophrenic?" Nashawna asked, her tongue acid.

"No, but a lot of them are devoutly religious. Muslims and Christians."

"And a lot of them are dead!" Aaron said. "The dead know!"

"Well, certainly there have been head injuries, trauma, people knocked into a coma by tear gas and police beatings."

"And," Lurlene said slowly, "Aaron has been talking about a pharaoh at every meeting. Maybe there's something to it."

"Egyptians worshipped the cat!" Aaron declared.

"There definitely is," Stewart said. He dug out his smartphone. "I just found this, this afternoon." He stood up and held the phone out to the women. If Aaron was interested at all, he didn't show it in his posture or attitude. His head was slumped over, and he was looking at a mark on the poured concrete floor.

"The media isn't going to air this, for the obvious reason." Stewart winced at his word choice, then pressed a button on the smartphone screen. It took the video a few seconds to load.

It was a protest video. A familiar one, at first. A crowd of mostly men, mostly bearded, mostly dark-skinned, chanting and pumping their fists. There were some women too — some in Western garb, others in veils of various lengths and cuts and fashions. The camera, probably one from a smartphone much like Stewart's, snaked through the crowd to the center of the protest. A young woman in a thick black robe was bound, in barbed wire, to a young man in khaki pants and a torn shirt. They were alive, groaning and wincing, and the man, whose face was not obscured by a cloth, was even occasionally calling out, looking at the camera.

And the chant was in English: "Reason! Reason! Reason!"

Aaron giggled. "Just like Romeo and Juliet," he said, his voice a piping squeak, like he had swallowed a little toy of himself and was letting it speak from inside his barrel frame.

"He's a Copt, she's a Muslim. They tortured them for hours. Both sides that is. Sectarian solidarity. The comments under the video, as best Google Translate can tell me, are that everyone was relieved to agree that something should be done, that these kids should be punished for, uhm, " — Stewart considered his immediate audience — "stepping out across religious lines. And there was this guy, some holy man from out in the desert, who suggested chanting in English, to get the attention of the world media."

"Not that that'll happen! It can't ever be allowed," Aaron said from the corner. Lurlene swore she saw the outline of an erection stirring in his sweatpants.

"So what do you want us to do?" Nashawna said. "How can we contact this guy? Email the person who put up the vid?"

"Tried that!" Aaron said. "Bounced!" He giggled again, and bounced himself, the aluminum folding chair straining under his weight.

"Well, I have some money saved. Maybe, Lurlene, you can take an equity loan out on the house, and we can all take a trip, do some research. Just meeting here isn't helping."

"Take out a loan? What would I tell my husband? In heaven's name, why? What possible reason could I give him for —"

"You don't need a reason," Nashawna said. "Remember. Nobody needs a reason to do anything anymore. It's like nothing happens for a reason. That's why everything is so darn crazy out there. But do banks even give loans to people anymore? My bank shut down last week. I didn't have much, but it was my savings, and I ain't getting it back."

"Please, we have to do something. Try to find the others," Stewart said. He was hollow-voiced, practically about to cry. "I think I'm going crazy."

"Oh, honey," Lurlene said. She didn't say anything else for more than a minute. Nobody did, except for the rioters shouting "Reason! Reason! Reason!" through the tinny speaker on Stewart's smartphone.

"I'm going to go upstairs for a second," Lurlene said, finally. "For some lemonade refills. And a beer for you, Stewart. I even went to the liquor store, and you know I don't like that awful place. The boys who hang around on the corner say such awful things to me. We have to talk more about this. Maybe we can have an emergency meeting after the weekend. But we can't make any rash decisions now."

"I'll help," Nashawna said, but Lurlene shot her a pleading look. Someone had to keep an eye on the men. They were both degenerating so quickly.

Once upstairs, Lurlene quickly grabbed her big quilt and hung it over the basement door, from hooks she had drilled at the top of the frame. She grasped a large and most peculiar switch bolted into the wall and was about to give it a turn when the cat meowed.

"Oh," she said. "Hello there, Nigger-Man."

"Hello," Nigger-Man said. "Did the meeting go well?" His voice was like a toddler's impression of a cat, or a cartoon character.

"Oh, definitely. Just about to gas the lot of them," Lurlene said. She cranked the switch.

"Did they come very close to figuring it out?"

Lurlene nodded, chewed her lip. "Oh, pretty close. The crazy fat ones with the mother born of a motherfucker often do."

Nigger-Man, lacking the organs to laugh properly, just schhz-schhz-schhzed.

"They wanted me to take out a second mortgage on the house, to fly to Egypt with them," Lurlene said.

"Speaking as your husband, I certainly wouldn't allow that," Nigger-Man said. "I keep my pussy close to home." He nuzzled up to Lurlene's ankles, and circled them, purring deeply, his tail tall.

"My little puss-puss," Lurlene said, bending over to stroke him. "It's like our job is never done. There are always a few rats to kill. And you tried to make everyone so happy, with your little adjustment."

"Some people feel better when they have something to worry about," Nigger-Man said. "A big ol' meanie setting up the universe like a billiard table."

"Yeah, knockin' 'em right into the corner pocket." Lurlene scooped up Nigger-Man and gave him a bunch of belly kisses, then a tongue kiss, the tip of her fat human slug of a tongue pushed into his little mouth, his needly teeth drawing blood.

Finally, she put him back down. "Tuna casserole for dinner?"

"My favorite!"

Nigger-Man turned and made to walk away from the basement door, Lurlene obediently on his heels. Then they heard a great yelp and a pounding on the door.

"Halp!" It was Aaron. It was probably Aaron anyway. It sounded like most of his throat was already gone, as it was. "Ev'ryone, dead! Halp!" The room shook. He was throwing his whole fat body against the door. Lurlene worried that he might upset the quilt, and then she'd really have to sell the house. The gas would melt the paint off the walls, get into the carpets, everything.

"Oh, darn it," she said. She went back to the big switch, cranked it counterclockwise to turn off the gas, and hustled over to the living room. Nigger-Man watched her go, then ran to the corner and cowered in his litter box as she came back.

"You know, I always end up using one of these things in the end," Lurlene said as she leveled the rifle at the door. "One little hole won't matter."

"Nothing does!" said Nigger-Man. Then he covered his ears with his paws as best he could.

Biographies

Kirsten Alene is the author of three books, most recently *Japan Conquers the Galaxy* (Eraserhead Press, 2013). Her fiction has appeared in a number of publications in print and online, including *In Heaven, Everything Is Fine: Fiction Inspired by David Lynch*; *Innsmouth Magazine*; and *New Dead Families*. She lives in Portland, Oregon, with her husband, dog, and cat.

David Yale Ardanuy, a native Floridian and American history graduate student, is an avid hiker of forbidden and lofty places, a known trafficker of hidden wisdoms and a dream weaver. His story in this collection reflects both the nature of his scholarly endeavors and his love of weird and terrifying fiction.

Asamatsu Ken is a writer and anthologist born in Hokkaido and presently residing in Tokyo, Japan. His pseudonym, a Japanese rendering of "Arthur Machen," reflects both his keen interest in the supernatural and his decidedly global literary tastes. Asamatsu was a 2006 nominee for the short story division of the Mystery

Writers of Japan Award and is the editor of the four-volume Cthulhu Mythos anthology *Lairs of the Hidden Gods*. Also available in English is his novel *Queen of K'n-Yan*, as well as short stories appearing in *Cthulhu's Reign*, *The Mountains of Madness*, and the 2011 charity anthology *Kizuna: Fiction for Japan*.

Nadia Bulkin writes scary stories about the scary world we live in. Two of her stories have been nominated for Shirley Jackson Awards, and one won the 2010 ChiZine Short Story Contest. It took her two tries to leave Nebraska, but she has been in Washington, D.C., for three years now. She works in research and tends her garden of student debt sowed by two political science degrees. For more, see nadiabulkin.wordpress.com.

Jesse Bullington wears the influence of Lovecraft on the pages of his three award-nominated novels: *The Sad Tale of the Brothers Grossbart*, *The Enterprise of Death*, and *The Folly of the World*. He has published numerous short stories, some of them Mythos-themed, as well as various articles and reviews; a full bibliography can be found at www.jessebullington.com. *Letters to Lovecraft* is his maiden voyage as an anthologist.

Chesya Burke's 2011 fiction collection, *Let's Play White*, was featured in io9 and received praise from Samuel Delany and Nikki Giovanni. She is also recognized for her critical analysis of genre and race issues, such as her articles, "Race and The Walking Dead" and "Super Duper Sexual Spiritual Black Woman: The New and Improved Magical Negro," published in *Clarkesworld Magazine*. Chesya is currently getting her MA in African American studies at Georgia State University and is a juror for the 2013 Shirley Jackson awards.

Brian Evenson is the author of more than a dozen books, including, most recently, the novel *Immobility* and the short story collection *Windeye*. Three times he has been a finalist for a Shirley Jackson Award, and he is the recipient of an International

Horror Guild Award for his collection *The Wavering Knife*. His novel *Last Days* won the American Library Association's award for best horror novel of 2009. He lives and works in Providence, Rhode Island, with his wife Kristen Tracy and their son Max.

Former film critic and teacher turned award-winning horror author **Gemma Files** is best known for her Hexslinger series (*A Book of Tongues*, *A Rope of Thorns* and *A Tree of Bones*, all from ChiZine Publications). She has also published two collections of short fiction (*Kissing Carrion* and *The Worm in Every Heart*, both from Wildside Press) and two chapbooks of poetry. Her next book will be *We Will All Go Down Together: A Novel in Stories About the Five-Family Coven* (2014, CZP).

Jeffrey Ford is the author of the novels *The Physiognomy*, *Memoranda*, *The Beyond*, *The Portrait of Mrs. Charbuque*, *The Girl in the Glass*, *The Cosmology of the Wider World*, and *The Shadow Year*. His story collections are *The Fantasy Writer's Assistant*, *The Empire of Ice Cream*, *The Drowned Life* and *Crackpot Palace*. Ford has published over one hundred twenty short stories, which have appeared in numerous journals, magazines and anthologies, from *MAD Magazine* to *The Oxford Book of American Short Stories*. He is the recipient of the World Fantasy Award, Nebula Award, Shirley Jackson Award, Edgar Allan Poe Award, Grand Prix de l'Imaginaire (France) and Hayakawa Award (Japan). His fiction has been translated into over twenty languages. In addition to writing, he's been a professor of literature and writing for over twenty-five years and has been a guest lecturer at the Clarion Writers' Workshop, the Stone Coast MFA program, the Richard Hugo House in Seattle and the Antioch Writers' Workshop. He lives somewhere in Ohio.

Orrin Grey is a writer, editor, amateur film scholar and monster expert who was born on the night before Halloween. He's the author of *Never Bet the Devil & Other Warnings* and the coeditor of *Fungi*, an anthology of weird fungus-themed stories. You can find out more at orringrey.com.

Stephen Graham Jones is the author of sixteen novels, six story collections, two novellas and a hundred and seventy or so stories in magazines (*Weird Tales*, *Cemetery Dance*, *Clarkesworld*, *Asimov's*, *Prairie Schooner*), anthologies (*The Weird*, *Creatures*, *Fearful Symmetries*), and multiple best-of-the-year annuals. Stephen's been a Bram Stoker Award finalist, a Shirley Jackson Award finalist, and a Colorado Book Award finalist, and has won the Texas Institute of Letters Award for Fiction, the Independent Publisher Book Award for Multicultural Fiction, This is Horror's Novel of the Year and an NEA fellowship. Stephen lives in Boulder, Colorado, with his wife and kids and various old trucks, and teaches in the MFA programs at CU-Boulder and UCR Palm Desert. More @SGJ72 and demontheory.net.

Robin D. Laws's most recent works of fiction are his collection of Chambers-inspired weird stories *New Tales of the Yellow Sign* and the fantasy novel *Blood of the City*. Other novels include *Pierced Heart* and *The Worldwound Gambit*. As creative director for Stone Skin Press, he has edited such anthologies as *Shotguns v. Cthulhu* and *The Lion and the Aardvark*. He is best known for his groundbreaking roleplaying game design work, as seen in *Hillfolk*, *The Esoterrorists*, *Feng Shui* and *HeroQuest*. He is one-half of the Golden Geek Award–winning podcast Ken and Robin Talk About Stuff, and can be found online at robindlaws.com.

Tim Lebbon is a *New York Times*–bestselling horror and fantasy writer from South Wales. He's had almost thirty novels published to date, as well as dozens of novellas and hundreds of short stories. His most recent releases include the apocalyptic *Coldbrook*, *Into the Void: Dawn of the Jedi* from Del Rey / Star Wars Books, *The Cabin in the Woods* novelization, the *Toxic City* trilogy from Pyr in the USA and the official Alien tie-in novel *Out of the Shadows*.

Future novels include *The Silence* (Titan UK/USA). He has won four British Fantasy Awards, a Bram Stoker Award and a Scribe Award, and has been a finalist for World Fantasy, International Horror Guild and Shirley Jackson Awards.

Twentieth Century Fox acquired film rights to *The Secret Journeys of Jack London* series (coauthored with Christopher Golden), and a TV series of his *Toxic City* trilogy is in development. His script *Playtime* (with Stephen Volk) is currently being developed in the UK.

Find out more about Tim at his website www.timlebbon.net

Livia Llewellyn is a writer of dark fantasy, horror and erotica. A 2006 graduate of Clarion, her fiction has appeared in *ChiZine*, *Subterranean*, *Sybil's Garage*, *Pseudopod*, *Apex Magazine*, *Postscripts*, *Nightmare Magazine* and numerous anthologies. Her first collection, *Engines of Desire: Tales of Love & Other Horrors*, was published in 2011 by Lethe Press. *Engines* received a nomination for the Shirley Jackson Award for Best Collection, and "Omphalos" received a Best Novelette nomination. You can find her online at liviallewellyn.com.

Nick Mamatas is the author of several novels, including *Love is the Law* and *The Last Weekend*, and the Lovecraftian mash-ups *Move Under Ground* and *The Damned Highway* (cowritten with Brian Keene). His Lovecraftian fiction has appeared in *ChiZine, Lovecraft Unbound, Shotguns v. Cthulhu* and many other venues. Much of it will be collected in *The Nickronomicon*, to be published by Innsmouth Free Press in the autumn of 2014. His non-Lovecraftian work has appeared in *Asimov's Science Fiction, Best American Mystery Stories 2013* and a wide assortment of magazines, websites, and anthologies. Also an editor and anthologist, Nick's latest editorial works include *Phantasm Japan* and the essay collection *The Battle Royale Slam Book*, both from Haikasoru.

Cameron Pierce is the author of nine books, including the Wonderland Book Award–winning collection *Lost in Cat Brain Land* (Eraserhead Press, 2010) and *Fantastic Earth Destroyer Ultra Plus*, a fairy tale for adults illustrated by artist Jim Agpalza (Sinister Grin Press, 2014). He is also the editor of the popular indie publisher Lazy Fascist Press. He lives in Portland, Oregon.

Angela Slatter writes dark fantasy and horror. She is the author of the Aurealis Award–winning *The Girl with No Hands and Other Tales*, the WFA-shortlisted *Sourdough and Other Stories* and the new collection / mosaic novel (with Lisa L. Hannett) *Midnight and Moonshine*. Her work has appeared in such writerly venues as *The Mammoth Book of New Horror 22*, Australian and US *Best Of* anthologies, *Fantasy Magazine*, *Lady Churchill's Rosebud Wristlet*, *Dreaming Again* and *Steampunk II: Steampunk Reloaded*. She was awarded one of the inaugural Queensland Writers Fellowships in 2013. She has a British Fantasy Award for "The Coffin-Maker's Daughter" (from *A Book of Horrors*, Stephen Jones, ed.), a PhD in creative writing, and blogs at www.angelaslatter.com.

Molly Tanzer is the author of the Sydney J. Bounds Award and Wonderland Book Award–nominated *A Pretty Mouth*, *Rumbullion and Other Liminal Libations*, and *The Pleasure Merchant* (forthcoming from Lazy Fascist Press in 2015). She lives in Boulder, CO, where she mostly writes about fops arguing with each other. She tweets @molly_the_tanz, and blogs — infrequently — at http://mollytanzer.com.

Paul Tremblay is the author of the novels *The Little Sleep*, *No Sleep Till Wonderland*, *Swallowing a Donkey's Eye*, the cowritten YA novel *Floating Boy and the Girl Who Couldn't Fly* (with Stephen Graham Jones), the forthcoming *A Head Full of Ghosts* (William Morrow), and the short story collection *In the Mean Time*. His essays and short fiction have appeared in the *Los Angeles Times*, FiveChapters.com and *Best American Fantasy 3*.

He is the coeditor of four anthologies, including *Creatures: Thirty Years of Monsters* (with John Langan). Paul is the president of the board of directors for the Shirley Jackson Awards. He lives outside of Boston, Massachusetts, has a master's degree in mathematics, has no uvula, loves his friends, and hates his many enemies.